RULER
OF THE
REALM

ALSO BY HERBIE BRENNAN

Faerie Wars

The Purple Emperor

THE FAERIE WARS CHRONICLES
BOOK THREE

RULER
OF THE
REALM

HERBIE BRENNAN

BLOOMSBURY

Published by Bloomsbury Publishing, New York, London, and Berlin
Distributed to the trade by Holtzbrinck Publishers

Library of Congress Cataloging-in-Publication Data
Brennan, Herbie.
Ruler of the realm / by Herbie Brennan. — 1st U.S. ed.
p.   cm.
"Book three in the Faerie Wars chronicles."
Sequel to: The Purple Emperor.
Summary: While simultaneously trying to prevent and prepare for war between the Faeries of the
Night and Faeries of the Light, Queen Holly Blue is kidnapped from her Uncle Hairstreak's home
by human Henry Atherton and learns she must face another, far greater enemy.
ISBN-10: 1-58234-881-2 • ISBN-13: 978-1-58234-881-0
[1. Fairies—Fiction. 2. War—Fiction. 3. Supernatural—Fiction.] I. Title.
PZ7.B75153Rul 2006   [Fic]—dc22   2006006430

First U.S. Edition 2006
Typeset by Dorchester Typesetting Group Ltd
Printed in the U.S.A. by Quebecor World Fairfield
2 4 6 8 10 9 7 5 3 1

Bloomsbury Publishing, Children's Books, U.S.A.
175 Fifth Avenue, New York, NY 10010

Another one for Jacks, with love

Prologue

Outside the great metallic cities – spell-protected and weatherproof – the climate of Hell was extreme. Surface temperatures rose to 860°F in the carbon dioxide atmosphere, a greenhouse effect so intense that it melted lead. A fifteen-mile layer of sulphuric-acid cloud blanketed the world at a height of thirty miles, casting the surface into perpetual gloom.

Because of the conditions, each member of Beleth's entourage was forced to take traditional demonic form – squat, immensely strong, with leathery skin and stubby wings – while Beleth himself had shape-shifted into the towering, slab-muscled Prince of Darkness whose horned face was so familiar to black magicians everywhere.

The party sat in the Great Hall of Beleth's keep, a basalt-built structure that clung to its lonely cliff face like a giant toad. Acid rain lashed the translucent window, driven by a hurricane that seldom ceased. Their faceted, adaptive eyes penetrated the heavily scarred glass and the deepening gloom beyond to give them sight of a gently rolling plain strewn with flat wedges of rock and broken to the east by an active volcano.

'The special portals …?' Beleth rumbled.

A smelly demon named Asmodeus said quickly, 'In place, Master.'

'All of them?'

'Yes, Master.'

'Troops?'

'On standby, Master.'

'Assault spells?'

'In place, Master.'

'Illusions?'

'In place, Master.'

'Blooms?'

'Matured, Master.'

The volcano to the east belched black smoke and erupted lava which flowed in a fiery river across the open plain. A small colony of steel-fanged niffs took fright and raced away.

Beleth leaned forward, his eyes dark. 'The boy?'

'In pl—' Asmodeus caught himself in time and changed his response. 'The boy, Master?'

Normally they would have communicated tele-pathically, with no chance of misunderstanding. But here, far from the amplifiers of the cities, it was easier to revert to speech.

Beleth growled impatiently, 'The boy! The boy! The stupid boy!'

Asmodeus licked his lips. 'Within days, Master.' He hoped fervently it was true. Beleth would have him flayed if anything went wrong.

But for the moment, Beleth seemed satisfied. He stood up and paced the length of the ancient hall. He turned. He glared. He smiled.

'So,' he said triumphantly, 'the conquest of the Faerie Realm may now begin!'

One

The smell of spice was overwhelming.

There were three open sacks just inside the door: one full of dried vanilla pods, one peppercorns, one golden-yellow *halud*, fine ground to release its perfume. Beyond the sacks were casks and chests, brimming with aromatics. Many glowed startling hues of orange, red and green. Behind them was the darkwood counter with its shelves packed with secrets – asafoetida for the control of demons, powdered lotus root, *tilosa* corms, cinnamon quills, cardamom pods, sesame seeds and mandragores specially compounded to open magical locks.

The Spicemaster was watching Blue from behind the counter. He was a small, thin man with a twisted spine who had either refused rejuvenation treatments or was so old now that nothing could colour his hair or take the wrinkles from his face. He had very pale, intelligent eyes.

Blue approached him warily, wondering if he could see through her disguise. No question of boy's clothes this time, of course – too much chance of a scandal. But the way she *did* look should have fooled anyone. The hand-crafted illusion spell had transformed her into a woman in her early thirties (more than twice her actual age!) and she was dressed in the anonymous garments of a harassed housewife. She might have had a couple of children dragging at her skirts, although – Blue shuddered – thankfully she didn't. But she *looked* as if she might, which guaranteed no one would imagine they were in the presence of their Queen. Most of the time it guaranteed nobody noticed her at all.

The only problem was her hair. In a moment of vanity, she'd commissioned waist-length, sex-goddess, brushed blonde hair which – duh! – ruined the effect, so she'd had to tie it up. Illusion or not, that hair was *heavy*. She felt as if she was wearing a military helmet. Would the Spicemaster notice? He had a fearsome reputation. Would he be able to see through the illusion as easily as he was supposed to see ... other things? Not that it mattered. She was expected.

She half thought he might say something, offer her fennel or chilli or a twist of taste powder, but he only stared at her.

Blue said very quietly, 'I understand the Painted Lady approached you about me, Spicemaster.'

For a moment he looked blank. Then he murmured, '*Ah*,' and came slowly round the counter to shoot the bolt on the door. She heard magical securities tinkle into place. The display window dimmed. They were alone in the shop. No one could see in.

The Spicemaster turned towards her. 'Your Majesty ...' he exclaimed. There was just the barest hint of a question mark in his voice, but he bowed deeply all the same. The twist in his spine pitched him sideways.

'Can we be overheard?' Blue asked.

He straightened painfully and shook his head. 'The privacy spells came into play when I closed the door.'

'Good,' Blue said. 'Spicemaster, I –'

'Memnon,' he murmured. He caught her expression and added, 'Forgive me, Majesty, but it is not fitting that the Queen should have to address me by my title.' He cast his eyes down. 'My name is Memnon.'

Blue suppressed a smile. Memnon the Spicemaster was another Madame Cardui, a stickler for good manners and precise protocol. No wonder she'd spoken of him so highly.

'Master Memnon,' Blue said, granting him one honorific to replace the other, 'Madame Cardui has told you why I'm here?'

He nodded. 'Yes, Majesty.'

'You know this visit can never be spoken of?'

'Yes, Majesty.'

'And you can do the thing I wish of you?'

This time there was just the barest hesitation before he said, 'Yes, Majesty.'

'What's wrong?' Blue asked at once.

'Majesty, may I sit in your presence?'

Blue blinked, then realised what he was asking. Memnon was a very old man and that spinal problem must make standing difficult.

'Yes, yes, of course.'

He moved even more slowly this time. 'I have a stool behind the counter, Majesty.' When he had perched, he said, 'I can do what you wish, but the Painted Lady has told me I must work without assistants.'

Blue said, 'The matter is confidential. No one must know but you and me.' *And even you won't know*, she thought, *if what Madame Cardui told me is true.*

He looked away as if embarrassed. 'Then *you* must assist me, Majesty,' he murmured.

She'd been warned this would most likely be the case.

'That will not be a problem, Master Memnon,' she said firmly. 'Just tell me what to do and I'll do it.'

'Yes, Majesty.'

There was something else: she could tell by his tone. 'What is it?'

The Spicemaster raised his head to look her directly in the eyes. 'Majesty, to stay with me alone in the labyrinth may prove dangerous.' He hesitated, then added, 'Very dangerous indeed.'

Two

Henry felt nervous visiting his dad.

He hadn't figured out why. You'd think he'd be glad to get away from Mum for a while. Which he was. But that still didn't stop him feeling nervous. Once he was inside the flat, Dad would give him the glad hand and the big grin and say, '*Come in, old man, come in!*' (Dad called him 'old man' all the time now since the split with Mum.) But for all that, Henry still felt nervous.

Maybe it was the area. Up to a year ago, you took your life in your hands going down by the canal. Now it was trendy. He hated to think what his dad had paid to live here. (He'd showed him the brochure once. It was a fat, expensive Metro-Goldwyn-Mayer production with tissue paper over a full-colour photo. And they didn't call it a brochure. They called it a *prospectus.*) At least he didn't have to stay long. He had the Hodge excuse ready. He was heading out to feed Mr Fogarty's cat.

Henry thumbed the bell and waited. After a minute, he thumbed it again. With a peculiar feeling of relief, he began to think his father might be out. He thumbed the bell a third time, deciding that if nobody came inside ten seconds, he was heading for the hills. He'd phone later, say he'd called, and collect the Brownie points with none of the hassle. Not that Dad meant to hassle. It was just that he kept asking about Mum. It wasn't the questions that upset Henry. It was the way his dad's eyes filled up when he asked them.

... Nine ... ten ... eleven ... twelve ... thirteen ... fourteen ... There was definitely nobody home. He was free and clear, duty done. He could go now. It was like being let out of school.

For some reason his hand reached out and pushed the door.

The door was off the latch. It swung open a few inches. Henry stared at it stupidly, wondering what that was all about. Nobody went out and left their door open, not when the flat was empty. It was asking for trouble. Even his dad must know that. This stretch of the canal might be trendy now, but the area around it was still pretty rough. The new waterside apartments had to be a target for every scumbag in the district.

Henry pushed the door again and it opened even further. A horrible thought occurred to him. Suppose Dad *hadn't* left the door unlocked when he went out. Suppose he'd locked it the way he always did. Suppose a scumbag came along and *picked the lock*! A scumbag who was inside now, rifling every drawer in sight ...

The nerves in Henry's stomach turned to a sick fear. He'd watched far too many horror movies. You pushed an open door and walked into an empty flat and something in a *Scream* mask lurched out of the shadows to smash your head in with a poker. But not all of the fear was for himself. He kept thinking maybe his dad might have come back and the thing in the *Scream* mask loomed up behind *him*. He kept seeing a body on the floor and blood staining the pale carpet.

Heart pounding, Henry pushed the door right back and slid into the flat.

The front door opened on to a postage-stamp hall with a coat rack, a wall mirror and a silly little polished table that was supposed to look eighteenth century. There were two doors off the hall. The far one led into what the prospectus called the 'Master Bedroom', which had shag-pile carpet, a double bed – what would Dad want with a double bed now he wasn't living with Mum? – and mean little French windows leading on to a tiny balcony with a fire escape. There was also, Henry knew, a connecting door to the living room and an en-suite bathroom. The closer door in the hallway led into the living room as well. The prospectus called it the 'Lounge'.

Henry cautiously turned the handle of the living-room door.

He was trying to move quietly, but his heart was thumping so loudly now you could hear it halfway down the street. It was making him feel sick in his throat as well as his stomach. The worst of it was he knew, he positively *knew*, he was going to find his father dead or dying on the floor. He wished he'd brought a weapon of some sort, but it was too late now.

The lounge was the largest room in the flat, furnished in poncy white leather with a squat spiral staircase winding up to a nun's cell the prospectus called a guest bedroom. There was a door to a kitchen, a door to a second bathroom, a door to a study his father never used (possibly because it was designed for a dwarf), a door to the master bedroom. There were windows that opened up to another balcony, this time without a fire escape, overlooking the canal. The carpet, he saw at once, was clean and bodiless.

Henry sighed and felt his heart wind down. 'Dad …?' he called, frowning. But the frown was just a habit – there was no body on the floor, no blood on the carpet. Maybe best of all, the whole place was bright and cheerful, without shadows for characters in *Scream* masks to lurk in. 'Dad …?' There was no reply. The place was empty.

It was a relief, except it didn't explain why his dad had left the door open. Maybe he was just getting forgetful. God knows he had enough on his mind these days. First there was Henry's mum having an affair with his secretary. Then there was Henry's mum kicking him out of his own home. (They claimed it was 'by agreement', but Henry knew better.) Then there was Henry's mum insisting both children – Henry being the reluctant one – stay with her. When you started to think about it, Henry's mum had a lot to answer for.

Henry supposed he'd better hang around for a bit. He couldn't very well just wander off now and leave the front door open. But he couldn't lock it either, in case his dad had gone out without his key, maybe just slipped down to the corner shop for a minute, taking his chances with Scumbags Anonymous. So the thing to do was make a cup of tea and wait. Once his dad came back he could say hello then go and feed Hodge.

He found the tea bags easily enough – Dad kept them in the fridge for some reason and there wasn't much else in there. He brewed up in a mug that said, *Beam me up, Scottie, there's no intelligent life down here.* Since there wasn't any milk either, he tried adding a spoonful of plain yoghurt and carried the mug into the living room. He sat down on the poncy leather couch and stared gloomily into his tea. The yoghurt had been a mistake. It had separated out and was floating on the top in uneven globules. He debated whether to risk tasting it or go back and make some fresh.

He still hadn't reached any conclusion when the bathroom door opened and a young woman walked out. She had wet hair, bare legs and a towel wrapped around her.

She caught sight of Henry and screamed.

Three

The Spicemaster's labyrinth was laid out on the floor of a cellar underneath the shop. Blue was surprised by its size. She'd imagined something larger. But she supposed he knew what he was doing. Madame Cardui said he'd been practising – largely in secret – for two generations.

Blue looked around the chamber. The labyrinth spiral was picked out in small rock-crystal chunks. At the entrance there was a brass incense burner on a tripod. Beside it was a low table with a burnished copper bowl and two glass vials, one containing spice, the other a clear liquid. Near the table was one of those old-fashioned backless chairs with a leather seat. To one side there was a cupboard or possibly a wardrobe: it was difficult to tell. That was all, except for the glowglobes fixed to the rafters in the ceiling. They looked fly-blown and dim.

'What do you want me to do?' she asked.

Memnon was in the process of locking the door. He seemed even more upset now. 'Majesty, are you sure you wish no one else present? Perhaps a trusted guard …?'

'No one,' Blue said firmly. It wasn't so much the fact she was here – what she planned wasn't illegal – as the possibility that her questions, and their answers, should reach the ears of … well … anybody. She would make State secrets in this chamber. As he turned away from the door, she asked, 'What danger is there? To me, I mean.'

Spicemaster Memnon looked positively distraught. 'I may try to kill you, Majesty.'

Blue glanced at the little old man and suppressed a smile. He hardly looked strong enough to swat a fly, let alone do her harm. But she appreciated both his concern and his loyalty, so she said soberly, 'Spicemaster, I take full responsibility for anything that happens. If you try to harm me, you will be absolved from criminal proceedings, charges of treason, anything of that sort.' The look on his face told her he was far from reassured, so she added kindly, 'Why don't you tell me exactly what takes place, so I can be prepared.' She smiled. 'Defend myself. If the need arises.'

Memnon sighed. 'The ceremony is very simple, Majesty. When I am cloaked, I swallow the spice and enter the labyrinth. By the time I reach the centre, the spice will have begun to take effect. When the god manifests, you may enter the labyrinth yourself to ask your questions.'

'And when am I likely to be in danger?'

'When the god manifests.'

Well, that was straightforward enough. But the god would manifest in the Spicemaster, using his body, so it wouldn't exactly be an attack by a raging bull. If it happened at all.

To distract him, she asked, 'How do you want me to help you in the ceremony?'

'Majesty, I shall need your assistance to cloak.

Beyond that, I would require you to play a drumbeat as I enter the labyrinth.'

And that seemed straightforward as well. She held his coat for him and played a drum. Not that you'd think he needed assistance for any of that, but even simple ceremonies had their formalities.

A thought struck her and she said, 'I've never played a drum.'

'It's no more than a heartbeat,' said the Spicemaster obscurely. He looked distracted. 'Majesty, are you certain –?'

Blue said *yes* and watched his resolve finally collapse. He didn't want to, but he was going to do it.

He said quietly, 'Take this, Majesty.'

For an instant she didn't realise what was happening, then saw he was holding out a small transparent packet of orange-yellow spice, little larger than a coin.

'What's this?' she asked as her hand closed around it.

'Mutated spikenard – it may offer you some protection.' He lowered his eyes. 'Shall we begin, Majesty?'

The cupboard turned out to be a wardrobe, and the cloak hanging in it was magnificent. It was a full, floor-length garment, made from the feathers of some exotic bird that would have put a peacock to shame. Even under the dim glowglobes, the colours danced and shimmered. A cloak worthy of a god, she thought, and wondered how the twisted old Spicemaster would look wearing it.

But it was a small, rather battered, wooden hand-drum he took from the wardrobe. 'Dragonskin,' he murmured as he passed it to her.

Blue glanced down at the worn green surface. 'Did you say *dragon*skin?'

'A small piece only, Majesty. The beast was in no way harmed when it was taken.'

Blue continued to stare at the drum. She couldn't imagine how you extracted a piece of skin from a dragon without harming it ... or getting yourself devoured, come to that. Perhaps he was lying. Dragons had been protected for years and the penalties for killing one were severe. But she had other things on her mind at the moment. She looked up at the Spicemaster.

'What do I do with this?'

'If Your Majesty would care to sit on the chair and –' he managed to look concerned, nervous and embarrassed all at the same time, '– place the drum between Your Majesty's knees ...' Blue did so without fuss, pushing down her skirt to make a lap. 'Now, Your Majesty, tap the drum gently: one-two.'

Blue tapped the drum with the tips of her fingers. For such a small instrument, it made an astonishingly loud, resonant note. She looked up at the Spicemaster.

'*Gently*, Majesty,' he emphasised. 'Let the dragon-skin do the work.'

She tapped it again, more gently this time. The note still sounded loudly, but the Spicemaster appeared satisfied.

'Now,' he said, 'one-two, like the beat of a human heart.'

Blue reached out to stroke the dragonskin. It looked smooth, but there was a coating of very fine green hair beneath her fingers. *Tap-boom*. She looked up at the Spicemaster. *Tap-boom*.

'Perfect!' he said. 'Like that. Exactly like that and at that speed until I reach the centre of the spiral. Then slower and more softly. Do you understand?' He blinked and added, 'Majesty.'

Blue nodded.

'Now, Majesty,' said the Spicemaster, 'if you will leave the drum on your chair for a moment and help me with the cloak …'

She was completely unprepared for the cloak. Although bulky, it was made from feathers so she expected it to be light, but the moment she tried to take it from the hanger, it writhed and twisted like a live thing and proved so heavy she needed all her strength to hold it. Glory only knows how the Spicemaster was going to manage.

'Fight it!' he commanded urgently. 'There's no real danger, but it will try to strangle you!'

How could there be no real danger if something was trying to strangle you? And why hadn't this silly little man mentioned the damn cloak if he was so concerned with her safety? But she fought the struggling garment gamely.

'My shoulders!' shouted the Spicemaster. 'Put it on my shoulders! It will quiet down once it gets hold of me!'

If I put it on his shoulders it will crush him to the ground, Blue thought. The thing felt as if it weighed a ton. But he was wriggling into position and the cloak was now so violent it almost wrenched itself out of her hands. Suddenly it was across his shoulders. The Spicemaster staggered a little, his knees buckled, but he managed to hold himself erect. The cloak, as predicted, settled down at once.

'Thank you, Majesty,' he said.

Blue sat on the leather seat, one hand absently caressing the dragonskin. It was almost like stroking a cat. The skin vibrated gently as if purring. But her eyes were on the Spicemaster, now at the entrance of the labyrinth. He looked magnificent in the cloak, far more magnificent than a man of his height deserved. The garment had changed him, lending him huge authority and presence. For the first time she found herself wondering if it might not, after all, have been a good idea to bring a guard with her. But she pushed the thought aside. Whatever the illusion of bulk, he was still the same frail little man underneath. She was perfectly safe.

He poured the contents of the liquid vial – was it water? – into the copper bowl, then unstoppered the second vial. At once a heady scent of nutmeg filled the air. Yet the spice wasn't nutmeg: she knew that instantly. There were citrus undertones and a heavy hint of musk that carried with it a curious note of corruption. The Spicemaster emptied the vial into the liquid and mixed the two together with a spatula. He glanced back at Blue.

'Drumbeat, please, Majesty.'

Blue jumped slightly, then tapped the drum. In one quick movement, the Spicemaster drank down the mixture in his bowl and stepped into the labyrinth.

four

If he'd been prepared to admit it, Pyrgus was afraid.

As Crown Prince, he'd never been allowed to visit Yammeth City – or anywhere else in the Cretch for that matter – and even when he'd run away, some natural caution kept him clear of the place. But he was here now; and he didn't like it.

The city wasn't at all what he'd imagined. It was cleaner, for one thing – far cleaner than the capital, which every Faerie of the Light touted as a shining example to the Realm. It was also – he hated to admit it – better laid out, although that wasn't surprising since it was a newer city. The capital was nearly two thousand years old. Yammeth City had been built no more than four hundred years ago, when the Cretch was ceded to the Faeries of the Night after the War of Partial Independence. They'd built it from scratch, with the help of demon labour, and laid it out, some said, to mimic the soulless metallic sprawls of Hael.

Maybe that was what made him nervous. Or maybe it was the level of the light.

Pyrgus was used to dark alleys. (Light's sake, he'd *lived* in one before his father's guards found him.) But this was different. Even the main streets of Yammeth were dim. And not just dim: the glowglobes in the street lamps gave out a blue-green illumination that left everything looking as if it was attacked by fungus. The lenses made it worse. Everybody here wore lenses, including Pyrgus, as part of his disguise. But the Faeries of the Night needed theirs because of their light-sensitive eyes. For Pyrgus, all lenses did was make things darker still. He'd already tripped twice, and tried to walk through a plate-glass door. He must have been mad to come here.

The traffic didn't help. The most popular form of transport among Faeries of the Night was something you just didn't see in other areas of the Realm: a single-seater flying pod you straddled like a horse. Unfortunately the pods were powered by cheap spells set for speed rather than altitude and most Nighters flew them at a breakneck pace around shoulder height. If you were on foot, as Pyrgus was, you ran an excellent chance of losing your head until your ears became attuned to the approaching hum. All of which meant he was avoiding the gloomy main thoroughfares and sticking to the even gloomier side streets. Getting anywhere took for ever.

All the same, he seemed to have reached the boundary wall of the Ogyris Estate. Even in the leprous light, he could see the distinctive red and gold of the Ogyris crest on the decorative frieze near the top.

Pyrgus glanced around. He couldn't afford to use the main gate, but he knew there were others and needed to find one in particular. What he wanted now was the statue of Lord Hairstreak. But that was carved from volcanic glass and nearly impossible to see in this light unless you were almost up against it. He certainly couldn't see it now. He could hardly see anything now.

In desperation he risked taking off his lenses – how many passers-by would be looking at him closely enough to discover he didn't have cat's eyes? – and there it was! At least there he thought it was: a black blob in a flowing cape. There should be an alley just south …

Yes! He had it now. There was the alley, bounded on one side by the estate wall.

Pyrgus put his lenses back on and slid furtively into the alley. Mercifully it looked empty. But how could anybody be sure through these damn glasses? He took them off again and the alley really was empty. He moved along it swiftly, one hand trailing on the wall, and reached the side gate in a moment. It was locked, of course, and the brown slick of spell coating suggested climbing it might be lethal. But it wasn't the gate that interested him. According to his information, there should be a small pedestrian entrance – no more than a narrow wooden doorway – just a little way …

Yes, there it was: a recess in the wall. He slipped in, tried the handle and – yes!!! – it was open, exactly as he'd been promised. Pyrgus went through, closed the door and uttered a triumphant prayer of thanks. He was in the Ogyris Estate!

Oddly enough, he could see better here, partly because the estate was open to the sky, partly because he was able to get rid of those damn lenses now. If anybody spotted him he was dead anyway, whether they discovered he was a Faerie of the Light or not. He looked around. He was on a narrow path that meandered through a stretch of lawn to disappear into a copse. There would be guards at the end of it, that was for sure. The Ogyris family might not be of noble birth, but they were fearsomely rich, which made them a magnet for every thief in the Realm. In fact guards were probably the least of their protections. He shuddered, thinking of the minefield that once guarded the old Chalkhill and Brimstone Miracle Glue Factory. You never knew how far Faeries of the Night might go.

Pyrgus found he'd stopped just inside the entrance and straightened his back to pull himself together. He was quite safe as long as he followed his instructions. Perfectly safe. Never safer.

The trouble was, they were *complicated* instructions.

He pulled the piece of paper from the pocket of his jerkin and discovered to his horror that even with his lenses off, he couldn't read his notes. What was *wrong* with him? It would have been so simple to bring a portaglobe or even a sparklight. But no. Perhaps he'd been a little … overexcited …?

Overexcited or not, he had limited choices now. He could go back to the street and reread the instructions under a street lamp for everyone to see. Or he could trust his memory. No contest, really. He couldn't run the risk of anybody finding out what he was up to.

Pyrgus left the path and cut diagonally across the lawn. He prayed he was heading for a rose bower.

The estate was a lot bigger than he'd imagined. After fifteen minutes he was still not in sight of the house, although he *had* found the obelisk, which was reassuring. He'd also avoided guards and traps, which was more reassuring still. Once he found the lake, he could follow the water's edge until he reached the boathouse.

The lake, when he found it, was also a lot bigger than he'd imagined. A private estate this size in the middle of a city must have cost an Emperor's ransom.

He was following the water's edge, eyes peeled for the outline of the boathouse, when a sudden blaze of light erupted on his left.

Pyrgus dived for cover. His first instinct was that he'd triggered a trap, but as he peered through the undergrowth, he discovered a large glasshouse had suddenly illuminated. He lay where he was, waiting. Chances were somebody had switched on the glowglobes. But he could see no moving shapes, no shadows, nothing to suggest anyone else was about. Glowglobes *could* be set to come on automatically.

After a while, he began to crawl forward. Cautiously.

The closer he got, the more he grew convinced there was no one in the glasshouse. Or if there was, they were keeping very still. He came to a decision and risked climbing to his feet. He waited. He was standing at the edge of the glow spilling out from the glasshouse, visible to anyone who happened to glance in his direction ... but still far enough away to make a run for it if someone did.

Nothing. No startled voice, no sound of an alarm. The glowglobes must have been set to automatic.

He realised he'd been holding his breath and released it with a sigh. Now that it seemed he was in no danger, he took time to look at the glasshouse properly. It was a far more sturdy building than he'd thought and, as he moved closer, he noticed the glass bore the telltale sheen of magical reinforcement. Something valuable inside. His mind suddenly went back to the time he'd freed Lord Hairstreak's phoenix. The bird had been penned in a glass cage with the same sort of spell coating. Was Ogyris holding some poor creatures here? The glasshouse was a lot bigger than Hairstreak's cage.

Pyrgus pressed his nose against the glass and saw at once that this was something very different. Inside, set in trays, were row upon row of delicate, exotic blooms, their petals glinting and sparkling under the lights. But even at a glance he could see these were not natural plants. Every stem, every bud, every blossom, every leaf was delicately sculpted from the very finest rock crystal. The entire content of the glasshouse was an artefact, an astonishing, priceless, near incomprehensible work of art, laid out in the whimsy of a natural setting.

Had each flower really been individually sculpted? The only other possibility was magic and he knew of no spell that could create such an effect. Illusions were far too coarse, transformations far too limited. Some master sculptor had lovingly created every piece and Merchant Ogyris had set them one by one in this vast glasshouse. There were hundreds of the crystal blooms. The cost must have been mind-numbing.

Pyrgus was still staring in awe at the crystal flowers when a hand fell on his shoulder.

five

'You're Tim's *son*?' the girl asked incredulously after Henry calmed her down. 'He never told me he had a son.'

Nice one, Dad, thought Henry. The girl didn't look much more than twenty-five, way too young for Dad who was positively *middle-aged*, for Pete's sake! She had auburn-red hair like – well, like somebody he knew in another place – and a terribly curvy figure and that towel didn't look too secure since she'd been screaming.

'He did tell you he'd a wife, though?' Henry asked, then wished he could have amputated his tongue. It was the sort of thing that sounded really, really mean; and if Dad *hadn't* told her, then Henry could have blown his nice new romance with the very first question he asked. He was fairly sure this *was* Dad's nice new romance, and even though the girl was way too young, Henry couldn't blame him. Not after what Mum did.

'Yes, of course,' the girl said, frowning, but not at all put out. 'But I thought his wife was a lesbian. I didn't know lesbians *had* children.'

It had thrown Henry a bit the first time it came up. 'Yes, they do,' he said earnestly. 'At least, Mum did.

But maybe she wasn't lesbian when she had us – that happens sometimes.' It came out so miserably he saw the girl's expression soften.

'I'm sorry,' she said. 'This is awful – I don't even know your name.'

'Henry,' Henry told her. He wished he'd foregone the Brownie points and headed straight for Mr Fogarty's house. 'What's yours?'

'You mustn't laugh – it's Laura Croft.'

Henry looked at her blankly.

'You know, like the computer game. And the movie. Except she's Lara.'

'Oh, yes …' Henry said uncertainly. He didn't play computer games and never seemed to have time to go to movies. 'Nice to meet you, Laura.' He held out his hand, then wished he hadn't because he was seriously worried what might happen if she lost her grip on the towel.

But she shook hands without mishap, then, either reading his mind or possibly just following his gaze, said, 'Look, let me get dressed. I was in the shower – that's why I didn't hear you. Your dad should be back in a minute. Make yourself a cup of tea or something –' She glanced at the mug in his hand. 'Oh, you have – that's good. Won't be a sec.' He noticed she went through the door to the master bedroom, not up the spiral staircase.

Henry sat back down on the couch, wondering how he was going to escape before his dad came back. What had happened was bad enough. The thought of a three-way conversation with his dad and his dad's new girlfriend was just too awful to contemplate. He sipped his tea and found it had gone cold, which didn't matter because it tasted foul anyway. But he decided against making himself a fresh mug. He also decided against mentioning any of this to his mother, even the fact he'd called to see his dad.

The girl came back wearing a mustard-yellow suit that would have been mad on most people, but somehow went with her colouring. Her hair was still wet, but she'd brushed it back off her face. She grinned suddenly.

'Know how I knew you really *were* Tim's son and not some axe-murderer just pretending?'

Henry shook his head.

'You're the image of him,' Laura said. Then added seriously, 'You have such sensitive eyes.'

'Look,' Henry said, embarrassed, 'I have to be going.' He nearly added, *I have to feed a cat*, but decided that sounded stupid.

'You can't go yet,' Laura told him firmly. 'Tim would kill me. Let me make you another cup of tea.' She glanced into his mug with its yoghurt globules. 'That one looks peculiar.'

Henry sat down again. He didn't see how he could just walk out, however much he wanted to. Laura went into the kitchen. He watched her through the open door, bustling about with the ease that comes when you live in a place.

'Do you take milk and sugar?' she called.

'There isn't any milk,' Henry said.

'Yes, there is.' And there was. She came back with a nice cup of tea in a proper cup, although he couldn't think where she'd found it. Or the milk.

He took a sip. 'Are you and Dad ... you know ...?'

She watched him for a moment, grinning slightly,

then helped him out by saying, 'An item? Yes. Yes, we are. He's not *that* much older than me.'

'No, I suppose not,' Henry said, even though he didn't suppose that at all.

Laura said, 'I'm not a gold-digger.'

Henry looked at her in surprise. It had never occurred to him his dad had enough gold to be worth digging. But now he thought about it, Tim Atherton was a successful company executive – he drove a Merc, for heaven's sake – which must mean he was pretty well off. And he had an expense account for entertaining clients, so he knew the best restaurants. For somebody who wasn't family, he probably looked rich.

Henry said, truthfully this time, 'I didn't think you were.'

Laura sat down beside him on the couch. She'd made herself a cup of tea as well. 'Just so you know,' she said. She hesitated, but only for a heartbeat. 'I don't know why he didn't tell me about you, Henry – I suppose it's the age thing: he's very sensitive about it – but I want you to know I love your father. I mean, I don't expect you to approve of me, or even like me – you love your mother, I know that. But I didn't break up their marriage: I had nothing to do with that. And it's important for you to know I'm not just some little floozy on the make.'

This was hideously embarrassing, but despite his discomfort, all he could think of was that he'd never heard anybody use the word 'floozy' outside of a black-and-white movie.

'I didn't think you were,' he said again. Maybe if he allowed her to get it off her chest, she'd let him go before his father came back. Henry didn't think he could cope if his father came back. To encourage her, he asked hesitantly, 'How did you two meet – you and Dad?'

'At a club,' Laura said.

For a moment he thought she must be making fun of him, then saw from her face she wasn't. His dad went to *clubs*? Oldest swinger in town? He opened his mouth to say something, couldn't think of anything to say and closed it again. Fortunately Laura was burbling on.

'I don't usually go to clubs, but my sister dragged me to this one. Said it would cheer me up, but actually she just wanted company. It was just as dreadful as they usually are. I don't really go for men my own age – they're always on the pull and the only thing they can talk about is football. I'd decided to stay half an hour just to please Sheila – that's my sister – then go home. But then I saw Tim on his own in the bar. He was drinking wine; all the other men – boys, really – were drinking beer. He looked so Byronic: you know, a tragic figure.'

That would be Dad all right – a tragic figure. Just lost his wife to his secretary, just lost his kids to his wife, just lost his home to a waterside apartment with a fancy prospectus. Not sure you'd call that Byronic, though. Henry set his cup down on the floor.

'Look, I'm sorry, but I really do have to go. Got something to do. It was – it was very nice to meet you and I'm sorry I frightened you when, you know, when you came out of the shower and everything. And thanks for the tea: it was great. Anyway, maybe you'd tell Dad I called –'

A door slammed shut somewhere. Laura said

brightly, 'You can tell him yourself. That must be him now.' Henry looked around, frantically searching for some means of escape, but then his father walked into the room and she smiled and said, 'Look, Tim. Look who's here!'

Six

As the Spicemaster reached the centre of the spiral, his whole appearance changed. His back straightened. He seemed taller. The feathered cloak expanded, giving him the illusion of fearsome bulk. But far more impressive was the way he moved. The hesitant, sickly steps of the old man were gone and he strode like a warrior. He spun round to look at Blue and hissed. His eyes burned.

With a chill, Blue saw his face had changed as well. He was still recognisable – if only just – but his features were florid and swollen, his lips thickened, with a bluish tinge. Worst of all were the teeth which had, incredibly, enlarged so that they seemed almost like those of an animal. He hissed again, a long drawn-out sibilant that cut through the air like a knife. Then his eyes rolled back in his head. He began to tremble violently.

'Spicemaster –' Blue murmured in alarm. The dragonskin drum slipped from her fingers and rolled across the floor.

The Spicemaster's trembling turned to something more violent, a sort of convulsion, like someone preparing to have a full-scale fit. His head began to snap back rhythmically with increasing force.

'Spicemaster!' Blue exclaimed again. He was dropping on all fours now, like an animal, but the convulsions were, if anything, more violent. It was the head-jerking that really worried her – the man could break his own neck. Despite a sudden eruption of fear, she started forward. Whatever was happening, he needed help.

'Back!' hissed the Spicemaster. His fierce eyes held hers for a moment, then the head resumed its jerking. He howled like a wolf and gripped his skull with both hands. 'Stay ... back ...' he gasped with enormous effort. 'You ... are not ... safe ... within the spiral!'

Blue halted, one foot just short of the entrance. Her mind was a turmoil. The spiral was nothing more than markings on the floor. Inside or outside surely made no difference. Besides, he needed help. She couldn't let him injure himself, no matter how important this con-sultation was to her. All the same, she hesitated.

But then, impossibly, the Spicemaster was on his feet again and he was no longer the Spicemaster. All vestige of the old man had disappeared. In his place towered a creature of gigantic proportions. For a moment it seemed as though it might be eight feet tall and vastly bulky. The thought of an illusion spell passed through her mind, but this was no illusion; or at least no magical illusion she had ever seen. Despite everything, the Spicemaster hadn't really changed. She could still make out the wreckage of his features, the poor distorted body. But it was as if some alien entity had got inside him and blown him up like a balloon. She half expected to see his skin crack and something huge emerge.

The creature that had been the Spicemaster began to dance.

It was a rough, raw dance, a stamping, shuffling dance that conjured scenes of swampland and evoked the rage of beasts. From somewhere on the edges of her mind, Blue imagined she could hear the savage rhythms of primeval music: click-sticks, toma and mercomba, growling voices.

The creature whirled to look at her ...

And smiled.

The voice that echoed through the chamber should never have emerged from the Spicemaster's throat. It reverberated like the dragonskin, but carried with it the infinite chill of deep space, a voice so alien, so *other* that she shuddered.

'I see thee, Faerie Queen,' it said.

Seven

Pyrgus whirled, one hand reaching instinctively for his blade. Then he saw the sweep of long black hair.

'What the *Hael* are you doing here?' Gela asked crossly. 'I told you the *boathouse*!' She had a gorgeous voice but a peculiar accent, probably due to the fact that the Ogyris family came originally from Haleklind.

'Got lost,' Pyrgus told her quickly. Which wasn't strictly true since he'd only been sidetracked while *looking* for the boathouse, but he'd discovered you had to be careful with Gela otherwise she buried you under a whole heap of questions. His heart was still pounding furiously, but now it had nothing to do with the shock of the hand on his shoulder.

'How could you get lost?' Gela asked. 'I gave you very detailed instructions. Don't you know you could get *killed* getting lost?'

It was happening again. Pyrgus decided to answer the first question and ignore the second.

'I couldn't read your instructions,' he said.

'Why not? You wrote them down. You can't complain about my writing.'

'No, I can't. And I'm not. I'm just saying I couldn't read the instructions – the instructions *I* wrote down.' He hesitated, then added, 'Because I –' He was going to say *Because I couldn't see them*, but realised that would just lead to another question and changed it to, 'Because I didn't bring a light with me.'

'You didn't bring a light with you?' Gela asked incredulously. She tossed her head in disbelief.

Pyrgus decided to stop this nonsense by asking a question of his own. 'What are those things in the glasshouse?'

Gela was a girl about his own age, but there any resemblance ended. Pyrgus was a prince who looked like a peasant, short and sturdy. No one would take Gela for a peasant in a thousand years. The clothes she was wearing had the understated stamp of designer flair. Her hair had the cut and sheen of expert styling and her face was finely featured. Her eyes were large for a Faerie of the Night, large and liquid. She was, quite simply, the most exotic creature he'd ever seen.

'Ah,' she said.

Pyrgus waited. 'Ah?'

'Those are something you shouldn't have seen.'

Pyrgus glanced through the glass. 'Why not?' he asked curiously.

'Oh, you know ...' Gela shrugged. She said casually, 'You haven't touched the glass, have you?'

'No ...' Or perhaps he had. Hadn't he pressed his nose against it? With Gela standing so close Pyrgus couldn't remember. He looked at her suspiciously. 'Why?'

'Daddy has it alarmed. Lethal force and all that.'

'Lethal force and all *what*?'

Gela shrugged again. 'You know. It would kill you.'

'Just *touching* the glass?' He couldn't believe it. This

was *worse* than Chalkhill and Brimstone's cobblestone minefield.

'I'm not sure,' Gela said. 'Maybe not just touching it. But if you tried to get in –'

'Well, I didn't,' Pyrgus said. 'Or touch the glass.' He frowned. 'Isn't that a bit ... extreme? I mean I know the sculptures must be very valuable, but –'

'Oh, it's not that. It's just stupid politics.'

Politics? This was getting more confusing.

'What's a glasshouse got to do with politics?'

Gela sighed deeply. 'I'm not supposed to know this, but Father's growing them for somebody.'

'Growing what?' Pyrgus asked, utterly bewildered.

She nodded in the direction of the glasshouse. 'The flowers.'

'Those aren't flowers,' Pyrgus said. 'They're sculptures.'

Gela tilted her head to give him a supercilious look. 'If they aren't *flowers*,' she sniffed, 'why do you think the lights are on?'

Pyrgus looked at her blankly.

Gela said with exaggerated patience, 'If they were just *sculptures*, why would Father set the growlights to come on in the middle of the night? Why would he want the place all lit up and attracting attention when he didn't have to? Why would he keep them in a glasshouse in the first place? Why wouldn't all his boring guards be beating you up this very minute?'

The only one of Gela's questions that really made sense was the last one. 'Why *aren't* his boring guards beating me up this very minute?' he asked. He didn't believe what she said about the flowers, but there were hundreds of crystal sculptures in there, each one worth a fortune. Why *didn't* Gela's father have a whole army of guards around them? He could certainly afford it.

Gela's face took on that dangerous look she got when she was impatient. 'Because guards attract *attention*. None of this is supposed to be happening, you know. You put guards around something and everybody knows it's important. Father just wants to grow his flowers quietly at night when there's nobody around. He makes the glass opaque during the day so you can't see what's inside.' She blinked slowly, covering and uncovering those magnificent eyes. 'Besides, he has some *really* dangerous spells on that building.'

'Why doesn't he opaque it at night? The growglobes are inside.'

'Something to do with starlight,' Gela said vaguely. She glanced over her shoulder. 'Look, are we going to stand here all night discussing horticulture?'

'Who's he growing them for?' Pyrgus asked. He still wasn't sure he believed they really *were* flowers, but it might be useful to play along with the story.

'That's a secret,' Gela told him severely.

'Do *you* know?'

'Of course I know – I'm Daddy's pet, aren't I?' She sniffed. 'But I've told you far too much already.' Her head went up again. 'Now, are we going to the boathouse for our meeting, or have you forgotten all the fuss you made about it?'

'We're going to the boathouse,' Pyrgus said.

It turned out the boathouse wasn't all that far – he'd remembered his instructions well enough before he'd sidetracked to the glasshouse. He followed her along the lakeside, then up a short path to a smallish jetty. There was a wooden building to one side of it. Gela pushed the door and disappeared inside. Pyrgus hesitated for a moment, then followed her.

It was pitch black inside. Gela's voice floated imperiously out of the darkness ahead.

'Close the door.'

Pyrgus closed the door behind him and at once a glowglobe illuminated overhead. It had the low light setting Faeries of the Night preferred, but he was able to see well enough. Gela was standing a few feet away beside two rowing boats and some fishing tackle. She looked stunning.

'Well,' she asked, 'are you going to tell me why we're here?'

Pyrgus walked across and kissed her.

Eight

Henry escaped eventually, slightly consoled by the fact that his dad was even more embarrassed than he was.

Henry could understand perfectly well why his father had neglected to mention his children to a girlfriend who was young enough to be his daughter. It was no big deal. But Dad went on a guilt trip – you could see it in his eyes. He saw his new squeeze sitting on the couch and Henry sitting uncomfortably beside her and you'd have thought he'd been caught with his hand in the till.

'*Ah, Henry, old man. Wasn't expecting you today. I see you've met my – my – see you've met Laura. She's, ah, staying over for a couple ...*'

And as he'd trailed off, Laura said mischievously, '*You never told me you had a son, Tim.*' Then blinked and added, '*Or a daughter.*'

And poor old Tim, who went to discos now he was on his own, launched into an explanation so convoluted Henry couldn't remember any of it. He'd probably still be explaining if Henry hadn't said, '*It's OK, Dad,*' and something in his voice convinced Tim it really *was* OK: if he'd done anything terrible, been disloyal or whatever, he'd been forgiven. He didn't seem all that worried about Laura, probably because it was clear from her grin she didn't mind at all.

With the explanation bit over, Dad had suddenly come over all hearty and started to talk about Henry staying the afternoon so they could all go out for a meal later, as if Mum wouldn't have gone ballistic if she'd ever discovered that cosy little arrangement. Henry just said no and muttered something about Mr Fogarty.

After that, it degenerated into one of those uncomfortable *How the hell are you?* conversations until Henry stood up and announced firmly he was leaving, which was probably a relief to everybody. Now he was at the head of Mr Fogarty's street and in a serious worry.

Up to now, he thought he'd taken it for granted that his parents would divorce. They were living apart, his mum had a new partner, so what else were they going to do? But Dad finding another woman somehow made it really *final*. If there was just the slightest chance Mum and Dad might get back together, it was gone now. Or would be, once Mum found out. Didn't matter Mum was the one who broke things up in the first place. Once she heard Dad was consoling himself with somebody – somebody young and pretty – she'd never forgive him. After that, it was just the legal formalities.

Including custody.

Henry wondered if he and Aisling would have to turn up in court. If they did, maybe the judge would ask them which parent they wanted to live with. Some nightmare that would be. Henry couldn't very well ask to move in with his dad now he was honeymooning with Laura. Not in a tiny flat – you were bound to hear stuff. But if he said he'd stay with Mum, he knew his dad would be hurt. Besides, he didn't want to stay with Mum. He hated Mum almost as much as he loved her and he was sure it was only a matter of time before Anaïs moved in.

But maybe the judge didn't ask you. Maybe he just decided what should happen and you had no say about it. Henry shuddered.

'Hello, Hodge,' he said mournfully as the old tom emerged out of nowhere to polish his ankles. It was gloomy in Mr Fogarty's kitchen so he flipped the light switch before taking a pouch of Whiskas from the cupboard. Then on impulse he took out a second. Mr Fogarty didn't approve of pouch Whiskas, which he claimed was far too good for a cat, but Hodge was looking thin lately – probably needed worming – and Mr Fogarty wasn't here. The story was that Mr Fogarty had gone to visit his daughter in New Zealand.

If that really *was* a story.

The thought struck Henry like a thunderbolt. He knew Mr Fogarty was Gatekeeper of the Faerie Realm. He knew Blue was crowned Faerie Empress. Henry had even visited the Realm himself. But standing here in Mr Fogarty's kitchen, feeding Mr Fogarty's cat, it all seemed … it all seemed …

The light went out as if the bulb had blown. Henry ignored it. It wasn't really dark yet and he could change it later. He'd be out of here in a minute anyway.

… It all seemed *mad,* was what he wanted to say. He was a *teenager*, for God's sake. How many teenagers did he know who believed in fairies? There were no such things as fairies, there was no such place as Fairyland. *No such place as Fairyland*. It echoed like a voice in his head.

The trouble was, he *remembered* Fairyland. Henry set the Whiskas pouches down beside Hodge's plate on the counter-top. If he remembered Fairyland, there had to be something wrong. There had to be something wrong with his memory. He stared down at the cat, who was staring up at him in beady expectation. There had to be something wrong with his *mind*!

All of a sudden, Henry felt very much afraid.

To Hodge's indignant howl, he walked out of the kitchen into Mr Fogarty's back garden. There was a constriction in his chest and he needed air. The twilight outside had taken on a bluish tinge and there was a slight vibration in the ground as if there were some heavy lorries passing. Henry felt like throwing up.

No such place as Fairyland, the voice repeated in his head.

It had all started to make a ghastly sort of sense. He knew stress could make you ill – his father had had a grumbling ulcer for years, just because he was in a high-powered job – and a lot of stress could make you *mentally* ill. Everybody knew that. You just thought it could never happen to you.

And he *had* been under a lot of stress, hadn't he? His mother was having an affair. His father had been thrown out of their home. (And had found himself a girlfriend, don't forget.) His parents were definitely going to get divorced, even though neither of them would admit it. Which meant Henry might be put into some sort of orphan's home until he was eighteen. Or he'd have to live with his mother and Aisling, which was worse. Of *course* he was under stress. He was under more stress right now than he'd ever been in his life. All he wanted was to get away, away from his rotten mother and his rotten sister and his stupid weak father and all the hassles at home …

And wasn't that exactly what he'd done? Hadn't he escaped from all of it? Hadn't he created a fantasy world and simply …

No such place as Fairyland.

… lived in it?

The more he thought about it, the more sense it made. The Fairyland of his imagination was nothing like the Fairyland you read about in books. His was full of heroes – the sort of people Henry longed to be and never was. And teenagers were in charge. Pyrgus was a prince and could have been Emperor if he'd been interested. Blue was Queen now, absolute ruler of the Realm. She could do whatever she wanted. If you were a teenage boy and needed to create a fantasy world, wouldn't you dream up one where teenagers were in charge?

The vibration underneath his feet seemed to be getting more pronounced. How many passing lorries could there be?

Henry stared at the buddleia bush where he'd first met Pyrgus. Where he *thought* he'd first met Pyrgus. It all seemed so real. But then dreams seemed real while you were dreaming them and hallucinations seemed real to a lunatic.

Blue seemed real. Henry remembered the first time he'd seen *her*. She was stepping into her bath at the time.

Suddenly he knew where *that* came from. He didn't have a girlfriend. Well, he had Charlie Severs, but she was a friend who just happened to be a girl. They weren't an item or anything like that. They didn't … well, you know. All the boys at school had girlfriends. Or at least went out with lots of girls. Most of them claimed they were doing it. Henry sometimes pretended he'd done it too, but he hadn't. He was a bit shy around girls when it came to that sort of thing. He couldn't imagine ever asking one to … But that didn't mean he didn't want to. You bet he wanted to! Every boy his age wanted to, whether they did it or not.

There was something else. Henry would have cut his thumbs off rather than admit it, but he was a bit of a romantic. He didn't just want one-night stands. He wanted a girl he could, you know (even in his head he mumbled the word shamefacedly), *love*. Run through fields of corn together, and rescue when she needed rescuing and hold hands with and bring her flowers and write poetry to and … and …

And all that.

Except girls weren't interested in that sort of thing any more. Start writing poetry and bringing flowers and girls took you for a stalker.

So he'd dreamed up a beautiful girl to fall in love with. An old-fashioned sort of girl, a fairy princess sort of girl. And Blue really *was* a faerie princess. At least until they crowned her Faerie Queen. And they'd done heroic things together, like rescuing her brother. And her brother was his best friend. And it all happened in Fairyland for cripe's sake, so he didn't have to deal with his rotten mother or his rotten sister or any of his *real* problems.

Henry was moving like a zombie as he left the blue light of Mr Fogarty's garden and walked up the street to the bus stop. There were no passing lorries any more.

When he got home, he found – despite all his mother's promises and protestations – that Anaïs had moved in.

Nine

'Who are you?' Blue whispered. She wanted to say, *What are you?* but it sounded rude and possibly dangerous. The creature at the centre of the spiral was no longer the Spicemaster. It loomed like a feathered giant and glared at her like a savage beast.

'I am Yidam,' the creature replied.

She'd never heard the word before and wasn't sure whether it was a name or a description. Madame Cardui said Spicemaster Memnon was possessed by a god when he made his predictions, but it was one of the Old Gods who walked the world before the coming of the Light. As far as Blue could make out, the Old Gods were so fierce they might as well have been demons. This one looked it.

'Lord Yidam,' Blue said, just to be on the safe side, 'can you see the future?'

'I exist beyond time,' the Yidam said.

Blue hesitated. She didn't want to irritate the entity, but it was important to be clear. 'Can you see *my* future?'

To her astonishment, the Yidam smiled. 'Come sit by me, Faerie Queen,' it said.

There was no sound in the chamber except the beating of her heart. After a long moment, Blue decided on honesty before diplomacy.

'The Spicemaster said you might kill me if I stepped into the spiral.'

'The Spicemaster was mistaken.'

And there it was, laid out in front of her. Four flat simple words. Did she believe the Spicemaster? Or did she believe the Yidam? Could she risk approaching it?

It occurred to Blue suddenly that the only thing between the Yidam and herself was a spiral pattern marked out on the ground. It could have covered the space between them in a bound. Any safety she felt was an illusion. She swallowed her fear and walked into the spiral.

As she squatted down beside it, Blue realised the creature had utterly transformed the old Spicemaster. The thing towered above her and, close up, its eyes were consumed by inner fires. She fought not to shy away as it reached towards her with enormous, strangler's hands.

But the hands gently placed themselves on the crown of her head. Blue felt the tingle of trapped lightning flowing down her spine and realised she'd received a blessing. 'Thank you, Lord Yidam,' she murmured. Any blessing was nice, but if the creature couldn't see her future, then she was wasting her time.

The Yidam leaned forward slightly. 'Thou art brave, Faerie Queen.' It seemed incredible, but for a moment she thought the fierce eyes took on the barest hint of a twinkle. 'But art thou brave enough to face what I may say?'

Blue blinked. The Yidam's words were disturbing. They brought up something that had been niggling at the edges of her mind ever since she decided to consult the Spicemaster. Did she *really* want to know the future? A future that might include the details of her own death? Or, worse still, the deaths of Pyrgus and Henry? Could she live with that knowledge?

Did she even want to know the future of the Realm? What if the Yidam told her it would fall to enemies or demon hordes? What if it was destined for corruption and disintegration? How could she go on, knowing that all her efforts would be in vain?

But she was here and needed guidance. Which over-rode everything.

'Lord Yidam,' Blue said, 'what will happen if I start a war against the Faeries of the Night?'

Ten

'Do you believe in fairies?' Henry asked.

'Sorry?'

Henry leaned forward. 'Do you believe in *fairies*?' he asked again, dropping his voice even further. They were sitting in a new coffee house called Ropo's that was proving extremely popular with everyone from school. There were at least eight pupils at nearby tables (several of them dressed as Goths) and he certainly didn't want *them* hearing.

'Fairies?' Charlie echoed, looking at him strangely. 'Like on top of the Christmas tree?'

Henry nodded. 'Except for real.'

'Except for real?' Charlie was obviously big into repeating everything he said tonight. 'Like, little people with wings who flit among the bluebells?'

Henry gave up and said, 'I thought I saw one once.'

'You thought you –?'

'Charlie,' Henry hissed, 'please don't keep repeating everything I say. Yes, I said I thought I saw one once.'

'You saw a little person with wings flitting among the bluebells?'

'I was under a lot of strain,' said Henry.

That caught her attention. Charlie knew all about the strain Henry had been under. She frowned. 'Your mum's not got you seeing things?' She sounded out-raged.

'I think so. I mean, what else could it be?' A thought occurred to him. 'It wasn't flitting among the bluebells: Hodge caught it.'

'Mr Fogarty's cat?'

Henry nodded. 'Yes.'

The ghost of a suppressed smile twitched Charlie's lips. 'Mr Fogarty's cat caught a fairy?'

'Look,' said Henry urgently, 'until today, I thought all this was for real. Then I went to see Dad and he's got a new girlfriend, and when I got home, Mum had moved Anaïs in.'

'Oh my God!' Charlie exclaimed, genuinely appalled. All hint of a smile vanished. 'You mean you'll have to live with your mum and Aisling and now this dreadful Anaïs woman as well?'

'She's not really dreadful. Quite nice, really. Like, she tries. But you know …'

'Oh, I know all right,' Charlie said fiercely. 'They're going to get divorced, aren't they? If your dad's got himself a girlfriend?'

Henry nodded miserably. 'I suppose so.'

Charlie reached out and took his hand. 'It's not as bad as you think, Henry. It's pretty awful, but it's not as bad as you think. And when it's over, it's over.'

Charlie's parents had divorced and Charlie's mum was married again to a man Charlie adored. Henry said uncertainly, 'Do you know what happens to the children? Like, me and Aisling? I mean do we have to go to court? And who says who lives where?' He swallowed. 'I mean, I don't want to live with Mum and Anaïs – that would be just too awful for Dad – but I can't very well move in with him if he's got a new girl: did I mention she was young? Just a few years older than we are. I couldn't move in there, not that he'd want me anyway, so do I have to go to an orphanage or something until I'm eighteen?'

Charlie said, 'I don't know, Henry. I was too young to remember much of it. Anyway, I think my mum and dad agreed everything between them and I was happy living with my mum – I hated my real dad. It wasn't like your situation at all.' She stared thoughtfully into the middle distance for a moment, then pulled her gaze back to Henry. 'What's the thing about fairies?'

Henry sighed. 'Oh, it's stupid.' He shook his head and tried to smile. 'It was after all this business started – Mum and Anaïs. Or at least after I heard about it. I suppose I just couldn't cope with it. I mean, how often do you find out your mum's a lesbian? I think I wanted to get away: you know, just get away from ... everything. And since there was no way I *could* get away, I suppose I ... I ... started to make up stuff. In my head. I suppose I made up a whole other stupid world in my head –' the weak smile again, '– and just, sort of ... went there.' The look on Charlie's face made him want to cry.

'But ... what actually happened?' she asked with a curious mixture of bewilderment and sympathy.

He'd gone too far to start backing off now. Besides, he trusted Charlie. He'd always talked to her, right since they were little kids. He took a deep breath and somehow managed to inject a note of briskness into his voice.

'I had this ... thing ... I don't know, hallucination or something, or dream, or false memory or –'

'Henry, just tell me what happened.'

Henry shifted uncomfortably. 'Well, after it came out about Mum, I went to Mr Fogarty's. I had to clean out his shed. And while I was there, Hodge appeared and he had a thing in his mouth. Like a butterfly. You know the way cats are. He'd caught it, but it wasn't dead so I tried to take if off him.' He hesitated, then added, 'That's when I saw it was a fairy.'

'You thought it was a fairy?'

'Yes.'

After a bit, Charlie said, 'Go on.'

'I suppose it was just a butterfly,' Henry said. 'But I made up this fantasy about the butterfly being a fairy prince called Pyrgus –'

'Pyrgus?' Charlie echoed.

Henry nodded.

'Did he have some other name?'

'Pyrgus Malvae,' Henry said.

'That's a butterfly name,' Charlie said. 'That's the Latin name for the grizzled skipper butterfly.'

'Is it?' Henry said, surprised. After a while he added, 'I suppose I must have known that. Subconsciously. Does a grizzled skipper have little brown spotty wings?'

Charlie nodded. 'Yes.'

Henry shook his head in wonder. 'I must have made it part of my fantasy. Grizzled skipper butterfly turns into a fairy and I give him his butterfly name.' He shook his head. 'I'm in a lot of trouble, Charlie.'

Charlie said quietly, 'I think maybe you are.'

Eleven

Henry missed his last bus home.

He lived nearly four miles outside town and when he called his mum in the hope she might collect him, all he got was the answering machine (Dad's voice still on it, which was a real bummer). So now he was walking in the rain. Not that he noticed it much. All he could think of was five words out of Charlie's mouth: '*I think maybe you are.*'

Charlie was the sweetest, kindest girl he knew. If there was any way of letting him down gently, she'd have found it. But Charlie thought he was in trouble. Charlie thought – she'd put it very diplomatically – that he might need 'help'. By which she meant psychiatric help, although she never actually said psychiatrist: she said 'therapist'.

There was engine noise behind him and the approaching glow of headlights. Henry stepped on to the verge without looking round: he was wearing a light-coloured jacket so the car should have no trouble seeing him. Charlie never said 'psychiatric problem' either. She talked very gently about 'emotional pressures' and 'strain'. Just the sort of thing he'd been thinking himself. She was calm and optimistic and reassuring, the way you were supposed to be with lunatics. But the bottom line was still the same. She thought he was nutty as a fruitcake.

The car sounded like it had slowed down, but didn't seem to be passing. Henry glanced behind him.

There was a glowing silver disc hovering above the road.

Twelve

It was just like the time he'd run away from his father. One minute you were minding your own business, trying to persuade the barman you were old enough to order ale. The next you were staring up at a bunch of hulking great soldiers who called you *sir* with exaggerated politeness, but were quite prepared to break your arms if you didn't do exactly what they said.

Only this time it wasn't his father who'd sent them: it was his little *sister*, for Light's sake! He'd always known being made Queen would go to her head. She was bossy enough while she was still a princess.

Pyrgus smiled at the six hulking great soldiers standing round his table at the inn and tried to sound more confident than he felt.

'Please present my compliments to Her Majesty,' he told their officer grandly, 'and inform her that I shall join her at the palace at my earliest, my *very* earliest convenience.' Even as he said it, he knew it wouldn't do.

'Beg pardon, sir,' the Captain said, 'but Her Majesty was insistent that you should come straight away, sir. We have orders to escort you, sir.' He blinked, slowly. 'Now, sir.'

Pyrgus knew what it was all about, of course. He'd already had two messages from Blue, hand delivered by an orange Trinian. The first was a friendly little note asking him to come to the palace 'to talk about something important'. When he ignored that one, the Trinian popped up again days later. This time the tone was less friendly. He was 'commanded' to attend at the palace forthwith 'to discuss matters of critical importance to the Realm'. He'd ignored that one too. It would do Blue good to realise not everybody was going to jump to attention every time she snapped her fingers. But now she'd sent the heavy squad.

He made one more try. 'If you'll just allow me to go home and change ...' he said and gestured vaguely, still smiling. 'As you can see, I'm not exactly dressed to attend a meeting at the palace.' Which was true enough. Since he'd abdicated the throne, he'd made a point of dressing like a scruff. At the moment, he was wearing a torn leather jerkin and a pair of brown breeches that would have disgraced a pig farmer. The sense of freedom was wonderful.

'Beg pardon, sir,' the Captain said, 'Her Majesty's orders said at once. Very clear she was on that point. No mention of a dress code.' He leered. 'I expect your clothes will be acceptable, sir.'

Pyrgus sighed. 'Oh, very well, Captain – I'll come with you.'

'Now, sir?'

'*Right* now, Captain.'

They had a golden ouklo waiting outside. It floated at knee height for easy access and hummed a little with the excess of energy that only came with a fresh spell charge. At least Blue thought about his comfort.

The carriage bobbed like a boat as he climbed on board. To his surprise, the Captain and two of his men climbed in as well and sat facing him with stony expressions. The remaining three guards swarmed quickly up on top with the driver. The coach pulled away smoothly as soon as the door closed. Pyrgus caught the *snick* of a magical lock and smiled a little. They were taking no chance of losing him.

'Don't suppose you know what this is all about, do you?' he asked the Captain conversationally.

'No, sir, 'fraid not, sir.'

'No crises? No wars about to start? No demons on the loose?'

'Wouldn't know anything about that, sir,' the Captain said stiffly.

'No,' Pyrgus murmured. 'I don't suppose you would.' Professional soldiers never knew anything about anything. He gave up on conversation, settled back and closed his eyes.

The seats were the new spell-treated ordofoam that shaped itself to your bottom and squeezed it gently now and then to prevent discomfort on long journeys. It felt as if you were sitting on a giant hand and Pyrgus wasn't altogether sure he liked it. No matter how much he steeled himself, every squeeze came as a surprise so that he gave a small, involuntary jump. It was like having an annoying facial tic, except not on your face.

As a diversion, he glanced through the carriage window. 'This isn't the way to the palace,' he said at once.

'No, sir, indeed not, sir. That's because we're not going to the palace, sir.'

'Where *are* we going?' Pyrgus frowned.

'Not at leave to say, sir. Security, sir.'

That was typical of Blue. She was nearly as paranoid as Mr Fogarty. All the same, it had to be something pretty serious for her to want to meet him somewhere other than the palace.

A thought struck him and he asked, 'Am I the only one coming to this meeting?'

'Couldn't say, sir,' said the Captain.

The seat squeezed Pyrgus's bottom distractingly. He ignored it and looked out of the window again. Maybe he'd been a bit hasty in ignoring Blue's first messages. She might be bossy, but she wasn't stupid and she *was* Queen now, with responsibility for everything that happened in the Realm. She knew how he felt about affairs of State, so she would hardly have sent for him if it hadn't been important. The very least he could do was give her a bit of support. He scowled. Now he was feeling guilty.

The carriage, he realised, was leaving the city through Cripple's Gate. Which meant Blue had called her little meeting not just away from the palace, but away from any of the official residences. In all probability she'd hired somewhere, or, even more likely, had Madame Cardui arrange a safe house. He wondered where it was.

Nearly twenty minutes later, it turned out to be a small manor house surrounded by trees and so many security devices it was all Pyrgus could do to keep from laughing. He'd really have to talk to Blue about all this nonsense. Except the figure on the doorstep wasn't Blue.

It was Black Hairstreak.

Thirteen

Henry froze. This was straight out of *Close Encounters of the Third Kind*. The craft was massive – easily the size of two or three articulated trucks – and hung, humming, perhaps six feet above the surface of the road (which was vibrating just the way the ground at Mr Fogarty's had done, he thought inconsequentially). It was like the fake photographs of every flying saucer he'd ever seen – a shining metal disc with a bump on the top and light streaming down from the bottom. There was a row of small, round portholes (although he couldn't see anything through them) and above them another circle of lights. Any minute now, if this was the movies, it would put down a silvery ramp and a little green man with a big head and enormous eyes would walk out.

The saucer put down a silvery ramp and a little green man with a big head and enormous eyes walked out.

Henry tried to run, then suddenly felt very calm.

In his calm, frozen state he became very much aware of everything around him. Particularly the silence. There was no traffic noise. The little background sounds of night animals and insects had stopped. The saucer was no longer humming.

It was a beautiful saucer. Very beautiful indeed.

The little man was definitely green, but not bright green or olive green or grass green or anything like that. If you were filing a report for the police (although it was silly to think of filing a report for *anybody*) you would strictly need to say he had a greenish tint to his skin, which was otherwise grey.

The little green man turned in his direction. His eyes were very big and very black and very beautiful. If Henry looked deeply into them, he could see stars and constellations. He could see the depths of Space. The little green man began to walk in Henry's direction.

Somewhere buried deep inside the Henry who was calm there was a second Henry screaming to get out. The second Henry was in a panic, hysterical, terrified. The second Henry wanted to fight, wanted to smash the little man down, mash him into the ground under-foot like a bug (and could probably have done it too since the little man's limbs were spindly as twigs). But most of all, the second Henry wanted to run away from the little green man and the big glowing saucer as if the devil himself were after him.

Henry screamed, but no sound came out. He couldn't move. The little green man was looking at him and he was completely paralysed. It occurred to him he might be about to die.

The little green man looked deep into his eyes and climbed into his head.

It was horrible having somebody inside his head: like an insect crawling relentlessly into his ear, only worse. The little green man crawled relentlessly into Henry's mind, lifting up flaps here and there to look at Henry's private thoughts. Look, there was Henry's sister Aisling with a dagger sticking out of her head. Look, there was Blue in her bath. Look, there was Henry's mum explaining why everything she did was actually for Henry's benefit.

The little green man seemed to be looking for something. Or maybe just making sure who Henry was. He crawled and crawled and poked and prodded. Once he watched a memory of Henry sitting on the loo. There was nowhere he couldn't go, nowhere he *didn't* go.

And then he withdrew.

A beam of bright blue light emerged from the flying saucer and played over Henry. Although he didn't move, he felt as if he was turned upside down to stand on his head. Then he turned the right way up again and began to tremble. The tremble became a vibration and the vibration became a scream. The blue light began to draw Henry up off the road towards the flying saucer.

Something in Henry told him he must be dreaming. It was the only thing that made sense. He must have got tired walking home and lain down by the side of the road for a little nap. Now he was dreaming. He had to be dreaming, because there was no door in the saucer and he was floating through the metal hull, which was impossible unless he was dreaming.

Henry was inside the flying saucer. The light was gone, the little green man was gone and there didn't seem to be anybody else in there. He was no longer paralysed either. He could move his hands and his arms and his legs. In fact he felt normal. But what was happening *wasn't* normal. He was on board a flying saucer and the aliens had toddled off somewhere. That meant he could escape.

He wanted to escape. God knew he wanted to escape. But ...

There was something wrong with him. He knew it for certain now. He wasn't dreaming. This was too real to be dreaming. But at the same time it was exactly like a dream. Things happened. Now the thing that happened was he found himself exploring, not escaping.

The saucer was even larger on the inside than it looked from the outside, like a tardis. He was in a room with silver walls and a soft, squishy floor that seemed somehow ... organic. There were no windows and he couldn't find the light source. (Although there *was* light: a friendly rosy glow.) There was a door without a handle, but as he approached, it slid open automatically the way doors did in *Star Trek*. Or Tesco's.

He was in a corridor that meandered like a stream. And little branches meandered off it – often only a few yards long – leading into other chambers. Some had doors, some hadn't. Henry meandered with the corridor and discovered chambers with metallic pods, chambers with weapons racks (the weapons looked like laser rifles), a chamber stuffed with giant eggs. (At least he thought they might be giant eggs, since they were large and white and egg-shaped.) He seemed to wander for hours, peering into chamber after chamber. The funny thing was, he never found a kitchen or a bathroom.

He found a horrible, scary room.

Henry opened the door and was half blinded by a sudden glare. Then his eyes adjusted and he was looking at banks of huge transparent tubes, each one larger than he was. There was a maze of wires and piping running from the tubes to a control console in the middle of the room. Nearly half the tubes were lit by violet light so you could see there was a thick, gooey liquid inside, bubbling like a great, slow fish-tank. Floating in the liquid were scores of naked human babies, their eyes tight shut, their little hands opening and closing together in a ghastly rhythm.

Henry tried to break open the tubes to let the babies out, but the tubes were made from some sort of glass that wouldn't break. He wondered if he could figure out how to open them using the console, but was afraid he might accidentally hurt the babies. After a while he left the chamber in an agony of frustration.

Behind him, the babies opened their hands and closed their hands ... opened their hands and closed their hands ... opened ...

Henry found a porthole and looked out. He expected to see the road where he'd been walking, but instead he was looking into a blackness peppered by the brightest stars. He was looking into Space. The saucer had taken off. There was no possibility of escape any more.

A great sadness overcame Henry and he lay down beside the porthole to have a little sleep.

He woke surrounded by little green men staring at him with enormous black eyes. They were directed by a tall, fair-haired woman who looked completely human and was very, very beautiful.

'*I want to show you something, Henry,*' said the woman, and he heard her quite distinctly even though she had not moved her lips.

The tall, beautiful woman looked at him sadly. '*I want to show you what will happen if humans do not learn to treat their planet with respect.*' She turned to gesture at a viewing screen built into the wall behind her.

The screen lit up with images of a devastated world.

He watched cities razed by nuclear war. He saw oceans curdled with pollution. There were children starving as the Earth was over-populated. (White children, too, not just the familiar wide-eyed, pot-bellied kids from Africa.) There were people whose faces were a crawling mass of cancers as the ozone layer finally collapsed. There were hurricanes and earthquakes, tidal waves engulfing entire continents. There were radiation mutants, no longer really human, crawling across barren wastelands.

Henry tried to look away, but could not move his head. *'Will you tell them?'* asked the woman. *'Will you warn them what will happen?'*

Other voices chorused in his head: *'Henry will be the Anointed!'*

Without warning, Henry was naked, lying on a gurney. He was surrounded by little green men, but now they were wearing white coats. To his embarrassment, the beautiful woman was there too. She was also wearing a white coat. Beside the gurney were trays of surgical instruments and some sort of machine with angled arms and drills and scalpels that looked as if it had been put together by a mad dentist.

The beautiful woman smiled benignly. *'You must be prepared,'* she said.

'Henry will be King,' the voices chorused. *'Henry will be the Anointed King.'*

Alien hands reached out to touch him. There was a flooding smell of antiseptic. A foam sprayed across his body, cool at first, then burning acid so he could hardly bear it until something else flowed over him and washed it off. The creatures probed his bottom and his genitals.

'*Leave me alone!*' thought Henry, but found he couldn't speak.

'*Prepare the implant,*' said a harsh voice in his mind, different to any of the voices he'd heard before.

The beautiful woman was leaning over him, still smiling broadly. In her hand was the dentist's drill, which spun with a high-pitched whine. But she wasn't bringing it towards his mouth: she was bringing it towards his *eye*.

Henry began to scream and couldn't stop.

Fourteen

'It makes sense,' Blue said.

They were seated among the orchids in the conservatory behind the Throne Room. It was a strange place for a Council of War, but her father had protected it with so many spells it was the most private chamber in the palace.

Blue's eyes moved from one to the other. Gatekeeper Fogarty still looked an old man, but the rejuvenation treatments were beginning to bite. There was an energy about him and he had better skin. Beside him, Madame Cardui was sitting with her eyes closed, but Blue knew she was very much awake. These two were her friends. The disapproving looks came from the three uniformed Generals: Creerful, Vanelke and Ovard. She wished Pyrgus would get here. She felt outnumbered.

Blue licked her lips. 'Look at it the way *they* will,' she said. 'Everything's been topsy-turvy for months. Uncle Hairstreak has tried to take over the throne twice and failed –'

'Which is precisely the reason why he's unlikely to try again, Majesty,' General Ovard put in patiently.

He'd been her father's closest military advisor. But she could not afford to show weakness. 'Let me finish, General.' Then, without waiting for a response, she turned to the others. 'Hairstreak's still ambitious. And even though he failed, the Faeries of the Night still back him.'

'They won't have much stomach for another failure,' Ovard muttered.

This time Blue ignored him. 'Now look at the other side of the picture. *We* came close to losing first time. What ha—'

'Oh, come, Your Majesty, I'd hardly say we came close to losing.' Not Ovard this time but General Creerful. They were old men. Senior military were always old men. Empress or not, they would never take her seriously. They looked at her and saw a little girl.

Blue glared at him. 'My father, the Purple Emperor, was murdered, General. I'd say that brought us pretty close to losing.'

Creerful dropped his eyes and said nothing. After a moment, Blue went on, 'What happened next was a clever plot that could have succeeded. In fact, it very nearly did. Don't forget my brother was banished from the Purple Palace. We were very, very lucky to find the allies we did. We could never have turned the tide without them. We can't count on that sort of luck a second time and my uncle knows it.'

Madame Cardui opened her eyes. 'The Forest Faerie are our friends,' she said gently. 'I'm certain they might be persuaded to help us again.'

Blue admired Madame Cardui hugely, but she fixed her with a steady gaze. 'The Forest Faerie are *your* friends,' she said firmly. 'That's not the same thing. When they helped us before, their own interests were involved. We can't be sure they'll help us again.'

Madame Cardui nodded mildly and closed her eyes

again. 'Perhaps you're right, Majesty.'

Blue turned back to the others. 'Now look at what's happened the way a Faerie of the Night would. The Purple Emperor was killed. The new Purple Emperor abdicated. Now there's a child on the throne. And a girl-child at that!'

Suddenly everybody was talking at once. Even Madame Cardui opened her eyes again.

Blue held up a hand for silence. '*Look* at it!' she said fiercely. 'I'm only just sixteen years old. I have no experience of politics or fighting wars or anything like that. And I'm a *girl*. It's only because my brother didn't want the throne that I'm here now. I'd never have become Queen. I was supposed to grow up quietly and marry some foreign prince and give him lots of stupid babies. I wasn't supposed to know about affairs of State. I was supposed to look pretty and get on with it. That's how my father saw me. That's how my uncle sees me. That's how I'm seen by the Faeries of the Night.'

Gatekeeper Fogarty spoke for the first time since the meeting began. 'She's right,' he said.

Blue glanced at him gratefully. 'Put yourself in their place. Your enemy has already been weakened and is now being led by a child who knows nothing about anything. Can you think of a better time to attack?'

Fogarty said stonily, 'So what's your solution?'

This was it. Despite his question, Mr Fogarty knew where she was heading. It was time the others did the same.

'I told you my solution before we started this meeting, Gatekeeper. We attack first.'

General Ovard choked, then rounded on her

apoplectically. 'That will start a civil war!'

Blue took a deep breath. 'Yes,' she said.

There was a long silence, which General Vanelke eventually broke. He was the oldest of the three Generals, a veteran of several campaigns and usually the first to voice an opinion. He'd been uncharacteristically quiet throughout this meeting, but now he cleared his throat.

'You *are* a child, Majesty,' he said bluntly. 'If we're honest, we all have to acknowledge that, and it's the job of older heads to guide you where we can. But far more important is the fact you've never seen a war. The first Nighter action was halted before it really got under way. The second was an act of treachery that produced one small battle. Neither time came to war. But it's war you're proposing now, Majesty.'

Watching him, Blue nodded. 'Yes. Your point being, General Vanelke?'

'My point,' said the old General soberly, 'is that those who have never experienced war are often fastest to *go* to war. They simply don't appreciate the enormity of the step.' He leaned forward. 'Let me explain to you, Majesty, what war – and especially civil war – will mean to the Realm. First and foremost, it will mean death. Not hundreds, but thousands, perhaps even millions would lose their lives. And not the old and the useless, but the youngest and finest, the very flower of our Realm, with the greatest potential and the very best of their lives ahead of them. The loss of just one such would be a tragedy. War multiplies that tragedy beyond calculation.'

Blue made to comment, but he held her with his eyes and pressed on. 'Secondly, there will be pain. To you,

Majesty, war is a decision, a stroke of the pen. To others, it may be the loss of their arms or legs, blindness, disability. And not just your soldiers, Majesty. They're arguably paid to accept such risks. But civilians will suffer too. In any civil war, civilian casualties are always enormous.

'Then there will be destruction. Even a short, decisive war – which civil wars seldom are – causes widespread destruction. Weapon spells have reached formidable proportions nowadays. Our enemy is well-equipped. Are you ready to inflict such spells on your people? Are you ready to count the cost that will be paid by future generations?' He squared his shoulders. 'And finally,' he said, 'although you may consider this treasonable, there is the possibility that we will not win.'

Blue said quietly, 'Our cause is just, General.' She knew what he said was true, every word of it, but what if the choice wasn't between war and peace? What if it was a choice between war and a greater war, a longer war, an even more bloody war? Although she fought hard to show nothing of her feelings, Blue was terri-fied. She'd thought long and hard about what she was going to do. She was certain – fairly certain – it was the right thing. But she was terrified it might not be. General Vanelke, if he only knew it, was voicing every doubt she had.

'Justice has nothing to do with it,' he went on relent-lessly. 'God sides with the strong and the victor writes the history books. You talked a moment ago about the Feral Faerie as possible allies – or at least the Painted Lady did. The Faeries of the Night have their own powerful allies – the demon hordes of Hael. The portals may be closed now, but war would produce an enormous incentive to get them open again. And when they open, we may find we have bitten off far more than we can chew.'

Which was true as well. The fact that the Hael portals were closed had been a big factor in her decision. But like Vanelke she knew they might not stay closed for ever. Everything depended on how fast they moved, how fast they won. Blue suddenly felt very old. Before she became Empress, it had all seemed so very simple. You had the Realm and you ruled it – what could be simpler? But once the crown was on her head, it all became so complicated.

'The problem, General Vanelke,' she said patiently, 'is that you talk as if it's a choice between war and peace. But I don't believe that's the choice we face. I believe my uncle will very soon decide to begin a war himself and we shall face all the horrors you describe and worse, with two added disadvantages: we won't be prepared and we'll have lost the element of surprise. At least if we strike first, we may get a quick victory and reduce the horrors to a minimum.'

'Perhaps we can avoid the horrors altogether,' a new voice interrupted.

Fifteen

'Where *were* you?' Blue asked crossly. They'd left the others in the little conservatory and were crouched together in one of the security cubicles behind the main throne.

Pyrgus said accusingly, 'You set your *guards* on me!'

'What else was I supposed to do?' Blue hissed furiously. 'I sent you two messages and you ignored them.'

'Yes, well, your little army got itself hijacked, didn't it?'

Blue stared at him. 'What?'

'Your guards. They got themselves hijacked. Where do you think I've been all this time?'

'That's what I just asked you,' Blue pointed out, exasperated.

'I've been with Uncle Hairstreak,' Pyrgus said. And that shut her up, he noted with satisfaction.

But after a moment she said, 'Hairstreak kidnapped you?'

'In a manner of speaking.'

'You're infuriating in this mood, Pyrgus. What do you mean "in a manner of speaking"?'

Pyrgus decided he'd had enough fun. 'He put a *lien* on your Guard Captain. Poor fellow took me directly to him instead of you.'

'What about the other guards?'

'They followed orders.'

Blue stared at him thoughtfully. A *lien* was a very costly spell, even for somebody with Hairstreak's wealth. He'd clearly wanted to get his hands on Pyrgus very badly.

'Tell me the worst,' she said.

'Actually ...' Pyrgus said, 'it may not *be* the worst. That's why I wanted to talk to you away from the others. He's sent you a message.'

'About what?"

Pyrgus, who was really getting a bit too tall for the security cubicle, slid down until he was squatting comfortably on the floor. After a tiny hesitation, Blue joined him. It was the sort of huddle they used to get into as children, when life was far less complicated.

'I don't know whether I believe it,' Pyrgus said quietly, 'but this is what happened ...'

Pyrgus still had his halek blade and was wondering about the political repercussions of using it on his uncle. But the very *fact* he still had his halek blade was peculiar. The manor was crawling with Hairstreak's men, yet he hadn't been searched once. That was not at all like Hairstreak, who was only alive today because he took security seriously.

For the moment, Pyrgus decided to keep his hands by his sides and wait. Hairstreak said shortly, 'Refreshment? Ordle, or something of that sort? Or would you prefer a drink? I suppose you're old enough for ale now, are you?'

Pyrgus thought he was, but you needed a clear head. Food held no appeal either. It was almost traditional to poison ordle when you wanted to get rid of an enemy. Four Purple Emperors had died that way in the past five hundred years. Pyrgus had been poisoned once already and had no wish to repeat the experience.

'No, thank you,' he said coolly.

They were standing together in what looked like a smallish dining room. There were logs burning in the grate and the smell reminded Pyrgus of the forest. Hairstreak had his back to the fire, an old trick to throw himself into silhouette and make him look threatening. But he made no attempt to sound threatening as he said, 'I suppose I should say I'm sorry to bring you here like this.'

It was the first time Pyrgus had heard Lord Hairstreak apologise for anything. He waited.

Hairstreak said, 'I should be talking to your sister, but she won't see me and, quite frankly, she's not as easy to get hold of as you are.' He contorted his face into what he probably thought was an avuncular smile. 'You really should pay more attention to your safety, Pyrgus.'

Pyrgus watched him, idly wondering if his uncle shouldn't take his own advice. Three steps, four at the most, and he could have the halek buried in his stomach. If it didn't shatter, that was that. Lord Hairstreak would be dead and the Realm would have one less problem. But it was only a very idle speculation at this stage. He waited.

Hairstreak said, 'In any case, I want you to deliver a message to your sister.'

It occurred to Pyrgus that his sister might be wondering where he'd got to. The longer he stayed with Lord Hairstreak the more worried she was likely to get.

Worried and irritated. He could live with worried, which was fun when it came to your sister. But she could get very stroppy when she was irritated.

'What's the message?' he asked brusquely.

'That the Faeries of the Nightside wish to negotiate,' Hairstreak said.

'Negotiate what?' Blue asked.

'A new relationship,' Pyrgus said.

Sixteen

Henry opened his eyes to find he was back on the road.

It wasn't dark any longer, it was full daylight. He looked around, wondering how that had happened. The last thing he remembered, he'd been walking home late at night after spending time with Charlie. He'd stepped on to the verge to let a car go past and suddenly the car headlights blended into daylight. Which didn't seem possible, yet here he was.

But where was *here*?

He looked around again. The road he was on seemed way out in the country. It meandered through a patchwork of small fields that didn't look at all familiar.

The sun was shining.

How did he get here? Clearly he'd walked all the way past the turning to his home and out into the country. The spooky thing – the *frightening* thing if he was honest – was that he'd forgotten everything between the car approaching and now. That couldn't be good. That had to be brain damage or something. Maybe the car hit him.

Henry stopped and cautiously felt himself all over. Nothing seemed to be broken and there was no sign of blood. All the same, a really bad jolt could affect your memory. He was fairly sure he'd heard about boxers going a bit funny after they'd been battered around the head. They got punchy and talked to themselves and probably couldn't remember things.

The problem was he didn't hurt. Not about the head and not anywhere. The side of his nose was a bit itchy, but that wasn't something you'd get from a car knocking you down and mangling your head.

Where was he anyway? There was a wall coming up and a sign that said *Stud Farm*. There *were* stud farms in the district, but none of them particularly close to where he lived. When he walked past his turning, he'd obviously *kept* walking. And walking. And walking …

It was peculiar his legs didn't hurt. He'd been walking all night.

The fear Henry felt sank to the level of a background ache. He didn't know where he was. He didn't know how he'd got here. Without very much emotion he realised he was going batty. He had to be going batty. First he saw fairies, then he got lost.

He turned round and started to walk back in what he hoped was the direction of home.

Seventeen

'What sort of new relationship?' asked Mr Fogarty suspiciously.

Blue looked at Pyrgus who said, 'Lord Hairstreak thinks it would be in everybody's interests if the Faeries of the Night and the Faeries of the Light signed a non-aggression treaty.'

Everyone in the room looked at each other. Most showed shock, with a liberal sprinkling of disbelief. After a moment …

'On what terms?' asked General Vanelke.

Pyrgus still wasn't sure how he felt about any of this. He mistrusted his uncle almost as much as Blue did, and the ease with which Hairstreak had snatched him left him more shaken than he was admitting. He shrugged.

'Basically each side agrees not to go to war with the other. If there are disputes, we settle them by negotiation or arbitration. He says the details can be worked out later, but if we agree the principle now it could open up a whole new era of cooperation that would benefit both sides and put our historic disagreements behind us. His words. More or less exactly.'

Fogarty said, 'Do you believe him?'

Tricky question. Nobody in their right mind would

trust Lord Hairstreak further than a perin's spit. But at the same time he'd *seemed* genuine. Pyrgus shrugged again.

'I tell the tale as told to me.'

'What's your opinion, Gatekeeper?' Blue asked.

'I'd want to think about it,' Fogarty sniffed. Then added, 'But as a general principle, I wouldn't trust Lord Hairstreak as far as I could throw a sack of dog crap.'

Pyrgus glanced at him in admiration. Analogue World similes always seemed a lot more colourful than the ones used in the Realm.

'I think we should talk to Lord Hairstreak,' General Vanelke said, unasked. He glared at Fogarty. 'As a general principle, I believe talking is preferable to war.'

'General Creerful?' Blue asked.

'On balance, I agree with Vanelke. What harm would talking do? Both sides could take endolgs as a token of good faith.'

The idea appealed to Pyrgus, who liked animals. 'Henry's endolg's still in the palace, isn't he?' he asked Blue. 'The one you made a chevalier?'

'I'm not convinced I should meet with my uncle,' Blue said, ignoring him.

General Ovard said, 'The details would be worked out by civil servants on both sides. You wouldn't have to be involved until the formal signing.'

'Assuming there is a signing,' Madame Cardui murmured lazily.

'So you're also in favour of talks?' Blue asked, looking at General Ovard.

Ovard nodded. 'Yes.'

Blue took in the sober faces. They were all so

mature, so experienced. Even Pyrgus was older than she was. Talks seemed reasonable. But suppose it was a trick? Hairstreak was capable of any deception. Her whole instinct told her not to trust him. Yet all three of her military leaders were agreed there should be talks.

In that instant, Blue suddenly saw her life as it might have been. If her father had lived, or Pyrgus accepted the throne, she'd have none of these worries now. She'd have time for the things she really enjoyed. She was a girl, for Light's sake. She should be thinking about clothes and music and seeing the world. She should be thinking about romance. She should be thinking about ... Henry. It was brutal that she should be facing life and death decisions about the future of the Realm.

Brutal or not, the life she was leading now was the life she'd chosen.

After a moment, she said, 'Thank you, Generals. I should like to discuss the matter further with my political advisors. I'll speak to you again when a decision has been made.' There was not a flicker of expression on her face as she added, 'In the meantime, I want you to make preparations for a military strike against Yammeth Cretch.'

Eighteen

Once the three old soldiers had left, Fogarty said, 'So you don't buy the idea of a treaty?' He gave a steely little smile. 'Obviously.'

Blue sighed. When the Generals were present, the meeting had to be formal. Now she was among friends, she could relax a bit. She looked at Gatekeeper Fogarty and shook her head.

'I think it's a trick. Or at least it might be.' Out of the corner of her eye she could see Pyrgus examining an orchid. He looked just like their father when he'd tended the plants.

'What do you think he's up to?' Fogarty asked her.

Blue didn't know what Hairstreak was up to. Didn't know for sure he was up to anything. What she did know was that she was afraid of making a mistake. That sick fear had been with her since the day she accepted the crown.

'Buying time,' Blue said with more conviction than she felt. 'I still think he's likely to attack before I've any real experience of ruling the Realm. But he may not be ready yet. Either that, or he just wants to keep us off our guard. If we're in the middle of peace negotiations, the last thing we'd expect would be war.'

Fogarty said. 'Our endolg would sense that right away.'

'He may not agree to endolgs,' Blue said.

'Wouldn't that be suspicious?'

'Yes, but it's happened in the past.' The one thing she had done was study politics. The history of the Realm was a long, miserable litany of treachery and deception. She looked at Mr Fogarty soberly. 'In fact, most treaties have been brokered without endolgs.'

'Actually,' Pyrgus said, 'I've been thinking about it and an endolg wouldn't guarantee good faith. General Ovard said the details would be worked out by civil servants. That's certainly what *would* happen. If Hairstreak's people think he's genuine, an endolg wouldn't pick up anything amiss.'

'There's still the formal signing,' Fogarty said.

'By then it might be too late.' Pyrgus looked from one face to the other. 'Honestly, endolgs aren't the answer.'

Madame Cardui suddenly said, 'That's not all, is it deeah?' Pyrgus glanced at her, but she was looking at Blue.

It was probably time to tell them. Blue was used to doing things on her own, had been since she was a little girl. But things were different now. Now she was responsible for the entire Realm. She had to start sharing. She smiled, a little shamefacedly.

'No, it's not. I went to the oracle.'

'Ah,' said Madame Cardui.

There was a long silence, then Pyrgus said, 'What oracle?'

'Blue saw the Spicemaster,' Madame Cardui said.

'Who's the Spicemaster?' Fogarty asked.

'Which god did you get?' Pyrgus asked in sudden

excitement. As an aside to Fogarty he added, 'He's an oracle.'

'Great,' Fogarty muttered.

Blue said, 'I asked him –' She hesitated. 'I got the Yidam. Is that good?' She looked from Pyrgus to Madame Cardui.

'Good, but dangerous,' Madame Cardui said.

'And tricky,' Pyrgus added. 'At least that's what everybody says. I'd never have the nerve to go to the Spicemaster.' He looked at his sister admiringly.

'I don't suppose anybody's going to tell me what this is all about?' Fogarty remarked sourly.

Madame Cardui reached out and took his hand. 'The Spicemaster is trained to call the Old Gods who ruled before the Light. They can sometimes tell you the future, if you're prepared to take the risk.' She reached over and patted Fogarty's knee. 'I'll explain it all later, deeah.' She turned to look expectantly at Blue. 'Did you ask about Hairstreak's intentions?'

Blue shook her head. 'No. I asked what would happen if we attacked the Nighters.' She found herself looking from one to the other for approval and stopped immediately. She had to be decisive. 'He said we'd win. And quickly.' When nobody spoke, she added, 'He also said I was in danger of betrayal from someone close.' She blinked. 'Actually I got on very well with him. The Yidam. I think he liked me.'

'In danger of betrayal?' Pyrgus echoed.

'That has to be Lord Hairstreak,' Blue said soberly. 'Nobody's much closer than an uncle. You can see why I don't trust his treaty.' She was looking for approval again. She couldn't help it. 'I still think we should attack.' Somehow she just managed to keep from turning it into a question.

Mr Fogarty's rasping voice broke the silence. 'Did this oracle thing actually *say* we would win? In those words: *you will win the war*?'

Blue said a little impatiently, 'No, not in those exact words, Gatekeeper. He said something like ... "*An enemy will be swiftly routed.*" Something like that. But it's what he meant.'

'Ah,' said Fogarty. He sniffed. 'Bloody oracles.'

They looked at him. Eventually Madame Cardui asked, 'What's that mean, deeah?'

Fogarty said, 'We used to have an oracle at home – well, at home centuries ago. Called the Delphic Oracle. Something similar to your Spicemaster, by the sound of it, except it was a woman. Got taken over by the god and predicted the future? That's what happened, was it?'

Blue nodded.

Fogarty said, 'The whole set-up was famous in the ancient world.' He drew in a deep breath and sighed. 'There was a king called Croesus who wanted to attack the Persians. The oracle told him if he attacked, a mighty empire would be destroyed.' He looked across from under his eyebrows at Blue.

'And did his attack succeed?' Blue asked, frowning.

'The Persians beat the crap out of him,' Fogarty said. 'The mighty empire that got destroyed was his own.' He stared at her with cold blue eyes. 'You have to be careful how you interpret an oracle.'

'Oh,' Blue said.

Pyrgus said, 'So you wouldn't attack the Nighters, Mr Fogarty?'

'Oh, I'd attack them all right,' Fogarty said. 'I don't believe in oracles.'

Nineteen

Hairstreak waited until the coach carrying Pyrgus was out of sight. The boy was tricky, but he could probably be trusted to take a simple message to his sister. What happened then was anybody's guess. Blue had been headstrong from the time she was a little girl. Now she was Queen ...

Well, now she was Queen, that headstrong streak could serve his plans very nicely.

He scowled as he turned back to the house. They'd be waiting for him by now, all of them. Waiting with their stupid questions. Not that it mattered. He could wait too, longer than the rest of them put together.

Pelidne was standing just inside the doorway. Hairstreak looked at him with a hint of distaste. Such a shame about Cossus Cossus. A damn nuisance training in a new Gatekeeper, but you could never trust a man with a worm up his bottom. And what Pelidne lacked in experience, he made up for in loyalty. Not to mention his interesting talents, which would certainly be useful.

'Are they here?' he snapped.

Pelidne nodded. 'I showed them down to the Conference Chamber, sir.'

'Are the securities in place?'

'Yes, sir.'

'Did they take precautions against being followed?'

Pelidne looked startled. 'I assume so, sir.'

'Assume nothing,' Hairstreak told him. 'They're idiots – all of them. Have a contingent of guards search the grounds. If they find anybody, interrogate them then kill them painfully. You can feed any bodies to my slith. Poor thing hasn't eaten in days.'

'Yes, sir.'

The Conference Chamber was more than thirty feet beneath the foundations of the manor, functional and spell-proof. There was a sudden silence when Hairstreak strode in, as if they'd been talking behind his back. Which they probably had. He allowed his eyes to drift coldly from one to the other, unsmiling. Old Duke Electo was there, dressed in his revolting magenta robes and looking more ancient than God. He seldom left his castle nowadays, which showed the importance he placed on the current developments. Hairstreak nodded an acknowledgement.

The rest, with a few notable exceptions, were the usual crowd – Anthocharis Cardamines, complete with irritating twitch, the ghastly Colias twins, Hecla and Lesbia, glaring at him malevolently, that imbecile Croceus who murdered his father, and all the other inbred weeds inflicted on him by reason of their titles. Their *inherited* titles. Not a real talent among them.

But the exceptions were interesting. Hamearis, Duke of Burgundy, was lounging in a chair at the end of the table. Darkness, but the man was enormous! Even seated he seemed to overwhelm the others. He played up to it, of course. Those shoulders were part due to his padded armour. But that didn't mean he should be underestimated. He'd fought more than his fair share of battles and attracted a huge following as a hero. He'd once been Hairstreak's closest ally. Now Hairstreak couldn't be sure. They had very different ideas about the current situation.

Then there was Fuscus, dear, sweet, baby-faced Fuscus, with his private army and wardrobe of military uniforms. They said he wore a different one each night and strutted round the battlements waving an amber sword. Such theatrics. Hairstreak doubted Fuscus had ever delivered a blow in anger. But the private army was a different matter. An elite force, well-trained, well-armed and ready to do their master's bidding. Which made Fuscus a power to be reckoned with. There'd been a time when Hairstreak thought he might have made a close ally, but he was Burgundy's man now and Hairstreak was no longer sure of Burgundy.

The final exception was more interesting still. Zosine Typha Ogyris, the only faerie in the room without a title. But what he lacked in breeding, he made up for in wealth. He sat there, a little, balding, toad-like creature with his hands calmly folded in his lap. He looked harmless, but he commanded more resources than six noble houses. The man was incredible. He'd actually arrived in the Realm without a penny, a refugee from Haleklind. Somebody claimed he'd laid the foundations of his fortune by hauling manure to market gardens. Manure! Hairstreak had had a hard time securing his place at this conference. The Great House representatives thought it beneath their dignity to sit down with someone who lacked a title. But Zosine was here now, oh yes. And whatever doubts he had about Hamearis, Hairstreak could count on Zosine absolutely.

Irritatingly, it was Hamearis who seized the initiative. 'Ah, Blackie,' he said, as if he were in command of the entire meeting, 'did you do it?'

Idly Hairstreak wondered if a poisoned stiletto might penetrate the padded armour. But he kept his face impassive, even managed a benign look, as he turned his gaze back to Burgundy.

'Of course,' he said.

'Any answer yet?'

'Hardly,' said Hairstreak easily. He pulled out a chair from the head of the table. 'The message has only just been dispatched.'

'Why the delay?' asked Hecla Colias sharply, ever ready to make trouble.

Hairstreak fixed her with a warning glance. 'Because *I* did not deem the time right before now.' He noted with some satisfaction that she dropped her gaze at once. He tilted the chair backwards to convey easy relaxation and swept the gathering with his eyes. 'Crown Prince Pyrgus –' He stopped, smiled a little, then went on, 'Or rather I should say *ex*-Crown Prince Pyrgus, has received details of our offer and is now on his way to deliver it to the young Queen. What I –'

'Is it in writing?' someone interrupted. Hairstreak recognised the voice as Cardamines, who wasn't so much an enemy as a nuisance. He had a pedantic streak.

Hairstreak forced a smile. 'Difficult to see the need, Anthocharis. At this stage we've merely offered to negotiate.' Cardamines nodded and grunted. Then twitched. Hairstreak turned back to the others. 'The purpose of this meeting is to refine our position should Her Majesty agree ...' he paused a beat, '... and define our position should she refuse.'

The purpose of the meeting was nothing of the sort, but it sounded good. He closed his mouth and waited for the inevitable reaction.

It came without a moment's delay. 'Thought we'd agreed on our position,' growled Electo's gruff voice. 'Both ways.'

'So did I,' snapped Lesbia, who was just as poisonous as her sister, but slightly better in bed as Hairstreak recalled.

'Perhaps not quite *both* ways,' Cardamines twitched pedantically.

And they were off. Hairstreak closed his eyes and let the discussion wash over him. Of *course* it had already been decided. It was the most serious defeat he'd ever suffered in the Council of the Faeries of the Night. Made worse because it had been utterly unexpected. Negotiate a peaceful solution? He almost shuddered. But once the proposition had been put – by some minor noble, obviously acting under orders – they'd forced his hand. Even Hamearis had deserted him and he was at a loss to understand why.

The end result was plain enough. There'd been a change of heart among the Faeries of the Night. Somehow they'd lost their backbone, lost the will to fight. He'd even been pilloried for his last two attempts to seize the throne. And now they wanted peace. Worse, they wanted it at any price. The offer of negotiation hid complete capitulation. If Blue wanted peace, she could have it. If she accepted quickly, there wasn't a damn thing he could do about it. He'd lost his backing and without backing he was nothing.

But Blue wouldn't accept quickly, not if he knew his

niece. She'd always had a deeply suspicious streak and now she was being advised by a Gatekeeper who was batty as a Border Redcap. She'd suspect a trap. She'd stall for time. She'd postpone the negotiations while her old harridan of a spymaster tried to find out what was behind them. And all that would give Hairstreak the time to shift Council members back behind him.

Starting now.

He glanced over his shoulder and saw that Pelidne had silently entered the chamber. 'Refreshment,' Hairstreak ordered shortly. He gave a small nod.

Pelidne nodded back, so subtly that no one else in the room could have noticed it. 'Of course, sir.'

He must have had a tray ready waiting, for he returned to the room at once. Croceus looked quickly – there were rumours he was a simbala addict – but selected a small tankard of ale when Pelidne reached him. Hamearis took one of the simbalas and tossed it down, then sat back, smiling as the music took hold. Both Colias twins drank wine, as did Fuscus.

When the guests had all been served, Pelidne offered the tray to Hairstreak. He was reaching for his tamarind juice when Fuscus began to cough. The discussion had already started up again, so most of them ignored him at first. But then he toppled his chair with a clatter, half stood and jack-knifed across the table. Lesbia Colias gave a little shriek and pulled away from him. Fuscus convulsed and vomited on the polished wood. The other twin, Hecla, stood up abruptly and watched him, her eyes huge. She gave a small moan that sounded suspiciously like pleasure.

'What's the matter with the fella?' demanded Duke Electo impatiently.

Something very unpleasant began to happen to Fuscus. Starting at the mouth, his head slowly split open. In a moment there was blood and brains all over the table.

The chamber exploded into uproar, although Hairstreak noticed Burgundy hadn't moved and was now staring at him intently. On cue, Zosine Ogyris climbed to his feet.

'Someone get a doctor,' he said in a curiously resonant voice. 'This man obviously has refinia.' Refinia was a disease of the tropics, but it was clear to anyone that Fuscus was far beyond the help of a doctor. All the same, the diagnosis had the required effect. Refinia was contagious. In seconds, the chamber was empty except for Hairstreak, Pelidne and the rapidly disintegrating corpse of Fuscus.

'Something in the drink?' Hairstreak asked quietly.

Pelidne shook his head and uncurled his left hand. A glistening needle point emerged from the band of his signet ring.

'Well done,' Hairstreak said. He felt a modest surge of satisfaction. Burgundy would not believe the refinia story for a moment. By now he must have realised his new friend had just been brutally and publicly murdered. Several of the others would soon reach the same conclusion.

It was an important message to send out. Before long, every Great House would realise Hairstreak was still a man to be reckoned with. Given time, the new policies would begin to be rethought. All he needed now was Blue to give him that time.

All he needed was Blue's refusal to negotiate.

twenty

'Do you think she's going to negotiate?' Pyrgus asked. There was a time when he'd have known the answer – he and Blue had always been close – but things had changed since she became Queen. She still *looked* like his little sister (most of the time) but there was something in her that had suddenly grown up. She'd become serious and a little hard. He wasn't sure he liked it. He certainly didn't understand it.

'I don't know,' said Gatekeeper Fogarty.

'Do you think she *should*?' Pyrgus pressed.

'Yes,' Fogarty said without hesitation.

'I thought you said you wanted to attack the Nighters, deeah,' Madame Cardui put it.

They were walking together in the grounds of the Purple Palace, along with Madame Cardui's orange dwarf Kitterick, who had long proved himself the soul of discretion; and was, in any case, their best security in troubled times.

'Not sure I do,' Fogarty said. 'I was just making a point about oracles.' He walked in silence for a moment, then said, 'I know you sent her to the Spicemaster, Cynthia, but Blue's impressionable. Hasn't learned to take things with a pinch of salt yet. And, of course, she hears what she wants to hear.

Things are tricky in the Realm just now. I don't want her making decisions on the advice of some spook.' He scowled. 'What are you grinning at?'

'*Take things with a pinch of salt.* It's such a *colourful* expression, deeah.'

'Common enough in my world,' Fogarty said shortly, but his expression softened. Pyrgus watched the exchange with interest. Fogarty said, 'Even if your oracle told you plainly *You'll squash Hairstreak like a bug,* that *still* isn't a green light. You have to remember what Blue asked. "What will happen *if.*" Telling you what will happen *if* doesn't mean you should do it. Maybe we *will* win if we attack the Nighters, but maybe we'll *still* win if we negotiate; and with a lot less loss of life.'

'You were impressed by General Vanelke,' said Madame Cardui, not unkindly.

'Yes, I was,' Fogarty admitted. 'I lived through one war in my own world. That's where I got the scar and lost the toe. Damn lucky to keep the leg at all. Knocks the nonsense out of you, that. War's not noble, not "an extension of diplomacy by other means".' His voice reeked with scorn. 'War's a mess. Usually started by some idiot who doesn't have to fight. It's the poor grunts on the ground who pay the price.'

'I didn't know you'd been a warrior,' said Madame Cardui.

'Warrior my arse!' Fogarty sniffed. 'I was just a miserable Tommy. Wouldn't have joined up if they hadn't made me.' He glanced away from them both and glared into the middle distance.

Pyrgus asked, 'Did you tell her she should negotiate?'

'Yes,' Fogarty said. 'I had a word just before we left.' He was still lost in his memories, for he added incomprehensibly, 'Churchill said jaw-jaw was better than war-war.'

'Do you think she will?'

Fogarty glared at him. 'You asked me that.'

'Yes, I know. But maybe we should be, you know, trying to *make* her.'

Fogarty gave him the benefit of a cynical look. 'Did you ever manage to *make* your sister do anything?'

In point of fact he hadn't, not even when she was little. He'd no doubt Blue loved him, but obedience wasn't in her vocabulary. All the same, he didn't like the way things were going.

In answer to Mr Fogarty's question he said, 'No, I didn't. But I think I know somebody who *could* persuade her.'

'Henry?' said Madame Cardui, and smiled. Pyrgus nodded. Madame Cardui said, 'Does he know she's in love with him?'

'I don't think so,' Pyrgus grinned. He'd been feeling good about Blue and Henry for a while now. He liked Henry.

Mr Fogarty stopped to stare at the distant horizon. 'Glands,' he muttered.

'Don't be so cynical, Alan,' Madame Cardui told him crossly. 'If you can't fall in love at their age, when can you?'

For some reason it warmed Mr Fogarty enough to make him grin a little. 'I suppose you're right.'

Pyrgus said quickly, 'Do you want to send for him, Mr Fogarty? Or should I translate and get him?' He quite fancied another trip to the Analogue World, even if he couldn't spend much time there.

But Mr Fogarty said, 'Mightn't need to.' He glanced from Pyrgus to Madame Cardui. 'You two got a minute?'

Since he'd translated permanently to the Faerie Realm, Mr Fogarty had moved into *Saram na Roinen,* the House of the Gatekeeper, an official residence that comprised a large lodge and some outbuildings on the edge of the Purple Palace gardens. As Fogarty opened the door, Pyrgus noted he'd wasted no time in turning it into a tip, but he led them straight through and out the back, then down a short path to one of the outbuildings.

The stone structure had once been an ornitherium, but the high latticed windows had been boarded up and all the external perches removed. Even the antique listening booth had been taken away. On the inside, only the vaulted ceiling remained of the original fittings. The rest had been gutted out and replaced by ... replaced by ...

Pyrgus blinked. They'd been replaced by Mr Fogarty's shed! Pyrgus remembered it from the time poor old Hodge mistook him for a mouse. But this was the original writ large. There was enough junk to fill a merchant's store and the workbench in the centre was enormous. Pieces of machinery were strewn all over it.

'It's something I've been working on,' Mr Fogarty said with enthusiasm. 'Any of you lot ever seen *Star Trek*?' He shook his head. 'No, of course you haven't – must be getting senile.' He ushered them inside and closed the door. 'It's a television programme we have back home. You can explain television to them, Pyrgus – you've seen *that*. *Star Trek*'s about space travel. They have a star ship and a thing called a *transporter*. It's just fiction, but that transporter got me thinking.' He moved towards the bench. 'The way it works is you *beam* people about the place, down to the planet, back to the ship, whatever, and the thing is, if you're *on* the ship, you can *lock on* to them down on the planet and beam them aboard.' He looked from one to the other. 'You see what I'm getting at?'

Pyrgus shook his head.

Madame Cardui said, 'No ...'

Kitterick said, 'I presume, sir, you feel there may be something in the process analogous to our portal technology, but possibly improved.'

Pyrgus blinked.

'Exactly!' exclaimed Fogarty. He focused on Kitterick. 'It's matter transmission, of course. You scan somebody down to his constituent pattern and beam the information to the destination where he can be reassembled using local atoms. The problem's always been what to do with the body.'

'What body?'

'The body you scanned at *this* end. And you *have* to do something about the body, otherwise you'd be in two places at once. You can see why matter transmission never became a commercial proposition. Imagine an airline that had to kill off each of its passengers to get them to their destination. You'd be ceiling deep in corpses by the end of the first week.'

'And no one else would wish to travel because of the smell,' Kitterick said blandly.

'Are you taking the piss?' Fogarty frowned.

'Indeed not, sir. Please go on.'

Fogarty relaxed his frown as the earlier enthusiasm

flooded back. 'Thing is, if you introduce a portal you solve the body problem. You don't have to beam information any more, you can beam the actual atoms. With the portal in place, that doesn't require any more energy.'

'Mr Fogarty,' said Pyrgus, who hadn't understood a word, 'what does this have to do with Henry?'

Fogarty nodded towards a small box on his workbench. 'That thing there's a prototype of a Mark II portable transporter. It doesn't just open a portal like the ones I made before, it lets you lock in on a target and pull them through it.'

'To here?'

Fogarty frowned. 'In theory.'

'Does it work?'

'I haven't tested it yet.'

After a moment, Pyrgus said, 'You mean you could lock in on Henry and translate him to your ornither— to your shed? Here and now?'

'Could give it a try,' said Mr Fogarty.

Twenty-one

Henry's legs were aching by the time he got to the end of his road, but his troubles didn't really start until he reached home. His mother must have heard the sound of the key in the door, for she met him in the hall. She was dressed for work in one of her hideous tweedy suits, but her blouse was rumpled and there were dark circles under her eyes. She looked as if she hadn't slept in months, but that did nothing to dampen her fury.

'Where the *hell* have you been?' she demanded. 'We were worried *sick*. Anaïs rang round all the hospitals and I've just reported you missing to the *police*. For heaven's sake, Henry, couldn't you just have *rung*? Why on earth do you think we got you a mobile phone? Don't you *ever*, for a *minute*, think about anybody else but yourself in your whole … selfish … life?' Then, to his intense embarrassment, she threw her arms around him and burst into tears. 'Oh, Henry, we thought you'd been *killed*!'

He'd never seen his mother cry before and he didn't know how to cope with it. She was holding him so tightly he could hardly breathe and he could feel her tears dripping from his jaw to run down the side of his neck.

'Where *were* you?' she sobbed. 'Where have you *been*?'

He couldn't answer that one either. At least not any way that was going to satisfy her. Where had he been? Walking all night and most of the morning, by the look of it. She was going to ask him *why* and he didn't *know* why. He might have been hit by a car, but he didn't *feel* like he'd been hit by a car. No bones broken, no headache, not so much as a bruise. His mind went back to an earlier thought. Maybe this blank in his memory was all part of his nervous breakdown, the business about seeing fairies and visiting fairyland.

'Mum ...' Henry said.

He'd been talking to Charlie about his nervous breakdown. And Charlie had said something about it, but he couldn't remember what.

'Mum ...' Henry said again, struggling a little.

Actually he didn't know why she was going on like this. He'd stayed out overnight before. Usually at Charlie's, where arrangements were often last-minute. He'd always rung, of course, but there'd been times when Mum and Dad had gone to bed – how worried could they be? – and he'd had to leave a message on the *answerphone*, for cripe's sake!

Henry suddenly remembered he *had* left a message on the answerphone the night before. He hadn't planned to stay out – he'd wanted a lift home. But nobody took his call, so he left a message. He could remember that quite clearly. *Mum, I've missed my bus. Any chance you could come and get me? If you don't pick up this message I'll be walking home.*

It suddenly occurred to him why she was so upset! She *hadn't* picked up the message. Not until this morning. And then she'd checked his bed and found he still wasn't home. She wasn't worried, she was *guilty*! That was so typical. She could never admit anything was actually her fault. She hadn't been worried about him at all. She'd gone to bed and didn't even *think* of him until this morning. Now she was making a fuss to cover up.

'Mum,' Henry said. He took her arms firmly and pulled away. 'Mum, you don't give a *damn* where I was.'

Then, with his own welling tears, he ran upstairs to his room and locked the door.

In its own small way, Henry's room looked much like Mr Fogarty's shed, except that strewn clothes took the place of tools and models of one sort or another stood in for the machinery. Henry sat on the edge of the bed thinking how *childish* those models looked. More than half the ships he'd made were *plastic*, could you believe that? And then there was that stupid cardboard model of a flying *pig*. Incredible to think that was the last model he'd made, and just a few weeks ago. Incredible to think how proud he'd been of it.

She knocked on his door almost at once.

'Go away, Mum,' Henry said dully.

A voice said, 'It's not Martha, Henry – it's Anaïs.'

After a long moment, Henry got up and unlocked the door.

twenty-two

'May I come in?' Anaïs asked quietly. She was dressed in sweater and jeans and designer runners. Henry shrugged and turned away. He walked back to sit on the bed, not looking at her.

Anaïs closed the door and stood just inside the room. Out of the corner of his eye he could see she looked concerned, maybe even a bit frightened. But her voice was steady enough as she said, 'Henry, we need to talk.'

He could imagine his mother saying the same thing. What it usually meant was *Henry, you need to listen*. After which his mother would tell what he'd done wrong, why he should never do it again and how he could do a lot better in the future. But, of course, this wasn't his mum. This was the *other woman* in the house.

He shrugged again, staring at his feet, and said, 'So talk.'

'Do you think I might sit down?' Anaïs asked lightly. She gave a little smile.

'Nowhere to sit,' Henry muttered. Which was true enough. The only chair in his room – an ancient sagging armchair – was so buried under junk it was scarcely visible.

'I could sit beside you on the bed.' Anaïs tilted her head to one side quizzically.

'I don't want you sitting beside me on the bed!' Henry snapped. He suddenly felt furiously angry and fought to control it.

The smile disappeared. Anaïs said, 'All right, I'll stand. And *I'll* talk. At least until you feel like it. I mostly wanted to say I'm sorry.'

It was the last thing he expected. He was so startled his anger disappeared and he actually looked at her.

She licked her lips and went on, 'Henry, I know how difficult this must be for you –'

'No, you don't,' Henry said quickly, his anger flaring again. 'No you bloody, bloody *don't*!' He looked down at his feet again. If he wasn't careful, he was going to cry.

'No, I don't,' Anaïs agreed. Part of the trouble was she looked so pretty. And so young. And she was so *nice*. That was the real problem. He wanted to hate her. He really, really wanted to hate her and she was so nice he just couldn't. Nicer than his mother, that was for sure. He couldn't imagine what Anaïs saw in her.

'Of course, I don't,' Anaïs was saying. 'But I *do* know you must be feeling awful. I wish you weren't, but there's not much I can do about that. But, Henry, running away isn't the answer.'

'I didn't run away,' Henry said. 'I just stayed over at Charlie's.' He glared at her defiantly. 'I've done it before.'

'Henry,' Anaïs said patiently, 'you didn't stay at Charlie's. It was the first place we checked. She said you wanted to stay, but they had cousins or something and there wasn't a spare bed. She was worried about you too.'

Bet she was, Henry thought. He'd just told her he'd been seeing fairies. What he hated was the way Anaïs said *we* as if she and Mum were an item. Which they were, of course, but he didn't need to have his nose rubbed in it.

'Did you call Dad?' he asked.

Anaïs blinked. 'Not right away,' she admitted reluctantly.

'Why not?' Henry demanded. 'Didn't you even *think* I might be staying with him?'

Anaïs said, 'But you weren't?'

'No, I wasn't, but that's not the point. The point is you all got so worried and none of you, not Mum, not you, thought the first thing you should do was ring up Dad. Well, did you?'

Now Anaïs was looking down at her feet. 'No.' She looked up suddenly. 'That was wrong. You're right, Henry: that was very wrong. But sometimes people just ... do the wrong things. We were worried. We didn't know what had happened. You were gone for three days and we were frantic. Your mother loves you, Henry. I love you –'

'Don't you say you –' Henry began furiously, then stopped. 'I wasn't away for three days.'

Anaïs moved across and sat beside him on the bed anyway. She looked into his eyes and reached over to take both his hands. 'Yes, you *were*, Henry. That's the whole point. We were out of our minds with worry – everybody was. Charlotte said you walked her home and then went off to go home yourself. She thought you caught the last bus. But that was Tuesday. Today's Saturday.'

'Today's not Saturday,' Henry whispered. For no

reason he was suddenly feeling afraid.

'What was it?' Anaïs asked him quietly. 'Were you doing drugs?'

'I wasn't doing drugs!' Henry hissed. 'I've never done drugs!' He couldn't have been away three days. It was just last night he'd missed the bus. Just last night.

There was something wrong. Not just confusion. Henry blinked several times and shook his head to clear it. He felt as if he really had been doing drugs. Something was happening to reality. The whole room was swimming around him. He looked at his hands to try to steady himself. They were clasped in Anaïs's small, well-groomed hands with bright red varnish on her nails. But his hands in her hands were disappearing.

Henry watched with horrified fascination. His hands were crumbling into tiny sparkles like a special effect. He felt a growing nausea. He raised his eyes to look at Anaïs's face. It was fading to white. And suddenly Henry was fading too.

He thought he must be dying.

twenty-three

The Imperial Suite was spacious and luxurious and Blue hated it. The chairs were too large, the bed was too soft, the tapestries were too rich.

The memories were too painful.

Everything reminded her of her father. She kept thinking she could catch a hint of his smell, the sound of his movements. Once, in the night, she thought she heard the low gurgle of his laughter.

She could see the bloodstain on the carpet, even though the servants had scrubbed out every particle, then, at her insistence, replaced the floor covering completely. But tradition dictated the replacement was the same colour and pattern and the bloodstain was still there, spreading liquidly in her mind.

The Queen must live in the Imperial Suite: that was tradition too. But she needed to think. How could she be expected to think when she saw her father everywhere she turned? She had to get away.

On impulse she triggered the secret panel Comma discovered during the few days he played at being Emperor. It opened on to a passageway that had offered an emergency escape to Emperors down the generations. In the old days they'd been fleeing for their lives. She was running from a ghost. Blue stepped inside and the panel closed behind her.

The passageway emerged on the edge of the Imperial Island beside the broad sweep of the river. It was growing dark now and she sat on some rocks watching the lights come on across the city. Closer to hand, torchlit traffic was milling over Loman Bridge. There were tens of thousands of her subjects out there and she'd never felt so alone. A wrong decision could leave so many of them dead. What was she going to do? What was the *right* thing to do?

A large patch of moss slipped off the rock beside her and splatted on the ground with an audible *thump*. 'Damn!' it muttered crossly.

Blue was on her feet in an instant, one hand scrabbling in the folds of her dress for the lethal little stimulus she kept as her last line of defence. It was stupid, stupid, stupid not to have alerted the guards where she was going, but she still wasn't accustomed to being Queen.

'Is that you, Blue?'

She strained her eyes in the half-light. The voice was terribly familiar. 'Flapwazzle?' She blinked. 'Flapwazzle?'

'I cannot tell a lie,' Flapwazzle said truthfully. He began to undulate across the ground towards her.

For some reason the burdens of State responsibility fell away and she felt a small bubble of delight welling in her stomach. 'What are you doing out here?'

'Gathering the *omron*.' It was something endolgs did at sunset. Blue had never really understood it. Flapwazzle said, 'When I was full, I fell asleep. Didn't think I'd find you here. Or anybody, really.'

Her problems came flooding back. 'I was trying to make up my mind about something.'

She thought he might ask her what – and wasn't sure she could tell him – but he only said, 'Must be tricky being Queen.'

It was almost funny. That was the very word for it – tricky. Not one of her courtiers or advisors would have used it, but that was the word exactly. For the first time in days she actually grinned.

'That's it, Flapwazzle. As tricky as it gets.' How did you decide what your uncle was up to? Tricky. How did you choose between war and peace? Tricky.

A thought occurred to her and flared into a rising excitement. 'Flapwazzle, would you do something for me?' she blurted. She couldn't order him – not that she would have anyway. Endolgs weren't strictly speaking her subjects, which may have been why she hadn't thought of something so obvious before.

'Sure,' Flapwazzle said at once.

Some of her initial excitement died, replaced at once by worry. 'It could be dangerous.'

Flapwazzle had draped himself over one of her feet, keeping it so warm she wished he'd move on to the other one as well. 'Danger is my middle name,' he said. Then added quickly, 'Just a metaphor, of course. Something I picked up somewhere. I don't actually have a middle name and if I did it certainly wouldn't be anything as pretentious as *Danger*.' He wriggled slightly. Endolgs lacked the capacity to lie, so metaphors were difficult for them.

Blue said, 'Would you pay a visit on my uncle?'

'Lord Hairstreak?'

'That uncle,' Blue said sourly. 'I want you to get close enough to use your truth-sense.'

'He won't like that,' Flapwazzle said.

Which was the understatement of the century. Blue had started to feel guilty – this really *was* a dangerous assignment – but the more she talked, the more her idea felt like a solution to all her problems. And Flapwazzle could do it. In fact, Flapwazzle was the only endolg she could trust with the job. He'd already proven himself several times over.

She took a deep breath and told him everything.

'You want me to find out if it's a genuine offer?' Flapwazzle asked.

Blue nodded. 'Can you?'

'If I can get close enough. I might have problems sneaking past his guards.'

'I can get you into his mansion,' Blue said, thinking furiously. She could make a State visit, except the formalities would put Hairstreak on his guard. If she turned up with her bodyguards, that might encourage him to increase his security precautions. But if she just turned up ...

Blue liked the idea of just turning up. It was the sort of wild thing she used to do before becoming Queen. She'd have to put precautions in place, of course, do it by the book. She'd order a Countdown, the way the old Emperors did when there was a risk of war. And she'd carry her stimulus. Actually, no, she wouldn't carry her stimulus – her uncle's security spells would detect the weapon at once. Best to appear innocent and empty-handed. The Countdown would be all the security she'd need. But she had to find some way of hiding Flapwazzle.

'He mustn't know you're with me. It's important he doesn't realise we're checking him out.'

'Besides which, he might kill me,' Flapwazzle said.

Blue nodded. 'Yes, he might.' It was impossible to keep anything from an endolg.

But clearly this endolg was prepared to take the risk. 'Whatever,' he shrugged cheerfully. 'When do we go?'

Now would be good, thought Blue. Once she instigated the Countdown and figured out a way of smuggling Flapwazzle.

As they walked together through the passage, Flapwazzle remarked conversationally, 'You know when I was asleep back there? Before I fell off the rock?'

'Yes,' Blue nodded.

'I was dreaming about Henry,' Flapwazzle said. 'He was in a lot of trouble.'

'I do that sometimes,' Blue told him.

twenty-four

Henry was in a lot of trouble.

He seemed to be hallucinating. There was a figure bending over him. After a moment he recognised it as Mr Fogarty.

'I thought you were in New Zealand,' Henry said dreamily.

'Don't be stupid,' said Mr Fogarty.

'What's the matter with him?' The voice, from somewhere to the left, was Pyrgus's.

'Bit disoriented, that's all. He'll be fine in a minute.'

'I want to talk to him. About Blue.'

'In a minute. He's had his atoms ripped apart and reassembled. You can't expect him to come out fighting.'

Henry tried to stand up and fell down. The ceiling looked very nice. It was vaulted like a church, only lower. The wood floor smelt of vanilla. His body ached a bit. Or quite a lot, actually.

'Perhaps I could be of assistance, sir …?'

A woman's voice said, 'He's really quite good at first aid, deeah.'

'Be my guest,' said Mr Fogarty.

An orange thumb dug into Henry's sternum. There was a sudden racking pain and everything snapped into focus. He jack-knifed into a sitting position, clutching his chest. The grinning face of Madame Cardui's dwarf was beaming at him.

'There, that's better, isn't it?' said Kitterick.

twenty-five

Henry felt as if he'd been run through a mincer. Everything ached, including, he noticed curiously, his hair. But worse than the ache was the confusion. He'd been in his bedroom a second ago.

He looked around. He was now in Mr Fogarty's shed. Or a Paramount Pictures version of Mr Fogarty's shed. It was huge and filled with really creepy stuff. There was a workbench scattered with equipment. There was a smallish portal full of blue fire that hovered briefly above his head, then popped out, shedding droplets like a bubble.

Pyrgus was grinning at him. Madame Cardui was smiling at him. Kitterick was looking at him. Mr Fogarty was frowning at him. He was back. Back in the Realm! It wasn't his imagination after all!

Henry pushed himself painfully to his feet. Through the window he could see the distant outline of the Purple Palace with its huge cyclopean stones weathered nearly black with age. It felt a bit like coming home. He took a step and nearly fell.

'Just aftermath,' said Mr Fogarty shortly, to no one in particular.

Henry put one hand out to lean on the bench. He found himself looking at Pyrgus, so he smiled at him.

Madame Cardui said, 'We can't bring him to the Queen in this state.'

Pyrgus said briskly, 'I know something that will perk him up.'

twenty-six

'What is this place?' Henry asked. Although it was his third visit to the Realm, he'd never actually been in the city before. It was a peculiar experience, like stepping back in time. He kept thinking of drawings he'd seen of Elizabethan London and the movie *Shakespeare in Love*. The city seemed to be entirely composed of narrow, dirty streets, tiny windows and overhanging buildings. The river might have been a wider version of the Thames. But despite the similarities, there were some spooky differences. This was definitely one of them.

'It's a Fizz Parlour,' Pyrgus said.

The frontage was decidedly garish. Spell coatings caused luminous bands of colour to crawl and intertwine with no concession to good taste. Above the door was a spinning spiral that had an hypnotic effect on passers-by. Henry noticed it was attracting a steady parade of insects and small birds.

'It's not some sort of tavern, is it?' Henry asked. 'Only I'm not allowed in pubs.' Even if it wasn't a tavern, he wasn't sure he wanted to go in. He was feeling a whole lot steadier now, but his muscles still ached and all he really wanted was to lie down somewhere and sleep. Somehow he doubted this was what

Pyrgus had in mind.

'No, it's not a tavern. We can go to a tavern if you like, but I thought this might be better for you.' Pyrgus frowned. 'Why aren't you allowed in taverns?'

'I'm too young.'

'You're the same age as me.'

'Yes, I know,' Henry said, and let it go. He eyed the entrance suspiciously. 'It's not … an opium den, is it?'

'I don't know what opium is,' Pyrgus said. 'But if you want a den, we can go to a saturation den. They're stimulating too.' Then he added brightly, 'But this is completely organic.'

'This'll be great, Pyrgus,' Henry said tiredly, belatedly remembering his manners.

The door beneath the whirling spiral opened into a winding tunnel that looked like the inside of an intestine. Walls, ceiling and floor were glistening pink and the whole thing undulated slightly as if pushing them along. Henry didn't like it much – he felt as if the building had digested him – but the intestine proved mercifully short.

They squeezed through a soft, squishy sphincter into a brightly lit open-plan chamber. There were white leather seats arranged in twos across the entire space with tiny little tables between them. Cables snaked from each seat into small black boxes bolted to the floor. Floating overhead was an immense, spell-driven sign in Gothic letters that announced:

THE ORGANIC FIZZ EXPERIENCE

'Grab those seats over there,' said Pyrgus. 'We want to be near the door in case there's a power outrage.'

'What happens in a power outrage?' Henry asked urgently, wondering what a power outrage was. But Pyrgus was already on his way to a booth, presumably to pay somebody.

Henry slid cautiously into one of the seats. It creaked and groaned a little when he moved, behaving exactly the way a leather seat should. He looked around. The Fizz Parlour – whatever it was selling – seemed to be doing mediocre business. There was a scattering of couples, seated facing one another, but the place was far from full.

Pyrgus returned and climbed into his seat, grinning broadly at Henry.

'What happens now?' Henry asked warily.

'They're sending somebody across,' said Pyrgus.

The somebody turned out to be a rather pretty girl with elfin features. She was carrying a tray with two tall glasses and, rather to his relief, Henry saw they were filled with nothing more threatening than carbonated fruit juice. He reached out as the girl unloaded her tray, but Pyrgus hissed urgently, *'That's for afterwards!'* as if he'd made some sort of social gaffe.

The girl smiled at Henry, reached down the front of her dress and pulled out a gleaming key on a length of string. She leaned forward to insert it into a small slit in the middle of the table.

'Enjoy your Organic Fizz Experience,' she said professionally, then left.

'What happens now?' Henry asked again. He hoped it was nothing strenuous.

'Just wait,' said Pyrgus, grinning.

Henry waited.

After a minute, Henry whispered, 'What are we waiting foRRR – YIPES!!'

A bolt of soft, smooth electricity charged up his spine. His head exploded like a Roman candle. His whole being shattered into colours dancing to the coolest music. It hurled the fractured pieces of his mind into a juggler's heaven and kept them there, whirling and plunging, while a heady excitement welled up in his stomach – where was his stomach anyway? – until he felt about to burst. Then suddenly it stopped.

'Wasn't that *great*?' Pyrgus exclaimed, his eyes shining.

Henry reached for his glass and discovered that his hand was shaking.

Once, on a holiday in Spain, Henry had been served tamarind juice and this had the same sweet-tart taste. But that was where any resemblance ended. From his first sip, the liquid wriggled in his mouth like a cat getting comfortable. It was weird to begin with, but after a moment he decided he liked it. In fact – he leaned back in the chair – he decided he quite liked a lot about the Organic Fizz Experience. He very much liked Pyrgus and the Faerie Realm. And talking. He wondered why he wasn't talking now.

'My aches have gone away,' Henry heard his voice say. He smiled.

'Really?' Pyrgus said. 'Have they really?' He took a large pull of his own drink.

They discussed Henry's pains for several minutes, or possibly most of the afternoon. They concluded Henry had been under a lot of strain and Mr Fogarty's new transporter hadn't helped a bit. They decided he was lucky it hadn't sent him mad. This struck them both as funny and they laughed a lot.

'Speaking of lunacy,' remarked Pyrgus later, 'are you in love with my sister?'

'Oh, yes,' Henry said at once. He felt no embarrassment, either at the question or his answer.

Pyrgus set down his glass. 'She's trying to start a war.'

'How peculiar,' Henry said.

There was a privacy spell around each pair of tables – or so Pyrgus claimed – so they felt free to discuss the matter at length. They discussed Hairstreak's offer and chewed around Blue's response. They considered how many people – *and animals*, Pyrgus put in quickly – might get killed if full-scale war broke out. They carefully examined Blue's attitude since she became the Faerie Queen.

'All power corrupts,' said Henry soberly. 'An asolute power corrups ... asolutely!'

'Wow!' Pyrgus exclaimed admiringly. 'That's *so* true.'

They discussed corruption for a while, then decided it was Henry's duty to persuade Blue to give peace a chance.

But when they got back to the Purple Palace, Blue was gone.

Twenty-seven

'Are you all right?' Blue asked.

'Yes, fine.'

'I think you may have slipped down.'

'Sorry.'

She felt him climb back. He had very soft, warm little feet, several hundred of them. Somehow they clung to her skin without hurting her at all.

'It's just that if you slip too far, it looks as if I'm wearing a bustle.'

'Sorry,' Flapwazzle repeated.

He felt more comfortable than some of her official garments, a little like a heat pad in the middle of her back. She was wearing a loose white shirt over him, which looked fine so long as he didn't move. But when she put on the tight-fitting jacket that went with her skirt – she twisted to see herself in the mirror of her bedroom – she looked as if she'd developed a hump.

'How is it with the coat?' Flapwazzle asked.

'Bit peculiar,' Blue said.

'Do I show?'

'Sort of …' She twisted again.

'Maybe I could breathe out. Endolgs can go quite a long time without oxygen …'

'Try it.'

'How's that?'

Blue frowned and shook her head. 'No ... it's not you – it's this jacket. I think I'll leave it off.' She peeled off the jacket and examined herself again. She was a bit underdressed for visiting. Would her uncle notice? Hairstreak noticed everything, but what was he going to do? He couldn't have her searched, not now she was Queen. Besides which, he'd never imagine she had an endolg clinging to her back, not in a thousand years. 'You can start breathing again, Flapwazzle ...' Yes, that looked all right. Just so long as he didn't slip down. 'You sure you can hold on? We'll be like this for a long time ...'

'No problem,' Flapwazzle said. 'It's an evolutionary trait. My ancestors clung to cliffs.'

This was *so* risky. If Lord Hairstreak discovered what she was up to, Flapwazzle was dead for sure. And Hairstreak might even be mad enough to kill *her*, especially if he thought he could make it look like an accident. Assuming he wasn't genuine about making peace. But that was what they were about to find out.

All the same, they were going to be entirely on their own. No back-up. No bodyguards. She wondered briefly if she should tell somebody what she was doing. But if she did, there'd be such a fuss she couldn't bear it. There was always a fuss about everything since she'd become Queen. You'd think becoming Queen would give you more freedom, but she'd found she actually had less. That's why she went to see the oracle alone. And that had turned out all right, hadn't it?

She straightened her back and Flapwazzle stayed stubbornly in place. She could order the Countdown to begin before she left the palace.

'OK,' Blue said. 'Off we go!'

Twenty-eight

'What's everybody looking at me for?' Pyrgus demanded.

'You're next in line for the throne,' Mr Fogarty said.

'No, I'm not – I abdicated!'

'You want me to go find Comma?' Mr Fogarty asked sourly. They were standing together – Mr Fogarty, Madame Cardui, Kitterick her orange dwarf, Pyrgus and Henry – in the Throne Room. Mr Fogarty had posted guards on the door.

'All right,' Pyrgus said, 'let's keep it between ourselves for the moment.' He looked around, still hoping to get out of taking charge. But no one else was volunteering. 'OK, are we sure she's not in the palace?'

Mr Fogarty said, 'She's not in the palace.'

Henry said quickly, 'You don't think she's been kidnapped, do you?' He looked worried.

Mr Fogarty shrugged. 'Could be, but her personal flyer is missing.'

Pyrgus blinked. 'She's got a *personal flyer*? How come I don't have a personal flyer?'

'You're under age.'

'Blue's a year younger than me! She can't have a personal flyer.'

'Blue's Queen. She can have anything she damn well likes.'

'You mean if I'd stayed on as Emperor, I could have had one?'

'You could, but you didn't, so you can't. Now can we get back to the point?' snapped Mr Fogarty. 'She's gone off somewhere, or been taken off somewhere, without telling anybody.'

'She's always going off without telling anybody,' Pyrgus mumbled, still stung by the business about the personal flyer. 'Did she tell anybody about that oracle thing?'

Mr Fogarty said crossly, 'No, she didn't. But given that we're on a war footing, don't you think it's just a little bit suspicious that she should disappear now?'

'We're on a war footing?' Pyrgus asked. He looked stunned.

'We're on a war footing?' Henry echoed.

Mr Fogarty strode over to the throne and absent-mindedly sat down. He sighed. 'Before she left, she called on Creerful and ordered a Countdown.'

'What's a Countdown?' Henry asked, but everyone ignored him.

Pyrgus stared at Mr Fogarty open-mouthed. His sister had gone power mad. It was one thing to prepare for war as a distant possibility. It was something else to put a Countdown in place. A Countdown gave the Generals a deadline. Once it passed, they launched an attack *without further orders*.

'How long have we got?' he asked.

'Three days,' said Mr Fogarty.

Pyrgus groaned. 'She's gone to see Hairstreak.' It was the only thing that made sense. Countdowns were a tradition established by a Purple Emperor named Scolitandes the Weedy, who'd had a horror of being kidnapped. Each time his duties forced him to visit an enemy, he ordered his generals to attack within a stated time if he didn't come back. He reasoned that if he was still alive he'd be rescued and, if not, revenged. That was close on five hundred years ago. As a strategy, Countdowns had been largely abandoned in recent years – they'd started far too many unwanted wars – but Blue was a stickler for tradition.

Pyrgus stared wide-eyed at Fogarty. 'If we attack Hairstreak, it'll start a war. What happens if she doesn't get back in time?'

'That's a problem,' Fogarty confirmed, nodding.

Henry said brightly, 'Perhaps she *hasn't* gone to see Hairstreak. Perhaps she's gone somewhere we could attack *without* starting a war.'

Mr Fogarty glanced at Madame Cardui, but said nothing. After a moment, Madame Cardui said uncomfortably, 'Actually, we ... ah ... we know she's definitely gone to visit Hairstreak.'

Three sets of eyes turned on her. She was wearing a lilac caftan that clashed violently with Kitterick, whom she was using as a seat. It was Pyrgus who spoke.

'We do?'

Madame Cardui nodded. 'We put a *follower* on her.'

'We?' Pyrgus demanded. 'Who's *we*?'

Madame Cardui shrugged and pouted. 'Very well, deeah, *I* put a *follower* on her. The day she became Queen.'

'You put a *follower* on a member of the Royal Family?' Pyrgus didn't even try to keep the outrage from his voice. *Followers* were illegal throughout the Realm and seldom used even by Faeries of the Night.

'You may be grateful I did,' said Madame Cardui,

not at all contrite. 'It means I can tell you exactly where she is at this precise minute.'

'Where is she at this precise minute?' Henry asked quickly.

'Approaching Hairstreak's new mansion,' Madame Cardui said blandly.

Pyrgus was still glaring at her. 'You haven't put a *follower* on me, have you?'

Madame Cardui smiled. 'Of course not, deeah – you're not *nearly* important enough any more.'

Mr Fogarty seemed suddenly to realise he was sitting on the throne and stood up quickly. 'We can argue about all this later,' he growled. 'Just now we need to decide how we're going to handle it.'

Henry said, 'This *follower* thing – can it tell you whether she's alone?' He was looking at Madame Cardui.

'She's unprotected, but not quite alone. She's carrying a concealed endolg.'

Henry said, 'Not Flapwazzle?'

Madame Cardui nodded. 'I'm afraid so, deeah.'

Mr Fogarty was shaking his head. 'It's obvious what she's up to. If she's smuggling in Flapwazzle, that means she's trying to find out whether Hairstreak's serious about his offer. Typical Blue manoeuvre – never considers repercussions, never considers the danger to herself.'

'Or Flapwazzle,' Henry muttered.

'Yes, or Flapwazzle!' Pyrgus echoed, glaring at Fogarty as if it was somehow his fault.

Mr Fogarty ignored them. 'The question is, what do we do about it?'

After a minute, Henry asked, a little anxiously, 'Do

we have to do anything about it?' He looked around at the others. 'I mean, she may pull it off. And if Lord Hairstreak's offer is genuine, he's not likely to harm her, is he? It's all right if she's back inside three days, isn't it?'

Fogarty favoured him with a contemptuous look. 'First law of politics: don't trust Hairstreak. What happens if he finds out what she's up to? Best case scenario, the offer's genuine and he's insulted by her lack of faith. Worst case, it's not genuine and he's got himself a tasty hostage.'

'But the difficulty,' said Madame Cardui, smoothly taking up the monologue as Mr Fogarty paused for breath, 'is that we can't simply send a contingent of troops to protect her. For one thing, that might start the very war we're working hard to avoid. For another, Blue obviously prefers *not* to have guards on this mission, and she *is* Queen after all. We have to take *some* account of her wishes.' She hesitated, then added, 'We need to move with subtlety. The situation is extremely delicate. My people have even had hints of demon problems.'

Fogarty glanced at her in surprise. 'The portals are still closed, aren't they?'

Madame Cardui nodded. 'All standard portals, yes. But –'

Henry cut across them both. 'Pyrgus and I will go after her,' he said firmly.

twenty-nine

Lord Hairstreak's forest mansion – now razed to the ground, alas – had been noted for its tight security. The forest was full of haniels so anybody who wandered in was likely to be eaten. His new home had no such natural defences. Although the house was surrounded by several hundred acres, the previous owner had set the grounds to gardens and cleared out any wildlife that was more dangerous than decorative. As a result, the previous owner had proven almost ludicrously easy to murder, a fate Hairstreak had no intention of sharing.

The new security system was state of the art. It was firmly centred on the mansion, spell-driven and globular. It cost a fortune to install and it looked like it would cost a fortune to run. But it had to be worth every penny.

'Is it active?' Hairstreak asked.

'Active but not armed,' Pelidne said.

'How do I see what's happening?' There were no viewing globes, no screens, nothing but a small bank of controls and a custom-made joystick that adjusted to the shape and size of any hand.

'The goggles, sir. On the table.'

Lord Hairstreak took off his lenses and replaced

them with the goggles, taking care not to disturb the parting in his hair. At once he seemed to be floating outside the mansion. The lighting was peculiar – rather like bright moonlight with a particularly bluish tinge – but everything was clearly visible. The three-dimensional effect was impressive.

'How do I change viewpoint?' he asked.

'The joystick, sir.'

Hairstreak glanced inadvertently in the direction of the joystick and discovered to his surprise he could still see it, despite the goggles. In fact, with a little effort, he could see everything in the cramped control room, including Pelidne. Yet at the same time he remained fully aware of the scene outside. It was an incredible piece of spell technology, one that clearly influenced the deepest levels of his mind. He reached out and gripped the joystick.

At once he was spinning out of control, tumbling and gyrating in the pseudo-body floating outside. 'Yark!' he snapped violently.

'Gently, sir – it takes a little practice.'

There had to be a printed manual somewhere. In the interim he steadied the joystick (and found to his relief he was no longer spinning) then inched it forward a hair's breadth.

At once he swooped down to the ground with a commanding view along the main avenue. He edged the joystick back and flew high into the air with a vast swathe of his estate spread out below him. The sensation was exhilarating in the extreme. If this wasn't a hideously expensive piece of equipment, it would make a great toy.

Under Pelidne's guidance, he worked the controls for

a few minutes until he got the hang of them. It really was extraordinary. With the help of just goggles and joystick, he could patrol every corner of his estate, spy on his groundskeepers, sneak up invisibly on his guards, even examine an individual flower that took his fancy. It was an illusion, of course, but astonishingly realistic. You even got used to the peculiar light.

'Are we set up for a test?' he asked.

'Oh, yes,' Pelidne assured him.

Hairstreak hesitated. 'What about our own people? Does it put them at risk?'

'No, sir, they're tagged.'

'What about outsiders?'

'It's outsiders the system's designed to attack.'

Hairstreak glanced round at him and scowled. 'It's just possible I might wish to entertain guests at some point,' he said sarcastically.

'It can be trained to ignore specific individuals,' Pelidne said. 'Or certain groups. Like all Faeries of the Night. Or people above a certain age. Or all males wearing pirate costume. Very flexible. Useful if you ever wanted to hold a fancy dress ball or something of that sort, sir.'

'But it hasn't been trained yet?' Hairstreak said. 'It will attack anybody within range?'

'Apart from our own people. After it's armed, of course.'

Hairstreak licked his lips. 'How do I arm it?' he asked.

'The switch to the right of the panel,' Pelidne said.

With a thrill of anticipation, Lord Hairstreak reached across and flipped the switch. A bank of seven telltales illuminated smoothly, one after the other. He turned his attention back to the scene outside and discovered the blue light had changed to a much more realistic hue, but set at a comfortable level for a Faerie of the Night.

'Release him now,' he whispered, his voice suddenly dry.

thirty

The boy was a Faerie of the Light by the cut of his eyes, a raggedy lad little more than thirteen years of age. The servants had discovered him wandering on the edge of the Hairstreak Estate – quite safely since the security system hadn't yet been armed. He claimed he'd got lost while collecting firewood for his mother, which might well have been true. There were several deprived Lighter families living on the edges of the estate and the nights were growing chill. But there'd been no fire in the cottage last night. Hairstreak's guards had grabbed the boy and put him in a cage. It was now hanging from a tree on the main avenue as a warning to others.

'It's not an exact test, I suppose,' Pelidne said quietly. 'He's hardly going to run *towards* the mansion.'

Hairstreak was watching with fascination as two of his servants lowered the cage to the ground, withdrew the bolt, then melted away into the bushes. Although he was free now, the boy stayed where he was, staring after them suspiciously.

'Going … coming,' Hairstreak shrugged. 'It doesn't matter so long as the system functions properly.'

Eventually, cautiously, the boy moved to the edge of his cage and tried the door. It swung open. Still he didn't get out. He looked up and down the main driveway as if expecting somebody to come along it and grab him.

'Where's the nearest node?' Hairstreak asked curiously.

'Less than thirty yards, sir.'

'Which direction?'

'Any direction. The grounds are peppered with them.'

The boy was leaving the cage now. His most predictable action would be to race along the driveway towards the main gate, but he was clearly too wary for that. He waited a moment, then seemed to make up his mind. Crouching low, he ran *across* the driveway in the opposite direction to the servants and disappeared between two rhododendron bushes. Hairstreak eased back on the joystick and rose to follow him.

From his new vantage point, Hairstreak could see the boy running full pelt over rough grass. As Pelidne predicted, he got less than thirty yards before a tracker emerged from its bunker and hurled itself after him.

The child didn't stand a chance. The tracker hit him full force from the side, knocked him heavily to the ground, then leaped on to his chest, growling savagely. The boy was game, Hairstreak had to give him that. He struck out wildly and twisted desperately in an attempt to break free, but the creature sank metal teeth into his shoulder and, seconds later, the boy's eyes rolled upwards and he lay still.

'What's our alert status?' Hairstreak asked curiously.

'Level 1, sir, for the purpose of the test: seek, hold and immobilise. At Level 2, the tracker would chew his arm off: seek, hold, immobilise and cripple. At Level 3 it kills him: lethal force authorised.' Pelidne hesitated. 'Would you like me to raise the alert level, sir?'

'No, let's wait until I have more time to enjoy it,' Hairstreak said.

'What do you want me to do about the boy?' Pelidne asked.

'When he wakes up, let him go. It'll do no harm at all if he talks about his experience – might discourage other trespassers.' Hairstreak began to pull off his goggles, then stopped. 'What's that noise?'

'Noise, sir?'

'High-pitched whine.'

Pelidne leaned across and made an adjustment on the control panel. A penetrating sound filled the little chamber. 'Aircraft alert, sir.'

A look of pleased surprise flitted across Hairstreak's features. 'How interesting. I hadn't realised the system detected aerial approaches.'

'The spell-field forms a sphere, centred on the house. It detects intrusion from the air and underground. This isn't likely to be an attack, of course – more like a commercial coach line or something of that sort. It's sensitive enough to pick up high-altitude disturbances.' Pelidne made another adjustment. 'If you relax your neck muscles, sir, the goggles will automatically turn your head in the direction of the intruder and simulate an image if it's too far away for visual detection.'

Hairstreak sat back in his chair and allowed his head to roll against the backrest. At once his perception was speeding through the air outside, zooming to a higher altitude than anything he'd so far achieved. He felt like a mountain haniel launching from a snow-covered peak.

'It's not a commercial coach line,' he said quietly. 'It's a personal flyer.'

The whining alarm suddenly began to pulse urgently. 'And it's just penetrated the detection sphere,' Pelidne said. 'Would you like to shoot it down, sir?'

Hairstreak raised an eyebrow above his goggles. 'Can I do that?'

Pelidne gave a bleak little smile. 'You can even do it *legally*, sir – the craft has now entered our airspace. Just press the red button on the top of your joystick. The system will do the rest.'

'Fascinating,' Hairstreak said.

His thumb stroked the red button.

Thirty-one

Blue's personal flyer was a dart-shaped single-seater finished in a stylish, high-gloss black with crimson interior trim. Voice-activated controls gave a hair-trigger response and newly installed spell compression meant it hurtled through the airways like a comet. Normally Blue adored using it, but this trip was an exception.

'Are you OK?' she asked.

'Yes, fine.' Flapwazzle wriggled reassuringly against her back.

'Sure?'

'I can't tell lies.'

The problem was she couldn't get comfortable. Usually she lay back in the crimson seat, overrode the safeties and flew at top speed. But with Flapwazzle anchored to her spine, she didn't want to lie back for fear of crushing him. And since she didn't want acceleration to *push* her back, she ordered the craft to maintain a boringly sedate pace. Unfortunately the flyer wasn't designed to be used in this way. It performed erratically, demanded constant attention. So she sat forward, frowning, and tried to coax it along while she developed a headache, sore back and a stiff neck.

Flapwazzle said, 'What's our plan?'

'What's our plan what?' Blue asked vaguely. The flyer was just beginning to pick up speed again, which was a relief, but looking down she discovered she'd lost track of where they were. The last thing she needed was a friendly chat with Flapwazzle.

'Our plan when we get to Hairstreak's place. What are you going to say to him? What's the excuse for paying him a visit?'

A good point, Blue thought, despite her problems. It was important Lord Hairstreak didn't get suspicious. He might be her uncle, but they weren't exactly on good terms, so she could hardly say she'd dropped in for a cup of ragwort.

After a moment she said, 'I'll tell him I want more details of his offer.'

'Wouldn't you just send a minion for that?'

Actually she probably would. Besides, what more details could he give her? It was an offer to negotiate. You either said yes or no.

'Besides, what more details can he give you?' Flapwazzle added, echoing her thought.

'Have you any suggestions?' Blue asked to shut him up. 'Bank starboard, avoid cloud,' she muttered to the flyer.

'Why don't you ask him how much backing he's got for negotiations?'

The flyer dropped below the level of the cloud and Blue realised two things. The first was that they were no longer over the city. The second was that they were definitely off-course. Lord Hairstreak's new mansion was the former Tellervo Estate which lay outside the city walls to the north-west, but not far.

You couldn't mistake the Tellervo Estate, even from the air. Old Zoilus Tellervo was obsessed with building follies – imitations of ancient ruins mostly – and there were dozens of them strewn across the estate. Hairstreak wouldn't have had time to demolish them yet. The ground below showed no sign of ruins, fake or otherwise, so clearly they weren't over the property yet.

The question was, what were they over?

Blue leaned back (Flapwazzle was just going to have to take his chances) and twisted her head to get the long view. The mountains were still clearly visible to port, so they couldn't be wildly off-course. But directly below seemed to be fairly featureless farmland. She could be anywhere.

'Why don't you ask him how much backing he's got for negotiations?' Flapwazzle asked again, his voice muffled now.

Then she saw the ridgeway! The ancient earthwork meandered like a snake towards a body of water that had to be Ormo Lake. Which meant she wasn't far from Hairstreak's new estate after all.

'Hard to starboard,' she ordered the flyer with a sigh of relief. As the craft swung right, she relaxed and turned her attention away from the controls. 'Why don't I ask him how much backing he's got for negotiations?' she asked Flapwazzle rhetorically. 'Yes, why don't I? That's a great idea.'

It was too. She should have thought of asking Hairstreak that anyway. How much backing *did* he have? It was one thing for Hairstreak to say he was ready to negotiate, but even if he was genuine, what good was that if the Nighter Great Houses didn't back him? Of course she'd have to ask him that. And it was sensitive enough for her to want to ask personally. Good old Flapwazzle!

An alarm sounded in the confines of the flyer's cabin and a red light began to pulse on the display in front of her.

'What is it now?' Blue asked tiredly. Probably another complaint that they were flying too slow or too low or too high.

'We have been targeted by ground-based missiles,' said the spell-driven voice of the flyer.

Thirty-two

It must be love, Pyrgus thought. That was the only thing could have changed Henry from the quiet, reserved boy Pyrgus knew to this take-charge character who snapped out crisp orders and wouldn't take no for an answer. It was Henry who organised the mission, Henry who drew up the plan, Henry who commandeered transport, Henry who led the three of them – Madame Cardui had insisted Kitterick go too – out of the Purple Palace.

'What do we do now?' Pyrgus asked.

They were hidden in some bushes, staring at the gateway to Lord Hairstreak's estate, which, surprisingly, was standing open and unguarded. Their transport, an unmarked delivery cart souped up with a turbo-charged spell drive, was parked around the corner looking innocent. A far cry from a personal flyer, Pyrgus thought sourly.

'May I suggest, gentlemen,' Kitterick put in, 'that it might be prudent to spend a moment reviewing the situation.'

Pyrgus glanced at the Trinian. It was probably good advice. 'All right by me,' he said, then glanced warily at Henry.

Henry seemed to be lost in his own thoughts. His

face had taken on that granite cast you saw in Mr Fogarty. 'We know Blue was headed towards Lord Hairstreak's mansion,' he said quietly, 'but we don't know whether she's got there.'

'Although it would seem very likely,' Pyrgus said, then added, 'Especially since she's travelling in a *personal flyer.*'

'If I might express an opinion, Crown Prince, Iron Prominent,' Kitterick said, 'I think we may take it that Her Majesty has arrived, for good or ill, at Lord Hairstreak's residence.'

'Our job is to save her,' Henry said.

'Our job's nothing of the sort,' Pyrgus said. 'At least not yet.' What was *wrong* with Henry? Blue – or anything to do with Blue – seemed to unhinge him completely. 'Our job's to make sure she's all right, hopefully without causing a diplomatic incident. And if she's all right, we leave her to it.'

'Our job is to save her,' Henry repeated as if Pyrgus hadn't spoken.

'Well, possibly,' Pyrgus said irritably. He was all for saving his sister, but since his father died he was beginning to appreciate that life wasn't all black and white. In the old days, he would have stormed in, just like the new, improved Henry. Now he could see that it wouldn't do anybody any good if they stormed in and Hairstreak killed them. Or, maybe even worse for the Realm, captured them. But it wasn't just a question of calling in the troops either – that would probably result in the civil war everybody was trying to avoid. On balance he favoured caution, combined with a sneaky approach.

'I note, sirs, that the gate is wide open and the estate

appears to be unguarded,' Kitterick said.

Pyrgus turned to him frowning. 'What would you deduce from that, Kitterick?'

'From our knowledge of Lord Hairstreak, I would say that appearances may be deceptive.'

'There'll be guards,' Henry predicted grimly. 'Just maybe not at the gate.'

'So do we go in or what?' asked Pyrgus.

'We go in,' said Henry firmly. 'Cautiously and stealthily, hiding in the bushes. We creep up to the house and peer through the windows until we find Blue. If there's the slightest hint of danger, we attack. We will succeed due to the element of surprise. Once we have her safe, you can flatten the whole place the way you flattened that glue factory. Spell bombs or whatever it was.'

'Alternatively, sir, we could simply walk down the avenue.'

They both turned to look at him.

Kitterick said, 'It might be argued that we are all here in a precautionary capacity. On the face of things, Her Majesty seems to have embarked on a diplomatic mission. We have – as yet – no reason to believe she is in any degree of personal peril. Should we approach covertly, *and be discovered*, Lord Hairstreak might appear justified in claiming we were engaged in espionage. On the other hand, an open approach has the benefit of complete transparency. If we are halted by guards – as I assume we will be at some point – we simply say we are a part of Her Majesty's retinue. We will then be escorted to the mansion where we can easily determine Lord Hairstreak's attitude towards the whole business. If we are not – halted by guards, that is – then we present ourselves at the front door and request audience with His Lordship and Her Majesty. Either way, we avoid all possibility of a diplomatic incident, show solidarity with Her Majesty, remain on hand to protect her physically, should that need arise, and simultaneously send a clear message to Lord Hairstreak that Her Majesty's whereabouts are known and any action he might be tempted to take against her would have ... consequences. Thus it would seem that walking down the avenue appears to be the most fruitful course of action.'

After a moment, Pyrgus shook his head. 'Oh, no, that's rubbish.'

Henry said, 'Complete nonsense. Wouldn't entertain it.'

They were creeping through the bushes when the first of Hairstreak's trackers took out Pyrgus.

Thirty-three

Hairstreak eased his thumb back off the red button. 'That flyer is showing the royal crest,' he murmured, as much to himself as Pelidne.

'Are we expecting an emissary from the palace?' Pelidne asked.

'No, but that doesn't mean they haven't sent one.'

'What are your orders, sir?'

Hairstreak pulled off his goggles. There was a thoughtful expression on his face. 'Standard procedure, Pelidne. Have our visitor escorted to the landing pad and treated with every courtesy. Alert me once his identity is established. If he has legitimate palace credentials, try to find out the purpose of the visit.'

'Then stall him?'

'Yes, exactly,' Hairstreak said. 'Offer him refreshment, get him drunk – whatever. Report back to me at once with any information. I shall be in my office.'

'And the flyer, sir?'

'Search it thoroughly once the pilot is clear.'

Pelidne hesitated. 'A royal flyer will have security spells in place. There would be no way of concealing the fact we'd searched it.'

Hairstreak shrugged. 'They'll expect us to search it – we'd be fools not to.'

'Yes, sir.' As Hairstreak pushed past him, Pelidne asked, 'The security system, sir?'

'What about it?'

'Shall I leave it armed?'

'Of course. Our visitor isn't likely to wander. And if he does, he deserves anything he gets,' Lord Hairstreak told him. He stood up. 'Contact my office once the craft is down.'

But he never reached his office. Halfway down the stairs to the main hall an excited servant caught up with him.

'Sir,' she said breathlessly, 'Lord Hairstreak, sir. It's Her Majesty!' Hairstreak turned to stare at her, his face expressionless. The girl waved her arms in something approaching panic. 'It's the Queen, sir. Outside, sir. Come in a flyer, sir, fastest landing I ever seen. Queen Blue, sir. What'll we do, sir?'

Hairstreak stared at her for a long moment. 'Queen Blue?' he said. 'That flyer was piloted by Queen Blue?'

'Yes, sir. The Queen, sir. She's standing outside now, sir. What'll we do?'

Hairstreak smiled chillingly. 'Get out of my way, girl. I shall welcome Her Majesty personally.'

Thirty-four

'That was the worst flyer landing ever,' Flapwazzle whispered.

'Were you frightened?' Blue asked.

'Petrified. You're the scariest queen since Quercusia.'

'I had to get out from under the missiles,' Blue said, grinning.

'Might have been more difficult if he'd fired them.' Flapwazzle made a peculiar movement and it took her a moment to work out that he was scratching himself. 'I'd like to know why he didn't.'

'Maybe I'll get the chance to ask him.' Blue said. 'Now hush – there's somebody coming.'

She was expecting the servant girl again, but the door swung back to reveal Hairstreak himself. He was a small man, dressed, as usual, in black. He made an elaborate bow and contorted his features into a smile.

'Your Majesty,' he said fulsomely, 'if you had let me know you were coming I would have made proper preparations.'

'Like shutting down your ground-to-air missiles?' Blue asked innocently.

Hairstreak smiled slightly. 'Standard security precautions, I'm afraid. Regrettable, of course, but in these troubled times ...' Something flashed in his eyes as he added, 'So fortunate they weren't actually launched.'

'For me or for you, Uncle?'

'For us both, my dear.' He squared his shoulders. 'But what am I thinking of, leaving you standing on the doorstep? Please come in. You grace my humble home with your presence.' As he stepped to one side, Blue suddenly noticed a slim young man standing in the shadows behind him. There was nothing untoward about his appearance, but for some reason she shuddered. Hairstreak may have caught the direction of her glance, for he said softly over his shoulder, 'Pelidne, have the servants prepare a meal for Her Majesty. In the main banquet hall.'

'That won't be necessary,' Blue said quickly. Now they were here, she was very aware she'd set a Countdown in motion. Three days was a good safety margin, but even so there was no sense taking any more time than she needed. 'This is a just a brief visit. But I would appreciate a few minutes in a secure room.'

'Of course,' Hairstreak said smoothly.

He led her down a corridor beside the main staircase and opened a heavy door. The chamber beyond was tiny and furnished only with two chairs and a small table, but it smelled strongly of privacy spells.

'The matter is confidential,' Blue said firmly when the Pelidne person tried to follow.

Hairstreak shrugged slightly and gestured with his head. Pelidne left at once. Throughout it all he had not spoken a single word.

As Hairstreak closed the door he said, 'I take it this concerns the offer I sent by way of your brother?'

'Yes,' Blue said.

'Then let us sit and discuss it.' He hesitated momentarily. 'Perhaps your endolg would be more comfortable on the floor than squashed up against the chair back.'

Blue froze. For a second she considered trying to bluff it out – *Endolg? What endolg?* – but Flapwazzle said audibly, 'He knows I'm here, Blue,' and slid out from under her shirt.

Hairstreak smiled a little grimly. 'Ah, it's Flapwoggle, isn't it? The endolg who famously infiltrated my obsidian maze?'

'Flapwazzle,' Flapwazzle corrected him sourly.

'Of course,' Hairstreak said.

Flushing a little, Blue said, 'I thought it might be a good idea to have an endolg present.' Despite the embarrassment, she held her uncle's eye. 'For both our sakes.'

But Hairstreak only said, 'Yes, of course,' and gestured her towards the nearest chair.

She waited until he'd taken the other seat before she said, 'Pyrgus told me the Faeries of the Night want peace – is that so?'

'It's all most of them have ever wanted, Blue,' Hairstreak said piously.

'And you're now offering to negotiate to that end?'

'To negotiate a treaty, yes.'

Blue took a deep breath. 'Is the offer genuine?' she asked bluntly.

She expected an angry response, but Hairstreak only shrugged. 'The offer's perfectly genuine. But ask the endolg. That's what it's here for, I presume.'

Blue flushed, hesitated, then said quietly, 'Flapwazzle?'

'He's telling the truth,' Flapwazzle said.

She suddenly realised the news had thrown her. Deep down she must have believed the whole thing was a ploy. But now, with a welling sense of excitement, the implications began to dawn on her. There was a genuine offer on the table. That meant the possibility of real peace in the Realm for the first time in centuries. The treaty negotiations were sure to be tough, compromises would have to be made, but the goodwill was there. Something absolutely unexpected had happened. She was Queen at a turning point in history. If nothing went wrong, her name would be remembered for a thousand years. It was a sobering thought.

If nothing went wrong ...

She suddenly remembered Flapwazzle's question. 'Uncle, what backing do you have to make this offer?'

'Enough,' said Hairstreak shortly. 'Every major House of the Faeries of the Night is behind it.'

'But there are dissenters? Some Houses don't agree?'

'As you say, some Houses disagree, but not enough to make a difference to the outcome. If a treaty is signed under the present circumstances, it will be implemented.'

She glanced at Flapwazzle, who said, 'It's true, but he's holding something back.'

'What are you holding back, Uncle?'

Hairstreak gave a hearty chuckle that sounded entirely genuine. 'Oh, come now, Blue, you don't expect me to reveal my negotiating position in advance of the talks, do you? You haven't even agreed to the basic proposal yet.'

It was reasonable enough. And he was right: she

hadn't even agreed to negotiations yet. At least not formally. In her head, she no longer had any doubt.

She opened her mouth to tell him so when there was a thunderous knocking on the door.

thirty-five

For no reason, Blue felt suddenly afraid. Her heart begin to thump wildly as Hairstreak strode across the room.

'What is it?' she whispered to Flapwazzle, who was now wrapped protectively around her feet.

'I don't know,' Flapwazzle whispered back nervously. 'It's Hairstreak's vampire – I can get that from the smell. And he's worried about something: I can get that from the smell too. But I don't know what. I can only sense truth, not read minds.'

Blue almost choked. 'Vampire? Uncle Hairstreak has a *vampire*?'

'The droopy young man lurking by the door – the one who tried to come in here. I forget what your uncle called him.'

'Pelidne,' Blue said. 'Pelidne is a vampire?'

'Didn't you notice how pale he was?'

Blue's voice had been rising. Now she modified it with an effort. 'Yes, but I never thought he might be a vampire.' Vampire servants were illegal, but it was stupid to think that would make much difference to her uncle. 'Why didn't you tell me?'

'I didn't think it was important,' Flapwazzle said.

'Not important?' Blue hissed. 'He might have drunk

our blood!'

'Wouldn't have drunk mine,' Flapwazzle sniffed. 'They're allergic to it.'

Lord Hairstreak had the door open now and it was indeed Pelidne outside. He leaned across to whisper something in Hairstreak's ear and Blue only just stifled the urge to shout a warning about the danger to her uncle's neck.

Hairstreak jerked away as if he'd been bitten. 'Three?' he hissed. He glanced back at Blue through the open doorway.

The man Pelidne – the *vampire* Pelidne – moved forward to whisper something else.

'I don't like the look of this,' Flapwazzle muttered. 'I think we should get out of here.' He began to climb up her leg.

Blue stood without waiting for him to anchor on her back again. 'Our business is done here, Uncle,' she exclaimed in her most imperious voice. 'I accept your offer to negotiate.' She tried to sweep from the room, an effect marred by Flapwazzle, who was clinging to her knee.

Lord Hairstreak moved quickly to block the doorway. 'Your Majesty,' he said formally. 'There has been a development you should know about.' He blinked slowly, like a lizard. 'If you don't know about it already,' he added softly.

Blue didn't, so the expression on her face was genuine. As was the panic building in her. She'd caught a hint of what Flapwazzle was sensing – he was on her thigh now, trembling slightly – and it was very frightening indeed. All she could think of was getting out of the mansion and into her flyer.

'I'm due back at the Purple Palace,' she said desperately, still trying to bluff it out. (Bluff *what* out?) 'They're expecting me and it's long past Flapwazzle's bedtime –'

Flapwazzle managed a little jump and wrapped himself around her stomach. 'Make a run for it!' he hissed.

She might even have tried, but Lord Hairstreak caught her arm. 'This way, *Your Majesty*,' he said angrily. He half dragged her out of the room and ten paces along the corridor. He stopped. 'Would *Your Majesty* care to comment?' he asked.

There were three bodies lying near the staircase.

Thirty-six

At first she didn't see anything except the limp, huddled corpses with their hideous wounds, then her eyes travelled upwards to the familiar shock of red hair.

'God of Light,' she whispered. 'Pyrgus!'

She tore away from Hairstreak and dropped on one knee. Pyrgus had been thrown almost casually across a body with orange skin – Madame Cardui's Trinian servant Kitterick. Blue felt a tightness in her chest that almost stopped her heart. Then her eyes moved to the third body.

Henry! It was Henry! She didn't even know he was back in the Realm. She twisted to look up at Hairstreak.

'You've killed them!' she gasped. 'You've killed all three of them!'

'Don't be stupid!' Hairstreak snapped. 'None of them is dead. The question is, what did your people think they were trying to do?'

Blue ignored him. Now she looked more closely, Pyrgus was breathing. So was Henry. But Pyrgus had a massive red stain oozing from his side and Henry's hair was matted with blood. She couldn't see the extent of Kitterick's injuries because of the way Pyrgus had been thrown on top of him, but from what she knew of the dwarf he was probably worse off than the other two. He always fought like a demon to avoid capture.

She forced herself to her feet and turned to face Lord Hairstreak, her eyes blazing. 'What have you done to them?' she demanded. If Pyrgus died or Henry died she would have Hairstreak hanged and to Hael with the political consequences.

'I have done nothing to them,' Hairstreak said impatiently. 'Your brother and his friends were sneaking about in my grounds, clearly intent on espionage or sabotage. They were detected and neutralised by my automatic security system.' His lip curled into a sneer. 'I cannot imagine they took action without your knowledge, *Majesty*.'

He doesn't know Pyrgus, Blue thought. But she was too concerned to let herself be bullied. 'Security system?' she snapped. 'Your security system may have killed them!'

'Oh, nonsense!' Hairstreak shook his head shortly. 'They're merely in a coma. The system uses a derivative of Trinian toxin.' He looked down at Kitterick with distaste. 'Ironically.'

'Trinian toxin is lethal,' Blue gasped, suddenly frightened again.

'A derivative, I said,' Hairstreak shouted, no longer even attempting politeness. 'The worst it does is send them asleep for a while.'

'He's telling the truth,' Flapwazzle murmured from the level of her belly.

Even after the endolg's reassurance, Blue felt murderous. 'They're injured!' she shouted at Hairstreak.

'Pelidne, fetch the staff physician,' Hairstreak

ordered over his shoulder. To Blue he said hotly, 'That damn dwarf broke four of my trackers, if we're starting to apportion blame.'

Blue didn't know what a tracker was, but assumed it must be a part of the security system. Hairstreak had a real cheek bringing that up. Like blaming somebody for making your sword bloody after you stuck it in him. All the same, now her initial panic was dying down, she could see he had a point. What *was* Pyrgus doing here? And where had Henry come from? Chances were they'd some romantic idea about rescuing her. Now, as usual, she was going to have to rescue *them*.

A fat, balding little man with a mandrake embroidered on his tunic came bustling from the bowels of the house. He looked like someone wakened from a nap.

'Fix them,' Hairstreak said shortly, nodding towards the bodies on the floor. 'Report to me when you've finished.' Without further preamble, he gripped Blue's arm again. 'Come with me, Niece – you have some explaining to – *yipes*!' He jerked his hand away as Flapwazzle bit him.

'Touching the royal person is forbidden,' Flapwazzle said from his position wrapped around the royal stomach.

Pelidne moved towards them and the way he moved was frightening in its speed and grace. But Hairstreak waved him away.

'The creature is quite right – I forgot myself.' He glared soberly at Blue. 'Nonetheless, Your Majesty, it is clear we need to talk, if Your Majesty will condescend to accompany me …?'

'Of course, Uncle,' Blue said lightly. Despite his new-found manners, she knew she had no option.

He led her back to the room they'd occupied before and closed the door carefully. Then he turned towards her. 'Well?'

It was exactly the tone her father had used when she'd irritated him, usually accompanied by the words *'young lady'*. Now it was her uncle who was angry and, while she was furious herself, she knew very well her situation was delicate. Pyrgus, Henry and Kitterick had no right to trespass on the Hairstreak Estate, let alone go creeping around in the bushes, looking for God knew what. (She had no doubt that what Hairstreak had told her was true – it was exactly the sort of thing Pyrgus *would* do ... and drag poor Henry along with him.)

Blue didn't think for a moment they were up to anything sinister, and all three had paid heavily for their silliness – their wounds looked horrible – but none of that changed the fact they were basically in the wrong ... or that Realm politics had hit a critical time. Would this stop the treaty? Probably not, but it would certainly give Hairstreak an advantage in the negotiations she'd much rather he didn't have. What she needed now was damage limitation.

'They were not here by my order, Uncle,' she said bluntly.

'Whose order *were* they here on?' Hairstreak asked coldly.

'I don't know.'

'You expect me to believe that?'

'Queen's telling the truth,' said Flapwazzle, in the process of sliding back down to the floor.

'Then you would have no objection to my questioning them?'

Blue took a deep breath. She had no intention of turning anybody over to Lord Hairstreak for questioning: his methods were notorious. But there was no doubt the three idiots needed to be questioned.

She said firmly, 'Let them go. I'll question them myself.'

Hairstreak shook his head. 'That,' he said, 'is not acceptable.'

The argument began in earnest then. They'd resolved nothing when the door opened silently.

Thirty-seven

Pyrgus opened his eyes to find a balding little man leaning over him. He shut them again. His head felt as if somebody had sandpapered the surface of his brain. But that was nothing to his stomach. It had turned into a churning, curdled sea that threatened to spew out of his mouth in an endless flood. (He wondered briefly if the little man would manage to get out of the way.) There was a pain in his side worse than anything he'd ever known, so deep and penetrating that he half thought somebody had left a knife in there.

He groaned. His mind moved like molasses and his body refused to move at all. The worst of it was, he had no idea what had happened. It occurred to him it might be best if he simply lay there and died quietly.

From somewhere he heard the familiar snap and fizz of a spell cone.

'What ...?' Pyrgus whispered with enormous effort. An acrid scent flooded his nostrils and made him cough, which made his head ache worse than ever. It reminded him of the time he'd been poisoned. They'd told him afterwards that if Blue hadn't given him the antidote when she did, his skull would have exploded. It felt much like that now. He wished Blue were here to give him the antidote again.

Then, quite suddenly, he started feeling better.

Pyrgus opened his eyes again. The little bald man was still there. 'That should help,' he said briskly. 'Now let me have a look at that side.'

Although his mind was clearer and his stomach had stopped churning, Pyrgus found he was helpless to resist as the little man pulled back his jacket and prodded at the wound in his side. The pain flared briefly, then died back to a dull ache.

'Looks worse than it is,' the little man muttered, half to himself. 'You've lost a bit of blood, but I expect you'll live. The worst of it will be the bruising. That's going to hurt like Hael for a while. What happened to you, anyway?'

It was a very good question and Pyrgus wasn't sure he knew how to answer it. One minute he'd been sneaking through the bushes at Hairstreak's mansion, the next he was here, feeling like a bear's intestines and probably looking even worse. What bridged the gap, he had no idea.

Henry and Kitterick!

He pushed himself painfully into a sitting position. 'My friends –?' he gasped.

'Your friends are in better shape than you are,' the little man said. 'The other boy has some bruising to his shoulder and a small cut on his head, but that's about all. He even seems to have been quite resistant to the poison – first one of you to wake up. The Trinian has a broken arm, but that's already started to knit – you know how it is with Trinians. You were the only one I was really worried about.'

Pyrgus looked around. 'Where are they?' He noticed his voice was getting stronger and his body felt a lot less weak. He thought he'd try standing up and, to his surprise, managed it without too much difficulty.

The little balding man – he had the insignia of the Physician's Guild on his jacket – watched him with interest. When Pyrgus was on his feet (panting a little and leaning against one wall) he said, 'They're cleaning up in the washroom.' He nodded towards a door. 'You'd better do the same – you're about to go visiting.'

They were in a smallish hallway furnished with barbarian antiques. 'Visiting?' Pyrgus echoed. 'Where?'

'Lord Hairstreak wants to see you,' the doctor said.

In the washroom, Pyrgus found Kitterick cleaning the blood off Henry's head with a towel. Neither of them looked too much the worse for wear.

'We're being taken to Hairstreak,' Pyrgus said without preamble. 'We'd better get our stories straight.'

Kitterick stepped back to admire his handiwork and threw the towel aside. He smiled briefly at Henry then said to Pyrgus, 'I suggest, sir, we had an urgent personal message for Her Majesty.'

'Nice one, Kitterick,' Pyrgus said admiringly. 'Why were we skulking in the bushes?'

'Skulking, sir? Hardly. We were making our way along the driveway as legitimate representatives of Her Majesty and the Purple Palace when we were set upon by mechanical devices governed by a faulty security system.'

Pyrgus frowned. 'Weren't we found in the bushes?'

'Indeed, sir, in all probability we were. At exactly the spot where we were driven by the mechanical devices.'

'You think he'll buy that?' Henry asked. He had a strange expression on his face.

'Of course not, sir, but he will be hard put to prove otherwise.'

'And it throws the blame on his stupid security system,' Pyrgus said, smiling suddenly.

Kitterick smiled back smugly. 'An added bonus.'

'Brilliant!' Pyrgus exclaimed. 'You happy with that, Henry?'

Henry shrugged and turned away as if their story was no concern of his.

'OK,' Pyrgus said briskly. 'Let's go see my dear uncle.' He pushed through the washroom door and stopped. The little doctor had been joined by a man Pyrgus had never seen before. He was young and tall and thin and blond.

His skin was very pale.

Thirty-eight

They came in together in a tight bunch, a wary look in every eye.

'Pyrgus!' Blue squealed. She made to run to him, then stopped. Hairstreak's vampire was standing directly behind her brother, one slim hand resting lightly on his shoulder.

Blue backed off a step. From behind her Flapwazzle gave a low, threatening growl. Henry and Kitterick were beside Pyrgus. None of them looked injured any more and there were no signs of ill-treatment.

Blue said quietly, 'Are you all right, Henry?'

Henry's face was expressionless. 'Yes.'

'Pyrgus?'

Pyrgus said, 'We have a confidential message for you, Blue.' He rolled his eyes in a peculiar way as if trying to signal something to her.

'Kitterick?'

'Never better, Madam. In the peak of my health, one might say.'

Hairstreak said, 'Now we have the niceties out of the way, *Your Majesty,* perhaps your people would care to tell us why they were trespassing on my land, and what –'

'We have a confidential message for Her Majesty,'

167

Pyrgus said loudly, interrupting him. 'We were proceeding along –'

'Shut up, Pyrgus,' Blue said, interrupting *him*. She had no idea what sort of cock and bull story Pyrgus had dreamed up to explain his presence here, but the situation was far too delicate to let him come barging in with hobnailed boots on. What she needed was to take control. She needed to stop Pyrgus saying anything that might make things worse. She needed to change her uncle's mind about questioning them. Everything was already in a bit of a mess, but she'd got what she came for. The Nighter offer was genuine and Hairstreak had the backing to make it stick. The thing now was to get back to the Purple Palace as quickly as possible and without provoking Lord Hairstreak any further. An idea occurred to her and she turned to her uncle.

'Lord Hairstreak,' she said formally. 'Perhaps if we –'

Henry detached himself from the little group by the door. 'It's time we left, Blue,' he said quietly, taking her arm. She stared at him in astonishment as he began to lead her from the room.

'Pelidne,' Hairstreak said sharply.

Pelidne stepped smoothly between them and the door. Henry moved with such superhuman speed that his arm blurred. Blue didn't even see the blow. But as Henry stepped back she saw Pelidne staring down with horror at the wooden stake protruding from his chest. He stumbled forward, eyes wide. Blood abruptly fountained from the wound, then just as abruptly turned to clouds of choking dust. Pelidne's handsome features wrinkled, turning in a heartbeat to those of an old, old man. His nose caved in, his lips thinned, then shrivelled over pointed, rotting teeth. Suddenly he was falling, crumbling on the inside of his clothes. A pungent smell of decay flooded the room.

'What –?' Blue gasped.

Henry had her arm again and was dragging her towards the door. Hairstreak looked stunned, but still produced a stiletto from a secret pocket of his jerkin. Pyrgus, mouth open, actually took a step backwards. Even Kitterick looked surprised.

Blue found her voice. 'No, Henry!' she shouted. This was a disaster. Her uncle's servant had been killed. In one brief instant the potential for a treaty lay tattered on the floor. She tried to jerk her arm away, but Henry's hand gripped her like a vice. 'Let me go!' she demanded.

Lord Hairstreak was already halfway across the room when Pyrgus recovered from his shock. He began to move towards Henry as well, but Kitterick was a pace ahead of him.

Then suddenly Blue and Henry were no longer there.

Thirty-nine

'What do you mean, *no longer there*?'

This was Madame Cardui as Pyrgus had never seen her before. He hadn't even realised she had an office in the Purple Palace until he went looking for her. But here he was, not simply in an office, but in a suite; and one that was all business. There was no sign of the mad colour schemes she had in her city apartment, or the lavish use of spells. Here everything was sharp, businesslike, functional. And while Madame Cardui was still the Painted Lady – purple hair, flowing gown, spandals that caressed her feet and smiled at you benignly if you looked at them – she had a hard edge now. No wonder Blue appointed her head of the Imperial Espionage Service.

'Just ... not there,' Pyrgus said feebly.

'You mean invisible? He used an invisibility spell?'

Pyrgus shook his head. 'No. You know the way you vanish with an invisibility spell – you sort of fade a bit and crumble and then dissolve into sparks? Well, there was none of that. I don't think it was invisibility. It didn't *look* like invisibility. Besides, Hairstreak's vampire thing closed the door when we came in. We'd have seen it open if they went out that way, invisible or not.'

'There was no other way out of the room?'

'Not even a window,' Pyrgus said. 'It was a privacy chamber.'

'What about some form of transportation?' Madame Cardui asked. 'Alan's been going on about his portable transporter modification – could it have been something like that?'

Pyrgus had been wondering the same thing. Where was Mr Fogarty, anyway? He hadn't been in the palace when they got back, or at his lodge. It was Kitterick who suggested they find Madame Cardui.

'I don't know,' he said. 'I don't think so.' Unless, of course, it was Mr Fogarty who transported them. Seemed too much of a coincidence that somebody else would have developed exactly the same technology at the same time. Unless it was stolen. The possibilities were confusing. 'You'll have to ask Mr Fogarty.'

'Yes, I will, as soon as I can find him. But you think it's possible?'

'I don't know,' Pyrgus said again, frowning. 'I suppose it might be.' The problem was he didn't know what you looked like when Mr Fogarty zapped you. Maybe you simply weren't there like Blue and Henry. Maybe you faded away like an invisibility spell. He just didn't know.

'I think Alan would have mentioned it if he'd planned to rescue them by transporter,' Madame Cardui said. Then, echoing an earlier thought of Pyrgus, she added, 'I can't imagine Hairstreak could have stolen it already.'

'You think Hairstreak is behind this?' Pyrgus asked.

'Not really,' Madame Cardui said. 'Why would he want to abduct them if he already had them in his power?' Her eyes drifted towards Pyrgus. 'I was just thinking aloud. How could Henry kill a vampire?'

'Pardon?' Pyrgus frowned.

'They're notoriously difficult to kill. Difficult and dangerous. I like Henry – he's a sweet boy – but he's hardly the action-hero type. Tell me *exactly* what happened.'

Pyrgus had already told her exactly what happened, but he told her again. There wasn't much to tell. The speed Henry moved at was impossible (and where did he find a wooden stake when he needed one?) and the way Henry disappeared with Blue was impossible as well.

Madame Cardui stared at him thoughtfully for a long time, then suddenly snapped her head round.

'Kitterick, were you recording?'

Kitterick was grooming her translucent cat, which was stretched in a louche manner on its cushions. He glanced round. 'Of course, Madame.'

Madame Cardui stood up. 'I think it's time we replayed this whole incident.'

Pyrgus followed them into a windowless room off the main office. It was filled with projection equipment and, as they entered, a reality globe expanded in the middle of the floor.

'I didn't know about this place,' Pyrgus said, looking around in awe.

'Your sister agreed the funding the day she became Queen.' Madame Cardui lowered the light level with a gesture. 'Kitterick, your seat, please.'

'Yes, Madame.' Kitterick climbed on to a large chair attached to the main projection equipment. As he settled himself, straps emerged to bind his wrists and ankles, while two gleaming metallic tentacles inserted themselves into his ears. He closed his eyes.

'Are you ready, Kitterick?' Madame Cardui asked.

'Yes, Madame.'

Madame Cardui leaned across him and extracted a small card from the tangle of cables that surrounded the machine. It was attached by three differently coloured wires, red, green and blue, to the body of the projector. She parted Kitterick's hair, and plugged the card into the slot in his skull. Then she threw a switch on the back of his chair.

The reality globe began to glow.

Pyrgus watched, fascinated, as a pretty young Trinian in a spangled bathing suit materialised within the globe.

'Concentrate, Kitterick!' said Madame Cardui sharply.

'Sorry, Madame.'

The pretty Trinian disappeared, to be replaced by a replica of Lord Hairstreak's privacy chamber. They were all there: Blue close to Hairstreak, Flapwazzle ... (Where had Flapwazzle disappeared to? Pyrgus suddenly thought. He'd accompanied them back to the palace.) ... Henry, Kitterick and Pyrgus himself, just inside the closed door. And behind Pyrgus, the slim form of Pelidne, Hairstreak's vampire. No one was moving.

'Run sequence,' Madame Cardui demanded.

The scene sprang to life, in three dimensions, full colour and stereo sound.

'Kitterick?' Blue asked conversationally.

'Never better, Ma'am,' Kitterick – the Kitterick inside the reality globe – nodded benignly. 'In the peak of my health, one might say.' Pyrgus noticed that the

real Kitterick, the one in the chair, mouthed the words silently.

Hairstreak said, 'Now we have the niceties out of the way, Your Majesty, perhaps your people would care to tell us why they were trespassing on my land, and what –'

'We have a confidential message for Her Majesty,' Pyrgus watched himself say loudly. *'We were proceeding along –'*

'Shut up, Pyrgus,' Blue said. She half turned towards her uncle. 'Lord Hairstreak, perhaps if we –'

And then it happened. Henry moved away from the door towards Blue and Hairstreak. He had a peculiar expression on his face, like somebody listening to distant music.

'It's time we left, Blue,' he said, and took her arm.

Pyrgus watched carefully. It was just possible Blue was in on this, but from her expression, he didn't think so. She seemed surprised and reluctant, maybe even shocked. Pyrgus would have bet his Halek knife that if it had been anybody but Henry she'd have pulled her arm away. As it was, she began to move with him – reluctantly – towards the door.

'Pelidne!' This was Hairstreak's voice.

The scene must have been influenced by Kitterick's concentration, because it narrowed in focus now so that Hairstreak, Kitterick himself and much of Pyrgus were cut from view. Pelidne grew in size, as did Blue and Henry.

'Slow motion,' Madame Cardui murmured.

There was an audible click from Kitterick's head as it rested in the chair. Within the reality globe, Pelidne slowly withdrew his hand from the one shoulder of

Pyrgus that was still visible and began to place himself between Blue and the door. Despite the fact that the scene was slowed, he moved with considerable speed. But nothing compared to Henry when *he* moved. Even with the scene creeping like a snail, Henry still blurred. Pyrgus watched his body twist as he pulled something from a pocket.

When it really happened, Pyrgus thought Henry had stabbed the vampire. Now he could see he'd actually *thrown* the stake. It entered Pelidne's chest like a driven sword and stuck there, buried all but a protruding inch.

What happened next was even worse than the reality, since every slow detail was replayed. The scene juddered as Kitterick jerked back his head to avoid the spurting blood. Then Pelidne slowly collapsed into a corrupt powder. His clothes must have been new for they fell to the floor in pristine condition.

'What –?' somebody said. Pyrgus thought the voice was probably Blue.

The focus of the scene narrowed again. From behind him, Pyrgus heard a sound like snoring as if Kitterick had fallen asleep. Blue and Henry were now the only two showing in the reality globe. Henry had hold of Blue's arm and was dragging her towards the door. He looked utterly calm. It was impossible to believe he'd just killed a vampire.

Blue shouted, 'No, Henry! Let me go!' and tried to pull away.

Pyrgus leaned forward. This was the point where they'd disappeared.

But they didn't disappear. Henry continued to drag Blue to the door, which he opened with his free hand.

He looked back briefly into the room, then pulled her over the threshold and closed the door behind him.

Pyrgus stared in disbelief. 'That wasn't what happened,' he told Madame Cardui.

forty

'Ah, there you are, Alan,' Madame Cardui said, as Fogarty swept in. 'Where were –?' She stopped. 'Why on earth are you dressed like that?'

Pyrgus glanced around, then blinked. Mr Fogarty was dressed in the full regalia of a Purple Emperor. Only the State Crown was missing. He scowled at them both.

'Heard the news about Blue. Somebody had to run the shop.' He sniffed. 'Even if it involves dressing like a ponce.'

Pyrgus felt a sudden surge of suspicion. He'd have trusted Mr Fogarty with his life, but sometimes a lust for power did strange things to people. He said cautiously, 'How did you hear about Blue, Mr Fogarty?'

Fogarty was staring at Kitterick, who was still strapped to the chair with the card plugged into his head. 'What?'

'How did you hear about Blue, Mr Fogarty?' Pyrgus repeated. 'Kitterick and I were the only ones who knew.'

Fogarty turned slowly to look at him. The barest hint of a smile curled his lips. 'You weren't the only ones who knew. I had it from the talking rug.'

'Oh, *Flapwazzle*!' Pyrgus exclaimed, relieved.

'We had a problem of protocol,' said Mr Fogarty briskly. 'With the Queen missing, supreme authority passes temporarily to the Gatekeeper. He can delegate it to the next-in-line for the throne, which is Comma. Do you want that? No, I thought not. Or it can go to the next closest relatives of Her Missing Majesty, which is you, Pyrgus – don't say it, I know you don't want it – or Queen Quercusia, who's mad and locked up, or – and you're going to love this one – Lord Hairstreak. Or the Gatekeeper can assume the throne himself for a period of one calendar month. I made an executive decision. For the rest of this month you curtsy to Emperor Fogarty. Any objections? Thought not. Now, what the hell are you doing to Kitterick?'

forty-one

The delegates arrived at Hairstreak's mansion grumbling, but they arrived. Most of them eyed Hairstreak with open suspicion. But their looks were tinged with respect. The assassination of Fuscus had done its job. There wasn't a soul in the chamber who'd consider opposing Hairstreak now. Except possibly Hamearis. The Duke of Burgundy had been too close to death too many times to fear anything any more. But he nodded amiably enough as he ambled in.

Would they notice Pelidne was missing? Hairstreak felt an impotent rage rise up to knot his stomach. It was incredible to think that human child had actually killed Pelidne. And hugely frustrating not to have worked out how. Burgundy, with all his military experience, would never tackle a vampire on his own. Old Duke Electo had dispatched one once, in his younger days, but he'd only managed the job with the backing of eighteen of his best men – and eleven of them were slaughtered in the process.

Probably Pelidne's absence wouldn't impinge. If they thought about it at all, they'd assume Hairstreak had sent him off somewhere. No reason for anyone to suspect he was dead, and Hairstreak certainly didn't plan to tell them unless he had to.

The really infuriating thing was that Pelidne was irreplaceable. Vampires were rare in the Realm, far more rare than they were in the Analogue World. It had taken Hairstreak years to find one – and months to negotiate a contract. He still shuddered to think of the cost. And what did he get in return? A few weeks' service, one miserable assassination and a hideously expensive security system nobody really understood. How had the brat killed him?

Hairstreak pushed the thoughts to one side. He had rather more urgent problems now. He waited until everyone was seated, then closed the door to trigger the privacy spells.

'Well, Blackie,' Hamearis said cheerfully, 'I hadn't expected to be back here quite so soon.'

Neither had the others, by the look of them. Hairstreak decided to dispense with the usual preliminaries. 'Queen Holly Blue is missing,' he said bluntly. 'Possibly dead.' The addendum wasn't for dramatic effect: if the boy could kill a vampire, he was capable of anything.

There was instant uproar. Hairstreak sat back and waited, scowling, as they tried to shout each other down. Eventually somebody would take charge and settle them. For the moment he didn't wish to do it himself. Best to wait for his important move: that way it would have more impact.

It was Electo who cut through the babble with his distinctive baritone. 'If you can all manage to keep quiet for a moment, we might find out what happened.' Then, as the noise died down, he turned to the head of the table. 'Hairstreak?'

Hairstreak told them succinctly what had happened.

For once he kept nothing back, except Pelidne's death.

'By God,' Electo snorted when he'd finished. 'You mean to say she was *in your care* when this young blighter seized her?'

'Hardly in my care,' Hairstreak said sourly. 'She was visiting my mansion, that's all. She chose to come without security. I can hardly be held responsible for what happened to her.'

'Not sure the Lighters will see it that way,' Electo muttered.

Hamearis, blunt as always, said, '*Were* you responsible, Blackie?'

Hairstreak managed a small, cold smile. 'Did I arrange to have her kidnapped?' He shook his head. 'No, I was surprised as anyone when it happened.'

Croceus, who'd never been the brightest glowglobe in the dungeon, said frowning, 'I don't understand how this child got away with it. Didn't you have guards, or locks or something? Was your security switched off? I see you've a new system installed – I noticed it as we arrived.'

'The usual precautions were in place. I told you. Both the boy and Queen Blue simply vanished.'

Cardamines said, 'I don't understand you. You mean they used an invisibility cone or something?'

'No, it was obviously some new spell technology.' Hairstreak fixed them with his gaze. 'But these are unimportant details. The fact is Queen Blue has been kidnapped – however it was achieved or by whom – and that changes the political situation.'

He thought for a moment he was going to have to spell it out for them, but then Hecla Colias asked the crucial question, probably hoping to embarrass him: 'Why was the Queen visiting you, Lord Hairstreak?'

Hairstreak smiled at her bleakly. 'She came to refuse our offer of negotiation,' he said.

forty-two

Kitterick's head was rattling alarmingly, but Madame Cardui ignored it. The re-run in the reality globe was set to close-up and slow motion with the result that the figures looked like exhausted giants.

'What's that?' Fogarty asked suddenly.

'What's what?' Cynthia asked him, frowning.

'That sparkle effect.' It was difficult to see because of the angle. 'And doesn't Henry have something in his hand?'

Cynthia leaned forward. 'Freeze it!' she told Kitterick. Then, 'Oh, yes, I think you're right ...'

'Can we run it again – just that segment?'

'Kitterick!' said Madame Cardui.

There was an unpleasant scraping sound from inside Kitterick's head, then the action in the reality globe repeated.

'You see?' Fogarty said. The problem was the relative positions of the people involved. Kitterick could only record what he saw, and sometimes bodies or furnishings got in the way. It looked as if Henry had taken something from his pocket, but he was sideways on so you couldn't see exactly what. And then there was the sparkle, for all the world like the edge of a trail of fairy dust in a Walt Disney movie.

'Yes,' Cynthia confirmed. 'Yes, there's something there ...'

'Spell cone?' Fogarty asked. He didn't know of a spell that would let you walk out of a room while everybody in it thought you'd disappeared, but they were bringing new spell cones on to the market all the time.

Cynthia frowned. 'I don't think so, Alan. It seems a bit big for a spell cone. And what are those particles – the glitter? You don't get glitter from a spell cone.'

'New type?'

'Don't know.'

'Can you go to extreme close-up, Kitterick?' Fogarty asked. Kitterick gave a strangled gasp, but the reality globe filled with a section of Henry's body. 'Do you think that could be the edge of a goblet, Cynthia?'

'Could be. A crystal goblet.' She hesitated thoughtfully. 'Or a Halek blade? It has the same sheen.'

'Where would Henry get a Halek blade? They don't make them in the Analogue World.' Fogarty straightened his back. 'Certainly looks like crystal, though.' He glanced across the room. 'OK, Kitterick, you can switch off now. Pyrgus, pull that thing out of his head before he croaks.'

'Thank you, sir,' Kitterick croaked.

As the scene faded to black and the reality globe collapsed, Fogarty said, 'The *follower* you had on Blue ...?'

'It lost them.'

'I thought that wasn't possible.'

'It isn't, but it happened, deeah.'

'Where did it lose them?' Fogarty asked.

'In the grounds of Hairstreak's mansion.'

'He has a vicious security system,' Pyrgus put in. 'Trackers that take you down, inject you with stuff that knocks you out.'

'You think they didn't get far?' Fogarty asked him.

'*We* didn't,' Pyrgus said.

'Interesting point,' Madame Cardui remarked. 'So you think it's possible Hairstreak may have them both now?'

Pyrgus licked his lips nervously. 'No, Henry was definitely up to something. I don't understand it and I don't understand how he did it, or why, but he definitely took Blue.'

'Yes, I know,' Madame Cardui persisted, 'but whatever he did, whatever he planned, is it possible that Hairstreak's security system trapped them when they left the mansion?'

'It's possible,' Pyrgus said reluctantly, 'but Henry knew about the security system. It got him as well as me and Kitterick.'

Fogarty cut across them both. 'This *follower*, Cynthia – could I talk to it?'

'It's a demon, Alan – you realise that?'

'Yes, I know. Presumably there are safeguards you can take …'

'Oh, yes,' Madame Cardui said. 'When …?'

Fogarty shrugged. 'Now. Can we do it now?'

Pyrgus said, 'I'll just go and –'

Fogarty said sharply, 'I want you with us.'

forty-three

Pyrgus watched nervously. The last time he'd had anything to do with demons was when a smelly old Faerie of the Night named Brimstone had tried to sacrifice him to one. It had never occurred to him there might be the wherewithal to evoke one in the palace. But Madame Cardui was full of surprises.

They were in a smallish basement library – another room he'd never known existed – packed with an astonishing assortment of rare books. Including several he could have sworn were Analogue World manufacture. His eyes glided over the titles – *The Hieroglyphic Monad ... Clavis Chymicus ... Mysteries of the Rosie Crucis ... Illuminations ... Liber Visionum ... Astral Doorways ... Ars Notoria* – before coming to rest on the circle/triangle motif inlaid in the tiling of the floor. He'd seen that design before, although Brimstone's circle and triangle had been picked out in animal parts. Pyrgus shuddered. He loved animals.

The circle here had a five-pointed star inscribed inside it. The whole room smelled faintly of some heavy, cloying incense.

Mr Fogarty was staring at the circle as well. 'You'd be put away for this stuff in my world,' he remarked.

'Put away?'

'In a lunatic asylum, Cynthia,' Fogarty said. 'Nobody believes in it any more.'

'More fool them,' said Madame Cardui mildly.

Mr Fogarty followed Pyrgus's example and looked at the books. He pulled one down from the shelves – Pyrgus noticed it was called *Conjuring Spirits* – and flicked it open.

'I thought the portals to Hell were all closed,' he said.

Madame Cardui was busying herself with an incense burner. 'They are, deeah,' she told him absently, 'but we won't be calling the *follower* out of Hael.'

'Won't we?' Pyrgus asked, surprised. 'I thought all demons came from Hael.'

Madame Cardui finished with the burner and lit the charcoal with a blue flame that emerged from the tip of one long painted fingernail. Perfumed smoke began to climb towards the ceiling.

'Yes, they do. Of course they do, deeah – ultimately. But this one has been pressed into service. It lives in our Realm now. Quite a few demons were trapped here when the portals closed – most of them in service to the Faeries of the Night, of course. They're based in limbos when they're not actually operational, but you control them exactly the same way you would if they were still in Hael.' She caught Pyrgus's expression and added, 'They're quite comfortable. The limbos are furnished. At least mine are: drawer bed, cushions … there's even a small entertainment globe. Black and white, of course.'

'Home from home,' Fogarty said, and gave one of his feral grins.

'Check the safeguards, please, Kitterick,' said Madame Cardui.

'Yes, Madame.'

As Kitterick scuttled to examine the tiling on the floor, Mr Fogarty said over his shoulder, 'You ready, Flapwazzle?'

Flapwazzle was draped over the back of a chair. 'Yup,' he grunted.

'No breaks in the circle, Madame,' Kitterick reported. 'No breaks in the triangle. All force fields active. Incense supplies sufficient. Asafoetida on standby. Black mirror in place.' Pyrgus looked around for a mirror, but couldn't see one. Kitterick went on, 'Rock crystals aligned. Anointing oil ready. Charged water ready. Fumigations ready. Purification vial ready. Sage bundle ready. Black candles ready. Timer set. Trapped lightning boxed.'

'Seems a lot of precautions for one little imp,' Mr Fogarty remarked.

'Can't be too careful,' said Madame Cardui. She looked from one to the other and beamed. 'All into the circle now, deeahs. You too, Flapwazzle.'

Obediently they trooped into the circle. Pyrgus found himself standing beside Flapwazzle and absently leaned down to tickle the endolg's ears.

'Reminds me of my days with the Great Myphisto,' Madame Cardui remarked. 'He used demons quite frequently in some of his most puzzling illusions.' She gave a small, girlish smile. 'He was a Faerie of the Light, so no one ever suspected.' The smile disappeared. 'Are we ready to begin the orison?'

'We don't actually have to do anything, do we?' Fogarty asked.

'Not a thing, deeah – just make sure not to step outside the circle. When you question it, don't look into its eyes.'

'OK,' Fogarty muttered. 'Do you need a book?'

'Oh, no, deeah – I've done this so often, I know it by heart.' She turned to face the triangle and raised both arms. Kitterick produced a fan with a flourish that would have done justice to the Great Myphisto and used it to direct incense smoke towards her. In a pleasant resonant soprano, Madame Cardui began the orison.

It wasn't at all like the way it happened when Brimstone called up Beleth. No distant orchestra, no gradual appearance. One moment the triangle was empty, the next there was an imp inside it, bouncing violently against the invisible force fields. The creature was little more than four feet tall, covered from head to toe in black fur and with a long, prehensile tail. It had pointed, upright ears, two small horns set in the middle of its forehead, luminously burning eyes and a snarling mouth packed with little needle teeth. For something even smaller than Kitterick, it was the most terrifying thing Pyrgus had seen since Beleth himself.

'Oh, come on, deeah,' Madame Cardui told it tiredly. 'I did say in thy full, fair and pristine form.'

The creature in the triangle changed at once. The fur fell away, the skin colour turned from black to greyish white, horns and tail both vanished and the head began to inflate alarmingly, like some monstrous balloon. In seconds, the change was complete. Pyrgus was staring at one of the frail, large-headed creatures with enormous black eyes that had captured him the time he found himself in Hael. He looked away quickly.

'This is Black John, Alan,' Madame Cardui said by way of introduction. 'Black John, this is Gatekeeper Fogarty. I want you to answer his questions truthfully, on pain of various hideous punishments, eternal torment and so on. You know the legalities as well as I do.'

'Of course, Madame Cardui,' Black John said. He had a tiny, pouting little slit of a mouth and nearly no nose at all. His voice was quite high-pitched, but it still managed to resonate inside your head, Pyrgus noticed.

Madame Cardui nodded briefly to Fogarty, who said, 'You're what they call a *follower*, is that right?'

'Yes, Gatekeeper Fogarty.'

'You were assigned to follow Queen Blue?'

'Yes, Gatekeeper Fogarty.'

'Which is what you did?'

'Yes, Gatekeeper Fogarty.'

'Just *yes* will do.'

'Yes, Gatekeeper Fogarty.'

Fogarty sighed. 'Did you follow her to Lord Hairstreak's mansion?'

'Yes, Gatekeeper Fogarty.'

'Did you follow her *inside* Hairstreak's mansion?'

'Yes, Gatekeeper Fogarty.'

'Did you follow her when young Henry Atherton took her out again?'

'Yes, Gatekeeper Fogarty.'

'Where did they go to?'

Black John said, 'I don't know, Gatekeeper Fogarty.'

Fogarty frowned. 'What do you mean, you don't know?'

'They left the mansion and walked north along the main driveway,' Black John said. A curiously mechanical tone entered his voice. 'Then turned north-east on the subsidiary driveway and disappeared in the vicinity of the Haleklind folly.'

Fogarty glanced at Pyrgus, who said quietly, 'There

are follies all over the estate, Mr Fogarty. The last owner ...' He kept his eyes on the imp. It made him nervous.

Fogarty said to Black John, 'What do you mean by *disappeared*?'

'I mean disappeared, Gatekeeper Fogarty.'

'You mean disappeared without a trace? One minute they were there and the next they were gone?'

'Yes, Gatekeeper Fogarty.'

'Did they use an invisibility spell?'

'No, Gatekeeper Fogarty.'

'You couldn't follow them any more?'

'No, Gatekeeper Fogarty.'

'Did Queen Blue go with Henry of her own free will?'

'Yes, Gatekeeper Fogarty.'

'And you have no idea where either of them are now?'

'No, Gatekeeper Fogarty.'

'Is he telling the truth?' Fogarty asked Flapwazzle.

'Lying through his teeth,' Flapwazzle said.

forty-four

Hairstreak watched the military preparations with a certain satisfaction.

He'd embarked on a risky course. But not, he thought, too risky. With the Queen missing, the Realm would be in chaos, at least for a while. Given any luck at all, his allies wouldn't discover he was lying until it was too late. There was even a slim chance that Blue hadn't told her advisors of her real decision – she was notoriously secretive – so even her people might not be able to contradict him until she turned up again. *If* she turned up again. Even then, he could probably bluff it out. It was her word against his, after all, and his word would carry more weight with the Faeries of the Night. Besides, by that stage, preparations for war would be at an advanced stage. Such events tended to take on a momentum of their own.

The only thing that really concerned him was the fact he didn't know yet who had kidnapped her – clearly the boy wasn't acting alone. It was a weakness in his position. But hopefully that might change soon. His entire espionage service was working to find out who was involved.

Meanwhile the combined armies of the Great Houses had begun stockpiling munitions and supplies in the vast caverns beneath Yammeth Cretch. Duke Electo, who knew about such things, estimated just days before the entire Nighter community was on a war footing.

Not that the timing mattered greatly. The Lighters had no idea at all what was happening. They were far too involved with looking for their Queen. Unless the rumours of a Countdown were true. But he very much doubted that. Not even his niece was mad enough to revive that old custom.

A soldier stacking crates – one of Burgundy's men, from his insignia – missed his footing, thrashed wildly for a moment, then succeeded in pulling the entire stack down on top of him. He made a thin mewling sound as the heavy equipment began to crush his chest. Hairstreak considered briefly sounding an alarm, then decided against it. Much more interesting to watch the man die.

There would be many more deaths in the coming weeks.

forty-five

Mr Fogarty hitched the imperial robes above his knee and sat scratching a blemish on one skinny shank. 'Well, that was a waste of time,' he said.

Pyrgus watched him warily. You could never tell what Mr Fogarty would do next, and now he was Acting Purple Emperor, that was a nerve-wracking situation.

'Couldn't you have forced it out of him?' he asked cautiously.

Mr Fogarty looked up from under steel-grey eyebrows. 'That was the old idea,' he said. 'Threaten them with torments. You heard Cynthia hitting him with the traditional formula. But know what, Pyrgus? I've been reading up on demons and I think they've had us all fooled – human and faerie – for an awfully long time.' He stopped scratching and flipped the robe back over his knee. 'You know the deal with demons, don't you? They're organised like insects.' He waved Pyrgus towards a nearby chair. 'Sit down a minute, will you?'

Pyrgus perched on the edge of a chair and waited. They were in the Gatekeeper's official office, having left Madame Cardui and Flapwazzle to clear up after dismissing the demon. Mr Fogarty said, 'You can't deal with insects. Not as individuals. You deal with the hive. It's the *hive* that's the individual. Same with demons. You think you're talking to this one or that one – Black John or whoever – but you're really talking to them all. They're linked inside their heads. They're all linked. And all the links join up in their king. So really you're always talking to Beleth.'

'Beleth?' Pyrgus wasn't sure he was following this.

'You're not following this, are you?' Mr Fogarty said. He sighed. 'Doesn't matter. Except you'll never get anywhere tormenting an individual demon. What does Beleth care about Black John? Poor little sod got sold into service, had to do what he was told while Beleth collected his pay. Torment Black John as much as you like, he's not going to tell you anything Beleth doesn't want him to. Beleth has his own plans.'

'But people – Faeries of the Night – *do* torment demons,' Pyrgus said. 'It's one of the ways of controlling them.'

Mr Fogarty gave a small shrug. 'Just a game, as far as I can make out. Just a way to make people think they're in control. But you're never in control with a demon. It's always got a hidden agenda. It's always following *Beleth*'s orders.'

Pyrgus said, 'What are we going to do, Mr Fogarty? About finding Blue?' He hesitated a beat, then added, 'And Henry?'

'Well,' Mr Fogarty said, 'Black John sure as hell isn't going to tell us.' He glanced sideways at Pyrgus. 'But you might.'

Pyrgus had one of those sinking feelings he got sometimes. 'What?' he asked uncertainly.

'What did Henry have in his hand?' Mr Fogarty asked. He waited a second, then said, 'Oh, come on, Pyrgus – I saw your face when Kitterick was on replay.

We were wondering if it was a crystal goblet or a Halek knife, but you knew what it was, didn't you?'

Pyrgus looked down at his feet, then glanced briefly behind him, then looked down at his feet again. 'Yes,' he said eventually.

Fogarty waited. 'Well, are you going to tell me or are you just going to sit there looking miserable?'

'It was a crystal flower,' Pyrgus said.

'And what was the fairy dust?'

Pyrgus blinked. 'Faerie dust ...?'

'That sparkling stuff. You could just about see it in the replay.'

'I don't know what that was,' Pyrgus said. 'I've never seen that sparkling stuff before. Maybe it's what you get when you crush something crystal into powder.'

'You ever tried to crush crystal into powder with one hand?' Fogarty asked.

Pyrgus shook his head dumbly.

'Thought not,' said Fogarty. 'What's going on, Pyrgus?'

Somehow Pyrgus couldn't drag his gaze away from Mr Fogarty's grey eyes. He swallowed. 'Maybe it was some sort of new magic or something. Maybe Henry –'

'Let's cut the crap,' Mr Fogarty said sharply. 'Henry doesn't do magic. He's allergic to it. I don't buy it, Pyrgus, and I don't buy the way you're acting. You know something you're not telling and I'm going to get it out of you if I have to wring your neck. We're on a Countdown here, for God's sake. Apart from your sister's safety, if we don't find her in three days – less now – we start a war!'

Pyrgus said, 'I've seen flowers like that before, Mr Fogarty.'

Fogarty released an explosive sigh. 'Ah,' he said. 'OK – where?'

Pyrgus licked his lips. 'There's a Faerie of the Night called Zosine Ogyris –'

'The merchant? Rich as Croesus?'

'I don't know Croesus, but he's rich.'

'What's he do?' Fogarty asked. 'Manufacture these things?'

Pyrgus shook his head. 'No, he grows them.'

'I thought you said they were crystal?'

'Yes, they are. Rock crystal. But Gel— somebody told me he grows them.' He hesitated, looking at Mr Fogarty. 'I don't know how that's possible either.'

Mr Fogarty sat quietly for a moment, then obviously decided not to worry about impossibilities. 'What's he do with them? Sell them?' He frowned. 'I haven't heard of crystal flowers.'

This was getting hideously embarrassing. Pyrgus wondered if he couldn't fuzz the rest somehow. But he was a bit afraid of Mr Fogarty and he'd a feeling he was in enough trouble already without making it worse. He drew a deep breath.

'I think he's growing them for Lord Hairstreak.'

Mr Fogarty looked at him, stunned. 'What's Hairstreak want with them?'

'I don't know,' Pyrgus said miserably.

Mr Fogarty got up and began to pace. Suddenly he turned on Pyrgus. 'Why the *hell* didn't you say anything about this before?'

Pyrgus couldn't meet his eyes. 'Cor ahr as seng is door,' he muttered.

'You were what?

'I was seeing his daughter,' Pyrgus said.

forty-six

At which point in waltzed Madame Cardui.

'Seeing whose daughter, deeah?' she asked cheerfully.

Pyrgus groaned inwardly.

'Zosine Ogyris's,' Mr Fogarty answered for him.

Madame Cardui's expression changed at once 'A Faerie of the Night?' She stared at Pyrgus in shock. 'You've been seeing a Faerie *of the Night*?'

'Yes,' Pyrgus admitted.

'And a Faerie of the Night *in trade*?' She made it sound like scrofula.

'Well, yes, her father's a merchant,' Pyrgus said, a little miffed by her tone. All the same, the Faerie of the Night bit was embarrassing.

'But you're a Prince of the Realm,' Madame Cardui said.

'Yes, I know,' Pyrgus said. He didn't know what else to say and so said nothing. For some reason he felt very young. He stood blinking in Madame Cardui's direction.

'Is this serious?' asked Madame Cardui. 'You're not ... you're not ...?'

'Of course he is,' Mr Fogarty sniffed. 'He's a teenager – it's all they ever think about.'

'I didn't mean that, Alan. Perfectly proper for a

young man of high birth to perk up the peasantry from time to time – the Royal Family's been doing it for centuries.' She turned back to Pyrgus. 'I meant you aren't thinking of *marrying* her?'

'Oh, no,' said Pyrgus promptly. Which was true enough, but not because Gela was a commoner or any rubbish like that. She was really, really gorgeous and he'd been a bit … well … bowled over when he first met her. But marriage never came into it. Which was just as well since he still hadn't sorted out how he felt about Nymphalis. Nymph was really gorgeous too, in a different way. And about as bossy as his sister, but he was used to that. The thing was, he couldn't imagine Nymph ever leaving her forest home.

'Well, I'm relieved to hear that,' Madame Cardui said, cutting through his thoughts. Her features softened. 'All the same, deeah, I do hope you've been discreet. I'm sure she's terribly pretty and quite accommodating, but a Faerie of the *Night*? And in these trying political times? Such an *embarrassment* for your poor, dear sister.'

'She *is* very pretty,' Pyrgus said. He could sense his chin begin to jut as a familiar feeling of rebellion rose up in his stomach. Who did Madame Cardui think she was anyway? She was starting to sound like his father. 'But that's –'

Mr Fogarty cut in before he could finish. 'Leave the kid alone, Cynthia. This could be a blessing in disguise. Pyrgus says Henry crushed a peculiar crystal flower before he disappeared and that Ogyris has been growing them for Hairstreak.'

Madame Cardui frowned. '*Crystal* flowers? You mean flowers that are transparent like crystal or flowers that are made from crystal?'

'I don't know,' Fogarty said. 'Do you, Pyrgus?'

'I think they're flowers made from crystal,' Pyrgus said, relieved that the interrogation about Gela seemed to be over. 'I know it doesn't make much sense: I'd never heard of them before.'

'Neither have I,' Madame Cardui said thoughtfully. 'I wonder what Hairstreak wants with them?'

'Well,' said Fogarty, 'I think that's what we'd better find out – these things are obviously connected with Blue's disappearance. If Henry had one, he's likely to have got it from Ogyris. I don't understand Hairstreak's involvement – he had her anyway – but I'm betting Ogyris knows something about it.' He hesitated thoughtfully. 'Besides, it's the only clue we have.'

Madame Cardui looked across at him. 'What are you planning to do, deeah?'

'Bring Ogyris in for questioning.'

'Do you think he'll talk?'

'He will when I've finished with him,' Fogarty said.

Pyrgus coughed lightly. 'How were you going to bring him in, Mr Fogarty?'

Fogarty raised an eyebrow. 'Contingent of Palace Guards should do it.'

'He has his own guards,' Pyrgus said soberly. 'Gel— somebody told me it's more like a private army. And his estate is right in the middle of Yammeth City. If you send in armed Lighters there's likely to be a fight, a big one. It might even start the war.'

'Do you have a better idea?' Fogarty asked.

Pyrgus hadn't, but he was used to thinking on his feet. 'Why don't I go there alone – to Merchant Ogyris's estate – and see what I can find out? One

Faerie of the Light isn't going to attract any attention. I know where the flowers are and I know my way around the estate ...' The last bit was a sort of a lie, but he'd found his instructions from Gela and the little gate might still be open. Besides, if anybody caught him, he could probably persuade them he'd come to see Gela. With luck they might even contact her before they killed him. He was fairly sure she'd vouch for him, despite what had happened. So long as he wasn't caught in the act, of course. Merchant Ogyris clearly didn't want anybody messing with his precious flowers.

'Much too dangerous, deeah,' said Madame Cardui firmly. 'Your sister would never forgive me if I let you do it.'

'No, just a minute, Cynthia,' Fogarty said, frowning. 'We need to know about those flowers, and he's right about trying to arrest Ogyris – that really *could* start the war.'

'We can send one of my operatives,' Madame Cardui said. 'Someone trained.'

'But if he's caught, they'll know the Imperial Espionage Service is interested,' Pyrgus said quickly. 'They'll get it out of him. Remember my uncle is involved, even if we don't know how. But if they catch me ...' He hesitated, but had to say it: 'I can just pretend I've come to see Gela.'

'Gela is the trollop of a daughter?' Madame Cardui asked sweetly.

'She's not a –' Pyrgus flared.

But Mr Fogarty cut across him again. 'He's got a point, Cynthia. It's perfect cover. We can't afford to make mistakes. Blue's been kidnapped and we're teetering on the brink of civil war. Volatile situation.

The last thing we need is to make it any worse. Only bit that really worries me is time. We're caught in a Countdown. Even as Acting Emperor I can't order the Generals to stand down – only Blue can do that. So we need results fast.'

'I could go straight away,' Pyrgus said. 'Now, if you like.'

'Yes,' Fogarty nodded, 'it would have to be now.'

'Take Kitterick,' Madame Cardui said. 'He's an excellent bodyguard. Just in case …'

'Yes,' Fogarty said. 'Take Kitterick. You can pass him off as your servant.'

'Yes, OK,' Pyrgus said. He headed for the door, then stopped. 'Madame Cardui …' He licked his lips. 'The business about me seeing Gela …?'

Madame Cardui looked at him. 'Yes?'

'You won't mention it to Nymph, will you?' Pyrgus said.

forty-seven

As the door closed, Fogarty said, 'Will you come to my room, Cynthia?'

'Of course, darling,' Madame Cardui said fondly. 'Have you taken over the Imperial Suite?'

Fogarty smiled faintly. 'No, the robes are as far as it goes. But I decided it was best for me to sleep in the palace until the emergency's over.'

'The robes suit you,' Madame Cardui said. Her smile was wide and warm. 'Emperor Alan has a nice ring to it.'

Fogarty sniffed. 'The robes make me look like a prat. But they get people to do what they're told.'

The room he'd commandeered was spartan, the sort of chamber usually reserved for unimportant visitors. But at least it was warm. Fogarty pulled the robes over his head and stretched out on the bed. He patted the counterpane beside him.

Madame Cardui crossed the room slowly and he watched her all the way. Weird where he'd ended up: actually living in another dimension of reality – the sort of thing they used to speculate about when he worked in quantum physics. But no more weird than meeting this marvellous woman. At his age.

She lay down beside him and reached across to take

his hand. For once the gesture didn't hurt. The rejuvenation treatments had cleared his arthritis completely from all five of the fingers and were already making inroads into the other hand. Some of his liver spots seemed to be fading as well and just that morning when he was combing his few remaining wisps of greying hair, he thought he noticed new growth. Give the wizards long enough and he'd end up looking like Robert Redford.

'You seem pensive,' Cynthia remarked.

'I was thinking of war,' Fogarty said.

'What were you thinking of war?'

'The way it seems inevitable,' Fogarty said, gazing at the ceiling. 'When I was at school, I had a teacher who told us we should never look on history as a period of peace peppered by outbreaks of war, but rather as a period of war peppered by outbreaks of peace. I think he had something there.' He rolled on his side so he could look at her. 'My father was in 14–18.'

'What's 14–18?' she asked.

'First World War,' Fogarty said. 'First war in my world that was fought by every country on the planet – at least every one that counted. We lost eight million soldiers in that one. Slaughtered as many more civilians. They called it the "War to End Wars". It ended my father all right – he caught a bullet at the Somme. But it didn't end war. We did it all over again twenty-one years later. I was in that one.'

'You told me,' Madame Cardui said, gently stroking his hand.

Fogarty said thoughtfully, 'Maybe I'd have enjoyed it more if I'd known I was going to survive. I was afraid all of the time, and exhausted most of the time and in pain a lot of the time after I was wounded. Do you know, it still plays up in wet weather? We destroyed whole cities in that one, whole countries really.'

'We have a spell like that,' Madame Cardui said quietly. 'Nobody's ever dared use it.'

'The thing is,' Fogarty told her, 'that wasn't the war to end wars either. Five years after it finished, we had another war in Asia, a place called Korea. After Korea was finished, we started another close by in Vietnam. Lasted twenty years. After that we had the Afghan War, the Arab–Israeli War, the Iran–Iraq War, two Gulf Wars, the Falklands War, the Angola War and God knows how many other civil wars they hardly bothered telling us about. You can see what my old history teacher meant, can't you?'

'It hasn't been quite that bad in the Realm,' Madame Cardui said. 'But close.'

'What gets to me,' Fogarty said, 'is that when things start to move towards war, nobody seems to be able to stop it. Once you mobilise your soldiers, you always seem to send them to war no matter what.'

'Is that what you think will happen here?' Madame Cardui asked.

'We've mobilised our soldiers,' Fogarty said. 'Blue pushed that button when she ordered a Countdown.'

'The Faeries of the Night are mobilising too,' Madame Cardui said.

'You have intelligence? That's definite?'

'Yes.'

'When were you going to tell me?'

'Tonight, when we were alone. I didn't want to mention it in front of Pyrgus.'

'Too much pressure on him?'

'Something like that.'

Fogarty rolled on to his back again. 'I want you to do something for me, Cynthia …'

'Anything, darling.'

'I want you to contact Queen Cleopatra of the Forest Faerie and persuade her to fight on our side.'

'You really think it will come to that?'

'Oh, yes,' said Fogarty, 'it will come to that.'

forty-eight

'Shall I order an ouklo to transport us, sir?' asked Kitterick.

'No way!' Pyrgus said. 'I want a personal flyer.'

forty-nine

Hairstreak opened the wine and sniffed the cork. 'Nearly fifty years old. Now it's the exact colour of blood.' He looked across at his guest and raised an eyebrow.

'Thank you, Blackie,' Hamearis said. 'I usually prefer ale, but I'll make an exception.'

The man was an oaf in many ways, but useful. He commanded massive respect among the Faeries of the Night and it was time to get him back on board. Hairstreak poured a generous goblet and pushed it across the table. He was less generous with his own portion. All negotiations required a clear head if you were sensible, and this, whether Hamearis knew it or not, was a negotiation.

The wine was superb. Hairstreak savoured it a sip at a time. Hamearis drank his down and pushed the goblet back for more.

'You and I have been through a lot together, Burgundy,' Hairstreak said as he poured. 'Enough to weather little disagreements, eh?' He forced himself to make it bluff and hearty, old soldiers talking of old times.

'No disagreements now, Blackie,' Hamearis said. 'Not since that little cow threw our offer back in our faces.' He watched Hairstreak's expression closely. 'If she threw it back in our faces.'

Hairstreak elected to ignore the implication. 'An historic opportunity for reconciliation,' he said smoothly. 'So tragic it has passed us by.'

'You were less enthusiastic when the matter was first raised, as I recall.' Hamearis took another enormous draught from his goblet.

'Oh, I grant you I had my doubts. To be frank, Burgundy, I feared my niece might react the way she did – a very stubborn child, very suspicious and just as set against the Faeries of the Night as her father ever was.'

Hamearis set his wine down on the table. 'What have you done with her?' he asked.

The question was not entirely unexpected. Hairstreak allowed himself the ghost of a smile. 'Are they saying I abducted her?'

'There's speculation ...'

Hairstreak held his eye. 'Let me tell you, here and now as an old friend, I had nothing whatsoever to do with Blue's disappearance. I did not plan it. I did not engineer it. I have not the slightest idea how it was carried out or where she is now.' He glanced away, then added, 'Although my people are working very hard to find out.'

After a moment Hamearis said, 'I believe you, Blackie.' He picked up his wine again. 'Frankly, I never thought you did it. Not that I don't think you're capable, but a cover story like that – *she simply vanished*. It just isn't your style.' He frowned. 'I'd like to know who did take her, though. What actually happened?'

'She simply vanished,' Hairstreak said, and smiled. His features sobered and he shrugged. 'That's literally how it happened. The boy from the Analogue World tried to take her out. Pelidne tried to stop him. The boy killed Pelidne, then both he and Queen Blue disappeared.'

'He couldn't have taken her to the Analogue World, could he?'

'I don't see how,' Hairstreak said. 'But I didn't ask you here to discuss mysteries. Blue is gone. Our proposals have been rejected. We need to plan our strategy.'

'We need to get the Queen back,' Hamearis said bluntly. 'There's a Countdown on.'

'I heard that rumour,' Hairstreak said easily. 'I doubt it's true.'

'It's true all right,' Hamearis said. 'I had it from my intelligence people.'

Hairstreak looked at him, thunderstruck. 'Are you sure?'

'Wonder why your spooks didn't tell you?'

Hairstreak was wondering the same thing. Heads would roll. Besides which, protocol demanded an active Countdown be reported to all interested parties. Blue should have done it when she put it in place. The Acting Emperor should have confirmed it the moment she went missing. Who was the Acting Emperor anyway? Pyrgus, he supposed – he didn't really know. He stared at Hamearis in horror. He could scarcely believe the enormity of the betrayal. Or of his own stupidity for not anticipating it. The blunt truth was he'd underestimated Blue. Came of thinking of her as a child.

'How long?' he asked.

'Three days.'

'From her visit or her disappearance?'

'Same thing, from what I gather.'

'Yes, you're right.' Hairstreak stared at him thoughtfully. 'This changes everything.'

Hamearis grinned. 'It certainly changes the timing. What were you up to, Blackie?'

'Up to?'

Hamearis moved in his chair. 'Oh, come on – you never favoured the offer of negotiation. You wanted to attack at once while the Faeries of the Light had a child as a leader. So did I –'

'So did you?' Hairstreak exclaimed. 'You voted against me in Council!'

'Of course I did,' Hamearis said easily. 'You had no backing. But that's all changed now. What's your plan?'

Hairstreak hesitated for a heartbeat, then said, 'Surprise attack. Catch them off guard.' He glanced away and added sourly, 'I didn't anticipate a Countdown.'

Hamearis leaned forward. 'There may be a way to regain the initiative.'

Hairstreak looked back at him at once. 'What do you suggest?'

Burgundy was every inch the seasoned warrior. 'Decapitate the beast,' he said. 'They've already lost their child Queen. I say remove the rest of their command structure. Assassinate Prince Pyrgus and any other royal in line for the throne. Kill the head of their Intelligence Service. That old witch has been a thorn in our side for far too long. Kill their Analogue

211

Gatekeeper – what's his name? Fogarty? Kill your sister Quercusia. She's mad, but she's royal blood and could become a rallying point. Once that's done, the way's clear to mount a pre-emptive strike on the palace and take out the Generals. With their command structure gone, the Lighters will turn into sheep. We can step in and take over – *you* can step in and take over. It's a limited operation, Hairstreak. I can organise it for you – I'll use the Assassins' Guild so nothing can be traced back to us. We can manage it easily before the Countdown expires.'

Hairstreak stared at him for a moment, then said, 'Do it.'

fifty

The room was a featureless white cube, about eighteen feet across. There were no furnishings, no doors or windows, no curtains or carpeting, although the floor was slightly soft underfoot. She couldn't see a light source, but there was light, a soft, white illumination that was neither too bright nor too dark. She still had no idea how they got here.

Henry was squatting on the floor, his back against one wall. His eyes were shut, but she knew he wasn't asleep.

'You can't keep me here for ever!' Blue exclaimed. It would have no effect, but saying something broke the *sameness* of the place. She was already beginning to lose track of time.

'They'll come for us soon,' Henry said, without opening his eyes.

'*Who'll* come for us soon?' Blue demanded, not for the first time.

Henry didn't answer. Henry never answered that one. Henry, Blue thought, had gone mad.

'I need a loo!' she said suddenly.

'The room will absorb waste,' Henry told her.

'You want me to go in the corner?' she asked angrily. She was furious with Henry, furious for the way he kidnapped her, furious for the way he was behaving now. There was nothing of the old Henry in him.

'I don't want you to go at all,' he said off-handedly. She couldn't believe the change in him. It was as if he didn't care. For her or for anything else. He'd been so dominant, so *aggressive* as they left her uncle's mansion. But since they arrived here he hadn't moved.

'I'm hungry!' Blue told him loudly, hoping for a sensible response.

'There's no food,' Henry said. 'But they'll come for us soon.'

Who'll come for us? Somehow she was afraid to ask the obvious question. She couldn't believe Henry might be working for Lord Hairstreak – it was unthinkable. But he had to be working for *somebody*. And they were coming soon.

Nothing made any sense. If her uncle planned to move against her – planned to kidnap or kill her, let's not mince words here – why involve Henry at all? Hairstreak already had her in his power. No guards at all at first, and later no better protection than one injured Trinian. He could have –

She stopped mid-thought. Hairstreak didn't want it known *he'd* kidnapped her. He couldn't do the deed in his own mansion. *That* was why he involved Henry! It was all so simple.

Blue suddenly realised she was thinking the un-thinkable. All the pieces fitted. Henry had betrayed her to her uncle. She looked over at him and felt sick to her stomach. What had Hairstreak offered him?

She wondered what he'd do if she attacked him. He was stronger than she was – there was a bruise on her arm where he'd gripped it at the mansion – but he didn't look very alert. Every so often he closed his eyes. He wasn't asleep. It looked more as if he was concentrating on something, almost listening. But all the same ...

If she waited until his eyes were closed, she could creep up and press the stimulus to the side of his neck. Well, she could. She definitely could. It would be simple. She realised she was arguing with herself. Could she *really* kill Henry whatever he'd done? Could she –

The inner argument abruptly deflated like a balloon. She didn't have the stimulus. She'd decided not to bring it in case her uncle's security spells detected a weapon.

Could she overpower Henry without a stimulus? Go for his eyes or strangle him until he passed out? She was being stupid. There was no way she was strong enough, even if she could bring herself to do it. And what would be the point if she did? What would be the point if she even killed him? She didn't know how she'd got into this creepy room and she didn't know how to get out of it again. There were no windows, no doors ...

Or were there?

It occurred to her suddenly that she'd been taking everything at face value. What she *saw* was a featureless room, but what she saw mightn't be the way it really was. She remembered the time she'd broken into Brimstone's lodgings. They hadn't looked the way they really were until she'd discovered the illusion spell. It could be like that here. An illusion spell might have changed the whole appearance. After all, the light had to be coming from somewhere, so clearly the source was disguised.

She glanced at Henry. He'd closed his eyes again. Would he sense it if she moved? Only one way to find out. Cautiously she began to feel her way along one wall. Henry didn't move.

She went carefully and very slowly. Henry could open his eyes again at any minute and, when he did, she wanted it to look as if she was just stretching her legs. That wasn't going to be easy. A really good illusion spell affected the character of an object, not just its appearance; but even the best of them weren't as good at fooling your sense of smell as your sight. If you took your time you could pick up the telltale signs. But that meant getting up close. *Really* close. If Henry opened his eyes while she had her nose pressed up against the wall he'd know at once what she was up to.

She looked back. His eyes were still closed, but his lips were moving silently and his body was tense as a coiled spring. His eyelids flickered.

Blue froze. She'd found a door! It wasn't even that well concealed, except to sight. She could feel the outlines quite plainly. She glanced across at Henry. He still hadn't opened his eyes.

Cautiously, Blue pushed the door.

It opened.

fifty-one

The personal flyer was *fantastic*. The top speed was about seven times faster than an ouklo. Just one word and you could make it loop the loop. It very nearly hovered without stalling and if you banked sharply it started up this amazing sonic hum. If Pyrgus hadn't been on a serious mission, he could have had a lot of fun.

The street grid of Yammeth City was underneath him now and he could see the amazing expanse of green that was their final destination. He put the flyer into a sharp dive.

'Do we plan to crash inside the Ogyris Estate, sir?' Kitterick enquired. 'If not, Merchant Ogyris may have a landing pad.'

'I think he probably has air defences as well,' Pyrgus said, frowning. 'Besides, I don't want him to know we're here. I thought we'd come down somewhere on the edge of the city and walk.'

'There is a public landing area quite close to the main gate of the estate, sir.'

'Is there? How do you know?'

'I have been equipped with maps of Yammeth City, sir.'

'You've got *maps*? You might have shown them to

me.' What with never having used a personal flyer before, he'd had some trouble finding the place.

'They're internal, sir. Imprinted on my brain. I'm afraid I only have visionary access.'

Pyrgus put the flyer into a holding pattern, describing a wide circle over the city. 'This public landing area – wouldn't a Lighter flyer be a bit conspicuous there? I mean, I don't want word getting around that we've arrived.'

'Oh, I don't think so, sir,' Kitterick said soberly. 'Faeries of the Night use far more air transports than we do, so there are scores of vehicles coming and going. One more will scarcely be noticed. Besides, this is an unmarked flyer.'

Pyrgus thought about it for a second. The last thing he wanted was a long walk through Yammeth City. If the public landing area really *was* close to the estate gate …

'OK,' he said. 'Where is this place?'

'The large rectangle rimmed in green, ahead and a little to starboard, sir.'

Pyrgus saw it. 'I'm on it,' he said. 'We're going down!'

Kitterick proved right about their not being noticed. Several hundred Nighter vehicles were parked in neat rows. People were coming and going all the time. There appeared to be no formalities at all. Pyrgus slipped on his lenses and handed a pair to Kitterick.

'What's this, sir?'

'Darkened glasses,' Pyrgus said. 'So people can't see your eyes and tell you're not a Faerie of the Night.'

Kitterick blinked. 'I'm four foot seven inches tall with orange skin. I think people might suspect I'm not a Faerie of the Night even with dark glasses, sir.' He folded the lenses neatly and handed them back. 'I don't think we need worry unduly, if I may say so, sir. There are quite a few Trinians in service throughout the Cretch. More so now, of course, since the Hael portals closed and demon servants are at a premium.' He began to tidy away the flying gear. 'May I enquire whether we have a plan on this mission or whether we will simply be crawling through the bushes until something attacks us as we did at Lord Hairstreak's?'

Pyrgus grinned. 'No crawling through the bushes this time, Kitterick. We do have a plan. We'll present ourselves at the main gate and ask for Gela.'

'Gela, sir?'

Pyrgus hesitated. 'My, ah, friend. My friend Gela. She's Merchant Ogyris's daughter.' He felt a lot less confident than he sounded. Gela might not be prepared to help. In fact, on balance, he thought it was a bit unlikely, but he didn't have a better idea and it was probably worth a try.

'I see, sir.'

'I thought Gela could get us in,' Pyrgus pressed on. 'Maybe ask us to the house for a cup of fume or something. I'd ask her not to mention the visit to her father. Then, while one of us engages her in conversation, the other could sneak out and take a look at the crystal flowers.' He hesitated. 'Probably you,' he added lamely.

'May I say, sir, that is possibly the worst plan I have ever heard?'

'It's the only one I've got,' Pyrgus told him sourly. 'We might as well try it.'

'Yes, of course,' said Kitterick.

The main gates of the Ogyris Estate were enormous ornamental bastions flanked by twin statues of grinning demons. The statues were in a garish pink-veined marble. The gates were wrought in lethal iron, hideously expensive, but impervious to faerie attack and with a thin, black spell coating to protect any legitimate visitor who might touch them accidentally. They were shut.

Pyrgus blinked. For some reason it had never occurred to him that the estate might be closed off, although now he was here it seemed the most likely thing in the world.

'What do we do now?' he muttered aloud.

'Allow me, sir,' said Kitterick and placed his palm squarely on the brass attention plate sunk into the left hand wall.

'Please state your name and business,' said the nearest statue.

'Please face the gate and speak clearly,' said its twin on the other side.

'Please refrain from touching the gates at any time,' said the first statue.

'The gates are made from iron,' remarked the other statue conversationally. 'Very dangerous to faeries.'

'The master coated it with spells, but they've worn a bit thin.'

'Need replacing, really.'

'So keep clear, or let the dwarf touch them. Iron doesn't work on Trinians.'

'It's Prince Pyrgus, isn't it?' the other statue said. 'You've been here before with young Mistress Gela, haven't you?'

'Yes,' Pyrgus said nervously.

'Thought I recognised you. Nice to see you again, sir. Careful of the gates.'

'You'll still have to state your name and business, I'm afraid, sir,' said the other statue. 'Just for the record. We have to log all visitors with Security Central.'

'Troubled times.'

'Purely a formality in your case, sir.'

'But one we must adhere to. Full name with titles, sir. Please speak clearly. Oh, and you should name the dwarf as well. He has to be stamped, since it's his first time.'

So much for Gela sneaking them in without her father knowing. 'Prince Pyrgus Malvae of House Iris,' Pyrgus said quietly, in case the name was heard by some passer-by. You could never tell what might happen to a Faerie of the Light in Yammeth City. You heard stories of them being lynched.

'Bit louder, sir,' the statue said.

'Prince Pyrgus Malvae of House Iris!' Pyrgus shouted, throwing caution to the winds. 'Knight Commander of the Grey Dagger, Honorary Arcond of the Church of Light, former Emperor Elect, former Crown Prince of the Realm, Chief Friend and Sponsor of the League of Decency to Animals, President of the Weirdling Congress, Honorary Grand Herald of the College of Heraldry, First Cooperdentoid of the Ancient and Honourable Order of the Immaculate Hand, plus various subsidiary honours.' He drew a fresh breath and added, 'And Kitterick.' He leaned across and whispered, 'You don't have any titles, do you Kitterick?'

'Afraid not, sir.'

'And the Orange Trinian Kitterick,' said Pyrgus loudly.

'And your business, sir? Succinctly. It just needs to be something like "Visiting Merchant Ogyris" or "Delivering ornaments for the house" or something of that sort, sir.'

'Visiting Mistress Gela Ogyris,' Pyrgus said.

'Passing on,' murmured the first statue. It closed its eyes to process the information.

'Would you like to step over beside me, Mr Kitterick?' asked the second statue in a friendly tone. 'Might as well get you stamped while we're waiting.'

When Kitterick moved beside it, the statue produced a large rubber stamp from the folds of its tunic and imprinted a luminous OG on his forehead.

'Just show that if you're stopped. It's valid for twenty-four hours. Don't wash until you want rid of it – rain won't affect it, but it comes off with soap. Some of the younger generation keep them on for weeks – it's a fashion accessory, apparently.'

'Cleared,' said the first statue.

There was an ominous click and the massive gates swung open.

fifty-two

Henry's eyes opened and flashed red. 'Won't do you any good,' he said.

Blue swung round, her heart pounding. He was still slumped squatting against the wall. There was no way he could get to his feet, cross the room and reach her before she dived through the open door. All the same she hesitated.

Henry said, 'It leads back here.' He closed his eyes again. There was something in his careless confidence that was absolutely terrifying.

Blue twisted round again and plunged through the open door. There was a soft *snick* as it closed behind her.

She was in another featureless white cube.

This room looked exactly like the one she'd left. White walls, white floor, white ceiling, the same concealed lighting, the same curious softness underfoot.

And Henry, slumped against one wall.

fifty-three

At almost four miles long, the winding driveway of the Ogyris Estate was clearly not meant for foot traffic. By the time Pyrgus and Kitterick arrived at the house, it was growing dark.

'You OK, Kitterick?' Pyrgus asked. His feet were sore and there was a knot in the muscle of one calf.

'Never better, sir,' said Kitterick annoyingly.

The Ogyris mansion was a relatively new building of curious construction. It combined the slim spires of a traditional Haleklind castle with a blocky under-pinning – so fashionable across the Cretch these days – that seemed to have been inspired by a troll's dungeon. The result was something that looked vaguely like a giant porcupine crouched to spring. In an ostentatious display of wealth, Zosine Ogyris had commissioned lavish spell coatings that transmuted the base material of the building into copper, into silver, into gold, into platinum, into orichalcum and back to copper again, endlessly, at seven-minute intervals. It was burnished copper at the moment and the reflected rays of the dying sun made it look as if it was on fire.

'Well, here we go,' said Pyrgus and stepped up to the massive door.

The woman who answered his knock – Pyrgus

assumed she was a maid – was short and plump with something about her eyes that reminded him of Gela. She had the greenish skin tone and nose wrinkles of a Halek peasant, which may have been exactly what she was, since Ogyris could have brought her with him from his native land. She wore a crisp blue-striped apron and there was a dusting of flour on her hands.

'Sorry to keep you,' she said cheerfully. 'Making scones.'

Pyrgus favoured her with an uncertain smile. 'I've come to see Gela,' he said. Time to find out whether Gela wanted to see him.

'Not here,' said the woman promptly. 'Father sent her 'ome.'

Pyrgus blinked. This was Gela's home.

'To Creen,' the woman said, using the native term for Haleklind. 'Thought it would be safer.' When Pyrgus looked at her blankly, she added, 'The war.'

'The war?'

'The war what's coming.' She said it so matter-of-factly that Pyrgus chilled. But before he could react, she began to tilt her body at an alarming angle. It took him a moment to realise she was trying to look past him. 'That you, Kitterick?' she asked, her face suddenly beaming.

'Yes, indeed, Genoveva,' Kitterick said smiling, as he stepped from behind Pyrgus. 'Nice to see you again.'

'Well,' said Genoveva, 'this is a real bootiful surprise! Come in, come in and bring your 'andsome young friend. I'll brew up some fume and you can try my scones, tell me if I've lost my touch.' She smiled broadly at Pyrgus and added, 'So Gela knows you – lucky girl!'

As they followed her along a flagstoned corridor towards the smell of baking, Pyrgus whispered urgently to Kitterick, 'I didn't know you knew Ogyris's servants.'

'Not his servant, sir,' Kitterick whispered back. 'That's his wife.'

'His wife?' Pyrgus exclaimed loudly, then repeated in a whisper, 'His wife? This is Gela's *mother*?'

'Yes, sir. Genoveva, sir. Very pleasant woman. Wonderful touch with scones, as I suspect we're about to discover. Married when she was sixteen and he was twenty-five. That was before he left Haleklind and got rich. Happy as two clams in gravy, I'm led to understand. Halek marriages are often like that. Something to do with the composition of the soil, I believe.'

'Why's she doing her own baking?' Pyrgus asked curiously.

He must have spoken too loudly, for Genoveva called over her shoulder, 'Because there's not a servant in the country can match my scones. So Zosine Typha says, anyway. I think it's a plot to keep me in my place, myself.' She chuckled.

'How is it you know her?' Pyrgus whispered to Kitterick.

'I fear I'm not at liberty to say, sir.'

Pyrgus blinked at him, then said, 'Oh. Some mission for Madame Cardui?'

'Something of that sort, sir.'

'But you know her well?'

Kitterick smiled a little, with his poison fangs retracted. 'Very well, sir. *Very* well indeed.'

Pyrgus opened his mouth to push further, then decided better of it. Instead he said, 'You don't think you could get her to tell you about the crystal flowers, do you?'

'Don't be silly, sir,' Kitterick said politely. 'She's extremely loyal to her husband. In certain matters. Besides, I doubt she'd know anything about them. Halek men are notoriously chauvinistic. They tell their wives nothing, nothing at all. I've often thought it a most admirable characteristic.'

'You two can stop whispering about my bottom,' Genoveva called cheerfully over her shoulder. 'Can't help it if I have a healthy appetite.'

'I would suggest, sir,' Kitterick said softly, 'in rela- tion to the crystal flowers, you tell Veva – Madame Ogyris – that you have an interest in Halek architecture and would like to see over the house. She will issue you with a pass that will permit you entry to any area you wish. If someone stops you, just produce it. I shall keep her chatting in the kitchen until you return.'

'She won't just let me wander through her home,' Pyrgus protested. 'She doesn't know me from Firstman.'

'Oh yes she will, sir,' said Kitterick confidently. 'It's a tradition of Halek hospitality.'

'What happens if she wants to go with me? Give me a guided tour?'

'She won't, sir. You can take my word on that.' Kitterick smiled.

''Ere we are, boys,' Genoveva said, opening the kitchen door. 'Fume and scones, and if you're very good I might find you a pot of my home-made squing preserve.'

'Try not to take too long, sir,' Kitterick whispered. 'I

don't know how long I can distract her.'

Pyrgus followed them into the kitchen. The plan seemed insane, but for the life of him he couldn't think of a better one.

fifty-four

'Hello, Blue,' Henry said and smiled coldly. 'I told you they were coming.'

He was flanked by demons. All but one of them was manifested in its spindly, grey-skinned form. They turned their huge black eyes upon her. Blue tried to jerk her head away, but moved too late. She felt her will begin to drain.

The exception was skinny and tailed and naked except for a covering of black fur. It had budded horns and pointed ears and sharpened teeth and glowing yellow eyes. It grinned at her and loped across to take her hand. Its fur felt soft and comforting, like a cat.

'Go with John, Blue,' Henry said.

Go where? It was a stupid thought but the only one that occurred to her in that chill instant. How could you go anywhere when the only door from the room led right back in again?

Then other thoughts were smashing down on her like a tidal wave. Henry wasn't working for Lord Hairstreak. Henry was working for the hordes of Hael. Which meant Henry *hadn't* betrayed her. Because nobody like Henry worked for Hael of his own free will. The demons were controlling him!

It was crazy, but she actually felt relieved.

The relief lasted less than a second. They were both in big trouble and Henry didn't even know it. If they were going to get out of this, it was up to her. But she was already caught up in the same web as Henry. Could she claw back control of her mind now she'd looked a demon in the eye?

Beside her, the foul little creature squeezed her hand encouragingly.

Blue looked carefully at what was happening to her. She didn't feel any different to the way she usually did, but that was an illusion – and a subtle trap. However she felt, she was standing quietly holding hands with a demon, in a room full of demons. She should be running or fighting or screaming – anything except standing quietly. So when the demons took control of your mind, they made you feel you wanted to do what *they* wanted you to do.

Could she use that insight? Did she have any of her own will left?

She tried moving her left arm a little. It moved easily. She pushed down the sudden surge of elation. What did that prove? The demons wouldn't care about her left arm. And why muck about with a small movement anyway? Why not try to run and see what happened? That would be a real test. Except she didn't want to try to run because she had to go with John, as Henry said.

The thought seemed so natural that she chilled.

There was a beam of blue light pooled on the floor. She couldn't see where it was coming from. The thing beside her crawled into her mind and fondled the surface of her brain.

'I'm Black John,' it told her silently. 'Let's walk together to the light.'

That was just what they should do, of course. She took a small step forward, then another. Henry was watching her. His eyes were closed to slits and he was smiling.

Blue tried to remember what Pyrgus had told her about being possessed by the demons. When it happened to him he'd tried hard not to think of his name, because once they knew your name, they had total control. Fat lot of good that information was. They knew her name already. Queen Blue, Empress of the Faerie Realm. Now walking like a child into a pool of light.

It occurred to her that this was not the time to resist them. They were actively controlling her, making her walk. Later, perhaps, when their attention was on something else, she might seize an opportunity to escape.

Hand in hand with Black John, Blue walked forward.

fifty-five

Blue was drawn elegantly along the beam. Such strange spell technology. There was nothing like it in the Realm. It made you so relaxed and dreamy, carried you so gently, up and up and up.

She reached the wall of the cubical chamber and passed through it as if it were mist. All the while Black John's little cat-claw hand held hers.

The sudden glare blinded her and hurt her eyes. She gasped and jerked her hand away. At once Black John gripped her mind savagely and she stood stock-still, unable to move, unable even to close her eyes. Black John took her hand again and her paralysis broke.

Blue stood blinking tears from her eyes. She felt icy calm. The incident had taken less than a second, but she'd learned something. While the demon creature held her hand, he could control her actions gently. When she jerked her hand away, his response had been close to panic. Locking up her mind and body was an overreaction. He still had control, but it was a crude, brutal control.

Blue forced herself to ignore the pain in her eyes and think. The problem was nobody really knew much about demonic possession. Faeries of the Night had techniques and spells to guard against it, but even they didn't know exactly how it worked. Henry was under demon control, obviously had been for some time, and nobody was touching *him*. Mr Fogarty had been possessed by a demon when he killed her father, but none of the creatures had been with him – touching him – at the time. Why did this thing need to touch her now? Henry and Mr Fogarty were both human. Perhaps it was different for faeries.

She wracked her memory to recall what exactly had happened to Pyrgus. He said the demons had jumped on him, so there'd been contact then. But had one held his hand after that? He hadn't mentioned it, although that didn't mean it didn't happen. Besides, Pyrgus had been possessed while he was in Hael – the demons' own world. It might work differently in Hael too.

No matter. She still thought she'd learned something. Here and now, the demons seemed to need contact to control her properly. That was knowledge she might use.

Blue turned her head, blinking the tears from her eyes. Her surroundings swam slowly into focus. She was in a strange metal chamber, lit by a pervasive violet glow. As her eyes adjusted, she could see the light was coming from a bank of huge transparent tubes, filled with slowly bubbling liquid. Floating inside were scores of naked babies, mouths open, eyes tight shut. To her sudden horror, she realised they were *breathing* the liquid. There was no way she could tell whether the babies were faerie or human.

'Neither,' Henry said, reading her mind. He was floating through the wall on another beam of blue light. Two of the black-eyed grey demons were following behind him. All three landed like thistledown.

When she looked at Henry, she was no longer looking at Henry. She knew that now. There was something else behind his eyes.

'What are they, then?' she asked angrily.

'Hybrids,' Henry said. 'Part of our breeding programme.'

Our breeding programme? The creature speaking through Henry was a demon. Keep it talking. Talk might distract it. Besides, any information could prove useful.

'Your breeding programme?' Blue echoed.

The thing dropped all pretence of *being* Henry now. Even the voice changed, dropping to a low growl that sounded even more frightening for coming from a boy's mouth. 'For stronger stock,' it said. Henry looked at her with cold, blank eyes.

Blue looked back at the babies floating in the tubes. Some were plump, some looked pale and sickly. All moved slowly in the liquid. Their hands opened and closed. A horrid realisation dawned on her.

'Those are –'

'Part Analogue, part Hael,' the demon said. Henry's eyes stared at her. 'Now we begin the second phase.'

The silence was so profound it was as if all sound had been sucked from the room. A sick fear rose in her stomach. She was afraid to ask but had to ask. Her voice sounded hoarse, scarcely louder than a whisper.

'What's the second phase?'

The thing inside Henry contorted his lips into a smile. 'A child of Hael born of a faerie mother.' His eyes flickered to Black John, who squeezed her hand.

Blue tried to pull away and scream, but the paralysis fell on her again.

fifty-six

Life was always so *very* difficult without Kitterick. Madame Cardui picked up Lanceline and stroked her translucent fur. The thing was, when one reached a certain age, one's faculties atrophied. A little pain here, a little ache there ... nothing that one couldn't cope with, of course, especially now they'd developed those *marvellous* rejuvenation patches. But the woolly-mindedness was a different matter. There wasn't a spell in the Realm would touch that. Which was why Kitterick was such a *boon*. Astonishing storage capacity. Lists ... records ... things to do ... old photograms ... new plans ... he absorbed them all. Honestly, you'd imagine his poor head would burst. But no, in it all went and out it all came at *exactly* the right moment. Remarkable. Even for a Trinian. She would be quite lost without him. She *was* quite lost without him. But Pyrgus's needs took priority.

Pyrgus. Such a bright young man. And so misguided, as young men often were. This involvement with a Faerie of the Night, for example. Quite dreadful. Alan was right, of course – the lure of the exotic. Forbidden fruit. Young men never thought of much else (except animals in Pyrgus's case, which was quite odd). She sighed as the ouklo pulled to a halt. She'd been just as bad herself when she was younger. How Daddy *squirmed* when she told him about the Great Myphisto. A stage career had seemed such a scandal in those days. And Myphisto was so much older than she was.

She stepped down from the carriage and tapped the side to send it on its way. She was sure she should have emulated Alan and stayed in the palace for the duration of the emergency. But honestly, one craved one's own bed in times of crisis. One's own bed and one's own home.

'I shall find you some minced mouse when we get in,' she promised Lanceline as she climbed the narrow staircase. The cat (who understood everything, absolutely *everything,* she said) began to purr.

Her Guardian triggered on the landing and she waved it away impatiently. Quite hideous how life had to be surrounded by so much *security* these days. She was quite sure things hadn't been nearly so bad when she was young. But, of course, when she was young she hadn't been involved in espionage. An occupation that brought its own risks. She sighed again as she reached the door of her apartment.

Lanceline growled softly.

Madame Cardui froze with her hand on the door. 'What is it, darling?' she asked.

Lanceline growled again.

With the cat still cradled in her arms, Madame Cardui retraced her steps and reactivated the Guardian.

'Report,' she demanded.

'Full or synopsis?' the creature asked.

'Synopsis.'

'Authorisation?'

'Codeword: Painted Lady.'

The Guardian placed his right hand on his turban. 'Accessing ...' Then, 'No visitors, Madame Cardui. No attempted access. No incidents, no accidents. Safeguards intact. Securities intact. No repairs necessary. Last system initialisation, twenty-two hundred hours. Situation normal. Shall I reset, Madame Cardui?'

'No,' Madame Cardui said absently as she turned back to the stairs. As she reached her door, Lanceline moved uneasily in her arms.

'It's all right, darling,' Madame Cardui told her.

Spell-driven securities were all very well, but even the most sophisticated system could be circumvented if one had enough resources. But Alan (dear Alan!) had taught her one very special trick – new to the Realm, although he claimed spies often used it in the Analogue World. She crouched down and felt for the invisible thread she'd stretched across the bottom of the door. It was intact. No one had come in this way.

Madame Cardui opened the door.

The apartment was in darkness. 'Lights,' she commanded. All systems activated at once, sending elaborate spell patterns crawling across the walls, switching on the soothing music, bringing up the soft pink lighting she favoured.

The killer was waiting for her in the middle of her living quarters.

He was dressed in black from head to toe and wore the dark glasses of a Faerie of the Night. Wrapped around his forehead was a sweatband bearing the insignia of the Assassins' Guild. Like most assassins, he was small and wiry, but he carried Halek daggers in each hand. He had been waiting – heavens only knows how long – in the Death Crouch, preparing for the moment she returned.

'Fang,' whispered Madame Cardui.

Lanceline launched from her arms in a blur of light. She hit the assassin at the level of his knee and streaked up his body to his face, attacking with all four paws simultaneously. The lenses flew across the room and he screamed in shock as she shredded his eyes. Then she went for the artery in his throat.

As the corpse lay twitching on the floor, Lanceline walked daintily away to leap back into Madame Cardui's arms.

'Minced mouse,' she murmured sensuously.

fifty-seven

The pass was working! Pyrgus hadn't really dared to believe it, but he'd been stopped by three different sets of guards now and each time he'd produced it, they'd waved him on with bows and smiles. Amazing the cultural differences with Haleklind. You'd never catch a Faerie of the Light letting a total stranger wander freely through his home, nor a Faerie of the Night, that was for sure.

Although it wasn't exactly *freely,* of course. Some doors were locked. The door to Ogyris's office, for example, and the door to Ogyris's private study. In fact, quite a few doors were locked. You could wave the pass at them as much as you liked, but they stayed firmly shut. No question of breaking in either, with guards likely to turn up at any moment. He might be allowed to go anywhere, but no pass gave him burglary rights. Which was a pity. There might have been interesting documents in the office or the study.

Still, no complaints. Kitterick was proving worth his weight in gold. The pass allowed Pyrgus to come and go as he pleased, which meant he could go outside and take a really close look at the glasshouse. He'd worry about getting into it when he reached it.

Pyrgus strode out the front door, waving his pass at

the portraits of Ogyris ancestors on the hallway walls.

He found the glasshouse easily enough. It was now fully dark outside and the building was illuminated as it had been on his first visit. He remembered Gela's comment that her father relied on magical protections rather than draw attention by posting guards, but even so he was cautious. He waited minutes, listening, before he approached too closely.

Nothing had changed. The crystal flowers were still inside, planted in neat rows. He peered through the glass (taking great care not to touch it), unable to believe they were living plants. But they still seemed beyond the skill of an artist. Every bloom was absolutely perfect, every crystal leaf and stem was a marvel in its own right. Each flower glowed softly underneath the growglobes. Starlight reflected in their depths.

He was wasting time. Poetic musings wouldn't get Blue back. He needed to know more about these flowers, and Gela said they were spell-protected.

Pyrgus stood trying to remember *exactly* what she said, and at the same time trying to figure out what spells *he* would use to protect something really precious. Since money was no object with Merchant Ogyris, you could be sure they'd be heavy-duty magic. And since the flowers were very special the chances were the protections would involve lethal force.

It would have to start with the glass. He was fairly sure that's what Gela had told him as well. *Keep away from the glass*, she'd said, or words to that effect. She thought the glass was dangerous. Pyrgus thought the glass was dangerous.

An idea struck him and he began to circle the

glasshouse, carefully examining the ground. Sure enough, when you looked closely, the grass hid the remains of insects in huge numbers and he came across the bodies of several dead birds with burn marks on their feathers. That made a lot of sense if his theory was right. Anything that flew into the glass was incinerated.

Which meant it had some sort of high-energy coating.

Pyrgus felt a sudden chill. You could short-circuit a high-energy coating with a Halek knife.

It was hideously dangerous, of course. Halek knives sometimes shattered when you used them, sending their energies back up your arm to stop your heart. (The reason they were more often used to threaten than to kill.) But a soldier once told him that if you used a Halek on an object with a spell charge, the chances of its shattering rose as high as one in three. Only lunatics used Haleks on an object with a spell charge.

But that sort of thinking wouldn't get Blue back and stop a civil war.

Pyrgus drew his Halek knife. The fine-wrought blue crystal blade reflected back the light from the glasshouse. Would it shatter, if he used it on the glass? One chance in three, the soldier said.

Pyrgus hesitated. What if he used it and it only broke through a single pane? That could easily happen if each one was coated individually. Some panes were large enough for him to squeeze through, but many of them weren't. He'd have to pick his target carefully – he certainly wasn't going to risk using his Halek blade more than once.

He circled the building again, paying close attention

to its structure this time. Then he circled it again and stopped in front of the entrance door. It was constructed of one large pane and several smaller. He could squeeze through the large pane provided it shattered entirely. But the thing was, if only part of it broke he might still be able to reach through and open the door from the inside. It was very unlikely that Merchant Ogyris would have ordered interior coatings. The point was to keep people out, not threaten anybody who happened to be working inside.

Pyrgus licked his lips and tapped the blade absently against the palm of his left hand. Did he have the courage to do this? He could feel the tingle of the trapped forces as they writhed beneath the surface. One chance in three that he was seconds away from death.

He thought of Blue and stabbed the glass.

The result was astounding. Magical energies surged from the blade, but the blade itself did not break. (It didn't break! *Yes!* Thank you, Powers of Light!) The pane cracked loudly, then fell in a tinkling heap at his feet. But before he could move, cracks were spidering across every surface of the building. Pane after pane shattered, sending shards tumbling. The snapping sounds grew louder. The cracks spread further and further. Huge plates of glass fell forward to smash into the growing heap of fragments on the ground. Whole panes fell out intact, then broke as they hit. In seconds, Pyrgus was surrounded by a tempest of broken glass. The noise was mind-numbing.

'Whoops,' Pyrgus murmured.

He was standing beside the naked skeleton of a glasshouse. Not one single pane survived intact. There was no way the noise could have gone unnoticed. He had minutes at best to do what was needed. After that, the guards were here for sure.

Pyrgus sheathed his blade and stepped through the empty doorway, his shoes crunching on the broken glass. The growglobes had survived, strung high above from the framework of the building. There was broken glass inside but the crystal flowers seemed miraculously intact.

He glanced around guiltily. It was a total mess. He was in so much trouble now. With Merchant Ogyris. With Gela. Probably with half the Realm. The destruction was *unreal*!

But no time to worry about that. Close up he could see Gela was right – the flowers were living things. Their stems were planted in rich earth with a new-fangled thread system providing nourishment and moisture. Some of them even had small shoots sprouting at the base.

He still had no idea what they were and precious little time to find out.

He'd already risked so much now that any other risk seemed small. He reached out, snapped the stem of the nearest flower and dropped it into his pocket. He'd never find the secret of the flowers here. His only hope was to carry some away and investigate them later, hopefully with some help from people who knew more about all this than he did.

He was reaching for another crystal bloom when the guards fell on him like a tree.

fifty-eight

Pyrgus fought like a fury. But guards were racing in from all directions until he was surrounded by a milling mass of close on a hundred. Even if he'd used the Halek blade again he'd never have broken out. In moments he was on the ground, wrestled down by the weight of bodies.

'Hold him, boys!' a coarse voice ordered.

Two of the boys grabbed his arms. Two more helped to drag him to his feet. Pyrgus stopped struggling. He was ringed by men now, every one of them a lot more heavily armed than he was.

'Shall I search him, sir?' someone asked. 'He may be carrying a weapon.'

'I'm carrying a pass from Madame Ogyris,' Pyrgus said.

'Pass, is it?' asked the officer. He looked pointedly at the massive wreckage of the glasshouse.

'Let me show you,' Pyrgus offered. There was no chance the pass would make a difference, but if he played for time he might think of something more sensible.

He felt one of the soldiers loosen the grip on his arm and jerked it free. The man didn't bother to grab it back: Pyrgus wasn't going anywhere.

'I have it here,' Pyrgus said. It occurred to him it might change things if he told them who he was. They could decide to kill him on the spot, of course, but he *was* still a Prince of the Realm, so they might think of handing him back to the palace authorities. Or they might decide to bounce on their noses all the way to Haleklind. But whatever. He had to do *something*.

He reached into his pocket for the pass and his hand closed over the crystal flower. As he began to draw it out, one of the soldiers shouted, 'Watch out – he's got a weapon!'

Half a dozen men hurled themselves upon him again. Pyrgus's arm jerked and his hand tightened convulsively. The bloom dissolved into glittering dust beneath his fingers.

All movement stopped. The guards stood frozen as if turned to stone.

fifty-nine

The demons carried Blue into a different room.

There was a strange bed with a bright red counterpane and ridged metallic tubes snaking from its underside to disappear into the floor. Glowglobes in the ceiling were set low to a soft pink light so that shadows crawled out of darkened corners. There was a viewscreen set into one wall. There was nothing else.

The demons withdrew. Henry collapsed in a heap on the floor.

'Oh God, Blue,' he wailed, 'I'm so sorry!'

Blue's paralysis broke and the slime of Hael control slipped from her mind. She spun round as the door slid shut. Henry was weeping now, but it was the old Henry, the one she knew, not the thing that had been talking through him. She knelt beside him, hesitated, then placed one hand on his shaking shoulder.

'What happened?' she asked softly.

For a moment he couldn't answer, couldn't even look up. Then he turned his tear-stained face towards her.

'They made me do it, Blue,' he said.

Blue cradled his head like a child. 'I know, Henry. I know.'

They stayed like that, huddled together on the floor, for a long time. Eventually the weeping stopped and

Henry pulled away gently.

'I'm fine now. I'm better.'

Blue said, 'I need to know what's happening. I need to know what's going on.' She hesitated. 'Do *you* know?' She wasn't sure how much he'd remember.

Henry started to climb to his feet. He looked wretched, almost ill. For some reason he avoided catching her eye.

'They told you about their breeding programme,' he muttered.

Blue shuddered, thinking of Black John. 'It won't happen,' she said firmly. 'I'd kill myself first.' She caught his expression. 'What's wrong? You can't believe I'd ...? With a *demon*?'

Henry said, 'It's not with a demon, Blue. It's with me.'

Sixty

'The flowers stop time!' Pyrgus announced dramatically. He could hardly believe it himself, but he was excited and frightened all at once. The only problem was he still didn't know where Henry had taken Blue. But now he knew *how* and maybe they could work it out from that.

Mr Fogarty, still in his nightshirt and bedsocks, glared at him. 'What's that supposed to mean?' he asked.

'They stop time!' Pyrgus repeated. 'I was surrounded by guards and I crushed a flower and it stopped time. The guards froze, but I could still move. That's how I got away.'

'Stasis spell?' Fogarty frowned.

'No,' Pyrgus said excitedly. 'The flowers *stop time*. Time stops for everybody except the person who crushes the flower. I just walked away, got into my flyer and zipped back here.' He looked at Mr Fogarty, grinning like an idiot. 'The trip back took *five minutes*! But that's because time was stopped for most of the journey. That's how I knew it wasn't a stasis spell. It's like the flower surrounds you with a bubble and the bubble's outside everybody else's time and you can race about and do things while they're all waiting for the next clock tick. If it hadn't worn off before I got here, I wouldn't be able to talk to you now.'

Fogarty said, 'Guards ...'

Madame Cardui said, 'You got into trouble with Merchant Ogyris's guards?' She looked away from him towards the window and smiled. They were in a private room of the palace, overlooking the rose garden.

'Another diplomatic mess,' said Mr Fogarty dryly, although he didn't look displeased either.

Madame Cardui turned to Pyrgus. 'By the bye, deeah, what did you do with Kitterick?'

'Ah,' said Pyrgus, suddenly embarrassed.

'Ah?' asked Madame Cardui, one eyebrow raised.

'I sort of ... left him,' Pyrgus said.

'Was that because he was outside your time?'

Pyrgus wasn't at all sure how he should put this. Eventually he said, 'No, actually, Madame Cardui. I mean, he probably was – outside my time – I didn't check. I just ...' this was definitely the tricky bit, '... sort of forgot about him.' It was hideously embarrassing, but no more than the truth. He'd had a lot of things on his mind when he left the Ogyris Estate. He looked sheepishly at Madame Cardui, waiting for the outburst.

But all she said was, 'Will he be all right?'

He will if Merchant Ogyris doesn't come home unexpectedly, Pyrgus thought. Aloud, he said, 'He's probably on his way back now. Kitterick can look after himself.'

'Well, yes, that's certainly true.'

'How long does it last?' Fogarty asked suddenly. He was looking at Pyrgus.

Pyrgus looked at him blankly. 'What?'

'The time-stop,' Fogarty said impatiently. 'That's what we're talking about, isn't it? How long? A minute? Five minutes? A couple of hours?'

'I don't know,' Pyrgus said. 'From my point of view it wasn't any time at all.'

'How many of these flowers were there?'

'Oh, dozens,' Pyrgus said. 'Hundreds. Maybe a thousand.'

'I don't suppose you brought any back with you?'

Pyrgus shook his head. 'No, Mr Fogarty.'

'I don't suppose you destroyed the rest?'

Pyrgus thought of the wreckage of the great glasshouse. 'I ... sort of broke the place they were growing in, so I don't think Merchant Ogyris can grow any more until he fixes it. But the flowers didn't wilt or anything. I think the worst it would do is stop them growing. I'm sure they won't really *die,* at least not quickly – they're made from rock crystal.'

Mr Fogarty didn't seem to be really listening. 'I don't suppose you found out where Blue is?'

Pyrgus said eagerly, 'Not exactly, but now we know how Henry took her away. He must have crushed one of those flowers and the bubble must have taken in Blue as well as him. Once you're in the bubble, you can go anywhere, do anything. Nobody can stop you.'

'Why would he have taken Blue?' Madame Cardui mused. 'I'm sure he wouldn't harm her. Don't you think so, deeah?'

Fogarty stood up abruptly. 'OK, you two, come with me.'

'Where are we going, dahling?'

Fogarty's face looked grim. 'I want you with me as Head of the Espionage Service, Cynthia. And you,

Pyrgus, as Crown Prince or the Queen's Brother or whatever your official title is now. We're going to see the Generals and try to talk them into stopping the Countdown. If the Faeries of the Night have flowers that stop time, it would be suicide to attack them tomorrow. Our forces would be wiped out to the last man.' He strode towards the door.

'Alan ...' said Madame Cardui gently.

'What?' Fogarty growled impatiently.

Her eyes travelled over his nightgown and bedsocks. 'I think you might be more impressive if you changed into your Emperor's robes, deeah.'

Sixty-one

All three Imperial Generals – Creerful, Vanelke and Ovard – were in the Situation Room deep beneath the bedrock of the palace. Their uniforms were immaculate, but they looked as if they hadn't slept in days. The place was a hive of activity. Messengers scurried to and fro carrying documents and updates. Military wizards crouched over concave mirrors. Soldiers in full combat gear guarded every door. They snapped to attention as Gatekeeper Fogarty entered.

He glanced around curiously. This was his first visit to the Situation Room and the twenty-minute descent by suspensor shaft had left him nauseous. But that did nothing to dull his interest. In the centre of the room was a huge Operations Table that somehow managed to display the entire geographical landscape of the Realm. The illusion was remarkable – clearly the very latest spell technology. It looked exactly like a model railway layout Fogarty had had as a child, right down to details like miniature buildings, roads and bridges, but impossibly larger. When your eye went in a particular direction, the landscape unfolded as if the Table somehow read your mind. Which it probably did. He found that simply thinking of a place brought it into focus. There were animated troop movements on many of the roads.

Fogarty tore his eyes away to look at the banks of crystal viewing globes. Most of them were focused on Yammeth Cretch, the heartland of the Faeries of the Night. About a third seemed to be trained on Yammeth City.

'Notice the globes on the bank to your left,' murmured Madame Cardui at his side.

Fogarty followed her gaze. Three globes showed alternate views of a vast subterranean cavern. Nighter soldiers were stocking it with munitions.

'It's directly underneath Yammeth City,' Madame Cardui told him. 'We only managed to smuggle three sensors inside.'

'Looks as if they're preparing for our attack,' Fogarty said.

She nodded. 'They know about the Countdown.'

'We have to stop this,' Fogarty said. 'It's madness.'

General Creerful detached himself from a tight group of uniformed women and walked towards them. He had the look of a man with scant time for interruptions, but he nodded politely enough.

'Crown Prince. Gatekeeper.' His face softened just a little. 'Painted Lady.'

'Get the other two over here,' said Fogarty shortly.

Creerful blinked. 'Pardon?'

'Vanelke and Ovard. Get them over. We have to talk.' Fogarty glared at him. In his experience, the only thing military men respected was toughness and in a situation like this he was prepared to give it to them in spades.

Creerful's eyes flashed angrily, but his gaze broke after a tense moment and he turned on his heel. In a moment more he was back with his fellow Generals. Ovard was the one who decided to push his luck.

'There's a lot to do, Gatekeeper. I hope this is important.'

'We can have a pissing contest next week, Ovard,' said Fogarty shortly. 'Right now I don't have the time. I want you to stop the Countdown.'

If Ovard was taken aback, he didn't show it. 'You know we can't do that, Gatekeeper.'

'You can and you will,' Fogarty told him firmly. 'I'm ordering you to stand down all Lighter forces. I'm ordering you in my official capacity as Acting Emperor. And that order is confirmed by Crown Prince Pyrgus and Madame Cardui, as Head of the Imperial Espionage Service.' He looked at the other two, who nodded confirmation.

Ovard sighed and allowed the tiredness to show in his voice for the first time. 'You can wheel in the whole royal family if you want, Gatekeeper. It doesn't change the law. The only faerie on the planet who can cancel an active Countdown is the reigning monarch. The last time I looked that was Queen Holly Blue.'

'Queen Blue is in no position to cancel it,' Fogarty said.

Creerful pushed forward slightly. 'Which is the whole point of a Countdown, Your Acting Majesty – you know that. Or you should.'

'I've discussed the situation with Madame Cardui,' Fogarty said grimly. 'Unless you comply with our demands, she will order her Service to withdraw all reconnaissance information.'

Creerful sighed. 'I'm sure Madame Cardui will do nothing of the sort,' he said, not looking at her. 'But if she did, we would be forced to arrest her for treason.'

Another bluff called. 'All right,' Fogarty said. He glanced around to make sure there was no one else within earshot, then locked eyes with Ovard again. 'Try this for size. The Faeries of the Night have a secret weapon, details on request from Prince Pyrgus, that means our people will be slaughtered to the last man before they can lift a finger to defend themselves.'

He waited, fully expecting arguments, doubts, demands for details. Instead, all three Generals looked at him with the eyes of old men who have seen far too much war and suffering. It was Vanelke who said softly, 'You're not of the Realm, Alan. We can't expect you to understand. It's a question of law and tradition. It doesn't matter if we're all wiped out.' He closed his eyes briefly, then opened them again. 'Unless Queen Blue returns to countermand her order, the Countdown must continue. At sunset tomorrow the war will begin.'

Sixty-two

Blue stared at him. 'With you?'

Henry looked hideously embarrassed. 'It's a bit complicated,' he said.

'Then you'd better explain,' Blue told him.

Henry went across to sit on the bed, then jumped up again as if he'd been stung. 'Sorry,' he said, without making clear what for. He glanced at Blue and licked his lips. 'They put a thing in my face.'

Blue waited. She wanted to put her arms round Henry and comfort him again, but she had to know what was happening and know it fast.

'Go on,' she said.

'They pushed it through the side of my eye.' He caught her expression and added quickly, 'It's like the way they can take you through walls with that blue light. It doesn't damage your eye or anything, but it's still jolly sore. And scary.'

'Go on,' Blue said again.

'It's a thing that links you with the Hellmind.'

She'd never heard the term before. 'What's the Haelmind?'

'It's the demon's Internet.' He caught her blank expression and said quickly, 'It's a sort of mental broad-cast thing that lets their leader tell them what to do.'

Blue frowned. 'You mean Beleth?'

Henry nodded. 'Yes, Beleth. The Hellmind is his communications network.'

'I don't understand this,' Blue said. She wasn't sure if she should be feeling impatient. Henry could sometimes be very roundabout when he tried to tell you anything.

'I'm not sure I do either,' Henry said. 'Not exactly, anyway. I think it's some sort of mental network. I don't know if it's natural or something they invented. But it lets Beleth pass on orders very quickly.' He hesitated, then added, 'And makes sure you obey them.'

There was a long silence. Blue was wondering why nobody had told her about the Haelmind before. But perhaps nobody knew. Faeries of the Light avoided contact with demons and even the Nighters didn't understand them entirely. Everybody knew demons were basically evil, but far more than that, they were *different*. Maybe faeries had never realised how different. Or maybe it was some new technology they'd invented, as Henry said.

Eventually she asked, 'They put something in your brain that links you to this thing?'

'They can activate it at a distance. It's off now.' He hesitated. 'When it's on, I'm a demon too.'

'You mean you're possessed?' She remembered the horrid sensation of Black John crawling inside her skull.

'It's worse than that,' Henry whispered. 'I get changed completely.'

It was beginning to sink in, and making Blue afraid. 'You *become* a demon?'

Henry nodded. 'Yes.'

Sixty-three

They were sitting together side by side on the hideous red bed. Henry held himself rigid, taking great care not to touch her. 'There's stuff you need to know,' he said.

Blue watched him and waited.

'I can only tell you while my implant's deactivated. I'm me now, but the thing is I remember. I know what the demons are doing. I know what Beleth has been planning.'

'What?' Blue asked.

'Total conquest,' Henry said. 'They're going to take over your whole world and mine.'

The plan had been in place for years, Henry said. The aim was demon mastery of both the Faerie Realm and its analogue, the human world. The means was to be a breeding programme. Beleth decided it should be tested first in the human world. Up to that time, there had been sporadic attacks by demons on humans. But the new plan meant an end to overt action. Demons no longer harassed humans openly, but concentrated instead on kidnapping selected individuals and breeding with them. It was a difficult process. The offspring were often sickly and many died. But enough survived to be infiltrated into positions of power in the human world.

'They started off with tribal chiefs and witch doctors in Africa,' Henry said. 'Then later it was European kings and their advisors, popes and priests and people like that. Recently it's been politicians and dictators. They're not all bad, of course, but some of them are demon children linked to the Hellmind by blood. They've been nudging humanity towards Hell for ages now.'

'Didn't anybody notice?'

'That was the really clever part,' Henry told her tiredly. 'As soon as they started infiltrating, they all worked hard to convince people demons didn't actually exist.'

'That's ridiculous,' Blue said.

'I know,' Henry nodded. 'Beleth didn't think even humans could be that stupid, but one of his advisors drew up a strategy. Instead of hiding, demons kept appearing to humans, but in silly forms. Leprechauns and boggarts and stuff like that. Anything that sounded dim. Lately it's been little green men from outer space. Nobody takes them seriously.'

'Wait a minute,' Blue interrupted. Something he'd said earlier was niggling her. 'If breeding with humans was so tricky, why didn't they just implant people the way they did with you?'

'New technology,' Henry said. 'They simply didn't have it when Beleth drew up his plan. They've started using implants now, of course. The British Prime Minister and the American President both have one. But the demons have to be careful. These things show up under X-rays. If humans found out what was really happening, it could sink the whole plan. Beleth doesn't want that – it's been working far too well already. So you see,' Henry added.

After a moment, Blue said, 'See what?'

'Why we're here,' said Henry.

Blue saw nothing of the sort. She wanted to take Henry and shake him, but she controlled herself.

'Why are we here, Henry?' she asked quietly.

'Infiltration,' Henry said. 'It's worked so well in my world, they want to try it in the Faerie Realm.' He hesitated, turned his head away from her and murmured, 'Starting with our child.'

Sixty-four

Travelling up in a suspensor shaft was a lot less intimidating than travelling down. You didn't have to step into space at the beginning of the trip for one thing.

As they floated side by side, Pyrgus said uncertainly, 'Do you think the Generals mean it?'

'They mean it,' Fogarty told him. He turned to Madame Cardui. 'Have you contacted the Ferals?'

'I do wish you wouldn't call them that, dahling.'

'Have you contacted the Forest Faerie?' Fogarty said tiredly.

'You really think it will come to war?'

'You heard the boys in uniform. We'll be at war from sunset tomorrow. We've tried to avoid it, Cynthia. The trick now is to win it. You've been in touch with Cleopatra, haven't you?'

Madame Cardui lowered her eyes and nodded. 'I got a message to her in the night. She was kind enough to send an immediate response.'

'Which you didn't tell me about.'

'My deeah, when did I have the opportunity? You were still in bed when Pyrgus arrived with his news and then we went directly to the Situation Room.' She shrugged. 'In any case, it gets us no further. Queen Cleopatra sends her profound regrets, but believes the present situation is a matter for the Faeries of the Light and the Faeries of the Night. It has no bearing on or relevance to the Forest Faerie and consequently she has formally declined to put her forces at our disposal.'

Fogarty snorted. 'Can you arrange for me to meet Queen Cleopatra later today?'

'You won't change her mind, Alan: I know her very well.'

'I'm not trying to change her mind,' Fogarty said. 'If she won't join us, she won't join us. But she might have some ideas where Blue has gone – the foresters know a lot about hiding places. And she might help us capture the time flowers. Or destroy them.'

They arrived at the surface and stepped out of the suspensor shaft. Pyrgus was suddenly animated.

'You mean a commando raid, Mr Fogarty?'

'Something like that.' Fogarty caught Madame Cardui's expression and added, 'Look, we'll be at war tomorrow. We need to start thinking about ways to win it.'

'That's a brilliant idea!' Pyrgus told him enthusiastically. 'I'll lead the raid!'

'No you won't!' said Fogarty and Madame Cardui together.

Sixty-five

'They want us to have a *child*?'

Henry nodded miserably.

Blue stared at him for a long, long time. There were so many questions boiling in her mind, but at the end of it all she simply asked, 'Why us?'

'You're Queen,' Henry said, a bit too quickly. 'If you had a demon child, it would automatically be in a position of power. When it grew up.'

He was hiding something. 'Why you?' Blue asked. 'Why not –' she thought of Black John with his fur and his tail and his clawed hand in hers, '– a real demon?'

'I am a real demon when they activate that thing. It's just my shape that stays the same. They thought you wouldn't ... accept ... something in demon form. Actually, they thought you might know it was a demon in *my* form. That's why they deactivated my implant.'

'They could have forced me,' Blue said coldly.

'No, they couldn't,' Henry said earnestly. 'Not something like that. The implants don't work on faeries.'

That was a bit of interesting information. But they wouldn't have used an implant on her anyway – they wanted a faerie mother, not some demon who looked like one. All the same, the demons could get into your mind, whether you were human or faerie. Why couldn't they control her that way?

Hesitantly she asked, 'What about ... possession?'

'Possession won't let them push faeries to do something against your deepest moral principles,' Henry said. 'They can only hold you still and make you walk and things like that. It's different with humans – they can make us do anything they want.'

Mr Fogarty was possessed by a demon when he killed her father. They could make humans do anything they wanted. Up to and including murder. Blue shifted uneasily. She still had the feeling Henry was holding something back.

'Why did they pick you, Henry?' she asked again.

Henry's face flared bright scarlet. His eyes went down to the floor and he drew away from her stiffly. For a moment she thought he wasn't going to answer, but then he mumbled quietly, 'They think you might be in love with me ...'

Blue wanted to hold him then, but it clearly wasn't the time. Besides which, her fury at the demons was consuming her.

'They think all they have to do is put us in a room together and we'll make a child just because I'm in love with you?'

Henry glanced at her strangely. After a moment he said, 'They don't really understand people.'

'No, they don't.' It was almost laughable.

'Of course –' Henry began, then stopped.

Something in his tone alerted her at once. 'What? Come on, Henry, I need to know everything before they turn you back into a demon. It's the only way we can survive this.'

Henry said slowly, 'If we don't ... if we don't ... you

know … if we don't, I mean of our own accord, they'll … they'll …' He swallowed. 'They'll force you. They'll hold you down.'

It took her a second to realise what he was saying. 'And you would …?' she asked, outraged.

'They'll change me back into a demon!' Henry wailed.

Suddenly, in the middle of it all, she realised what he must be going through. She softened her tone. 'So they'll try that anyway, if we don't … of our own accord?' She almost added, *Because I love you.*

Henry nodded. 'Yes.'

She sighed, stood up and walked across the room to the viewscreen. 'That's what this thing's for, isn't it?' she said, stroking the screen. 'To see what we do.'

'Yes.'

She was holding herself together with a massive effort, exhibiting a calm she didn't feel because she had to be strong enough for the two of them.

'What happens if I don't conceive?'

'It doesn't matter,' Henry said. 'They'll know that right away – they have some sort of probe that tells them. If you aren't pregnant, they'll invade the Realm.'

Blue stared at him. 'The portals are all closed,' she said foolishly.

'They've opened new ones,' Henry said.

Sixty-six

The approach to the suspensor shaft involved a series of heavily guarded checkpoints. Fogarty, Madame Cardui and Pyrgus were all known by sight, so formalities were minimal, but it still meant their conversation went in fits and starts.

'The thing is,' Fogarty was saying to Madame Cardui, 'with the Forest Faeries' spell technology, we could get into the Ogyris Estate undetected. I think they can travel direct from tree to tree. Are there any trees near your crystal flowers?' he asked Pyrgus.

'It makes sense for me to lead the raid,' Pyrgus said. 'I know the estate. I've been there. And I know where the flowers are. They're very difficult to find, you know.'

'And even if they can't,' Fogarty said stonily, 'we know they can pass through solid surfaces far better than we can. More men, less danger.'

'It certainly makes sense, deeah,' Madame Cardui said uncertainly. 'It's just that Cleo may not agree.'

'And I'm the only one who's actually *touched* a time flower,' Pyrgus said. Apart from Henry, who wasn't here and anyway was the cause of half the trouble in the first place.

'She'll agree all right,' said Fogarty with utter certainty. He lowered his voice as they passed through yet another checkpoint.

'And I'm the only one who knows how to destroy them,' Pyrgus said, wondering if they would fall for it.

'What are you going to do?' Madame Cardui asked Fogarty suspiciously.

'Charm her,' Fogarty said shortly.

They emerged from the checkpoint corridor into the vast basement suite that abutted it. Madame Cardui gave him an endearing smile.

'Well, you could certainly do that to any woman, dahling, but apart from charm ...?'

Fogarty said, 'I thought of pointing out it's hardly in her interests if they win – which they will if we don't find Blue and destroy the time flowers. Hairstreak has already brought demons to the forest once. He could easily do it again, once he gets the upper hand. The Hell portals won't stay closed for ever, you can be sure of that.' He sighed. 'I could also promise to leave them in peace if we win – that seems to be the one thing that really interests them. We could offer a treaty that guarantees it, both from us and the Faeries of the Night.'

'Do you think the Nighters would agree?'

'They will if we win – what's left of them.'

'You see,' said Pyrgus, 'you can't just smash them up. I mean, I only crushed one flower and that stopped time for –' he didn't actually know how long it had stopped time for, but pressed on anyway, '– *hours*. If you smash up hundreds of them, there's no way of telling how long time would stop for. You might stop it *for ever*. You might interfere with the very fabric of our univer—'

Men in black appeared by the far entrance of the huge chamber. They assumed an arrow pattern and took up a fighting stance.

'What are those yo-yos up to?' Fogarty asked.

Madame Cardui peered at them a little short-sightedly. 'They look like Assassins' Guild, deeah. I expect they've come to kill you and Pyrgus.'

A large group of swordsmen appeared and hurled themselves on the intruders.

'Think so?' asked Fogarty.

'Oh, I would imagine so, deeah. One tried to kill me yesterday.'

'Really?' said Fogarty, concerned. 'Are you all right?'

'Oh, yes,' said Madame Cardui. 'I had Lanceline with me.'

The clash at the far side of the room was turning into something of a Battle Royal. Pyrgus noticed the swordsmen were concentrating on capturing the assassins rather than killing them – not altogether successfully, since the assassins themselves fought with suicidal intensity.

'Who hired them?'

'Lord Hairstreak's man, the Duke of Burgundy, according to the one who attacked me.'

Fogarty frowned slightly. 'I thought you said Lanceline killed him.'

'I interrogated the corpse.'

Fogarty tore his eyes away from the fight. 'I didn't know you could interrogate a corpse.'

'You can if it's fresh.'

'Oh,' said Fogarty. He frowned again. 'You should have told me you were attacked.'

'I didn't want to worry you, deeah. Besides, what more could you do? I ordered an immediate alert throughout the entire Espionage Service. We knew the Guild's plans for you and Pyrgus and the Generals. As you can see.' She waved her hand vaguely towards the mass of struggling men.

The fight was almost over, its result a foregone conclusion. Madame Cardui's men far outnumbered the assassins and were, in their own way, just as skilled. One or two bodies were dragged out. The remaining men in black were overpowered and led away.

'You can see the logic of my position on this raid,' Pyrgus said. He took a deep breath. 'And besides which I outrank you, Gatekeeper.'

'Do you indeed?' muttered Fogarty.

They had reached the bottom of the broad stone stairway that led to the upper levels of the palace.

'You know I do,' Pyrgus said impatiently. 'I'm still Crown Prince. Sort of.'

'And I'm still Acting Emperor. Sort of,' growled Fogarty. His voice softened. 'But you're right. You found those damn flowers and you know where they are and you know more about them than anybody else, so it makes sense for you to take part in the raid.'

'Lead the raid,' Pyrgus said quickly.

'All right – lead the raid,' Fogarty said irritably. He glanced across at Madame Cardui. 'We can send some of your people to keep him safe, can't we? If they can sort out assassins, they shouldn't have much trouble with Ogyris's guards. I'll try to get the Forest Faerie involved. Queen Cleopatra won't begrudge us a small contingent. Might even send –' He stopped.

Madame Cardui was looking at Pyrgus. 'What is it, deeah?' she asked. 'What's the matter?'

Pyrgus was looking up the stairs, his jaw slack with astonishment.

Sixty-seven

Blue sat beside Henry, put her arms around him and kissed him.

'What are you doing?' Henry gasped. He jerked away and stared at her in astonishment.

Blue pulled him close again, but this time whispered in his ear. 'They're watching us. We need to make them think something's going to happen.'

'Why?' Henry's mouth was muffled by her hair.

'To play for time, you idiot!' Blue said in exasperation and kissed him again. After a moment he began to react as if he might be enjoying it. As they drew apart she murmured, 'OK, let's not overdo it.' She manoeuvred so her body was between him and the screen. 'Turn out your pockets.'

'What?'

'Turn out your pockets!' Blue hissed. 'We have to get out of here and I want to see if you have anything that might help.' A thought occurred to her. 'Where is here, anyway? Do you know?'

'We're in one of the demon ships. A transport. On Earth we call them flying saucers.' He began obediently to turn out his pockets.

'Was that funny square room part of it?'

Henry shook his head. 'That was a storage cube in

271

limbo,' he said incomprehensibly. 'The saucer picked us up from there.'

Blue stared at him with a sinking heart. 'Where is the saucer now – in space?'

Henry nodded. 'Yes, probably.' He caught her expression. 'What's wrong?'

'If we're in space, we can't escape. Unless you can fly a saucer.'

'No, I can't,' Henry said. 'But I remember how to work the blue light.' He saw her blank look and added, 'The light that pulled us out of the cube.'

'We don't want to go back to the cube!' Blue hissed. Then, in a moment of uncertainty, 'Do we?'

'I don't think so,' Henry said. 'But the light will send us anywhere, if I can figure the coordinates. There ...' He looked up at her and gave a little smile. He'd finished emptying his pockets.

Blue stared at the little heap on the bed. There were several unfamiliar coins, a piece of paper with writing on it, a small white packet of something that might have been a snack and several pieces of string. Not exactly commando gear to break out of – what did he call it? – a flying saucer.

She forced herself to think. The limbo cube place had been packed with demons, but she could only remember seeing three in the saucer – the two that accompanied Henry and the Black John creature. There were probably others – how many demons did it take to crew a saucer? She needed to know what she was up against.

'What have you got?' Henry asked in a whisper. He glanced around him. 'You don't think we should go back to ... you know ... kissing?'

'What have I got what?' Blue asked crossly, ignoring his second question. 'Look, do you know how many demons are on this ship? Twenty? Thirty? A hundred? What?'

'In your pockets,' Henry said. 'You might have something useful too. There's just three.'

Did he mean what she thought he meant? 'Just three of a crew?'

'It's all you need. Most of the ship is automatic. And, of course, they have me when the implant's activated.' He shifted to block the viewscreen. 'Go on, you must have something.'

'I have this,' Blue said; and showed him the slim, sleek shape of the stimlus half concealed in her hand. She was feeling suddenly elated. Just three. There was a chance they might get out of this yet.

Sixty-eight

'What is it?' Henry asked.

Stimlus, Blue mouthed. It suddenly occurred to her that even whispers might be overheard. There was no way she wanted to throw away the element of surprise.

Stimlus? Henry mouthed back, frowning.

Oh, for Light's sake, Blue thought. She scrabbled in the pocket of her tunic for a writing tablet and found the ornate purple thing she was supposed to carry at all times as Queen. She held it away from the viewscreen and stroked the spell coating. Words began to crawl across the surface.

Kills on contact.

Henry looked at the writing, then at her. 'The stimlus kills on contact?' he asked.

'Kills on contact' disappeared and was immediately replaced by glowing red capitals: DON'T SPEAK ALOUD. IF YOU WANT TO SAY SOMETHING, PLACE YOUR THUMB ON THE SURFACE OF THE TABLET AND THINK CLEARLY.

'Cool!' Henry murmured. He got the hang of it at once, for the tablet cleared, then showed the words, *Will it kill them all?*

Blue pushed his thumb to one side with hers. *Kills one only. Single charge. Must have contact.*

Henry moved her thumb aside. *Better than a kick in the teeth from a wet haddock.*

Blue looked at him in bewilderment.

'It's all right,' Henry said sheepishly. He put his thumb back on the pad. *What's the plan?*

Sometimes, Blue thought, it would be nice if someone else took charge. She shifted his thumb and her words began to fill the pad again. *Stand by the door. We lure them in, then attack. Take them by surprise. Kill them.*

'Kill?' Henry mouthed. His eyes were wide.

'Oh, for heaven's sake!' Blue exclaimed aloud. 'What did you expect to do – invite them to a ball?'

Henry gripped the tablet. *There are three of them and only two of us.*

They're little skinny things.

I've never killed anything before.

You'll be fine if you don't look in their eyes.

Henry stared at her as if trying to make up his mind. After a while he nodded suddenly and moved beside the door. Blue walked over to the viewscreen and shattered the fragile glass with a single kick. The spell coating turned magenta and howled. She spun round and raced to join Henry at the door.

The plan unravelled at once. The demons burst in at a run, but only Black John was in his original form. The other two had transformed themselves into creatures from a nightmare, muscular and huge.

'Yikes!' Henry exclaimed.

He has no weapon, Blue thought. That was stupid. I should never have started this until he had a weapon. But there was no weapon for him, nothing in the room that might even have served as a club. She stepped forward and pressed the stimulus into the side of the nearest demon. There was a loud hiss and the smell of burning flesh, then the creature toppled, its eyes blank.

Blue spun round and saw to her surprised delight that Henry was clinging to the second nightmare demon, apparently trying to strangle it. The creature was threshing to and fro, trying to dislodge him. She winced as Henry's knee cracked against the wall, but noted he never slackened his grip. Blue flung herself at the demon.

The stimulus was useless now, burned out after its single discharge. She knew she didn't have the strength to kill the brute, not even with Henry hanging on to it, so she went for its eyes, the most vulnerable point.

The demon jerked upright and roared, scrabbling for her hands. 'Good girl, Blue,' Henry murmured. There was sweat beading on his forehead as he fought to increase the stranglehold. There was no way he could kill the thing like that, of course, but he might manage to distract it until she blinded it. A blind demon was almost as helpless as a dead one.

She reached for the eyes again, then there was a demon on her back, the furred imp with budding horns and pointed ears. Black John clutched her shoulders with slim, taloned fingers. 'No more, Majesty,' he hissed malevolently into her ear.

Blue flung herself backwards at once. They rolled together across the floor, Black John still clinging to her back. She could feel his claws shredding her clothing, then the sharp pain as they reached her flesh. She jerked her head back in the hope of connecting with his face, but missed. One of his slender arms went round her throat and tightened.

Almost at once, her vision began to darken. His other hand came round and raked her face. Blood spurted, half blinding her. In desperation she hurled herself backwards against the nearest wall. There was a sickening thud, the grip on her throat loosened and she felt Black John slide off her back. Blue stumbled and fell, then picked herself up. The black demon lay on the floor beside her. He was still breathing but looked dazed from his fall. Blue reached down and took his head and broke his scrawny neck. Then her knees began to give way.

The last thing she saw before losing consciousness was Henry standing over her. He was grinning broadly. Against all odds, he'd strangled his demon.

Sixty-nine

'Good God!' Fogarty exclaimed.

Blue was floating in a beam of light at the head of the stairs. There was a livid bruise on her right cheek and dried blood on her face. Her hair was matted, her clothes in tatters. But the worst of all was her eyes, which were glazed, blackened and bloodshot.

'Blue!' Pyrgus shouted. He began to run up the stairway.

There was a figure floating through the wall behind her. To Fogarty's astonishment, it resolved itself into Henry.

Blue landed lightly and tried to step forward towards Pyrgus. She spun slowly around and began to fall.

'Blue!' Pyrgus shouted again.

Blue toppled forward.

Her eyes snapped open. Waves were lapping gently on a golden beach. The calls of seabirds blended with the strains of soothing music. Blue felt awful. Her face hurt, her head hurt, her nose hurt, her body ached from neck to toe.

'Oh, excellent – you're awake, deeah.'

Blue turned her head to one side with enormous caution. Jags of crimson pain forced her eyes closed briefly, but she opened them again to look into the smiling face of Madame Cardui.

'It's all right, deeah, don't try to talk.'

Blue wasn't sure she *could* talk. But at least some of her confusion was fading away. She was lying under crisp, clean sheets tucked beneath her chin. The beach was an illusion painted on the ceiling, the soothing music played by elementals trapped in jars beside her bed. This had to be the palace Infirmary. The spells were standard treatment for recovering patients.

'You're quite safe now, deeah. You've been through a difficult experience, but it's over now and everything's all right. Are you in pain? Just blink once if the answer's yes.'

Blue blinked once.

'The healers will bring you something for that in a moment. They're just waiting for the results of your final tests. You're suffering from demon poisoning, but there's nothing else – no broken bones, no organ damage, nothing of that sort. You're very lucky, really. If Pyrgus hadn't been so quick off the mark, you might have broken your neck.'

Blue's tongue felt too large for her mouth and all her teeth hurt. Her lips were swollen to twice their normal size. 'Ooo ahs Prus, Am Siya?'

Madame Cardui reached out to place a soothing hand on her forehead. 'Don't try to talk just yet, Blue deeah. Here's Chief Wizard Surgeon Healer Danaus now. I expect your test results are in – yes, they are: see, he's nodding. You'll soon be feeling so much better, and while Chief Healer Danaus does his work, I'll try to bring you up to date – all right?'

Blue wondered why even sensible people like

Madame Cardui felt obliged to treat you like an imbecile the minute you felt ill. She could see Chief Wizard Surgeon Healer Danaus now, a tall, fleshy figure with the shaven head and blue robes of his profession. He was carrying an energy globe in one hand and a vial of miniature elementals in the other.

'Try to let go, Majesty,' he boomed. 'A relaxed body cannot harbour a negative emotion.' A professional smile creased the full moon of his face. 'We'll soon be feeling better, I assure you.'

Blue wondered vaguely if she could order him beheaded. All the same, when he cracked the vial and allowed the little elementals to swarm into her body, she did indeed begin to feel better almost instantly.

Madame Cardui clearly noticed the difference for she laid a warning finger on Blue's lips (no longer swollen now, incredibly) and said gently, 'Perhaps delay our conversation until we are alone ...?'

Blue nodded and waited. Chief Wizard Surgeon Healer Danaus checked his handiwork, pronounced himself satisfied, warned Her Imperial Majesty not to overtire herself, then withdrew backwards, bowing awkwardly.

As he closed the door, Madame Cardui said, 'I've had this room secured – we can talk freely.'

Blue said, 'That was rough. Where's Henry? Did he get through?' His idea had been to use the demon transporter to beam her directly back to the palace. Then, when she was safe, he was going to try to set it on automatic so he could follow her.

'He was right behind you,' Madame Cardui said a little grimly. 'Where did he take you?'

Blue pushed down on the bed to help herself sit up

and was surprised to discover she was no longer feeling weak. 'I'm not sure. Somewhere cubed.' The truth was, despite the elementals in her bloodstream, her mind was still foggy. But Henry had made it through, so that was all right.

Madame Cardui frowned. 'What do you mean – cubed?'

Blue shook her head. 'It's not important.' She was very definitely feeling stronger. She pushed back the bedclothes and swung her feet on to the floor. 'Where are my clothes?'

'What you were wearing has seen better days, I'm afraid,' Madame Cardui said. 'I had them destroyed. There some fresh things in the wardrobe.' She hesitated, but no more than a fraction of a second. 'You *do* look much better, deeah, since Danaus unleashed his little helpers. I certainly don't want you to overdo it, after all you've been through, but there are one or two rather *pressing* matters ...'

'In a moment,' Blue said firmly. She had to get her mind clear. She had to call her people together and explain to them about Beleth's plan. 'Where's Pyrgus?' she asked.

'He's not in the palace just now, deeah. We had to send him –'

Blue cut her off. 'Where's Henry?'

'In the dungeons,' said Madame Cardui. 'I had him arrested, of course. He's currently awaiting execution on a charge of treason.'

Seventy

'Who the hell are you?' Fogarty asked crossly. He was in the forest, just about to start another round of talks with Queen Cleopatra, and resented interruptions. Especially now things were going well. She'd already agreed to help in the raid on the time flowers – couldn't leave them in Hairstreak's hands, even if Blue was home now. Given a bit more of the Fogarty charm and she might even agree to a formal alliance.

'Nyman, sir,' the intruder told him. 'Madame Cardui's new dwarf, sir.'

Fogarty frowned. 'Where's Kitterick?'

'Still missing, sir. Whereabouts unknown. Herself promoted me *pro tem* on account of the Emergency. I was always good at running errands, taking messages, that sort of thing. I expect it's back to the kitchens for me when Kitterick turns up again, but in the meantime it's a hike in pay, a change from peeling spuds and here I am, sir.' He smiled, showing a missing tooth.

'And what do you want?' Fogarty asked, still frowning.

Nyman glanced around, then jerked his head and scuttled into the shade of a large oak. 'Confidential, sir, Herself says,' he remarked when Fogarty caught up with him. He began to make little jumps up and down.

'What are you doing?' The creature was insane.

'Trying to get on a level with your ear, sir, yourself being a fine big tall man and me being vertically challenged as you might say.'

'Oh, for God's sake!' Fogarty exploded. He bent down until his ear was at the level of Nyman's head.

'Herself says you're to get back right away, sir,' the dwarf whispered. 'Bit of a problem, like.'

'What sort of a problem?'

'Ah, Herself would never tell me that, sir. Nothing dangerous or too confidential on account some miscreant might squeeze it out of me. I'm not what you'd call stoical under pressure, sir.'

'You're not a Trinian, are you?' Fogarty said.

'Indeed and I am not, sir, as a fine, big, clever man like yourself could probably tell by the colour. Don't hold with those lads at all, to tell you the truth: far too well organised. I'm what you might call a Lep.'

'Ah,' said Fogarty, without the slightest idea what a Lep was. 'Well, now, listen, Mr Nyman, I want you to get back to Hersel— to Madame Cardui – and tell her I'm in the middle of some very delicate negotiations –' He stopped: Nyman was shaking his head solemnly. 'What is it?'

'Herself said you might be a bit troublesome, begging your pardon, sir, and if you was, I was to tell you one thing –' He beckoned Fogarty to bend over again and when he did, whispered, 'There's big trouble, sir. Regarding Henry.'

Seventy-one

It was brilliant leading a commando raid. Pyrgus was wearing full camouflage fatigues with a helmet sporting so much greenery than it looked like a vegetable patch. His face was painted in olive and brown stripes. But that wasn't the really good bit. The really good bit (as he wriggled on his stomach through the undergrowth) was that there were twenty heavily armed men right behind him, all tough as nails, all ready to lay down their lives for the mission.

And every one of them called him *sir*.

'Freeze!' Pyrgus ordered in a whisper.

'*Sir!*' they snapped in whispered unison; and froze. It was so, so *cool*.

He wished Nymph could see him now.

Or maybe not. He raised his head carefully above the level of the grass to discover he was still lost. The problem was that crawling on your stomach changed your whole perspective. Things that looked one way when you were standing up looked completely different when you were lying down and peering through a shrub. But what was he to do? He couldn't just march his men down the main avenue of the Ogyris Estate. This was a raid, not a frontal attack. You didn't mount a frontal attack with twenty men, no matter how tough they were.

Besides which, a frontal attack would start a war and they'd only just averted one now Blue was back to stop the Countdown. But at least Mr Fogarty and Madame Cardui hadn't called off the raid. So Pyrgus got to lead *twenty men.*

He hadn't told them they were lost, of course. Wouldn't want them demoralised so early in the mission. Besides, he had to concentrate on meeting up with Nymph. How good was that? The Forest Faerie had agreed to send some people and Nymph was leading them. Blue back safe, no war, he was leading twenty men and going to meet up with Nymph again. Life could not get better than this.

He was about to bring his head down and press on regardless when he caught a glint of something from the corner of his eye. He swung his head round. Water! It was sunlight glinting on water. The lake! If they got to the lake, he could find his bearings eventually. He was bound to. He'd been able to follow the lakeside path even in pitch darkness, so daylight had to be a doddle, even crawling.

'Left turn!' he hissed, and swung himself round.

'*Sir!*' his men responded and fell in behind him.

Seventy-two

Blue said, 'Have him released, Madame Cynthia. And get that thing out of his head.'

Madame Cardui frowned. 'My deeah, you *do* recall it was Henry who kidnapped you?' She hesitated. 'What thing?'

Blue was sitting on the edge of the bed pulling on her boots. 'Henry didn't know what he was doing,' she said firmly. 'He was taken over by Beleth.'

'Beleth?' Madame Cardui exclaimed. A look of sudden comprehension crossed her face. 'I *wondered* if that was a demon transport beam. My deeah, I think you'd better tell me everything.'

Blue told her. It took surprisingly little time.

'Poor Henry,' Madame Cardui said when Blue had finished. She moved to the door and gave instructions to one of the guards outside. When the man hurried off, she turned back to Blue. 'I've ordered Henry released. He'll be taken directly to the infirmary to have Beleth's implant removed.'

'Thank you,' Blue said. She had almost finished dressing.

Madame Cardui sat down heavily on the bed. She seemed suddenly very old. 'I'm losing my edge, deeah. I was looking in the wrong place.'

Blue glanced at her, but picked up her meaning at once. 'So was I, Madame Cynthia. I thought Uncle Hairstreak was behind all our troubles. Not that he wasn't behind *some* of them.'

Madame Cardui said, 'Speaking of which, you need to cancel the Countdown.'

'Yes, of course. I'll do it at once.'

Madame Cardui hesitated. 'There's one thing ...'

'Yes?'

'I'll make this quick, deeah,' Madame Cardui said; and told her about the time flowers.

'So that's how Henry got me out of Hairstreak's mansion – he never told me. I thought it might be some sort of stasis spell.'

'The thing is,' Madame Cardui went on, 'when you disappeared with a Countdown in place, we – that's to say Gatekeeper Fogarty and myself – decided we could not possibly permit the Faeries of the Night to retain such a powerful weapon – you can easily imagine the military implications, of course. So we ordered a commando raid to destroy the flowers. Pyrgus is leading it as we speak.'

'Why Pyrgus?' Blue asked quickly. He was her older brother, but she'd always been protective of him.

'Pyrgus knows exactly where the flowers were being grown. I just hope this is the *only* place they're being grown.' She waited.

After a long moment, Blue said, 'You did right, Madame Cynthia. Flowers that stop time would change the entire balance of military power. How many men has Pyrgus taken?'

'A score of our finest,' Madame Cardui said, 'but he's meeting with an equal number of the Forest Faerie.

Alan persuaded them to help us.' Rather surprisingly, she thought; but it never did to underestimate Alan.

'I suppose the Forest Faerie are being led by that Nymphalis creature?' Blue said sourly.

Madame Cardui smiled slightly. 'I imagine they might be. I'm not yet privy to the arrangements.'

'Where is Gatekeeper Fogarty?' Blue asked. 'I should like to know more about this raid.'

Madame Cardui looked at her fondly. One moment an injured girl, the next every inch a Queen. Blue was her father's daughter all right – especially when there was the slightest danger to her family.

'I'm afraid he's still with Queen Cleopatra.'

'Have him come to see me as soon as he returns,' Blue commanded and stood up. 'I think I'll visit our Generals in the Situation Room. After I cancel the Countdown, we need some urgent talk about our Hael strategy.'

'Perhaps not so urgent,' Madame Cardui murmured gently. 'The demons' plans for you have failed abysmally.'

Blue looked at her directly. 'Henry said if they didn't succeed with me, they would invade the Realm.'

Madame Cardui blinked. 'The portals are closed.' She hesitated. 'Aren't they?'

'That's what I said,' Blue told her. 'Henry says they've opened new ones.'

After a moment, Madame Cardui asked, 'Where?'

'That's the problem,' Blue said. 'We don't know. What I do know is we need to contact Uncle Hairstreak and accept his offer of a treaty. We can't afford to squabble amongst ourselves with Beleth at the gates.'

'I agree entirely,' Madama Cardui told her. 'If you really feel strong enough, we can get that under way at once.'

But as they left the room, a military messenger arrived with news that turned their situation upside down.

Seventy-three

Pyrgus stood up cautiously.

He and his men – *his men!* – were at the rendezvous spot, a small ornamental grove on the far side of the lake from the main house, but there was no sign of Nymph or any of her Forest Faerie. It was a worrying development. If she was late, she was late, but if she wasn't coming at all, how long was he supposed to wait? By now Ogyris would know about the shattered glasshouse. There'd be new security in place – a contingent of crack guards at the very least. Which meant a fight. One Pyrgus would rather tackle with the Forest Faerie at his side.

There was something at his back. Pyrgus jumped half out of his skin when a hand fell on his shoulder.

'Nymph!' he exclaimed. He fought down an almost overpowering urge to throw his arms around her and kiss her. Instead he simply stood there, grinning like an idiot.

'What's that thing on your head?' Nymph asked curiously.

Seventy-four

Somehow it all went far more smoothly now the Forest Faerie had arrived.

Nymph seemed to have an instinct for where they should be going. She gently herded Pyrgus in the right direction when he got lost again, which wasn't all that often now since he was spending a lot less time crawling on his stomach.

In five minutes they were back on the lakeside path, heading in the general direction of the boathouse. Pyrgus should definitely have been feeling good about the mission. But he wasn't. It was much too quiet.

Actually it had been much too quiet all along, Pyrgus thought suddenly. For Light's sake, Ogyris was a Faerie of the Night, the most ruthless breed in the Realm. The crystal flowers were his big thing. He might have relied on secrecy and spells at first, but Pyrgus had knocked his entire glasshouse down. The whole estate should have been crawling with guards by now. New securities should be in place to protect the flowers. He remembered what they'd faced when they called on Hairstreak, and that was just a routine system. Ogyris should have had a thousand trackers heading for them by now.

But nothing.

'What's the matter?' Nymph whispered.

'It's so quiet here,' said Pyrgus. 'Much *too* quiet.'

'That's just nerves,' Nymph shrugged. 'Are we close yet?'

'It should be over the next rise.' Pyrgus frowned. He was still uneasy.

Then they topped the next rise and he discovered why Ogyris hadn't ordered more security. The shattered remnants of the glasshouse had been cleared away.

Not a single crystal flower remained.

Seventy-five

Fogarty hit the palace like a whirlwind, issuing orders. 'Change of clothes – can't see people with loam on your backside. Get me an appointment with the Queen. Find somebody to brief me on what's been happening. Send a formal thank-you to the Forest Faerie. Have those bloody Generals come and see me. See if you can find out where Madame Cardui is hiding. Take –'

'Ah, sure, these were fresh on last month and not a pick of loam on any of them,' Nyman said.

Fogarty stopped to glare at him, frowning in bewilderment before it dawned on him the Lep was talking about clothes. 'Not for you, you idiot – for me!'

'Ah, I get you now, sir. You leave that to me: I'll have something brought up from your Lodge and you can change here.' Nyman drew a notepad from the pocket of his jerkin and licked a stub of pencil. 'Now what was the rest of it, sir ...?'

It brought Fogarty up short. He'd been so energised by good news that he'd been going off inside his head like a firecracker. His rejuvenation treatments must be affecting his hormones.

'You're not as stupid as you look, are you, Nyman? All right, let's see ... Clothes first. And a sonic shower. Then find me Madame Cardui – she can fill me in on what's been happening. After that the Queen, then the Generals.'

'She'll be in the Situation Room, sir,' Nyman said. He looked at Fogarty's blank expression. 'Herself, sir. Situation Room, sir. That's where she told me to bring you.'

'Yes, of course,' said Fogarty.

The guards stopped Nyman at the first checkpoint – he'd insisted on accompanying Fogarty even though he had no security clearance whatsoever. Fogarty went on alone. His earlier ebullience had been replaced by a curious feeling of unease. For a palace that was no longer on Countdown, there were a lot of military personnel in the corridors and he even had to wait his turn at the suspensor shaft listening to stiffly apologetic guards as a stream of messengers took priority over the Realm's Gatekeeper.

But when he did step into the shaft, his build allowed him to sink so quickly that he caught up with one group that had gone down before. They wore the armbands of reconnaissance messengers.

'What's all the activity about?' Fogarty asked at once.

'Wouldn't know, sir.'

'Couldn't say, sir.'

'Brass never tell us anything, sir.'

'Thanks,' Fogarty growled shortly, his head now on a level with their ankles.

'You're welcome, sir,' the messenger's voice floated after him.

What the hell was going on? With Blue back, the Countdown would be stopped at once. Unless there was some other factor he didn't know about. It looked as though he'd come back only just in time.

He'd know soon enough.

At the bottom of the suspensor shaft, the lead corridor to the Situation Room was a bustle of activity as well. Fogarty used his elbows vigorously to push through the throng. Then the door guards spotted him and moved to clear a way. He pushed through the door and took in the scene at a glance. The war preparations had ratcheted up to high gear. Everybody was moving at the double. All three Generals were shouting orders. Every viewglobe in the place was live. Cynthia was reclining near the door issuing instructions to several of her agents.

'Ah, there you are!' she exclaimed as she caught sight of him. She must have been using some sort of suspensor technology on her gown for she floated towards him in the reclining position before rising gracefully to her feet.

Fogarty looked around him. 'What the hell's going on, Cynthia? Hasn't Blue cancelled the Countdown?'

'The Countdown is no longer relevant, dahling. Our friends the Faeries of the Night have launched a pre-emptive strike.' Madame Cardui looked at him soberly. 'I'm afraid the Realm is at war.'

Seventy-six

Hamearis Lucina, the Duke of Burgundy, projected a bluff, down-to-earth demeanour, but he had a romantic streak that showed in his taste in architecture. His keep was a Gothic nightmare, full of gloomy towers and turrets, pointed arches, flying buttresses and a host of gargoyle guards poised to spring down on the unwelcome. The whole structure clung to the edge of a remote, lonely cliff, constantly buffeted by the breakers of an angry sea.

Since a lifetime of military campaigns had collected loot aplenty, alongside several interesting scars, Hamearis could well afford the weather spells he needed to enhance the eerie atmosphere. Where others sought the sunshine, his lavish outlay brought perpetual fogs and rains, with frequent thunderstorms and howling winds.

It all meant his keep was the least visited of all the Great Houses ... and the perfect place to hide a military secret.

Hairstreak's black ouklo followed the cliff road, jerking erratically in the grip of the prevailing wind. His feeling of unease had nothing to do with the storm outside. The Faeries of the Night were united again. The war was under way. Burgundy was a staunch ally once more. In theory everything was going exactly as he'd planned and, with the element of surprise, victory was all but guaranteed.

Yet for all that, he had a feeling in his gut that the situation was somehow slipping away from him. It was a feeling that had been with him since the young Analogue boy had killed his vampire and disappeared with Blue. How had he managed that? There were aspects of the situation Hairstreak didn't understand; and what you didn't understand you couldn't control.

The ouklo pulled into the keep's cobbled courtyard – Hamearis kept horses because a horse had once saved his life and he'd been superstitious about the stupid creatures ever since. Hairstreak waited until his guards arrived to surround the carriage before getting out. He pulled his cloak around him and ran through the freezing rain to the great entrance door where Burgundy was already waiting for him.

'Darkness' sake, Hamearis, don't you ever switch off this bloody weather?' He threw his sodden cloak to a footman.

Hamearis looked at him in genuine surprise, then said, 'Know what, Blackie – I hardly notice it any more.' He placed a friendly hand on Hairstreak's shoulder. 'Come in and we'll dry you off at the fire with a hot toddy before we get down to business. If you send your guards to the kitchens, the girls will entertain them. Last time I looked they had an ordle stew in the cauldron.'

Hairstreak ran his fingers through his hair and scowled when they came away wet. 'I'd as soon we went straight to the tower.'

Hamearis shrugged. 'As you wish.'

The tower was a remnant of the original keep. Some experts believed it dated to the time of the original Purple Palace. It certainly featured the same cyclopean stonework, on a larger scale by far than anything a modern spell could handle. Hairstreak always thought of it as one of those structures that would stand for ever, resisting everything that men and time could throw at it. He sometimes found himself wondering about the forgotten culture that built it. What sort of faerie had they been?

Small ones by the look of it. The only entrance to the tower was through a tiny oak door that gave access to a narrow spiral staircase. He wasn't a particularly tall man himself, but even he found it cramped. Hamearis, who'd gone ahead, had to bend almost double and turn sideways. But at least it kept them safe from attack. An army would have to tackle those steps one man at a time.

He was sweating and his hair had steamed dry by the time they reached the turret room. Despite his discomfort, Hairstreak felt a tingle of anticipation. This was the real nerve centre of the Nighter attack. And what a contrast to the Situation Room beneath the Purple Palace.

Once, years ago, Apatura Iris, the late lamented Purple Emperor, had taken him to see the Situation Room in a misguided attempt at intimidation. Such scurry. Such bustle. So many people ... soldiers on guard, women in uniform, messengers with bits of paper, aides to aides and aides to the aides of aides. There were *three* Generals, who looked old even then, and God alone knows how many wizards. There were viewing globes – scores of them – and cabinets full of elemental engineers. There were signallers and code-breakers, winter-makers and spell-breakers. There was a running armament tally. (What a mistake it had been to let him have sight of that!) There was a strategy table. There were seventeen communications consoles. All this and not even a war on. What folly! What incredible folly, exactly the sort of brute-force overkill the Faeries of the Light had always favoured.

How different to the turret room.

It was pleasingly spartan. It was pleasingly *empty*. There were no guards on the door to constitute a security hazard, no staff to listen in on every decision. None were needed, none were wanted. None could have gained access – the spirit guardians set along that exhausting staircase would strip the meat from the bones of anyone who set foot on it, excepting only Hamearis and himself. Thus Nighter secrets were kept to the Nighters.

But the real joy of the turret room was its equipment. The messengers, the communications consoles, the view globes, the signallers, the code-breakers, the spell-breakers and all the other fractured nonsense were replaced by a single sphere of polished crystal set in an amethyst bowl. Just two spell-driven pieces and they took the place of everything – and everybody – you might find in the Lighters' Situation Room.

The entire war effort of the Faeries of the Night could be controlled, absolutely, by a single man.

Hairstreak pulled up a chair and sat down, placing his hands, palm downwards, on the mount of the amethyst bowl. The moment contact was made, the crystal sphere began to glow, the bowl itself began to hum.

'Access granted,' murmured the bowl in a soft, feminine voice.

Hairstreak glanced up at Hamearis and smiled. The access setting, geared to his personal vibration, was his ultimate security. What political manoeuvring that had taken. But the agreement was in place now. Hairstreak and only Hairstreak could control their forces. Oh, he could delegate, of course – and had delegated to Hamearis and one or two other trusted underlings – but only for a limited time and with the option of his own remote override. He licked his lips and savoured the delicious taste of power.

'Let's see how our attack is going,' he said aloud. 'Sit down, Hamearis, dear fellow – this will take a while.'

The system, linked to the thoughts behind his words, delivered a chair for Hamearis on the other side of the globe and expanded an aerial view of the Yammeth caverns within the globe itself.

It was incredible how much had been done in the short time since he'd inspected the place personally. The vast caverns were packed full now with munitions: crates of concentrated foodstuffs, weaponry, cases of spells, stacked bottles of trapped lightning, lead-lined containers of imps, djinn and other military elementals, engineering equipment, advanced bivouac gear. And beyond it all the patiently waiting troops in their city of tents pitched in neat rows on the cavern floor.

Well, they wouldn't have to wait long. The front line was already pushing forward. These reinforcements would join it at the crucial time. Nothing could stop the Nighters now.

'You know they have spy eyes in the caverns,' Hamearis remarked. 'Seven by our last count.'

'Seven, is it?' That was three more than when he'd personally inspected. Old Cardui's people were getting better. 'All neutralised, I take it?'

'As subtly as you ordered, Blackie.' Hamearis grinned. 'Our magic boys crafted an evolving illusion – nicest one I've ever seen. They knew we were making preparations, all right, but slowly and largely defensive. They had absolutely no idea about our real level of readiness.' The grin broadened to a smile. 'Or our offensive capacity.'

'Nicely done,' Hairstreak murmured. 'Let's see what the opposition is doing,' he told the amethyst bowl.

'Connecting ...' said the bowl.

The crystal globe flared briefly, then presented a scene of the Situation Room itself. Hairstreak felt a glow of pride. The idiots had assumed their Situation Room was impregnable because of the quartz-loaded granite that surrounded it. No spell could penetrate quartz – everyone knew that. And Cardui's people combed the place hourly for smuggled spy eyes. Such foolishness. Someone had remarked to him just the other day that Generals always seemed to fight the last war, not the current one. It was certainly true here. The Faeries of the Light took precautions against anything that had been used against them in the past and never once, in their arrogance, imagined their enemy could develop new approaches to be used in the present.

Hairstreak bent forward. His stealth spy eye showed the Situation Room was busy, but then the Situation Room was always busy so far as he could see. Even when peace reigned supreme, it crawled with activity. But all three Generals were there, as they had to be when they were on a war footing. He concentrated and the globe took him closer to what he wanted to see; and there it was, view globe within view globe. The Lighter troops were engaged and they were losing!

Hairstreak leaned back in his chair. Nothing worried him in what he'd seen. He didn't underestimate the Faeries of the Light. It would be a hard fight but he was certain he could win it. And victory would bring spoils beyond imagining. Victory would give him the Realm.

'Shall we sample our new toy?' he asked Hamearis cheerfully. 'Fully operational, I presume?'

'Oh, yes,' Hamearis confirmed. 'Has been for almost a day.'

Hairstreak murmured a codeword. At once the scene changed in the crystal globe. He was looking down on an area of forest, the same area where he had once built himself a mansion. The place was in ruins now, razed to the ground, with the forest itself already closing in to conceal the remains, like some giant animal healing a wound. But though there was nothing much to see any more, that scarcely mattered. The area was purely a reference point, of no strategic importance. As a reference point, it allowed him to explore ...

Everywhere!

He was finding it difficult to contain his excitement. The technology was not as flashy as the surveillance system around his home – no illusion of flying, no sensation of movement: just a three-dimensional image within the crystal globe – but its extent was breath-taking. Until now, surveillance had always been limited by things like the placement of spy eyes or the establishment of area markers. But this device ... this device gave him the Realm! What was he thinking?

This device gave him the world!

It was as good as he'd dreamed it would be. With a thought, the scene pulled back from the area of his old mansion and suddenly he could see the entire forest. Then the plain surrounding it. Then the mountains beyond and the coastline and the sea. If he'd wished, he could have examined the curvature of the planet. In a godlike vision he could have watched its stately journey round the central sun. But godlike or not, that vision was of little practical importance. He conjured an aerial view of the Lighter capital, followed the river beyond the Loman Bridge and hung for a moment above the Imperial Island.

Then he swooped down to enter the Purple Palace. It was incredible. There were no limitations. He could actually see *inside* the Purple Palace. He could examine corridor after corridor, room after room. No secret in the Realm was safe from him any more. Grinning with delight he watched a kitchen cook drop vegetables into a pot.

What a joy this was going to be when the war was over. He could spy on every enemy, keep record of every subject. He could foil plots before they began, ensure total, absolute obedience from everyone, for ever. This incredible device had placed more power in his hands than any Emperor had ever enjoyed in the entire history of the faerie. Ah, what a time he would have when the war was over.

And before then, how easy it would be to win. This was the ultimate tactical weapon. No enemy troop movement could be hidden from him. There would be no enemy decision to which he was not privy. He could oversee whole battles, place his own forces with unparalleled accuracy. He could craft his victory like an artist.

Hairstreak called up picture after picture in a manic travelogue that took him far beyond the Realm to Haleklind and Borderland and Feltwell Spur and Graphium and Wallach and then back to the Realm itself, where he examined the southern provinces and Yammeth City and the great grain-growing fields to the west, and the swathe of heavy industries and transportation yards to the north and beyond, then eastward from Yammeth Cretch to the desert wastes of –

He froze the picture with a thought and leaned forward. 'What's that, Burgundy?' he asked, his heart suddenly pounding.

Seventy-seven

Henry opened his eyes.

He was in a strange bed in a strange room with a weird ceiling that made it look as if he was outdoors. Soft music was playing somewhere, but there was a funny smell that reminded him of hospitals. Was he in hospital?

He tried to sit up, but the bedclothes were so tightly tucked around him that they held him like straps. He struggled and while they loosened slightly, the effort showed him he was feeling weak. He had to be in hospital. Except it didn't *look* like hospital. There were jars beside his bed full of misty things that writhed and floated, like those novelty aliens they made for little kids.

Maybe the car had knocked him down.

He made another effort to sit up and this time succeeded in loosening the bedclothes. He could remember having to walk home because his rotten mother didn't pick up the phone. He could remember the headlights of a car behind him. After that ... nothing.

There was a dull ache along one side of his nose and a shooting pain into his eye. Maybe he'd fallen down and hit his head.

There was a small mirror on the far wall. He tugged at the bedclothes and finally managed to swing his legs on to the floor. He was wearing some sort of silken gown that left his bottom bare, which meant he had to be in a hospital. But the bed didn't look like a hospital bed and there were no machines or stuff like that in the room.

He walked over to the mirror. There was a bandage running along the side of his nose to the corner of his eye. Otherwise there was no sign of any injury, not even bruising. He was feeling stronger by the minute too. If he *was* knocked down by a car, it hadn't done him much damage.

But where was he?

Underneath the hospital smell there was another smell that seemed strangely familiar. It was almost like the smell of the *Lethe* cones he used on his mother to make her forget when he –

Henry stopped dead in a moment of rising excitement. He couldn't be, could he?

He didn't want to try the door in case he met somebody with his bottom bare, but there was a wardrobe in the room and when he opened it, there were his clothes all freshly washed and neatly pressed and there were other clothes – his size! – like this cool green tunic and that meant he had to be, he just had to be back in the Realm, back in the Purple Palace, although he'd no idea how he got here.

Henry threw away the silken robe and got dressed faster than he'd ever done in his life. Then he threw open the door and stared down the sumptuous corridor and knew, with absolute certainty, he was in the Purple Palace. This was so, so good.

He thought he might see if he could find Blue.

Seventy-eight

'What do we do now?' Pyrgus whispered. He felt really stupid having to admit it in front of Nymph, but he hadn't an idea in his head. He'd been so thoroughly focused on finding the crystal flowers that it never occurred to him they might have been moved.

'I'm not sure,' Nymph whispered back. They were lying side by side in tall grass staring at the remnants of the Ogyris glasshouse. The broken glass and flowers were gone, but the foundation wall and portions of the skeleton structure remained. Their men were sprawled out in various concealments behind them. 'Do you think Mercer Ogyris may have stored them in the house?'

Pyrgus didn't know, but it occurred to him that if Merchant Ogyris *had* taken his flowers into the house, they'd need a lot more men to mount a successful attack. He decided suddenly that while commando raids were fun, he wasn't really cut out to be a military leader. He turned on his side to look at Nymph and opened his mouth to say something when Nymph asked, 'How did you find out about the flowers in the first place, Pyrgus?'

He couldn't have felt more chilled if Hairstreak's whole army had marched over the horizon. To his hideous embarrassment, he felt himself suddenly blush crimson.

'Happened to be visiting the estate,' he muttered. Then added quickly, 'Do you think it would be a good idea to –?'

'Mercer Ogyris is a Faerie of the Night, isn't he?' Nymph interrupted.

'Yes,' Pyrgus said. 'I was just thinking –'

Nymph's face was expressionless. 'Why would a Prince of the Light just happen to be visiting a Nighter estate?' she asked.

Pyrgus gave up his attempt to divert the conversation and went back to muttering. 'Bit of business,' he said. He looked away, unable to hold her eye.

Nymph wouldn't leave it alone. 'With Mercer Ogyris?'

'If is orter,' Pyrgus mumbled into a nearby bush.

'I'm sorry?' Nymph said politely.

'With his daughter,' Pyrgus said, marginally more clearly.

'Oh,' said Nymph, 'Mercer Ogyris has a *daughter*?'

This was turning into a major disaster. First the time flowers were missing and now Nymph was on the point of finding out about Gela. He decided to brazen it out.

'Oh, yes, I believe so. I mean, I know so. Met her. Once or twice. Not often. Plain little thing. Very plain. Quite young. Just a child, really.'

Nymph said, 'And what ... business did you have with this very plain little young child thing?'

'Oh, you know ...' Pyrgus shrugged.

'No, I don't know,' Nymph said coolly. 'Why don't you tell me?'

To Pyrgus's intense relief one of the soldiers wriggled through the grass and came to a halt beside them. He snapped off an awkward salute.

'Channel, sir,' he said.

'Channel?' Pyrgus echoed. It had been fun while it lasted, but he *definitely* wasn't cut out to lead a military operation.

'Yes, sir. Channel, sir,' the soldier repeated. He was a small, wiry man with sunken eyes. He may have seen the blank look on Pyrgus's face, for he added, 'Incoming, sir.'

Nymph must have seen the look as well. She leaned over to whisper in Pyrgus's ear. 'He's a communications medium. There must be a message from the palace. Or possibly my mother. Tell him to go ahead.' She hesitated, then added, 'You call him CC. Official title. Stands for *Communications Channel*.'

'Go ahead, CC,' said Pyrgus briskly.

'Have to sit up, sir – can't do it lying down.'

Pyrgus glanced around. Thanks to the cock-up about the crystal flowers, there wasn't a guard in sight. They'd probably be safe doing a Circle Dance, let alone just sitting up.

'What's your name?'

'Woodfordi, sir.'

'Go ahead, Woodfordi.'

The little CC sat up and crossed an ankle over each thigh in an impossible contortion. He placed his hands palm upwards on his lap and circled his second fingers to touch his thumbs. His eyes squinted alarmingly as he focused on the tip of his nose. He breathed deeply and his eyelids began to droop.

After a moment he trembled, then announced in a

deep, booming voice, 'Military Guide Communications Headquarters here, acting as Spiritual Gatekeeper to this human vessel. Incoming message for His Royal Highness Prince Pyrgus Malvae.'

'Go ahead,' Nymph instructed, apparently giving up on Pyrgus entirely.

The CC trembled again and his features sagged. 'Is that you, deeah?' he asked.

Pyrgus looked at Nymph who nodded encouragingly. 'Yes,' he said uncertainly.

'Have you secured the flowers yet?'

'Actually ...' A pained expression locked itself into Pyrgus's features.

'Never mind that for the moment, deeah,' said Madame Cardui's voice, deepened a little by the CC's vocal cords. 'There's been a small change of plan. Are you alone?'

'Nymph's here,' Pyrgus said. 'And the CC, of course.'

'The CC won't remember anything,' Madame Cardui said. 'I'm glad Nymph's there – how are you, deeah?'

'Fine, thank you, Painted Lady,' Nymph said easily.

Even through the Channel, Madame Cardui's tone turned crisp. 'Now, Pyrgus, the situation has changed since you left the palace. The Faeries of the Night have launched a pre-emptive strike against our forces, and –'

'What!?' Pyrgus exclaimed; and even Nymph looked shocked. 'We're at war? A civil war?'

'Believe me, I was taken as much by surprise as you are, deeah. I'm afraid fighting has already started. It's a tragedy, but now we have to deal with it. What –'

'Where's Blue?' Pyrgus interrupted.

'She's here beside me, deeah. She's safe and completely –'

'I want to talk to her,' Pyrgus said.

Blue's voice came through immediately. She sounded brisk as well. 'Pyrgus, I want you to –'

'How are you?' Pyrgus asked.

'I'm fine,' Blue said. 'Henry was … look, that doesn't matter now: I'll tell you all about it when you get back. I want you to listen to Madame Cardui. We've spotted something that may be important to the war effort.'

War effort, Pyrgus thought. It had happened. The greatest disaster in the history of the Realm and now they summed it up in two words.

'Yes, OK,' he said.

Madame Cardui's voice replaced Blue's. 'I take it you haven't found the flowers?'

'Not really,' Pyrgus admitted, thinking it sounded a little better than *Not at all*.

'That doesn't matter for the moment. This is more important. Do you know how to get to the Eastern Desert?'

'I do,' Nymph whispered.

'Yes,' Pyrgus said loudly, glaring at her: he wasn't a complete idiot.

'How long will it take you to reach it from where you are now?'

Pyrgus frowned. 'Not very long – we've flyers inside the estate and we're right inside Yammeth City. Once we get back to the flyers, it's only fifteen minutes to the wasteland.'

'That's what I thought,' said Madame Cardui. 'You're the closest people we have. Now, this is what I want you to do: fly to the desert at once. You and

Nymphalis and your CC. No one else. This mission is top-secret – above top-secret, really. I'd prefer it was just you and Nymphalis, but you must get word back to me as quickly as possible, so the CC goes too. The rest of your people will just have to find the time flowers on their own – appoint a temporary officer commanding and leave them to it.'

'Madame Car—' Pyrgus began, but Madame Cardui wasn't listening.

'Your triangulation is 38/17/105. Will you remember that?'

'Yes, of –'

'I will, Painted Lady,' Nymph put in, interrupting him.

'Good. Thank you, Nymphalis: it's such a relief to have someone mature and experienced on this mission – I did clear it with your mother, of course.' Even from the CC's mouth it was possible to hear the change of tone as a worried note crept in. 'You can land at that triangulation, deeahs, but I'm afraid you'll have to make the rest of your way on foot. I would have preferred you to stay in the flyer, but the volcanic thermals make it quite impossible for you to travel further by air. But this is a dangerous mission and I want you to be extremely careful.'

'I'll look after him,' Nymph promised, to Pyrgus's fury.

'Thank you, deeah. Now, from your landing coordinates, you should proceed north-east – directly north-east. The good news is it isn't far – an hour's march, two at most, and you may get some help from the nomads, although I wouldn't count on it. The worst will be the hills: there's a range of low, volcanic hills. But once you top that, you should have a clear view of what is happening.'

'But what *is* ha—?' Pyrgus tried to ask.

'I want no heroics, Pyrgus. No guerrilla tactics, nothing like that. In fact, I want you to make sure you aren't even seen. Just use the CC to report back to me at once.'

'What am I reporting *on*?' Pyrgus blurted desperately.

'It looks as if Lord Hairstreak may have found some allies,' said Madame Cardui.

Seventy-nine

Unexpectedly, Madame Cardui stood on tiptoe to kiss him gently on the cheek. 'I need to see you in my office, Alan,' she whispered. 'Door on your right – I'll join you in a moment.'

You learned a little every day, Fogarty thought. An office in the palace upstairs and now an office off the Situation Room. A remarkable woman by any measure. Sometimes he got luckier than he'd any right to ask for. All he needed now was time to enjoy it.

He looked around. Madame Cardui's office was small, but remarkably well-appointed. She had a desk and one of those expensive new-fangled chairs that moulded itself to your bottom and squeezed it every so often to remind you you were still alive. A biological storage unit oozed and bubbled in a cauldron in the corner. A spell-driven food butler stood ready in case she wanted a snack. There was even a reproducing chair for visitors, lurking on the floor ready to clone itself indefinitely depending on how many visitors there were – you could tell its talent from the creepy black material that covered it.

But the thing that caught his attention was the miniaturised view globe sunk into the desk. That was a levitator for sure, hence state-of-the-art. It had to be linked with the view globes in the Situation Room, but there wasn't a wire or cable in sight. Little gizmos like that were always hideously expensive, but the tax-payers were probably paying for it.

He was reaching for the reproducing chair when Madame Cardui bustled in and closed the door carefully. She pressed a thumb on the built-in spell cone and the leathery smell of privacy enchantments filled the room. Well-oiled locks slid into place.

'I thought it best we talk on our own, dahling,' she told him as she walked across the room. 'The Generals are fine men in their way, but you can never be sure how they'll interpret the concept of loyalty. And with so much bustle, you never know who might listen in. Besides, I suspect Hairstreak has a spy eye in there despite our sweeps.'

'Trust nobody,' Fogarty growled. The chair had sensed his singularity and inhibited its tendency to reproduce. He parked his bottom with a scowl. The surface felt dank and unappealing, an effect he suspected was deliberate. Cynthia was exactly like himself. She did nothing to encourage visitors to outstay their welcome. 'What's happening?' he asked.

She walked across the room to take her own seat. 'There's something I want you to look at …' She set both hands on her desk and the globe levitated to eye level. As it began to glow, she said, 'Pull your chair over, Alan: this isn't awfully easy to see, even close up.'

Fogarty set his jaw and pulled the chair across. He leaned forward. A scene began to form as the globe heated and suddenly he was staring into a scorched wasteland of barren rocks and smoky fume.

'You haven't managed to get a spy eye into Hael?' he

asked, using the Realm pronunciation. If she had, he was impressed.

But Madame Cardui was shaking her head. 'No, deeah. That's not Hael. It's a segment of the desert to the east of Yammeth Cretch. Fumaroles ... gas vents ... lava flows ... boiling mud springs – they tell me it's the most volcanically active area on the face of the planet. Nobody lives there except a few nomadic Trinians and even they find life hard going. The Nighters look on it as a protection for that flank of their city – try to march men across that and you'd lose nine-tenths of them before you met a single enemy. But look ...'

After a moment, Fogarty asked, 'What am I looking for?'

Madame Cardui's slim hand floated forward to point. 'See that ridge? There's a break – some sort of opening, quite a large one, deeah, except that it's partly hidden by the dust that's venting. The view varies, but keep your eye on ... *here*, just here. It'll clear in a moment, then you should catch a glimpse ...'

'Can't you get a close-up?' Fogarty asked. 'Zoom the lens or whatever it is you do here?'

Madame Cardui shook her head again. 'We don't actually have a spy eye *in* the desert – there's so much sulphur venting that any moisture turns to acid. The eyes are moist, of course, so it eats through their spell coating in a matter of hours. Simply isn't worth installing them. And for what, usually? A few wandering Trinians? No, the eye you're looking through is on the eastern gate of Yammeth City. It's normally turned on the city itself: there are a few spell factories in that quarter we like to keep an eye on, forgive the bad pun. But one of them blew up last week – some sort of industrial accident involving sprites, I believe. In any case, the energy discharge turned the eye around. No damage, just turned it so it was looking out across the desert. What with everything that's been going on, we didn't get round to sending an agent to correct it. Then earlier today, a monitor noticed this –'

'Noticed what?' Fogarty asked.

'Just keep watching where my – there, see the dust is clearing. Watch there. There's a break in the ridge. When you see it, look *through* it.'

Fogarty watched. The dust plume did seem to be thinning a little, but he still couldn't see the break in the ridge. And then suddenly he could. For scarcely more than a second he was glimpsing what seemed to be a plain covered in black dots. The trouble was, you couldn't work out the perspective. You didn't know if you were looking at ants or armoured cars.

'Did you see that?' Madame Cardui asked.

'Think so. Not sure.'

'What do you think it is?

Fogarty shrugged. 'I don't know. What do *you* think it is?'

'I think it's Beleth,' Madame Cardui said.

Eighty

'Beleth?' Fogarty echoed. 'The King of Hell?'

'Well, technically his title is Prince of Darkness, deeah, but yes, *that* Beleth.'

Fogarty shook his head, frowning. 'The Hell portals are closed.'

'There may be new ones. Blue says the demons have been planning an invasion.'

'How does Blue know what the demons are planning?' Fogarty asked.

Madame Cardui stared at him, then shook her head impatiently. 'I'm sorry, deeah. I forgot you were with the Forest Faerie when Blue came round. Blue was kidnapped by the demons using Henry as their agent.'

'Good God!' Fogarty exclaimed. He did a double take. 'Using *Henry*?'

'They implanted him. We've just had it removed. I'll tell you the whole story when we have more time,' Madame Cardui promised. 'Just now, the important thing is Blue has information about a possible demon invasion. I'm worried this might be it. If Beleth's troops join up with the Faeries of the Night, we're finished.'

'I take your point,' Fogarty said. He leaned forward to peer into the crystal ball again. 'But are you *sure* those dots are demons?'

'No, of course not. That's why I've sent Pyrgus to find out.'

'You sent Pyrgus?'

'Yes.'

Fogarty blinked. 'Bit dangerous if you happen to be right.'

'He was close and I can trust him. This is no time for niceties – we're at war and I need to know what we're facing. Besides, Nymphalis is with him: next to Kitterick I don't know anyone who could protect him better.'

Fogarty tore his eyes away from the scene in the globe. 'Does Blue know?'

Madame Cardui withdrew her hands and the globe sank back down into the recess in her desk. 'About Pyrgus? Yes, she was with me when I sent him.'

'Where is Blue anyway? Shouldn't the Queen be running her own war?'

'She certainly agrees with you on that,' Madame Cardui said. 'She was in the Situation Room until she came close to collapse. I finally bullied her into taking a rest – she's still recovering from the effects of demon poisoning. But I expect she'll be back before long.'

'But she knows about these demons, does she?' Fogarty waved his hand towards the globe.

'Assuming they really *are* the demons,' Madame Cardui sighed, 'and not a figment of an old woman's imagination. No, she doesn't and I don't plan to worry her until we know for sure.'

'Maybe we –' Fogarty began, but was interrupted by a thunderous knocking at the door.

'Oh, dear, what *now*?' Madame Cardui sighed. She walked across and thumbed the security lock.

A florid-faced General Creerful was standing with his hand raised to knock again. He ignored Madame Cardui completely.

'Gatekeeper, Lord Hairstreak's at the palace gates. He demands to see Queen Blue.'

Eighty-one

The heat hit him like a wall. Then came the smell. 'Whooo!' Pyrgus exclaimed, and began to cough helplessly as some acrid fume caught in the back of his throat. Nymph, who was hard on his heels, began to cough too. Only Woodfordi, bringing up the rear, seemed unaffected.

Pyrgus looked around, still coughing. This was his first visit to the Eastern Desert and, if he had anything to do with it, it would be his last. He'd heard about this area, but nothing prepared him for the reality. A barren, rocky pavement stretched as far as the eye could see, broken at intervals by plumes of smoke and dust. A criss-cross of cracks glowed dull red from the lava flows beneath, casting a peculiar glow across the entire scene. Not a hundred yards from where they landed, he could see a softly bubbling mud lake.

Woodfordi handed him a flask. 'Try this, sir, begging your pardon, sir. And the lady too.'

'What is it?' Pyrgus asked between coughs.

'Little something for the throat. Army issue. They tell you it lines the passages and prevents permanent damage. Don't know about that, sir, but it does help.'

Pyrgus took a brief swallow and handed the flask to Nymph. The liquid was viscous and tasted foul, but his

coughing eased at once. He turned to lock the flyer –
no sense in taking unnecessary chances – then said,
'North-east, wasn't it?' He glanced up at the sky.

Woodfordi smiled slightly. "Fraid I don't remember,
sir. Part of the training.'

Nymph confirmed, 'Yes, north-east.'

'I'll lead the way,' said Pyrgus and strode off.

It proved heavy going, even on the flat, and after half
an hour he began to wonder about Madame Cardui's
estimate of their timing. The trouble was the fumes.
Although Woodfordi's liquid stopped the coughing,
there was no way of avoiding noxious gases getting
into your lungs. He'd read somewhere that if you
stayed a little too long in this wasteland you started to
hallucinate. (And if you stayed a lot too long, you
died.) But even before that happened, the desert sapped
your strength.

The irritating thing was that neither Nymph nor the
little soldier Woodfordi seemed to be as badly affected
as he was, so he had to push himself to the limit to keep
up the stupid pace he'd set. The two of them walked
after him easily. They even had breath for a chatty
conversation.

'How did you get to be a CC?' Nymph asked.

'Born to it, I think, Miss,' Woodfordi told her.
'Parents found me chatting to my nan when I was a
kid. Only trouble was the old girl died before I was
born. Well, they didn't know what to do with that, did
they? Simple people, my folks – Dad worked on an
ordle farm, Light rest him. So they sent me off to a
special school: I think they were a bit scared, to tell the
truth.'

'Was this some sort of training school?'

'Not really, Miss. But one of the teachers realised what I was and raised enough funds to get me a year in the Psychic's Academy – you know, the one off Flannelmaker's Square. That's where the military found me. Only way a titch like me could get into the army. My wife says I need to stand on a box to kiss her anywhere above the knee. So you couldn't imagine me in combat, could you?'

'Can you still talk to dead people?' Nymph asked curiously; and Pyrgus's ears pricked up, even though he was pretending not to listen.

'Heavens no, Miss. Army knocked that out of me. No use to them, see? Troops would waste their time chatting to their fallen comrades. They trained me to contact the Military Guide instead – some sort of angel, I think he is, although you'd never believe it when you hear him swear – and he showed me how to do the messages. Receiving was easy, right from the start, but sending's a bit tricky until you get the hang of it.'

'Can you send a message to anybody?'

Woodfordi shook his head. 'Oh, no, Miss – only another channel. We make up a sort of network, you might say. When the Painted Lady called you before, she was talking in the ear of a mate of mine called Weiskei.'

Pyrgus stopped dead. They had entered a boulder-strewn area and he was certain there was something moving behind a rock.

'Quiet!' he hissed.

Nymph responded at once and unslung her bow. Pyrgus pointed silently to the rock and she began to circle behind it. As much for a diversion as anything else, Pyrgus said, 'Better take cover, Mr Woodfordi.'

'Sir!' Woodfordi acknowledged briskly.

Then Pyrgus abruptly realised Nymph might be moving into danger and started to run towards the rock, reaching for his trusted Halek knife.

And then suddenly, incredibly, they were surrounded.

Eighty-two

Blue woke with a start. For just the barest moment she didn't know where she was, then saw she was in her Imperial Quarters, in a comfortable chair where she must have fallen asleep. How long ago? Minutes? Hours?

She felt better. Various pains had drained from her body, leaving only a residue of stiffness, and her mind was a great deal clearer. She started to push herself out of the chair when the memory flooded back. The war. She'd be needed in the Situation Room.

Then as the knocking came again she realised what had wakened her. 'Come!' she called and her voice pattern released the spell securities.

It was Gatekeeper Fogarty, along with Madame Cynthia and –

'What's *he* doing here?' Blue demanded. Her heart was pounding suddenly. For a mad moment she thought he might be a prisoner of war.

'My deeah,' said Madame Cynthia cautiously. 'Your uncle has something to say to you.'

Lord Hairstreak was already striding forward, arrogant as always, dressed in his favoured black. 'Your Majesty –' he began formally.

What in Hael was he doing here? No guards. No

uniform. He might have been on a social visit.

'I'm here to offer an immediate truce,' he said.

Blue stared at him, certain she'd misheard. Nobody would offer a truce so soon. It had to be a trick.

'Why?' she asked him simply.

Hairstreak's face remained unreadable. 'Because,' he said, 'if we do not cease fighting at once, the Realm is doomed.'

Eighty-three

Pyrgus slid his knife slowly back into its sheath. From the corner of his eye, he could see Nymph carefully setting her bow and arrows on the ground. Then she stood up and raised both hands to show they were empty. A little to his right, Woodfordi had ignored the order to take cover and was standing with his empty hands exposed as well.

'We come in peace,' said Pyrgus, feeling stupid.

There were maybe twenty-five nomadic Trinians in plain sight and Light alone knows how many more still hidden in the rocks. They were wearing only loincloths on account of the heat and all three Trinian types were represented. Violets predominated as you'd expect in a hostile environment, but there was a goodly scattering of orange and even one or two green. None of them was armed. They didn't need to be – all three breeds were toxic. A Trinian bite was almost always fatal and even a venom spit – which travelled several yards – could incapacitate you for months. Pyrgus noted with relief that the leader – you could tell he was a leader from the feathers – was orange.

'Ayre ning?' the leader asked solemnly. His face was striped with white and purple paint.

Pyrgus looked at him blankly. Trinians – even

nomadic Trinians – were supposed to speak Faerie Standard and perhaps this one did, but his accent was so thick it might as well have been the click-speech of High Halek.

Nymph said, 'North-east, Plainsman,' and pointed. *Plainsman* was an honorific, roughly equivalent to saying *sir*.

'Ou eek our yolader?' asked the Trinian chief.

'Yes,' Nymph told him promptly. She gestured. 'Pyrgus.' Then, pointing to the third member of their party, added, 'Woodfordi.'

The Trinian struck himself forcibly on the chest. 'Nagel!' he said explosively and coughed.

It was clearly introduction time. 'We come in peace,' Pyrgus said again, rather feebly.

One of the greens pushed forward, accompanied by the strangest little animal Pyrgus had ever seen. It was short and squat, hairless and wrinkled, much like its master. The Trinian launched into what sounded like a stream of invective, the content of which Pyrgus couldn't even guess at. It had a galvanising effect on the rest of the tribe, who advanced muttering, and on the leader, who began to wave his arms about.

'What's going on?' he asked Nymph helplessly.

Nymph smiled a little. 'It's all right,' she said. 'He just wants to marry me.'

For an instant Pyrgus thought he'd misheard. 'He wants to *what*?'

'He wants to marry me,' Nymph repeated. 'He says he'll give you forty placks.'

'He can't –' Pyrgus began, then asked, 'What's a plack?'

'That little creature he has with him. He makes

them. He's the tribe's witch doctor.' Nymph's smile broadened. 'It's a terribly good price for a wife. I think I'm flattered.'

'But he can't marry you!' Pyrgus protested. 'I won't have it!'

'You'd better tell him,' Nymph said blandly. 'Just speak slowly and pronounce your words carefully.'

'You can't marry –' Pyrgus shouted at the witch doctor, then aside to Nymph, 'What's his name?'

'Innatus, I think.'

'Now listen, Innatus,' Pyrgus began again. 'There's absolutely no way I'm going to let you –'

'Best not to threaten,' Nymph put in quietly. 'He carries a lot of weight.'

But Pyrgus was already losing it, '– marry this girl, and if you so much as lay one of your ugly little fingers –' he drew his Halek blade again to a chorus of '*Oooh*'s and wide grins from the surrounding Trinians, '– on a single hair of her –'

Nagel's voice cut across him, talking not to Pyrgus, but Innatus.

'Oh, how sweet,' said Nymph. 'He wants to marry me as well.'

'Is he out of his –?'

Woodfordi touched Pyrgus's elbow. 'Beg pardon, sir, but I'd suggest you give her to the chief. Army policy in situations like this. Always give the girl to the most important man in the tribe. Witch doctor's a big noise, OK, but the orange one with feathers and stripes is definitely the Chief.'

'Are you out of your –?'

Woodfordi backed off, hands raised. 'Just telling you the army way, sir.'

Nymph said, 'Forty placks, seven bales of ordle and a full service contract.'

'What in the name of Light are you talking about?' Pyrgus exploded.

'That's what Nagel's offering,' Nymph said. 'You can tell he's an orange Trinian, can't you? A full service contract! A Violet would just kill you.'

Pyrgus's panic-stricken gaze jumped from one Trinian to the other. 'You can't marry this girl!' he shouted desperately. 'Neither of you! Because ... because ...' He looked around for inspiration. This whole thing was insane. 'Because she's engaged to marry me!' he screamed at last.

'Oooh!' exclaimed Nymph, and moved over to stand beside Pyrgus, her chest pushed proudly forward. She was grinning broadly.

Pyrgus still had the Halek blade in his hand, but to his astonishment, the crisis defused at once. Innatus turned and walked away, the funny little plack creature at his heels. Nagel simply shrugged, as if the matter was of no importance. He murmured something to Nymph, who said, 'Yes.'

'What's he saying? What's he saying?' Pyrgus demanded.

'He says we can't go north-east,' Nymph told him.

Pyrgus bristled again. 'Who does he think's going to stop us? A pack of lunatic dwarves who want to marry everything in sight? You just tell him –'

'He's not trying to stop us, Pyrgus,' Nymph told him patiently. 'We can't go north-east because there's a magma flow blocking our way.'

'Oh,' said Pyrgus, deflated. He had a feeling he'd made a complete fool of himself and not just about travelling north-east. As leader of the little party, events seemed to have slipped away from him entirely. 'What are we going to do?' he asked Nymph.

'It's all right,' Nymph said cheerfully. 'He's offered to show us a way round.'

Travelling with the Trinians proved very different to travelling alone, and Pyrgus quickly found that in this territory the shortest distance between two points was not always a straight line. The dwarves constantly skirted areas that looked perfectly safe to him. Conversely, on two memorable occasions, they led the way through mud and lava pools he would never have dared to tackle on his own.

They were right about the magma flow as well. Before cutting temporarily southwards, he caught a glimpse of it in the distance, a simmering, crimson river that absolutely defied passage by anyone.

At one point in their eccentric progress, Woodfordi, who seemed to understand the Trinians almost as easily as Nymph, whispered in Pyrgus's ear, 'There's talk of enemies ahead, sir.'

'What sort of enemies?' Pyrgus whispered back.

'Search me, sir – I just caught a snatch of conversation.'

'Keep your ears open,' Pyrgus ordered. 'And report back anything you hear.'

But it turned out there was no need. Only moments later Nymph appeared at his elbow. 'Nagel says we must proceed with caution – there are enemies ahead.'

'Who?' asked Pyrgus quickly.

'Somebody they call the *Fluid Dark*. I've never heard of them before – have you?'

Pyrgus shook his head. 'Probably another tribal grouping. Not our fight. Unless we get caught up in it.'

'I don't think Nagel's planning to fight – he's hoping to avoid one. He wants us to keep low, keep under cover and keep still whenever he gives the signal.'

'Suits me,' Pyrgus said.

The order to keep low and keep still came nearly fifteen minutes later. Pyrgus found himself crouched behind a rock with Nymph. He peered cautiously around, but could see nothing of the Fluid Dark. All the same, every Trinian seemed to have vanished. The way they blended with this countryside was uncanny. He wondered suddenly how they lived here. Since he stepped into the wasteland he'd not seen a single plant; nor animal, come to that, except for the thing Innatus was supposed to have made.

Nymph said casually, 'Did you mean it?'

'Mean what?' Pyrgus asked.

Nymph said soberly, 'That we were engaged to be married.'

Pyrgus felt a flaring of emotions, not least of them panic. 'I, ah – I, ah – I, ah …' he said.

'Oh, I know you only said it to save me from Nagel and Innatus, and that was very chivalrous of you.' She hesitated. 'But I was wondering …'

'You were wondering?' Pyrgus echoed.

Nymph nodded. 'Yes, I was.' She held his eye.

When he realised she wasn't going to say anything else, Pyrgus said, 'I, ah …' He licked his lips and then surprised himself. 'I'd … like to.' He grinned sheepishly and felt like an idiot and didn't care. If this went any further, Blue would kill him. His grin widened. He still didn't care.

'What about Gela?' Nymph asked him.

Pyrgus's grin disappeared. She already knew about Gela, so denial wasn't possible. He sorted quickly through a hundred lies, then heard his mouth say something that was very nearly true. 'Nothing happened.'

'But you were attracted?'

'Yes, but nothing happened.'

'So you didn't ...?'

'Oh, no. Oh, no, definitely not.' Then, because truth between them was suddenly important, he said, 'Well, I kissed her once, sort of, and she ...'

The ghost of a smile was playing across Nymph's lips. 'Kissed you back?'

'Punched me on the nose,' said Pyrgus; and this time they both laughed out loud.

Eighty-four

They were hand in hand as they crept to the top of the rise to spy out what the Trinians called the Fluid Dark.

Pyrgus froze. Beneath them, stretched for miles across the desert plain, were Beleth's demon legions. They stood waiting with inhuman patience, armed and armoured. Hell hounds crouched by every foot. Lines of giant transport beetles carried heavy armaments. A city of tents provided shelter.

The red reflection of the magma flows on metal surfaces made it look as if they'd never left their native Hael.

Eighty-five

Blue asked, 'Do you trust him?'

Fogarty shook his head. 'Hairstreak? Of course I don't trust him.'

Madame Cardui said, 'Except he's telling the truth about Beleth's legions. They've already entered the Realm.'

Blue stared at her in surprise. 'Why didn't I know about this?'

Madame Cardui said mildly, 'Pyrgus only called in and confirmed it a few minutes ago. After Lord Hairstreak arrived. From his description, it's not just a few demons. It sounds like the entire demon army – a much stronger attack force than anything they've ever mustered here before. With that amount of help from Beleth, the Faeries of the Night will win the war. Probably within weeks.'

Blue felt the entire weight of her office pressing down on her. This was a mess. It was getting worse. And a small voice deep inside her kept insisting it was all her fault. If she hadn't put a Countdown in place, her uncle might not have ordered the Nighters to attack. But if she hadn't gone to see her uncle in the first place, the demons might not have had a chance to kidnap her and she wouldn't have learned about their plans.

Except she didn't know enough about their plans. She couldn't remember Henry saying anything about whether Beleth's plans involved the Faeries of the Night. Or when he planned to attack. She needed Henry here to make it clear, if he could. In the meantime ...

'You don't believe Lord Hairstreak then?'

Madame Cardui sighed, shook her head, then shrugged. 'I simply don't know. None of this is making much sense. The Nighters have been allied with Hael for generations. Why should it be any different now?'

'Why would Hairstreak *claim* it's different now?' Gatekeeper Fogarty put in. 'He says the demon invasion has nothing to do with him or any of the Nighters.'

'My deeah, I would not believe a thing Lord Hairstreak said if he swore it on his mother's grave.'

'Neither would I normally,' Fogarty agreed. 'But that man is frightened and I've never seen him frightened before. You heard what he said. He doesn't just want peace between the Lighters and Nighters – he's asked for an alliance against Beleth. He's never done that before.'

'Or ever needed to,' Blue mused thoughtfully. She looked at Madame Cardui. 'Get Henry here.'

'Henry, deeah?'

A horrifying thought leaped into Blue's mind. 'You have released him, haven't you? He's not still under sentence of death?'

'No, of course not, deeah. He's in the infirmary recovering from his little operation.'

'Then bring him here now, Cynthia,' Blue hissed impatiently. 'He's the one who can tell us if this offer's genuine. He'll know exactly what the demons are planning – he was linked to the Haelmind.'

'What's the Hellmind?' Fogarty asked.

Blue ignored him. She was still looking at Madame Cardui. 'What's wrong?'

'I'm afraid Henry will be under sedation.'

Much as she loved Madame Cardui, Blue could have killed her. But murder was a luxury she couldn't afford at that moment. 'When will he wake up?'

'Probably not soon enough,' said Madame Cardui. 'It may be that we're going to have to make this decision without him.'

Blue fought hard to get her anger under control. 'Very well. Send somebody to check. In the meantime, what's your opinion?'

'Beleth's forces are massed in the Eastern Desert,' Madame Cardui said. 'Exactly where they need to be to aid Yammeth Cretch.'

'Or invade it,' Fogarty pointed out. He parked his backside on the arm of a chair and said, 'Let's just look at what we've got, see if that makes it any clearer. OK with you, Blue?'

Blue nodded.

Fogarty began to tick points on his fingers. 'First, Beleth's army is camped in the Eastern Desert. His whole army; a massive attack force.'

'Yes.'

'Lord Hairstreak says this has nothing to do with him. He didn't call on Beleth, he didn't ask for Beleth's help, he didn't know the Hael portals had reopened. When he found out the demons were there ... what? ... he decided Beleth was about to attack him and came here to ask for our help? That doesn't make sense.'

'Which is what I said, deeah. Surely if your old ally turns up again, you race out to welcome him with open arms? Why did His Lordship not do that?'

'Is Hairstreak still in the palace?'

Madame Cardui nodded. 'Refused to leave, even after Blue dismissed him. He's in an antechamber now, hoping we will talk to him again.'

Fogarty said, 'Then let's ask him.'

Hairstreak, when he entered, looked as if he hadn't slept for months, but he still managed to retain his composure.

'Have you seen sense yet?' he snapped at Blue.

Fogarty cut across him. 'When you discovered Beleth had arrived, why didn't you send someone to meet him?' he asked bluntly. 'He's your old ally, after all.'

Hairstreak gave a small, cold smile. 'Oh, I did. Of course I did. I assumed he was here to help our cause – the Nighter cause, that is. So I sent Burgundy to greet him, escort the demons into Yammeth City.' The smile turned into a chill, hollow laugh. 'It seemed like an extraordinary piece of luck.'

After a moment, Madame Cardui said, 'And what happened?'

Hairstreak looked her directly in the eye. 'He sent me back Burgundy's head in a sack.'

Eighty-six

It was strange, Blue thought: Hairstreak suddenly looked small. He was still the same man, but he seemed strangely shrunken, as if life was leaking out of him like a punctured balloon. As Mr Fogarty said, there was fear in his eyes. She'd never seen her uncle afraid before.

Madame Cardui said, 'They have not attacked Yammeth City ...?' She was speaking of Beleth's demon hordes. It was half musing, half a question.

'Not yet,' Hairstreak said.

'Or anywhere else in the Cretch?'

Hairstreak shook his head. He was answering Cynthia, but his eyes were on Blue.

Blue said nothing, watching and waiting. She was hoping against hope something would come out of the discussion that would clear her mind. But all she could think of was that here they were, holding a strategy conference with her *uncle*. Even as a child she'd been taught to think of him as her *wicked* uncle, like a character in a mythic tale. Now, suddenly, he wasn't the enemy any more and nor were the Faeries of the Night. Or so it seemed.

'Why do you think that is?' Madame Cardui asked. 'It seems he has his forces well in place. No more than an hour's march from your city walls from what I understand.'

'And why did he tip his hand by killing Burgundy?' Fogarty put in. 'Why not just accept your invitation, bring his whole army in from the cold and then attack you by surprise from inside your defences? That's what I'd have done.'

Hairstreak shrugged. 'Perhaps he is waiting for you to do his dirty work.'

Fogarty leaned forward. 'Assuming I believe you, why should he turn against his old friends? Faeries of the Night and Hell have been pals for centuries. Beleth has provided you with demon servants, demon labour, God knows what else, in return for ...' He trailed off, suddenly unsure.

'Not quite an accurate assessment, Gatekeeper Fogarty,' Hairstreak said coldly. 'Beleth never willingly *gave* us anything. Generations ago, our wizards developed techniques for *compelling* demons into certain pacts. The filth have been our servants ever since. Faeries of the Light could have had the same benefits, but they elected not to do so out of some ... misplaced sense of morality, I suppose. I've never understood the thinking myself.' He turned his attention back to Blue. 'I'm no historian, but I understand it was the demon question that caused the split between us in the first place.'

'I don't suppose you can *compel* them now?' Blue asked suddenly.

Hairstreak smiled coldly. 'There are more than a million demons in the Eastern Desert. That is a number well beyond compulsion.'

'So you think this is his revenge for centuries of

exploitation?' There was a wicked glint in Fogarty's eye.

If her uncle had a sense of humour, it didn't show. 'Oh, I don't think it's us he's after,' he said soberly.

'Very well,' said Fogarty briskly. 'What *do* you think he's planning?'

Hairstreak looked from one to the other. 'I think he was waiting for war to break out between the Faeries of the Night and the Light.'

'Which it has,' Blue put in. 'Thanks to your pre-emptive strike.'

Hairstreak's eyes flashed. 'I was not the one to instigate a Countdown, niece.'

Madame Cardui said smoothly, 'Perhaps we should allow your uncle to continue, Majesty. After all, he has more experience of demons than we have.' She glanced at Hairstreak and smiled sweetly.

'Go on, Uncle,' Blue said shortly. 'Beleth's plans …?'

Hairstreak said, 'I do not believe he will intervene in the war. I think it is completely irrelevant to him who wins it. When the war is finished, he will attack the victor, confident in the knowledge that the victor has been weakened by the conflict. In that way, Beleth plans to take the entire Realm.'

It sounded hideously plausible. But then many of Hairstreak's most devious schemes had seemed hideously plausible too. Blue still wasn't sure she trusted him.

'How do you think we can stop him?'

Hairstreak shrugged. 'You know my proposal. An immediate military alliance between the Nighters and the Lighters. Our combined forces can then attack Beleth in the desert and, hopefully, drive him back to

Hael where he belongs.'

Gatekeeper Fogarty suddenly asked, 'Why don't you use your time flowers against him?'

'What time flowers?' Hairstreak asked.

Eighty-seven

'Do you believe him?' Gatekeeper Fogarty asked as soon as they were alone.

'I don't know,' Blue said. 'I wish Flapwazzle was here.' A thought struck her and she asked, 'Where is he? Did he get away from Lord Hairstreak?'

Madame Cardui nodded. 'Came back safely, then went out hunting. They do that when they're tense. I think the business with Henry and the vampire unnerved him. He's terribly fond of Henry.'

'Light's sake, isn't Henry awake yet?' Blue demanded.

'Soon, deeah, I promise.'

Gatekeeper Fogarty said impatiently. 'We can check with Henry later. In the meantime, do we believe Hairstreak?' He looked from one face to the other.

Madame Cardui said slowly, 'I suspect I do.'

They turned to look at her. 'Including the bit about the time flowers?' Fogarty asked.

'I'm not sure about that, Alan. But I suppose what he says *could* be true. Pyrgus had his information from Ogyris's daughter, who's scarcely more than a child – not the most reliable of sources. Perhaps Merchant Ogyris was growing the flowers for his own use. Perhaps he planned to sell them to the highest bidder.'

'Perhaps the highest bidder was Beleth,' Blue suggested. In the present situation, almost anything seemed possible.

Fogarty blinked. 'Henry used a time flower to kidnap Blue. We assumed he had it from Lord Hairstreak, but we know now that Henry was working for the demons. He had to have it from them, which means Ogyris *was* supplying Beleth.'

Madame Cardui shuddered. 'If that's the case, we are all lost.'

Blue said, 'This is ridiculous. We need Henry. How can I be expected to decide something like this when he can tell us the answer? I'm going to the infirmary myself to see if his sedation has worn off. If it hasn't, I'll order the wizards to wake him.'

'We'll go with you,' Fogarty said hurriedly.

They found Henry wandering the corridors outside the infirmary. He had a bandage on his nose and a vacant expression on his face. He smiled shyly when he saw Blue.

It took them less than a minute to discover he had no memory of anything that had happened to him after the demons inserted their implant.

Blue sighed deeply. 'Tell my uncle he's going to have to wait until tomorrow for his answer. I think we need to sleep on it.'

Eighty-eight

Hairstreak left the palace in a fury. How dare that stupid child treat him in this manner! How dare she refuse to listen when the future of the Realm was at stake! Time was running out – couldn't she see that? The demons might attack at any time, perhaps in an hour, perhaps tonight. Yet he was supposed to wait another day before he could act – or however long it took the brat to make up her mind. No wonder the Empire was in such a mess. No wonder Beleth had decided to seize his opportunity.

The thought of Beleth increased his anger. The treachery of the creature was almost beyond belief. Except that he should have anticipated it. You could never trust a demon. But self-recriminations were pointless. The question was, what to do now?

His escort fell in around him as he left the Purple Palace. Hairstreak was under no illusions: the situation was grim, far more grim than young Queen Blue realised. The trouble was, Lighters never appreciated the truth about demons. Demons were dangerous. You could never afford to forget they had their own agenda. Which was exactly what he'd done himself. It was going to take some very fancy footwork to avoid paying dearly for that small mistake.

He ordered his transport to be flown directly to the caverns – the western entrance was just big enough for him to land. If anything resembled a stroke of luck in the present sorry circumstances, it was the fact that Hamearis was now dead. Not that Hairstreak wouldn't miss him – they'd been through a lot together – but with Burgundy out of the way, Hairstreak was now unequivocally in charge of the entire Nighter military effort. No one would question his decisions. Or his orders.

He left the flyer and strode out on to the main cavern floor. The Nighter reinforcements were stretched before him, waiting as patiently as the demons in the desert. There was much less of a bustle than the last time he'd been here. All the preparations had been made, all supplies and armaments laid in and readied. It was an army awaiting final orders, as close to action as a drawn bow. The question was, what order to give.

So far, Hairstreak had held this vast army in reserve. But he would have to commit it soon. He was furious with Blue. If she'd only understood the urgency of the situation, his decision was made. An alliance against the demons was the only sensible course. Everything else was madness. Yet that madness might be forced on him. Could he afford to wait until tomorrow? And what if Blue decided to reject a treat? Should he throw the rest of his forces against the Faeries of the Light? Or should he turn them first on Beleth's legions?

There were close on a million demons waiting in the desert. The creatures had no fear of death. Once they marched, they were relentless as ants. They kept coming, wave after wave, however many you killed. More to the point, if Beleth had managed to portal in an entire army, he could portal reinforcements if the need arose. There were an awful lot of demons in Hael. Another million fighting demons would be nothing to him, or another two, or three or even ten. The possibilities were too hideous to contemplate. The only hope would be to score a fast, decisive victory, then *close the portals* before Beleth could react. Close them, sabotage them, keep them closed. For ever, if possible. The Nighters could do without their demon servants. The price had just grown too high to pay.

The other obvious approach was to throw his entire might against Blue herself, hope to score a quick victory there before Beleth moved. But what were the chances of that? He was fairly sure he could overrun the Faeries of the Light eventually. But soon ...? Unlikely. And even if it only took him days, there was no guarantee Beleth would not attack at once.

General Procles, the senior field commander, had already emerged to greet him, flanked by three of his aides. Hairstreak waited until he was within earshot, then called out, 'Send your men away, Graphium – this is private.' He dismissed his own people with a casual wave.

Procles was a tall, thin man, slightly stooped for a soldier. There was a deferential air about him that belied a steely character beneath.

'I take it the mission was unsuccessful, Lordship?' he said promptly.

Hairstreak shrugged. 'My niece will not give her decision before tomorrow. Perhaps not even then.'

'Will she stand down her forces in the interim?'

Hairstreak shook his head.

'Do we know why?' He was a shrewd General.

His question really meant, *Is there room for compromise or negotiation?*

'She does not trust us.' Hairstreak sighed. 'Perhaps we have given her some cause.'

Typically, Procles let it go. 'Do you have a contingency plan? In the event of her refusal?'

Hairstreak sighed again, more deeply this time. 'A desperate one, Graphium. That's why I sent our people away. I want you to hear what I have in mind and I want your opinion. Then, unless you can convince me there is another, better way, I want you to take immediate action. Immediate,' he stressed. 'I cannot say how much time we have, so speed is essential.'

Procles nodded gravely. 'I understand, Lordship.'

Hairstreak held his eye. 'This is how I analyse the situation. If we are overthrown by the Faeries of the Light, that will be a tragedy. If we are overthrown by Beleth, that will be the greatest disaster in the history of the Realm. Neither ourselves nor the Lighters would ever recover. Our world would become a slave state with the demons as our masters. Do you concur so far?'

Procles nodded again. 'Yes. *If* we are overthrown.'

Hairstreak said, 'Clearly, we will endeavour to secure ourselves against either eventuality. We may even succeed, but I doubt it. I believe we might defeat Beleth or we might defeat Blue, but we will not defeat both. Anyone who thinks so is a fool.' He stared at Procles, who shrugged slightly. Hairstreak went on, 'It is my conclusion that, in such circumstances, we must ensure the defeat of Beleth as our absolute priority. Do you concur?'

'Of course. This is precisely why you have offered an alliance to the Queen.'

Hairstreak said. 'She may easily refuse it. Blue is obsessed with fighting us. She does not – *will* not – see the greater threat. And it may be too late by the time she comes to her senses. Let me speak frankly with you, Procles ...'

'Of course,' Procles murmured.

'Our pre-emptive strike has not been as successful as I anticipated. The Faeries of the Light are now counterattacking Yammeth Cretch. Our troops are holding them at the moment, but if Beleth moves, we are lost. Thus –' he took a deep breath, '– it is my conclusion that we must throw every available man into a massive attack on Beleth's forces in the desert. Not merely the reserve troops here, but our forces presently engaged with the Faeries of the Light.'

'Even though the Queen has not agreed a ceasefire?'

'Yes.'

Procles looked stunned. 'You're prepared to leave the Cretch and city undefended?'

Hairstreak nodded sourly. 'Effectively, yes.' He shrugged. 'Oh, we can deploy a few militias of men who are too old or too ill to take part in the main offensive. They may delay the Lighters a little, but frankly I am prepared to sacrifice the entire Cretch – should it come to that – for the sake of a quick victory over Beleth.' He hesitated. 'But there is one more thing ...'

Procles waited.

Hairstreak said, 'Not all Nighters live within the Cretch. Simultaneous with our attack on Beleth there must be an immediate uprising by every loyal Faerie of the Night throughout the Realm. We can set the Realm alight within hours and with luck this may keep the Lighters occupied just long enough for us to dispatch

Beleth. If that happens and if we can close down the portals again and if we don't lose too many men in the process, we may then turn our attention to the problem of Queen Blue. Possibly we may have enough strength to depose her, if we cannot defeat the Faeries of the Light completely.' He stared at Procles. 'I would appreciate your comments.'

'There are a great many *if*s in your plan, Lordship.'

'Do you have a better one?'

Procles shook his head. 'No, Lordship.'

'Then set the contingency in place. Our commanders are to act on it as soon as they are able. Preferably tonight.' Hairstreak turned on his heel and strode back to his flyer. As he climbed aboard, he added half to himself, 'And pray to Darkness this is the right decision.'

Eighty-nine

Pyrgus stopped, locked by a weird, almost over-powering sensation of unease.

'What's the matter?' Nymph asked at once.

'Something's wrong,' Pyrgus said. By his reckoning they were very close to where they'd left the flyer, so close all he'd been thinking about was getting back. But now ...

He looked around. The Trinians, who'd been escorting them cheerfully until now, had disappeared. The desert stretched endlessly behind them, rocky, desolate and bare.

'Nagel ...?' he called out urgently.

The orange dwarf materialised at once from behind a rock. 'Eeper dahn!' he hissed, glaring.

Pyrgus looked at Nymph.

'He wants you to be quiet,' she told him.

'Ask him what's going on. There's something wrong.'

Nymph started to speak, but before she could utter a word, Nagel put a finger to his lips, caught her by the hand and led her crouching up a rocky outcrop. Pyrgus stared after them for half a second, then followed.

It was almost a repeat of what had happened when they topped the rise and saw the Hael legions camped in the deep desert. Following on Nagel's urgent signs, they raised their heads carefully.

A small contingent of men wearing the grey-black uniform of the elite Nighter Scout Regiment was moving grimly across the desert in the direction of Beleth's waiting legions.

'God of Light,' groaned Pyrgus. 'Those are messengers. Hairstreak's joining up with Beleth. He has to be. We'll be facing them both now.' He looked around for Woodfordi. The palace needed to know about this new development at once.

Nagel said something in a whisper.

'We must pull back from this position,' Nymph translated. 'There may be more following. If we stay here we'll be discovered.'

The Trinian was already on his way to lower ground. Pyrgus and Nymph scrambled after him. For a frustrating fifty minutes they followed the Trinian tribe, moving silently from cover to cover, until Nagel called a halt in a shallow crater ringed by a sulphurous fumarole fog.

'He says we're safe here,' Nymph explained.

Pyrgus's nose wrinkled. 'I can see why.' To Woodfordi he said, 'Can you talk to my sister – Queen Blue? Can you talk to her directly?'

Woodfordi shook his head. 'Doubt it, sir. Her Majesty doesn't usually have a CC handy. Word is she doesn't hold with us for some reason, sir.'

'OK, put me through to Madame Cardui again. She can relay the message.'

'Yes, sir.' Woodfordi sank down into his impossible squat and crossed his eyes. After a while he uncrossed them again. 'Can't seem to make the connection, sir.'

'Why not?' Pyrgus demanded. 'Doesn't the Painted Lady have her CC handy?'

'It's not that, sir. It's Orion. He's not responding.'

'Who in Hael is Orion?'

Woodfordi said soberly, 'Hardly in Hael, sir. He's the Communications Angel. So it's more like "Who in Heaven is Orion", sir, if you get my meaning. Calls himself Military Guide and Spiritual Gatekeeper, but that's only because he likes wearing uniform. Most of them go nude up there, on account of the balmy weather.'

Despite the urgency of his situation, Pyrgus frowned and said, 'I didn't know we were in touch with Heaven?'

'Military secret, sir.' Woodfordi tapped his nose. '*Need to know* sort of thing. Shouldn't really have told you, but I expect it's all right, you being royal and all that.'

'Why can't you get through?' Pyrgus asked, getting back reluctantly to the matter in hand.

'Think it might be this place, sir,' said Woodfordi earnestly. 'Reception wasn't great earlier, to tell you the truth. Lot of volcanic activity round here. Ground stresses always influence the energy flow, throw up trapped lightning fields. Affects the network. Sort of like transportation portals in reverse. I'll keep trying if you like, sir, but my guess is it won't improve until we get out of the deep desert.'

But suddenly Pyrgus wasn't listening. He had the look of somebody struck by a sudden idea.

'What?' Nymph asked.

'Portals!' Pyrgus said. He looked around urgently. 'Nagel, you called the demons *Fluid Dark*. Does that mean you've seen them in the desert before?' That's what it had to mean. Nobody had names for things they'd never seen before.

Nagel nodded. 'Yar,' he said.

'Where do they come from?' Pyrgus asked. He had the air of somebody pushing down a rising excitement.

Nagel pointed. 'Ohr ere way yorboat hores alk sides tha ate if.'

Pyrgus's ears must have been starting to attune because it almost made sense to him. But he turned to Nymph all the same.

'Over there, the direction he's pointing, about an hour's walk away. Apparently it's beside something they call the Great Cliff.' She stared intently at Pyrgus. 'What is it?'

'Look,' said Pyrgus excitedly. 'There's an army of demons in the desert: we saw that. But we never thought to ask how they got here. Well, did we?'

'No ...' Nymph said uncertainly.

He gripped her shoulder. 'It has to be portals. There's no other way you could transport so many troops in so short a time. Well, you could ship them in, but not without being noticed. So it's portals. But it can't be the regular portals – we'd have known if they got them open again – right?'

'Right ...' Nymph confirmed, even more uncertainly.

'So Beleth must have set up new ones!' Pyrgus exclaimed. 'I know what Nagel means by the Great Cliff. It's a geological feature in the deep desert, about as inaccessible and far away from anywhere as you're likely to get. Perfect for Beleth's portals and perfect for his demon troops – they *like* volcanic conditions. But don't you see, Nymph ...?'

'See what, Pyrgus?' Nymph asked him patiently.

Pyrgus was actually grinning. 'We can't do anything about the troops Beleth already has here. But if we sabotage the portals, we can stop him sending any more! No reinforcements. No fresh supplies. It could mean the difference between victory and defeat.'

Nymph looked interested at once. 'Do you know how to get to this Great Cliff?'

Pyrgus shook his head. 'No, but Nagel does – he knows this desert inside out. And his people might be able to help. Violet Trinians are warriors. They could support us if the portals are guarded. And Green Trinians are great with technical stuff – Innatus made that little clack, remember – they could help with the sabotage. This is an incredible opportunity, Nymph. All of us together could make such a difference. And if we move fast, we could do the job before nightfall.' He turned to Nagel. 'Will you do that, Nagel?' he asked urgently. 'Will you help us?'

'Oh yar,' Nagel said.

Ninety

Pyrgus was getting a bit tired of approaching places crawling on his face, but he had to admit it was better than being spotted by demons. He raised his head cautiously.

The Great Cliff towered above him like the central spine of the wasteland, a sheer sandstone massif that climbed so high it created its own mini-climate, whipping up dust and sand from the desert floor in confined swirls that looked like whirling djinn.

He turned his head slightly and his jaw dropped. Set at intervals no more than a yard or two apart were the portals he was expecting. But there were more of them than he could have imagined in a nightmare. There were portals by the score, by the hundred, by the thousand and more. They stretched like sentries along the base of the cliff as far as the eye could see. There was no way so many portals could have been constructed in the time since the standard portals had closed down. Beleth must have been secretly building these gateways for years.

There were no visible guards. But perhaps Beleth felt none were needed. Destroying so many portals would need an army of men and even then would certainly take days, maybe weeks. Besides, his secret had been safe for so long he probably thought the work would never be discovered. No one ventured this far into the deep desert: even the Trinian nomads avoided it as much as possible. It was the perfect base for a demon invasion.

Pyrgus allowed his eyes to travel desolately along the line of portals. 'So much for sabotage!' he muttered between clenched teeth. Even if they managed to close down one or two, thousands would remain. The effect on Beleth's war effort would be a gnat's bite.

'Wouldn't be so sure,' remarked Nymphalis, stretched out on the ground beside him. She turned to Woodfordi, who was lying beside her. 'What do you think?'

'Distance apart you mean, Miss?' Woodfordi asked.

Nymph nodded silently.

'Tricky to say from here,' Woodfordi frowned. 'But they *could* have been set too close together ...'

'What are you talking about?' Pyrgus asked.

'Chain reaction,' Nymph told him. 'Portal technology is inherently unstable. Basically you're creating a hole in reality, so it has to be. Inside any given portal the instability is under control, but it's still there. You see what that means?'

'No,' Pyrgus admitted. He hated it when Nymph lectured him.

'If we were to sabotage one portal – blow it up, that is – we would trigger the portal's own instability,' Nymph said. 'So our sabotage explosion causes the portal itself to explode; and that's a much larger explosion. But if there's *another* portal nearby, another portal that's *close enough*, the explosion in the first portal will cause that one to explode as well.' She glanced towards the row of portals underneath the cliff. 'If those are close enough together, we only have to blow one up for the whole lot to go off like firecrackers, one after the other.'

Pyrgus was staring at her in astonishment. 'How do you know all this technical stuff?' he asked. 'Forest Faeries don't even *use* portals.'

Nymph just smiled at him.

Pyrgus said, 'Pity we don't have anything to blow up the first portal.' When he'd suggested sabotage he'd been thinking of blocking them up with rocks, an old guerrilla trick that would have left transported demons locked inside the stones.

'Think we might have, sir,' Woodfordi said. He rummaged in his kit and brought out a length of painted willow about nine inches long.

'What's that?' Pyrgus asked.

'Exploding wand, sir. You snap it in half to distress the spell coating, then leave the pieces beside the thing you want to blow up. You've got eight seconds to get out of range.'

'I thought CCs were non-combatants,' Pyrgus said.

Woodfordi smiled. 'Still issue you with the kit and give you the basic training,' he said. 'Just in case.'

Nymph, who was looking at Woodfordi, said, 'What's the problem?'

Pyrgus glanced at her in surprise. 'Why should there be a problem?'

Woodfordi said, 'Thing is, Miss, eight seconds is plenty of time to get out of range of the wand explosion. But if the wand triggers the portal, that's a much bigger explosion. *Much* bigger ...'

'So whoever blows up the first portal might not get

away in time? Might be caught by the larger explosion?'

'Might be killed, Miss, yes,' Woodfordi nodded soberly.

'I'll do it,' Pyrgus told them promptly.

'No you won't,' said Nymph at once.

'I'm the soldier,' Woodfordi said. 'Has to be *my* job.'

'You're our Communications Channel,' Pyrgus told him fiercely. 'We need you to get word back to the palace.'

'Can't get word back from here,' Woodfordi pointed out. 'Orion isn't answering.'

'That's only because we're in the deep desert. We can use you later.'

'I'll do it,' Nymph said. 'I can run faster than either of you.'

'No you can't!' Pyrgus bristled.

'Oh yes I can,' Nymph told him confidently. 'Besides, I know what a portal explosion is like and I think I can be out of range within eight seconds.'

'How do you know what a portal explosion is like?'

Annoyingly, Nymph only smiled at him again.

The argument went on until Nagel crept up beside them and suggested, 'Ace or aht.'

Pyrgus blinked. 'Race for it?' He'd understood Nagel this time and it sounded like a good idea. He didn't think he'd have any problem beating a girl and Woodfordi had only little short legs.

'From here to that rock,' Nagel said, pointing. 'I'll count you down from three.'

They raced and Nymph won easily. 'You can help me set the wand,' she told them reassuringly (and without the good grace to breathe heavily). 'I'll let you get clear before I set it off.'

'We need to be sure the portals are close enough together for any of this to work,' Pyrgus said a little sulkily.

Nymph beamed at him. 'Then let us go and inspect them properly,' she said. 'Coming, Nagel?'

The Trinian shook his head. 'If you're going to blow things up, I have to get my people out of the area. They hate explosions.' He moved away to disappear between some rocks.

'I'll come with you,' Woodfordi said. 'I've got a measure and I know the distance we need.'

The three of them were on their way to the nearest portal when a group of rocks transformed themselves into a Goblin Guard.

Ninety-one

Henry's face was on fire. 'I did *what?*' he exclaimed.

'That's not the worst of it,' said Fogarty. His face was unsmiling as ever, but there was a glint in his eye that might have meant he was enjoying this.

'What's the worst of it?' Henry asked with trepidation.

'You tried to get her to mate with you,' Fogarty said.

There was a war on and the world was falling apart around them, but since there was nothing they could do about it, Fogarty and Henry had gone to Fogarty's lodge where they were drinking Analogue tea from a dwindling supply while Fogarty brought Henry up to speed on what had happened to him.

Henry was not enjoying the experience.

He stared at Mr Fogarty, his mouth opening and closing like a fish. Eventually he squeaked, '*Mate?*'

'What don't you understand?' Fogarty asked. 'Your parents forgot the talk about the birds and bees?'

Henry's hand had begun to shake so he set down his mug. 'I couldn't have,' he said.

'You could according to Blue. And you did. I don't know what you're making such a fuss about – I thought you fancied her.'

'I did – I *do*! But –' He picked up his mug and set it down again immediately. 'I *respect* her!' he blurted out.

Maybe it was his tone, but Mr Fogarty's face softened. 'Look, Henry, you can't take this stuff personally. Beleth had you fixed. You didn't know what you were doing. From what Blue says, the implant turned you into a demon.'

After a minute, Henry said, 'Like ... with horns?'

'Oh, for God's sake, Henry!' Mr Fogarty exclaimed impatiently.

When Mr Fogarty was appointed Gatekeeper of the Empire, his official residence became the Gate Lodge of the Purple Palace, an imposing structure by any criterion. But since he'd moved permanently into the Realm, he'd gradually turned it into as much of a tip as the little house Henry was looking after. The room they were in at the moment was almost a replica of his original back kitchen, complete with rusting old tin biscuit boxes and half-finished bits of electrical machinery.

Henry said, 'Well, I don't know, do I? I can't remember *any* of this!' He didn't mean to, but the last few words came out in a wail.

Mr Fogarty waved a hand. 'You weren't yourself, and Beleth has a breeding programme.'

It was almost unbearable. He loved Blue so much and all the time he kept getting into stuff like this with her. Jeez, the first time he saw her, she had no clothes on, stepping into a bath. She had to think he was a complete pervert by now. Henry wondered if he shouldn't just go home and never come back to the Faerie Realm again. If he stayed and this sort of thing kept happening, she'd hate him for sure.

'Mr Fogarty –' he began.

But Mr Fogarty cut him short. 'Nutshell, OK?' When Henry nodded, he went on, 'This is flying saucer business, Henry. You study that like I have and you know the demons have a breeding programme –'

'I thought it was aliens who had flying saucers,' Henry said, bewildered. 'You know, from outer space and stuff.'

'Same thing,' Fogarty said shortly. 'Demons … aliens … same thing. Christ, Henry, you were *abducted*. They do that. They've been doing it in our world for years. I've told you about this before, if you'd just take your thumb out of your ass and *listen*. What the hell do you think they abduct people *for*? All the self-appointed experts will tell you there's something wrong with their genes and they want to improve the stock, but it's a lot worse than that. They're infiltrating us, Henry. They make babies with human women, then put them into positions of power when they grow up. They look like ordinary people, but they're actually demons in human form.' He glanced behind him and lowered his voice. 'Half the Cabinet, Henry, and don't get me started about the Yanks – they've lost most of their Senate.' He fixed Henry with a gimlet eye. 'Now they want to do the same in the Realm. They thought they'd start with you and Blue.'

'Me and Blue?' Beleth turned him into a demon so he could have a baby with Blue and the baby would grow up to be the next Purple Emperor and Beleth would have a demon on the throne? Henry thought he was about to vomit, but it was as much embarrassment as disgust. He didn't want to hear the details, but he had to hear them anyway. This was so bad it couldn't get any worse. 'And I actually asked Blue to … to … you know …'

'Yeah, you did,' said Mr Fogarty.

'What did she say?' Henry heard his mouth ask.

Mr Fogarty looked at him without expression. 'She didn't tell me.'

After a moment Henry said, 'But we didn't do anything?' If they did anything, he would have to leave the Realm. He could never face Blue again. He could never face himself again. He'd have to join a monastery.

'Did quite a lot from what I gather,' Mr Fogarty told him. 'You killed a demon, for one thing. Wrung its neck or something.'

That was so stupid he didn't even bother questioning it. 'We got away.'

'Oh, yes.' Mr Fogarty gave him a ridiculous nod and wink. 'You're a bit of a hero, Henry.'

But he wasn't a bit of a hero. He wasn't any sort of a hero. How could he ever face Blue again after what he'd done to her? Beleth had turned him into a monster.

Henry stopped. When had he turned back? 'Mr Fogarty,' he said, frowning, 'if the implant turned me into a demon, how come I helped Blue escape?'

'They deactivated it,' Mr Fogarty said. 'They reckoned Blue would know it wasn't you when you tried to jump her bones, so they switched it off.' His mouth twitched slightly as if he was trying to suppress a smile. 'Beleth figured the two of you would get it on of your own accord if he just left you alone long enough. Do his dirty work for him.' The smile actually appeared now. 'That's really something, Henry. People must be talking about you and Blue all the way to –'

But Henry was still frowning. 'Wait a minute, Mr Fogarty.'

'– Hell!' Fogarty concluded.

Henry said, 'There's something wrong.'

Ninety-two

Pyrgus had never seen a Goblin Guard before. This contingent was the traditional grouping of five – four male, one female, all dressed alike in one-piece silver jumpsuits and thick-soled silver boots. They were demons in their original unshifted form, grey-skinned, large-headed and with enormous jet-black eyes. Not one of them stood much higher than his waist, but they were by far and away the most dangerous creatures on the surface of the planet. They gambolled forward on spindly legs like playful monkeys, chittering with the sound of clacking lobster claws.

'Don't look at their eyes!' Pyrgus screamed. But it was already too late. Nymphalis had set down her weapons and was walking blank-faced towards the demons.

Pyrgus hurled himself forward and struck her at an angle with his shoulder. The blow was so severe it took her off her feet and she fell heavily on the stony ground.

'Sorry,' Pyrgus murmured, but the move had the desired effect: Nymph rolled and sprang to her feet again, eyes clear.

And weaponless.

Woodfordi, eyes firmly fixed on the ground, was

scrabbling for something in his kit and emerged with a coated short sword, one of the few effective weapons against a Goblin Guard. The blade writhed with military grade offensive spells. As it appeared, the female goblin stopped dead and closed her enormous eyes. Woodfordi began to groan.

'What's wrong?' Pyrgus shouted.

'CCs ... particularly ... particularly susceptible,' Woodfordi gasped. 'Even without ... eye contact. Take ... take the sword. Halek ...' He shook his head.

'Nagel!' Pyrgus howled, then remembered the Trinians were running away from the planned explosions. They were probably already out of earshot.

The four male goblins were closing in on Nymph. They had tiny pouting mouths and slits for noses, but there was a look of triumph on their faces. Woodfordi was pouring sweat now. The sword in his hand was turning towards his own throat.

'Help me,' he said weakly.

But it was Nymph Pyrgus ran to help. He met the goblins and stabbed the nearest with his Halek knife. The blade swept upwards between the creature's ribs to pierce its heart.

The energy discharge was astonishing. Blue fire enveloped the goblin in a writhing aura so that its body jerked and twitched like a beached fish. For just the barest moment its eyes clouded, then it reached down, gripped the blade and snapped it with a single movement.

Pyrgus had no time for surprise. The backlash of pure energy lifted him off his feet and threw him backwards for several yards. He hit the ground with mind-numbing violence, but at least the pain convinced him he was still alive. Perhaps it was the discharge of energy into the goblin that had saved him. Whatever the reason, he was still in the fight.

Like a flock of birds, all five demons whirled to run towards him.

Woodfordi's body straightened, but he was trembling so violently that he dropped his sword. Now Nymph was beside him.

'Take it!' Woodfordi gasped. 'I can't use –'

Nymph swooped on the sword and spun round in a single movement. Moving with that superhuman speed Pyrgus remembered so well from the time he'd fought her himself, she lashed out at the nearest goblin and severed its arm at the shoulder.

The creature set up a howling that issued not just from its mouth but from its mind. Woodfordi slapped his hands over his ears and sank to his knees. Pyrgus, who was climbing to his feet, jerked uncontrollably and staggered. His body felt as if someone had punched him in the stomach. His own shoulder was on fire. Only Nymph seemed unaffected. She was still on her feet, still moving swiftly as she attacked the remaining demons.

But fast as she was, the demons were faster. One ran towards her and, to Pyrgus's astonishment, jumped like an insect right over her head. The move clearly took Nymph by surprise as well, for she hesitated. The goblin landed, bounced and turned. The other four fanned out. To his horror, Pyrgus saw that the one with the missing arm was still on his feet, moving as a greenish ooze solidified to close up his wound. In an eye blink, Nymph was surrounded.

With no weapon now, Pyrgus picked up a rock and

threw it at the nearest goblin. It struck the creature violently on the back of her hairless head, causing her to stagger. She turned to look accusingly at Pyrgus, who jerked his head to avoid the mesmerising eyes. It was obvious the goblin was more surprised than injured, but it was all the opportunity Nymph needed. She jumped to push the creature to one side and broke free from the circle. She still had Woodfordi's sword.

Pyrgus had picked up another rock and was running towards the goblins now. Even the shattered Woodfordi had straightened up and seemed to be searching his kit for another weapon. Pyrgus was now beside Nymph, who seemed less pleased to see him than he'd have hoped.

'Stay away!' she hissed. 'Your blade is broken.'

The goblin who lost the arm opened its lipless mouth to reveal needle teeth. The others produced short swords. The weapons had polished obsidian blades. The demons' eyes focused on Nymph and they moved towards her in a single unit. She lashed out with her blade, but this time the goblins parried easily.

'Nagel!' Pyrgus shouted again in desperation.

Woodfordi tossed Pyrgus a military dagger then rolled something along the ground into the midst of the goblins. 'Clear!' he shouted urgently. 'Run clear!'

Nymph swung away from the goblins, grabbed Pyrgus and hauled him away at a run. Woodfordi was running too. There was a curious clicking sound, then the familiar scent of raw spell craft. Pyrgus glanced over his shoulder in time to see the multicoloured flash. Vast quantities of smoke and dust rose up.

It was a self-limiting explosion, military magic designed for mass destruction at close range. There was no noise, no shock wave, no rolling blast. Pyrgus, Nymph and Woodfordi all stopped and turned to watch. The devastation was incredible. Where the demons had stood was a huge, blackened crater with wisps of smoke still rising towards the relentless sky.

'Well done, Woodfordi!' Pyrgus exclaimed admiringly.

Then, at the edge of the crater, a goblin head emerged, reddened by the dust of the desert but otherwise intact. It was the creature Nymph had injured, pulling itself up with its one remaining arm. Another head appeared, then another. The liquid eyes were filled with hate.

Beyond the crater, a second group of rocks was morphing into another Goblin Guard. Then another appeared and another. The wasteland was filled with the *clack* of lobster claws.

'Good grief!' Nymph exclaimed, eyes wide.

'Run!' Pyrgus shouted.

But Nymph failed to move. 'Run where?' she asked.

Pyrgus looked around him desperately. Behind them towered the Great Cliff, sheer, unclimbable, impassable. Before them Goblin Guards approached. Beyond them, more Guards morphed out of their disguises. The creatures were walking towards them with a terrifying, slow deliberation. This time there was no escape.

Pyrgus moved beyond all thought of consequence. He grabbed the arms of his two companions and, dragging them behind him, plunged into the nearest Hael portal.

A tightly knit three-man Goblin Guard was on their heels.

Ninety-three

There was a discreet knock on the bedroom door before it opened silently. Madame Cardui, who suffered most fearfully from insomnia, was propped up in her bed, resplendent in a flowing peignoir, reading some State papers. She glanced up over the top of her spectacles at the figure who slipped in.

'Ah, Kitterick, you're back.'

'Indeed, Madame,' Kitterick confirmed.

'We are at war, Kitterick.'

'So I understand from your guards, Madame.'

'You saw nothing of it?'

'I was fortunate in the route I took to return.' He began to tidy the room, a routine that came easily to him.

'You've been away a long time. Mrs Ogyris, I presume?'

'I fear so, Madame. Did Pyrgus not inform you directly?'

Madame Cardui sighed. 'He was the soul of discretion. Were your efforts fruitful?'

'In a manner of speaking, Madame.'

'Information on the war?'

Kitterick shook his head. 'I fear not, Madame. It was not a development I anticipated, so I concentrated on the time flowers.'

Madame Cardui removed her spectacles and pinched the bridge of her nose. 'It was not a development any of us anticipated, Kitterick. Will the time flowers prove our undoing?'

Lanceline, Madame Cardui's translucent cat, appeared from underneath a table and wound herself around Kitterick's ankles. He reached down and absently fondled her ears.

'No, Madame, they will not,' he said emphatically.

'Ah,' said Madame Cardui and waited.

'Pyrgus appears to have destroyed them,' Kitterick said.

She frowned. 'Pyrgus told me they had been removed.'

Kitterick shook his head. 'Not then – on his previous visit. When he shattered the glasshouse.' He moved deferentially towards the bed, produced a single crystal bloom from the pocket of his jerkin and presented it almost gallantly to Madame Cardui.

'Why, thank you, Kitterick. This is one of the actual flowers?' The thing was exquisite, like some wonderful artwork.

'Yes, Madame. But it no longer functions to control time. None of them do. For that one needs a living flower and this one, like the others, is now dead. They require a special atmosphere to grow. When picked they can be preserved for several hours by means of a sealant spray. After that they become inert. The glass was supposed to be impervious – Merchant Ogyris never imagined anyone would be idiot enough to attack it with a Halek knife. When Pyrgus broke it, there was no one to spray the preservative. The entire harvest died within minutes.'

'I see,' said Madame Cardui. She felt a small well-spring of relief. One less problem for the morrow. Lanceline jumped on to the bed, curled herself into a question mark and fell asleep.

'There is one thing, Madame ...'

Something in his tone alerted her at once. 'Yes, Kitterick?'

'The flowers were not grown for the Faeries of the Night, as Pyrgus believed. They were to be exported to Hael.'

The relief was replaced by a sudden chill. This was what she had feared. 'For Beleth to use against us?'

'It would seem the Realm owes Prince Pyrgus a considerable debt of gratitude, even if he didn't know what he was doing. Madame Ogyris was not privy to the details, but it appears the demons have been considering a strike against the Faeries of the Light and believed the time flowers would tip the military balance. They approached Merchant Ogyris some time ago, before the portals closed.'

Madame Cardui leaned forward slightly. 'So this was a long-term plan?'

'Very much so. The flowers themselves are a Hael plant. In their natural state they control time for no more than a second or so – a defence against insects, I believe. The hybrids Merchant Ogyris was growing could only be produced in the Realm. The light spectrum makes it impossible for them to grow in Hael. So the demons did a deal.'

Madame Cardui shuddered. Beleth was proving an implacable enemy, one far more dangerous than Lord Hairstreak could ever be. If the Realm survived the current crisis, the Intelligence Service would have to pay far more attention to the demons than it had done in the past. If the Realm survived …

She said drily, 'Madame Ogyris seems to have been most forthcoming, Kitterick.'

Kitterick lowered his eyes modestly. '*Most* forthcoming, Madame,' he agreed.

Ninety-four

Blue climbed out of bed.

The strange thing was she'd actually been sleeping, but she was wide awake now and excited. The glow-globes responded to her movement, but she switched them off with a whispered command. Best to alert no one just yet. She walked to the window and silently drew back the curtains. The twin moons of the Realm hung low on the horizon and bathed the room in a soft glow, enough light for her to get dressed.

She moved to the wardrobe, pulling her nightgown over her head. Most of her outfits were severely functional. She'd long preferred boys' clothes and even now she was Queen her taste hadn't really changed. But tonight was a special occasion and she had to look her best, so she selected the dress of spider silk she'd commissioned for Pyrgus's coronation. It was formal, but well suited. Her only regret was that it wasn't new, but she'd yet to commission another and until she did, the Silk Mistress's creation was by far the most fetching thing in her wardrobe.

As the slick material flowed over her body, she felt the familiar enchantment. Even without the aid of a mirror she knew she looked superb. She certainly felt elegant and confident. Exactly how she should feel on such an important night. She wondered briefly about make-up, but decided she really needed no illusion spells. She was young, she was fresh, and in the spider silk she knew she was attractive. Nobody needed more than that.

As she left her quarters, her personal guard moved to accompany her, but she waved them away with a gesture. They'd talk, of course. They'd speculate about her midnight wanderings. But that didn't matter. In an hour or two, everyone would know anyway.

The Purple Palace was a building so gigantic that new servants often disappeared for days while they wandered its passages and corridors. Ten years ago, one unfortunate actually starved to death in a disused wing, unable to find a food store. When the emaciated body was discovered, Blue's father, then the Purple Emperor, ordered maps placed at strategic locations with spell coatings that would locate the individual and plot a course to any major spoken destination. Blue, who had wandered the labyrinth since the time she learned to walk, had no need of them. Besides which, none of the spell coatings contained *her* destination.

In the carpeted corridors with their heavy curtains, night staff flattened themselves against walls, bowed and curtsied as she passed. But she soon passed into the old quarter of the palace where carpeting gave way to stone flags and the velvet curtains turned to cotton pennants, then nothing at all. The air grew noticeably chill away from the central furnaces. There was condensation on the walls. She'd need to do something about that later. No part of the palace should be cold. But for the moment she had other things on her mind.

She turned a corner, hesitated for a moment – even she was not familiar with much of this wing – then saw what she was looking for. The doorway was oak, banded in iron and so small a grown man would have had to bend almost double to pass through it. The wood smelled of ancient spells. The lock looked rusted and disused.

Blue produced a heavy key, but knew better than to use it. The protections might be ancient, but they were still lethal. She was dealing with something crafted in the olden times, long before any faerie acceded to the Peacock Throne. This entrance was forbidden even to a Queen. She would never have dared to use it without help.

From the same pocket as the key, Blue fished out a scrap of parchment and squinted at the runes that squirmed across its surface. The light here was not good. The old quarter of the palace drew its illumination from the stonework of the walls, which contained a residual luminosity nobody quite understood. It was cheaper than glowglobes and perfectly adequate for an area that had been disused for generations, but it was an irritation now when she wanted to be certain of the shapes she was seeing. To help, she traced them with the tip of her finger, feeling the warm tingle of the magic they contained. She whispered the words beneath her breath and almost caught their meaning.

After a moment, something inside told her she was safe. Without hesitation she inserted the key in the lock. There was no howling, no spell-driven outrage, no attack. But the lock itself was stiff with age so that it took all her strength to turn it.

The little door swung slowly open. Blue bent her head and stepped across the threshold. She licked her lips. She was standing at the top of a narrow, spiral, stonework staircase that wound its way downwards into darkness.

Ninety-five

Pyrgus struck the cliff-face with such force that he dropped his weapon, winded. Then Nymph careered into him, followed immediately by Woodfordi. All three went down in a tangle of arms and legs. Nymph recovered at once and was on her feet again in an eye-blink, spinning a defensive sword. Pyrgus jumped up gasping, blood steaming from scratches on his face and hands.

The Goblin Guards were gone. Not just the demons who'd been close to them, but all the others. The rocks were just rocks.

'Where did they go?' Pyrgus asked.

'They have gone into hiding,' Nymph told him confidently, her eyes wary.

'Why?' Woodfordi asked. He climbed carefully to his feet, feeling his arms and legs for broken bones.

'Yes, why?' Pyrgus echoed. 'They had us. They were right there, just behind.' But it wasn't the goblins that concerned him. 'That portal didn't work,' he said.

They were still in the desert, caught in the long rays of the dying sun. No blue fire, no gut-wrenching translation. The portal was inert. Cautiously he reached out to where the force field should have been. It was a dangerous move that might have cost him a fingertip, but there was nothing.

Nymph said sharply, 'Pick up your weapon, Pyrgus. The demons will be back!'

'I haven't *got* a decent weapon,' Pyrgus told her crossly. He was getting fed up with losing expensive Halek knives. Woodfordi's dagger was just no substitute.

'What's wrong with it?' Woodfordi asked. He was looking at the portal.

Something was totally weird. 'Guard me,' Pyrgus said to Nymph. He wiped blood from his eyes and trotted to the next portal in line.

'Careful,' Nymph called. She was moving nervously, her head jerking around as she searched for the attacking demons.

The second portal was inert as well. Close up he could see something clearly he hadn't seen before. The portal looked genuine enough from a distance, but now it was obvious the thing could never work. There was no control technology at all.

'The demons don't exist,' he whispered. He spun round. 'This is an illusion!' he shouted to Nymph.

She glanced in his direction, but did not drop her guard. Woodfordi was still at the first portal, examining it closely.

'That wasn't a real Goblin Guard,' Pyrgus said, his eyes wide. He shook his head.

'I cut its arm off,' Nymph snapped.

'We should have known when they survived the explosion. *Nothing* could have survived that explosion.'

Woodfordi stepped back and looked along the line of demon portals. 'Reflective spells,' he said.

'Blue told me about it. She was attacked by a Goblin Guard when she broke into Brimstone's lodgings, but it was an illusion.'

'Who's Brimstone?' Nymph asked annoyingly.

'Doesn't matter,' Pyrgus said. 'An illusion can kill you. It's real enough as long as it lasts. But it's still an illusion. You set them up as securities.'

He must have started to get through to her because she relaxed a little. 'What were they guarding?'

'The portals,' Woodfordi suggested. 'Except they're some sort of an illusion too.'

'There has to be a real one somewhere,' Pyrgus said, staring at the portal in front of him. 'Should we look for it?'

Woodfordi shook his head. 'It'll just be a framework. This doesn't even have works.'

'What are you two talking about?' Nymph asked, irritated.

'This is all a set-up,' Pyrgus said excitedly. 'The portals are a fake. Somebody built one, then set up a reflective spell so it looks like thousands. It's like standing between two mirrors, except there aren't any mirrors.'

'Then set up a Goblin Guard illusion to stop anybody finding out,' Woodfordi put in. He looked around. 'It's all you'd need. The most you get out here are a few wandering Trinians.'

It hung together nicely, but it made no sense. Why go to the trouble of setting up elaborate – and costly – illusions in an area of desert where, as Woodfordi said, the only people around were a few wandering Trinians?

'This doesn't make any sen—' Pyrgus stopped as a new thought struck him like a thunderbolt. 'Wait a minute,' he said. 'If these portals are all fakes, how did Beleth bring in his army?'

The three of them stood looking at each other blankly.

'Perhaps –' Nymph said; and stopped.

'Maybe he used –' Woodfordi said; and stopped.

They continued to look at one another in silence.

Pyrgus said thoughtfully, 'Unless Beleth's army is an illusion too.'

Ninety-six

'It doesn't make any sense,' Henry said. 'You just told me Beleth's implant actually turned me into a demon. Like I became a demon, then shape-shifted back so I looked like Henry – something like that?' He was staring intently at Mr Fogarty.

Fogarty said, '*Exactly* like that. At least that's what you told Blue and she thought you should know.'

Henry took a nervous sip from his mug of tea and found it cold. He licked his lips. 'The idea was I should … you know … with Blue.'

'Yes, *breed* with her,' said Fogarty harshly. He seemed to be losing patience with Henry's sensibilities.

'And that was so the demons could get a demon child – or a half demon child anyway – into the Purple Palace?'

'That was the plan, yes.'

'And the demon had my – Henry's – appearance so Blue wouldn't suspect she was going to be kidnapped?'

'You're just repeating everything I told you,' Fogarty said impatiently. 'Is this going anywhere?'

'But when they put us in the room to …' he swallowed, '… breed, they deactivated the implant and I turned back into the *real* Henry. That doesn't make sense.'

'Yes, it does,' Fogarty said. 'Blue's very sensitive. They were worried she might figure out she was mating with a demon, even if it had your shape.'

Henry said, 'If I was really me again, how would that produce a demon child?'

Fogarty blinked.

After a moment he said, 'Well, you – I suppose if you –' He stopped, staring at Henry. 'You're right. That doesn't make any sense.'

They stared at one another.

Eventually Henry asked, 'Are you sure you got it right: what Blue told you?'

'I'm not *that* senile.'

'Then are you sure *Blue* got it right?'

'How should I know?' Fogarty snapped. 'I'm only telling you what she told me and Cynthia. She said that's what you told her. When you were a demon. Or rather when you weren't: when the implant was deactivated. She's not likely to get that wrong.'

'Unless I was lying to her,' Henry said.

Mr Fogarty got it right away. 'You mean the implant *wasn't* deactivated?'

'I don't know,' said Henry. 'But it's possible. Suppose –'

'I'm ahead of you,' Fogarty cut in thoughtfully. 'Suppose the demons wanted to fool Blue by *pretending* the implant was deactivated when it wasn't. Suppose they were trying to sell her on some bill of goods that wasn't what was really happening at all.'

'That's what I think,' Henry said. 'Maybe the whole story about the child was just a cover-up for something else.' He felt simultaneously relieved and just a fragment disappointed.

'What?' Fogarty asked. 'A cover-up for what?'

Henry said, 'I don't know.'

'This could be important, Henry.'

'I know it could be important, Mr Fogarty! But I can't *remember.* You *know* I can't remember. I can't remember anything since you took the transplant out. I can't even remember how I got to the Realm.'

'Maybe I could make you.' Fogarty frowned.

There was something in his tone that made Henry think of rubber hoses and lights in your eyes. 'How ... how would you do that?' he asked warily.

'You're not the first,' Fogarty said.

'I'm not the first what?'

Fogarty got up and began to pace around the room. 'You got your implant in a flying saucer abduction,' he said. 'You're not the first. The demons have been abducting people from Earth since 1961. They lose their memory as well, but we know how to get it back again. Been done hundreds of times.'

Henry wondered who *we* were. But all he asked was, 'How ... how do we do that, Mr Fogarty?'

Mr Fogarty rounded on him and grinned triumphantly. 'We hypnotise you!' he said.

Ninety-seven

Torches flared in wall sconces as Blue set a hesitant foot on the top step. She stopped for the barest second. This wasn't any technology she knew. The torches didn't seem to be spell-driven. They were lit by some sort of mechanical device that produced a spark. Yet this area of the castle had been locked up for centuries. How could any mechanical device still work after so much time? How could any torch still burn in this dampness?

She pushed the questions from her mind and concentrated on keeping her footing. The stone steps were worn and slippery. How things happened didn't matter. The important thing was that they did. She was here now and she was happy.

The spiral staircase was so narrow she twice smelt her hair singe in the torch flames, but she reached the bottom at last. She was in a tiny vestibule, facing a single door flanked by painted statues of fanged guardians, their colours faded with age. The door itself was crudely made from planks of some black wood, but beaded here and there with slivers of obsidian. There was no handle and she could not see a lock.

She reached out to push the door and metal claws sprang out at once to grip her hand. Blue froze, her heart pounding suddenly, and forced herself not to panic. If she had jerked back her hand, the claws would have ripped the flesh from her bones. As it was, one of them had pierced the skin so there was a welling of a single drop of blood. She looked at it, fascinated.

Something else emerged from the door, not a mechanical device this time, but a sinuous ribbon that had a strangely organic look to it. It slid across the surface of her hand and licked the blood like a tongue. Blue waited, suddenly aware of what was happening. Apparently the sample proved satisfactory, for the claws suddenly withdrew and the entire doorway shattered, collapsing in dusty shards at her feet. She stepped across them daintily.

She was standing in an immense black lacquer box, its polished surfaces reflecting a small flame that erupted from a stone dish in the centre of the floor. The effect was oppressive, but this was obviously no more than an antechamber to some other room. Blue hurried across it towards an open archway, then hesitated at some inner prompting. There was an unlit lantern of archaic design on the floor beside the stone dish. The archway was dark – it seemed to absorb what little light there was – and she would need some illumination if she was to go through. It was ridiculous to imagine the lantern could be fuelled and functional after all these years, but she picked it up anyway.

It took her several minutes to discover how the lantern worked, but she finally managed to light it from the open flame. She walked towards the archway, holding it aloft.

The room was like nothing she'd ever seen before. It was like stepping out beneath the night sky, but a night sky peppered with alien stars. A lazy inlaid river, sparkling in the lamplight, crawled across the mosaic floor. There were living creatures on its banks, insectile and carapaced, but something told her they were harmless so long as she left them undisturbed.

Blue stepped on to the river itself, convinced it represented a safe pathway. Three paces further on, her lantern flared and she saw the godform.

The figure was so foreign to anything she'd known that her every instinct was to throw herself cringing on the floor. Its blood-red lacquer representation arched across the star-ways above her, sickeningly naked and deformed. Its outstretched arms defined the archway through which she'd entered. Its sturdy legs outlined an open doorway ahead. But it was the face that appalled her. It leered down obscenely from the gloom above her head, an open maw that seemed designed to swallow her alive.

Blue tore her eyes away and concentrated on her breathing. She had to remember why she was here. If this was a test, then she must pass it. What she had to do was far more important than some stupid relief carving of an archaic god, however much ancient power it radiated.

After a while she grew calm enough to walk through the doorway between the godform's straddled legs.

The third and final chamber was the strangest of them all. Its proportions were colossal, as if it had been constructed to accommodate a giant. Walls and ceiling were completely lined with plates of brass, green with age now, but still reflecting the light from her lamp. Inlaid in the polished granite floor was a brazen circle, inscribed with an enormous pentagram of brass. In the exact centre of the figure rose a double cube altar carved from porphyry. On the altar lay an open, ancient book.

Blue's eyes glazed as she walked forward.

She crossed into the circle and at once the entire chamber emitted a high-pitched whine which rose to a brief crescendo, then dropped to a background hum. She set her lantern on the ground and began to move towards the altar. She had the look of a sleepwalker, but she was smiling.

The altar dwarfed her. She had to stand on tiptoe to reach the book, but that, while large, was at least of manageable proportions. She pulled it down, taking care not to lose the place where it had opened. The pages were crafted from the skin of some unfamiliar animal and smelled of grave dust and dank earth. The binding was of heavily tooled leather.

For the barest moment she experienced a pang of panic. The book was handwritten in an ornate and unfamiliar script, delicately illuminated around the edges with scenes and creatures so alien they almost twisted the mind. How could she read from this? There was nothing about it that she understood.

But then, as if the book had a life of its own, the words began to rearrange themselves subtly. Nothing really changed character, but now, with an effort, she found a degree of comprehension:

Micma Goho Mad Zir Comselha Zien Biah Os Londoh Norz Chis Othil Gigipah Vnd-L Chis ta Pu-Im Q Mospleh Teloch ...

The words were in a language so archaic she could not even guess its roots. It bore no resemblance to anything she had ever known, yet somehow the meaning resonated in her mind:

Behold, saith your God, I am a circle on Whose Hands stand Twelve Kingdoms. Six are the Seats of Living Breath. The rest are as Sharp Sickles or the Horns of Death ...

Carrying the open book carefully in both hands, Blue took a step backwards, then another. In a moment she was standing just outside the brazen circle with its inlaid pentagram and altar. Her chest felt tight, but she ignored it. She took a deep breath. Although she had never heard the words spoken before, Blue commenced to intone the evocation on the page before her:

'*Micma Goho Mad Zir Comselha Zien Biah Os Londoh Norz ...*'

The flame of her lantern flickered wildly and the background hum rose noticeably in pitch and volume.

'*Chis Othil Gigipah Vnd-L Chis ta Pu-Im ...*'

In a moment the brazen pentagram began to glow.

Ninety-eight

It was fully dark by the time Pyrgus and his two companions managed to retrace their steps to the rise from which they'd spied on Beleth's army, but the moons rose early at this time of year so they had light enough to see.

The demon encampment stretched below them.

Pyrgus lay propped on his elbows with Nymph to his right and Woodfordi on his left. He could see the flickering campfires and the rigid, robotic movements of the sentries.

'Looks real enough to me,' Woodfordi murmured, echoing Pyrgus's very thought.

'As I understand it,' Nymph whispered formally, 'such illusions are meant to look real.'

'Well, all illusions are meant to look real,' Pyrgus said. 'But there are illusions and illusions.' When Nymph gave him a long-suffering look, he added, 'I mean, the Goblin Guard is an illusion that can kill you. When it's triggered, the goblins might as well be real for as long as the illusion lasts. They can attack you and cut you up and react in every way as if they were really there except you can't kill *them*. But you couldn't do that with a whole army.'

'Why not?' Nymph asked.

'Costs too much,' said Pyrgus simply.

'Beleth's hardly short of money.'

Pyrgus shook his head. 'It's not just money – it's the energy cost. All spells need energy. You can't just keep making them bigger and bigger. After a while the spell needs more energy than your technology can handle. An illusionary army that could actually fight is way beyond anybody, no matter how much money they have.'

'Excuse me, sir, this is all very interesting,' Woodfordi said, 'but it doesn't help us figure whether that army down there is real or not.'

'No,' Pyrgus agreed. He began to climb to his feet. 'Only one way to find out ...'

The arguments started at once. 'You can't go down there,' Nymph said. 'It's too dangerous.' She glanced towards the demon encampment and added, 'I'll go.'

'My job,' volunteered Woodfordi. 'I was trained in espionage.'

Pyrgus looked at him in surprise. 'Were you?'

Woodfordi shook his head. 'Not really, sir. But the lady's right – can't have a prince taking that sort of risk.'

They bandied it back and forth for a while, then reluctantly agreed they'd all go, but only on the strict understanding there would be no heroics.

In the event, none were needed. Beleth's entire army proved to be as insubstantial as a moonbeam.

Woodfordi passed his hand right through a patrolling sentry. 'What's going on here?' he whispered, half to himself.

'I don't know,' Pyrgus told him. 'But I do know we need to tell the palace about this. Are you still out of communications range, Woodfordi?'

'Afraid so, sir.'

'Then we have to get back to the flier right away.'

Ninety-nine

Henry said, 'I don't think I can be hypnotised, Mr Fogarty.'

Fogarty was scrabbling about in one of his tin boxes. 'What makes you say that?' he asked.

'I went up on stage once when I was a little kid. The Illustrious Svengali couldn't put me under.'

'The Illustrious *what*?' Fogarty snorted.

'I don't think it was his real name,' Henry said.

'Ah!' Fogarty exclaimed. He dragged an old pocket watch out of the box and began to free its chain from a tangle of electrical wiring. To Henry he said, 'Little kids aren't all that easy – attention spans of goldfish. Might do better with you now.'

Henry watched with trepidation as Mr Fogarty liberated his watch. Despite his negative experience with the Illustrious Svengali, he had a nervous feeling Mr Fogarty might just manage it. 'You won't ... make me *do* things?' he asked.

'Christ sake, Henry!' Fogarty exclaimed impatiently. 'We've a war on, the demons are invading, you got implanted by the Prince of Darkness and you're worried I'll make you stick your finger up your bum and bark like a dog? This is serious.'

'Sorry, Mr Fogarty,' Henry said. It didn't matter. It

probably wouldn't work. 'What do you want me to do?'

'Just sit there and watch the watch.' Fogarty began to swing the ancient timepiece on the end of its chain. 'Let your eyes follow the watch.'

The Illustrious Svengali hadn't used a watch. He'd just stared into people's eyes and made peculiar hand movements. Henry hoped Mr Fogarty knew what he was doing. What happened if he *did* put Henry under, but couldn't wake him up again? All the same, he did let his eyes follow the watch, which was swinging like a long, slow pendulum.

'Heavy,' Mr Fogarty remarked. 'Your eyes are getting heavy …'

Henry's eyes actually *were* getting heavy, but that wasn't exactly surprising. If you kept swinging your eyes back and forth, they got tired and when they got tired, they felt heavy. Didn't mean you were being hypnotised.

'So heavy you can hardly keep them open,' Mr Fogarty intoned.

Henry found his eyes were sliding shut and jerked them open wide. He knew if he let his eyes close he was in trouble. He'd watched Paul McKenna on television. They didn't show you how he did it – probably to stop people at home getting hypnotised by accident – but his subjects always ended up with their eyes shut doing stupid stuff. When you had your eyes shut you were putty in Paul McKenna's hands. He wasn't sure he wanted to be putty in Mr Fogarty's hands.

Then he remembered why they were doing this in the first place. It was important to find out what Beleth and his demons were really up to. Because there was definitely something wrong with the story they'd told Blue.

'Heavy,' Mr Fogarty repeated in a heavy sort of voice.

Heavy, Henry thought as his eyelids slid south again. He felt really comfortable. He'd always thought of hypnosis as a battle of wills, but it wasn't like that with Mr Fogarty. Interesting that he'd never noticed Mr Fogarty had such a nice voice before.

'So heavy you can't keep them open,' said Mr Fogarty in his nice voice.

Henry gratefully allowed his eyes to close. It didn't really matter that his eyes were closed. Mr Fogarty might be a nut, but he was a nice nut and Henry trusted him. Sort of. No, completely. He had such a nice restful voice. And besides which, Henry wasn't putty yet. If he wanted, he could open his eyes at any time. It was just that he didn't want to. He didn't want to offend Mr Fogarty by opening his eyes.

'Falling,' said Mr Fogarty. 'Falling backwards into darkness, safe, warm darkness. Safe and well. Happy and relaxed.'

Henry felt safe and well, happy and relaxed. He was floating through the darkness, a safe, warm darkness inside his head that came about when you closed your eyes and listened –

'Listen to my voice,' Mr Fogarty droned.

Henry wasn't under, of course. He knew that. But he didn't want to contradict Mr Fogarty because that would be rude. Much better to float in the safe, warm darkness and let Mr Fogarty think he was asleep when actually he was wide awake and knew everything that was going on and could open his eyes whenever he wanted, even though he didn't want to just yet.

Mr Fogarty reached across and touched his right arm. 'Heavy arm,' remarked Mr Fogarty; and immediately Henry's arm felt as heavy as lead. It was very peculiar.

He tried to lift it, but it was too heavy to lift.

'But now it's growing light,' said Mr Fogarty. 'Lighter than the air. So light it's floating in the air.'

Henry almost giggled. His arm really did feel light, like a gas-filled balloon. It was lighter than the air. It wanted to float in the air. Henry relaxed and watched, eyes closed, as his arm began to move of its own accord. First it twitched, then it shifted, then it lifted. Mr Fogarty was right – it was floating in the air! How cool was that?

'Your arm will now float of its own accord until your hand touches your face. And when your hand touches your face, you will fall at once into a deep … dreamless … sleep.'

Henry knew he wasn't gone, of course. He was absolutely wide awake and in complete control. He could do anything he wanted, say anything he wanted. He could jump up and do a tap dance if he wanted. But best not to mention that to Mr Fogarty, who was working hard to put him under. Besides, it was interesting to sit with your arm floating in the air.

'Deep … dreamless … sleep,' repeated Mr Fogarty. 'When your hand touches your face.'

There was no way at all he was going to fall into a deep, dreamless sleep. That was very obvious. Henry wasn't sleepy, wasn't remotely sleepy, just warm and safe and very, very relax—

Henry's hand touched Henry's face.

'Open your eyes!' commanded Mr Fogarty firmly.

Henry opened his eyes. Madame Cardui was standing behind Mr Fogarty – when did she come in? – and both of them were looking grave.

'Didn't work, eh?' Henry remarked sympathetically.

Mr Fogarty said, 'Beleth has implanted Blue.'

One hundred

There was so much pressure in her skull that Blue's head began to ache. The background sound in the chamber of brass had become a howling, like the cries of lost souls trapped in agony. The glow of the pentagram increased, reflecting in the ceiling and the walls. The immense porphyry altar began to shake.

'*Od commemahé do pereje salabarotza kynutzire fabaonu, od zodumebi pereji od salabarotza ...*' Blue read aloud from the book, her voice rising clear and true above the din. Although the language was unknown to her, it seemed she understood it: *And I bind thee in the fire of sulphur mingled with poison and the seas of fire and sulphur ...*

The words were a blasphemy, drawn from the time of the Old Gods, but she did not care any more than she cared about her pain. What she was doing was important, vital for the welfare of the Realm. Nothing was more important than that.

'*Niisa, eca, dorebesa na-e-el od zodameranu asapeta vaunesa komesalohé!*' she intoned. *Come forth, therefore, obey my power and appear before this circle!*

The howling rose to a crescendo and the brass plates of the chamber took up the resonance in a hideous vibration. The pain in Blue's head was so intense now that she could scarcely focus on the words that writhed and crawled across the pages of the book.

'*Niisa!*' she called again. *Come forth! Come forth!*

The brass plates in the ceiling shifted and a trickle of dust poured down. The whole chamber was shaking now, as if caught up in a violent earthquake. Her lantern flickered, then went out, but the chamber remained illuminated by its own reflections. Behind the howling there arose a deep subsonic drumbeat, then, incongruously, the music of a distant orchestra. The cacophony gripped body and brain, drawing her towards the point of madness, but she did not hesitate for an instant.

'*Niisa! Niisa! Niisa!*' *Come forth! Come forth! Come forth!* she shrieked.

All noise and vibration stopped. There was an instant of deep silence. Then the massive altar cracked and shattered into rubble.

From its depths stepped Beleth, Prince of Darkness.

One hundred and one

As the flyer swooped low over Yammeth City, Nymph said suddenly, 'Look over to the east.'

Pyrgus glanced in the direction of her pointing finger. Below them tens of thousands of Nighter troops were streaming through the city, accompanied by heavy ordnance. He had never seen so many soldiers together at one time in his entire life. He felt his spirits sink.

'I hope our men can hold back that lot.'

'They're moving in the wrong direction,' Nymph said.

Pyrgus blinked. Woodfordi moved out of his seat and stood behind him to look over his shoulder. After a moment, Pyrgus said, 'You're right.' The forces were pouring out of their city gate into the Eastern Desert. He turned round, frowning. 'What's that all about? Are they retreating from our troops?'

'Does that look like a retreat?' Nymph asked.

It didn't look anything like a retreat. The men were marching in good order with no sign of casualties at all.

Pyrgus said thoughtfully, 'Maybe Uncle Hairstreak's joining up with Beleth's army.'

'Beleth's army doesn't exist,' Nymph said.

'He may not know that.'

'Unlikely,' Nymph said shortly.

Pyrgus glowered at her. 'All right, what do *you* think's happening, smart boots?'

Nymph shrugged annoyingly and turned away. 'I don't know.'

To Woodfordi, Pyrgus said, 'I don't suppose you're back in contact with your network yet?'

'Afraid not, sir. Should have been by now, but I'm not and that's the fact of it. I think the Communications Angel must be sick.' He craned round Pyrgus's head to get a better view of the city below. Almost every street was full of men now, marching like ants towards the eastern gate. 'Why do you ask, sir?'

'Because the sooner the palace knows about this the better.'

'Your people will already know about it,' Nymph said. 'From their Generals.' She sat down and added, 'Since Lord Hairstreak is obviously disengaging.'

'Why would he be disengaging?' Pyrgus asked belligerently.

'I don't know that either.'

'The palace still needs to be told as soon as possible,' Pyrgus muttered.

'We'll soon be back there anyway,' Woodfordi said in a conciliatory tone.

Pyrgus wheeled the craft around and increased speed to maximum, ignoring the spell-driven voice that claimed it wasn't safe.

One hundred and two

Henry stared at him. 'How do you know Blue's been implanted?'

'You just told me,' Mr Fogarty said.

'I wasn't under,' Henry said.

'Oh yes you were, sunshine – deepest trance I've ever seen. You'll remember soon – I gave you the suggestion, but it sometimes takes a minute or two to kick in.'

'But you were right, Henry,' Madame Cardui said.

She must have joined them while he was in a trance. It was spooky: he hadn't even noticed. He licked his lips.

'Right?' he echoed.

'The story about Beleth wanting you to mate with Blue, deeah. It was all a nonsense.'

'It was?' Henry asked. There were maybe about a hundred more appropriate emotions at this moment, but the one he actually felt was relief.

Madame Cardui smiled. 'Just a story they implanted in Blue's head and yours to distract us from the invasion.'

'None of it really happened?' Henry asked. But Mr Fogarty was right. He was beginning to get little flashes now. 'I wasn't put in a bedroom with Blue?'

'No.'

'I didn't kill a demon?'

Mr Fogarty snorted. 'Thought that was a bit far-fetched from the start.'

Madame Cardui said kindly, 'I expect you could easily have killed a demon, deeah, but none of it actually happened. Blue didn't kill hers either – she didn't have her stimlus with her. Those were all false memories.'

'So I didn't kidnap Blue?'

'You kidnapped Blue all right,' Mr Fogarty said. 'The way it worked was Beleth had you kidnapped and implanted. Then they programmed you to kidnap Blue and implanted her as well. The business about the demons breeding half-human babies is true enough, but it won't work in the Realm – the DNA is too dissimilar. But they gave you and Blue the same false memories and sent you back as a distraction from their real plans. Cunning little ploy.'

It was coming back to him now, exactly as Mr Fogarty said. He could remember the implant and the creepy, slimy feeling as black-eyed demons in white lab coats carefully layered the false memories into his brain. He started to feel guilty about the kidnap all over again. Because of him, Blue's brain had been tinkered with as well. The thought of it left him agitated. Actually quite a lot agitated.

'You have to get that thing removed,' he said.

'My deeah, it's already *been* removed. That's why you lost your memory completely.'

'Not me,' Henry said urgently. 'Blue. You have to take the thing out of her head.'

'Blue's asleep now,' Madame Cardui told him. 'I shall make arrangements to have her implant removed first thing in the morning when she's rested. Then Alan can hypnotise her too and restore her proper memories.'

'No, now!' Henry insisted. He wasn't quite sure why, but it was vital they removed the implant at once.

'Henry, deeah, what's wrong?'

He didn't *know* what was wrong, but he could feel the panic with a vengeance. They couldn't wait until morning because if they waited until morning –

He didn't know what would happen if they waited until morning. Something bad would happen, but he didn't know what. Something bad would happen to Blue. Something bad would happen to the Realm. The panic was so strong now he could no longer sit still. He pushed himself out of the chair.

'Henry –' Mr Fogarty said.

'Something bad –' Henry began. Then the memories flooded back and he stopped, his eyes wide. 'Oh my God!' he said. He launched himself abruptly through the door.

'Henry, what's *wrong*?' Madame Cardui called after him.

But Henry was already outside, running full tilt towards the Purple Palace.

One hundred and three

One of the best things Pyrgus ever did was to appoint Henry a Knight Commander of the Grey Dagger. It allowed him to pass freely through the Purple Palace and often earned him salutes from guards.

He crashed down the corridor of the imperial quarters and gasped breathlessly, 'I must see Queen Blue at once!'

The guards saluted to a man, but their Captain said apologetically, 'Afraid she's not in her rooms, sir.'

'Where is she?' He had a horrified feeling he already knew the answer.

'Couldn't say, sir. She refused an escort.'

'When did she leave her quarters?'

'Little while ago.'

It had to be! It had to be! 'How was she dressed?'

The Captain blinked. 'Dressed, sir?'

'Dressed, man – dressed!' Henry shouted into his face. 'What was she wearing?'

The Captain looked at him in bewilderment. 'Nice-looking gown, sir. Like she was off to a party. Not the sort of thing she usually wears.'

Dear God, he was too late! He'd remembered too late!

The Captain frowned. 'Is something wrong, sir? Sir –'

But Henry was already racing back down the corridor. How could this have happened? How could he have let this happen? Why hadn't he remembered sooner? Blue could be lost by now – lost for ever. *And it was all his fault!*

Savagely, Henry pushed the guilt and self-pity out of his mind. There might still be time. But he needed a clear head. If he managed to catch up with her in time, he could stop the whole disaster, even if he had to force her. He'd kidnapped her before. He could do it again. Once they got the implant out, she'd be fine. And she'd understand.

He was moving by instinct now, twisting and turning through palace passageways he'd never seen before. Except it wasn't really instinct, however it felt. He knew he had to be following the memory of the instructions the demons had planted in his head. He knew where Blue was going, because he was supposed to go there with her. And if his implant hadn't been removed, that's exactly what he'd have done. But now maybe he could turn Beleth's own plan against him.

He was in the old quarter of the palace now, running like a demon himself. Pyrgus once told him this part of the building dated to a time before faeries ruled the Realm. It contained chambers that hadn't been opened in millennia and there were rumours of ghosts. Most palace residents avoided it, but Henry was too desperate to feel any unease.

Part of him hoped he might catch up with Blue before she went too far, but by the time he reached the corridor that housed the little door there was still no sign of her. A horrid thought struck him. What if the door was locked? Beleth's demons had given Blue the key, but as far as they were concerned, Henry had no need of one since he would be with her. But now ... what happened if she'd closed the door behind her?

Henry skidded to a halt. The door *was* closed, but when he tried it, he found it unlocked. He almost groaned with relief as he hurled himself down the narrow spiral staircase.

But his relief was short-lived. Even before he reached the bottom, he could hear the howling. Blue had begun the obscene ceremony that would finally unlock the gates of Hell.

One hundred and four

Pyrgus overrode the safeties as the flier reached Imperial Island. He sent out a single burst of code that would neutralise the palace security system, then pitched the nose of the craft towards the lawn outside the main entrance doors.

'Straps,' he ordered. Nymph and Woodfordi were immediately secured to their seats by body-netting. Woodfordi's knuckles showed white where he gripped the arms. 'Dive,' Pyrgus muttered.

There was an elemental scream as the flier went into a steep descent with no loss of speed. Pyrgus kept his eyes firmly fixed on his target, a level area between two flowerbeds. The ground rushed towards him with indecent haste. He waited, heart thumping, until it seemed he could almost reach out and touch it, then commanded, 'Land!'

The flier attempted to comply, but Pyrgus had left things far too late. The *tulpa* thought-forms built into its propulsion system read the situation in an instant, re-instated the safeties and hurled the craft back upwards. It banked, struck a tree branch and cracked open like an egg. Pyrgus fell out to drop in a heap on the ground. Nymph and Woodfordi dangled from their netting.

'That was exciting,' Nymph remarked. She pulled a

knife from her boot and cut herself free, holding on to the seat with one hand. Then she clambered on to the branch and released Woodfordi.

'Thanks, Miss,' he murmured gratefully. 'I thought I was a goner for sure.'

'So did I,' Nymph told him. She swung from the tree and dropped nimbly to the ground, leaving Woodfordi to his own devices. Pyrgus was already on his feet, limping towards a running guard contingent that had just emerged from the palace.

'I'm all right!' he called over his shoulder.

Nymph smiled a little to herself.

'Escort us to Queen Blue!' Pyrgus called grandly to the approaching guards. He suddenly noticed a tall figure on the palace steps. 'Mr Fogarty, can you arrange to get Blue and the Generals together – and Madame Cardui. There's news.'

To his surprise, Mr Fogarty ignored the urgency in his voice and came down the steps towards him. The guards fanned out and surrounded them both, then parted to allow Nymph and Woodfordi through.

Fogarty said, 'Christ, it's all happening tonight.' He looked beyond Pyrgus at the wreckage in the tree. 'Have you any idea what those bloody things *cost*?' He looked back at Pyrgus. 'Henry's just gone off his head as well.'

Pyrgus gripped his arm and leaned across to whisper, 'Beleth's army is an illusion! The portals aren't real either. There's no demon invasion and Uncle Hairstreak's marching all the Nighter forces into the desert.'

Fogarty stared at him blankly for a moment, then shook his head. 'I'm getting too old for this,' he said.

One hundred and five

Beleth was shifted into his most powerful form. Curling ram's horns grew out of his forehead. His teeth were smiling fangs, his body knotted muscle. Only his height was curtailed, perhaps because of having been encased in the altar: he was little more than six feet tall. A blood-red cloak swept from his shoulders to his ankles. His feet were bare and Blue could see that each toe ended in a wicked talon. His eyes bored into hers.

Beleth shook himself as if to throw off any remnants of the porphyry block. The brass wall at his back was changing, each plate flowing liquidly into its neighbour before sliding downwards. For just the barest instant Blue wondered if the pentagram circle might contain him, but he threw back his cloak and strode towards her.

Blue took a step forward and threw herself into his arms.

'My darling,' she whispered breathlessly as she stretched up to kiss him.

One hundred and six

'*Nooo!*' Henry screamed. Beyond Blue and the devil, the wall had disappeared so that the chamber opened up, impossibly, on to a scene that chilled his blood. He was overlooking a vast metallic plaza, surrounded by squat, black buildings underneath a lowering sky. Set to one side of the plaza were twin thrones carved from obsidian and ornamented with complex inlays of what might well have been gold. Ranged before the thrones, row upon row, were thousands, tens of thousands, of horned demons. All were on their knees.

Henry ran. He had no weapon, but he struck Beleth with his shoulder so violently that the creature staggered. 'Leave her alone, you bastard!' Henry screamed. He punched and kicked the demon with a flurry of blows.

Beleth brushed him off like a gnat.

Henry was thrown violently across the floor. His foot caught in the remnants of the porphyry altar so that he stumbled and fell heavily. Beleth strode across and kicked him violently with one taloned foot. Henry's clothing ripped and blood welled from the gash across his stomach.

'Henry!' Blue gasped. She felt a jolt as if she'd been kicked herself.

Henry's eyes glazed, then slowly closed.

Beleth turned back to Blue with a smile.

'Is he dead?' she whispered.

The devil shook his head. 'Not yet. Perhaps we should keep him as a sacrifice to celebrate our marriage.' His eyes bored into her. 'Would you like that, my dear?'

After a moment, Blue said dully, 'Yes.'

Beleth took her hand and led her through the open wall. There was an instant of transition as the ancient magics gripped, then they were standing on the metal plaza. The kneeling demons prostrated themselves at once, foreheads pressing on the metal pavement. Beleth's voice rose to the intensity of thunder.

'Behold my new consort and your Queen!' The kneeling demons roared approval.

Blue glanced behind her. Two of Beleth's demons had entered the pentagram chamber and were dragging out Henry's prostrate body. He looked more dead than alive. There was a sickness in her stomach, but she pushed it down savagely. Nothing must interfere with her duty to the Realm.

'Not quite the truth,' said Beleth quietly, 'but soon you will be both.'

He led her to the smaller of the two thrones and waited politely until she was seated before sitting himself. She looked out over the sea of demon backs as the creatures began to climb to their feet and moved in regimented segments to take their appointed places.

The demons loved formality and ceremonial, that was for sure. All Beleth's closest attendants were robed, horned and cloaked, their faces sharp and eyes aglitter. Beyond them stood rank upon rank of demon guards, naked for the most part, with the low light reflecting dully on their scales. Four enormous devils who moved to occupy the cardinal points sported barbed, prehensile tails.

The atmosphere was sulphurous, oppressive and very, very hot. Blue felt a bead of perspiration trail down one side of her face. Two ancient chamberlains carried a sturdy oak-wood table across the plaza and placed it directly in front of the thrones. This would be for the signing of the marriage pact, she thought.

The sense of occasion was heightened by the standard-bearers who moved quickly to surround the table on three sides. They were all imps dressed in eye-jarring motley where complementary colours flashed and clashed without the aid of a single woven spell. For the banners themselves, scarlet and black predominated, reflecting the heavy brocade now being spread across the table.

She forced herself not to look directly as the two demons dragging Henry dumped him in a heap against one table leg. He was still alive but unconscious, his breathing laboured. She had an uncomfortable feeling she might be required to drink his blood as part of the ceremony. If any of his blood remained. His clothes were already saturated from the wound in his stomach.

Beleth cleared his throat and stood on his throne to give himself more height. He looked imperiously around the assembled throng. 'This is an auspicious occasion,' he intoned in a voice that seemed too large for both mouth and chest. 'A formal Marriage Pact – the first of its kind – between a ruling Prince of Darkness and a ruling Queen of Faerie.' He was forced to pause by the spontaneous cheering of his subjects.

The noise died down eventually and Beleth continued with a speech that was liberally peppered with words like 'historic', 'proud', 'significant' and 'era'. Blue listened politely, but when he at last climbed down and sat back on his throne, she leaned over and said quietly, 'What about the boy?'

Beleth glanced at her and frowned. 'What about him?' he rumbled.

'He's still unconscious,' Blue hissed. 'If he's to be a sacrifice, shouldn't he be awake so he can suffer?'

Beleth contrived to look surprised and pleased at the same time. 'Quite right, my dear. Our tradition calls for a slow and agonising death. Quite pointless if he sleeps through it.' He turned to growl something at one of his attendants. In moments, two demon healers were kneeling at Henry's side. Blue noted with satisfaction that his eyes opened almost at once, but the healers did nothing for his wound.

A creature that was mostly arms and legs scurried forward to deposit an enormous leather-bound tome on the table. Blue stared at it with interest. This was almost certainly the fabled Book of Pacts which recorded every significant treaty the devils ever made, dating back five centuries. She'd heard that somewhere, stored in fireproof chests hidden in the deepest depths of Hael, was an entire library of such books from even earlier times. She doubted anything they recorded was likely to match what was planned here.

'Never a contract such as this one,' Beleth boomed, almost as if he'd picked up her thought. She glanced at him quickly, but his expression betrayed nothing. Blue forced herself to relax. This was a vital moment for the Realm.

It was time. Blue could feel anticipation in the waiting demons like a physical fog. In minutes, she and Beleth would be married. She prayed Henry would understand what she was doing.

An ancient ceremonial pen was produced now; and a sheet of virgin parchment. It was all tradition at this stage. The pen was a sharpened eagle's quill, the parchment made from lambskin, carefully cured, bleached and dried. It had a creamy colour and a pleasing texture. The writing was black ink in a strong copperplate hand outlining the terms of the marriage contract. Once signed, the document would last for ever.

'The Pact,' said Beleth smugly to a murmur of appreciation from the gathered throng. In his reverberant voice he began to read it, clause by clause.

Blue paid little attention. Their agreement was simple enough in its essence. It committed her to obey her future husband in return for his protection. *Obey in all things* was the exact wording. While the terms were personal, the implications were political. The Pact would deliver the demons control of the Faerie Realm.

'Do you agree the terms?' Beleth asked her formally.

From the corner of her eye she could see Henry turn to look at her. She hesitated. Could there be another way?

'My dear ...?' Beleth urged.

Blue straightened her back. 'I do,' she said.

One hundred and seven

There were howls of excitement from the assembled demons. Blue sat stiffly on her throne. She could see the look of shock on Henry's face, although he must have known what was happening. A part of her wanted to shout to him to run, to save himself. But that would achieve nothing now.

Besides, she was certain he would never leave her.

'Then let the Pact be signed!' Beleth announced grandly.

The verbal agreement was nothing. Hael tradition required a written contract, signed in blood. Blue knew where her duty lay.

Heralds blew a fanfare of sinister trumpets. The sound reverberated chaotically off the surrounding metal buildings. A minion scurried forward with a razor and a tiny golden bowl.

Beleth turned to look at her and smiled. Then he took the blade and without hesitation, slashed the palm of his left hand so that a quantity of greenish blood flowed into the bowl. He seized the quill, dipped it and signed his name on the lambskin with a flourish.

The demons cheered. Beleth bowed his head slightly in acknowledgement. He smiled at her again. 'Now you, my dear. Be brave.'

The minion wiped out the bowl with a clean piece of linen, then handed the razor to Blue.

With one last longing glance at Henry, Blue leaned across the thrones and savagely cut Beleth's throat from ear to ear.

'Goodbye, *my dear*,' she said.

One hundred and eight

They convened in the Throne Room.

'I don't *know* what's going on,' Pyrgus was saying. 'All I know is that Beleth doesn't have real troops in the desert. Or real portals either. It's all a big bluff.'

'To do what?' Fogarty asked him crossly. 'What's the point?'

'You could try asking Henry – he's the one's been spending time with demons.'

'Henry's not here,' Fogarty snapped. 'I told you that. We were talking about Blue and he ran off.'

Madame Cardui arrived a little late. 'Blue's not in her rooms,' she said at once. 'I'm worried.'

Pyrgus said, 'She'll be safe in the palace.'

Madame Cardui looked at Fogarty. 'You haven't told him about Blue's implant?'

Pyrgus looked from one to the other. 'Implant? What implant?'

'So I forget things,' Fogarty said irritably and shrugged. 'He'd just crashed his flier into a tree, for God's sake!'

Madame Cardui said, 'Beleth had Blue implanted like Henry. To give her false memories.'

'Wait a minute –' Fogarty said suddenly.

'What's an implant?' Nymph asked. It was the first

time she'd spoken since their dramatic arrival.

'Wait a *minute* –' Fogarty said again. He was frowning. 'That's not making sense. We assumed the false memories were a diversion to distract attention from Beleth's invasion. But Pyrgus has just told us the invasion is phoney too.' He stopped and looked from face to face.

Madame Cardui took it up. 'So what was the *real* reason for Blue's implant?'

'And where is Blue now?' Pyrgus whispered.

'Right behind you,' Blue said grimly.

One hundred and nine

There was blood on her dress, blood on her hands, blood splattered along her bare arms. There was blood smeared on her face. Henry was a pace or two behind her. There was blood oozing through his clothes.

'Get Henry to the infirmary,' Blue said.

'You're hurt, deeah!'

Blue shook her head. 'This isn't my blood.' Pyrgus ran to throw his arms around her. She began to shake violently. Tears cut through the bloodstains on her face.

'What the hell happened to you?' Fogarty demanded.

Blue clung to Pyrgus and her tears turned to a ghastly, gurgling giggle. 'I'm Queen of Hael now, Mr Fogarty,' she said; and fainted.

She awoke in the infirmary, feeling hugely better despite the pain in her head. She raised a cautious hand to touch the bandaging.

'It's out,' said a familiar voice.

Blue turned slowly. 'Where's Henry, Mr Fogarty?'

'He's fine. Had to have stitches, but he's fine.' He held a small metallic cylinder between his finger and thumb. 'They planted this inside your brain. Interesting, eh? Henry got off easier. His was just lodged in his sinus cavity. Beleth must have wanted them to do two different things.'

'Yes,' Blue agreed.

Fogarty said, 'There are an awful lot of demons in one of the palace cellars.'

'They won't give you any trouble,' Blue said.

'I noticed that,' said Fogarty. He cocked his head to one side and looked at her. 'Can you remember?'

'Yes. Everything.'

'Henry lost his memory when we took out his implant.'

'It must be different with faeries.'

'So what happened?'

Blue looked past him through the picture window into the morning sunlight. She had clearly been unconscious for hours. 'Beleth wanted me to marry him. That way he could control the Realm. The deep brain implant meant he could manipulate my thoughts and emotions.'

'That's what Henry told me,' Mr Fogarty said. 'The business in the desert was a diversion.'

'More like a distraction,' Blue said. 'He wanted to keep everyone so worried you wouldn't suspect what was really happening. It was a very complicated plan.'

'What went wrong with it?' Fogarty asked.

'I'm not sure,' Blue said honestly. She pushed herself up in the bed and gave a small, bleak smile. 'When they put that thing in my brain, I actually felt attracted to Beleth. But it was more than that. I thought the marriage would be good for the Realm. It felt as if it was my duty.'

'When did you stop feeling that?'

Blue said, 'When Beleth attacked Henry.'

Fogarty rolled the cylinder in his fingers. 'Know what's interesting? I had a look at this thing when they took it out. The insides are burned out.'

'Are they?' Blue asked mildly.

'It takes a lot to burn out one of those implants – almost impossible, in fact. You must love him very much,' Fogarty said quietly.

'Yes,' Blue said. 'Yes, I do.'

After a moment Fogarty said, 'Henry says you cut Beleth's throat.'

Blue's eyes glazed slightly as she nodded.

'Weren't you afraid?'

'Very.'

'You must have thought the demons would tear you limb from limb – you and Henry.'

'Yes.'

'Why didn't they?' Fogarty asked curiously.

'It's their custom to accept any new leader strong enough to kill the old one. Beleth ate his father to accede to the throne.'

'Strange creatures,' Fogarty said. 'Are you going to leave the portal open?'

'It's not a portal,' Blue said. 'It's old magic from the time before the faerie. I don't know how Beleth got hold of it. But no, I'm not going to leave it open, not if I can find out how to close it down.'

Fogarty pushed himself out of his chair. 'Feel strong enough to get up yet?'

'I think so. Why?'

'The others are waiting. We need you to talk to the Generals.'

'Hand me that dressing gown, Mr Fogarty,' Blue said.

One hundred and ten

General Creerful bowed mutely as they entered the Situation Room. He nodded briefly to Pyrgus, ignored Mr Fogarty and Madame Cardui completely, and said, wooden-faced, to Blue, 'Lord Hairstreak's main forces are in retreat, Ma'am. There was some opposition, but we have now penetrated deeply into the Cretch and are approaching Yammeth City. I anticipate we will have captured it within hours.'

There was no protecting Yammeth City now, Blue saw at once. One of the largest globes showed the entire city from an elevated perspective. For a capital at war the place looked tranquil, its streets largely deserted. Until, that is, you looked towards the eastern sector where Nighter troops and engines of war were concentrated in vast numbers. Clearly her uncle still had not realised the demon forces in the desert were an illusion. It occurred to her suddenly that Beleth must have murdered Burgundy because he had found out.

She said bluntly, 'We must withdraw.'

Creerful's shock was palpable. 'Withdraw, Majesty?'

'Immediately.'

'Queen Blue, the Faeries of the Night are at our mercy. We may never have this opportunity again.'

Blue said tiredly, 'The Faeries of the Night are our

cousins, not our enemy. Our real enemy has already been defeated.' She glanced at the globe again. 'Are we in communication with Lord Hairstreak?'

A wary look sprang into Creerful's eyes. 'No, Majesty.'

'How long before we can contact him?'

'Perhaps an hour with runners – the CC network is closed down. It will depend where he is.'

Madame Cardui asked quickly, 'What's happened to the CC network?'

General Creerful was joined by General Vanelke, who fielded the question: 'We suspect sabotage. There have been several acts of rebellion by Faeries of the Night living in the capital. We're working to repair the damage, but it may be some time before we're operational again. Runners might be faster at this stage.'

Blue said, 'Dispatch runners then, General. Coded message, of course. Inform my uncle of our withdrawal. Tell him his offer of an alliance is accepted.'

Epilogue

They were walking together in the gardens of the Purple Palace. It was evening and pinpoints of light were just beginning to flare in the distant city streets. Night stocks were releasing their scents, an alien medley that had now become familiar.

Blue asked, 'What's wrong, Henry?'

What was wrong was that he'd soon have to go back. He'd have to explain to his mother where he'd been. He'd have to explain to Anaïs how he'd managed to disappear before her very eyes. He'd have to live with the guilt about what he'd done to Blue. She was being very nice, but he was certain she could never forgive him.

He shrugged. 'Oh, you know ... going home,' he mumbled. He didn't want to go.

Unexpectedly, Blue said, 'I'd like to meet your family.'

Henry glanced at her in surprise, then suppressed a lunatic urge to giggle. He thought of his mother and her lesbian lover. He thought of his father, now living with a girl young enough to be his daughter. He thought of Aisling, his selfish brat of a sister.

'Oh no, you wouldn't,' he said with heartfelt emphasis. 'Take my word for it, you wouldn't!'

'Don't you like them?' Blue asked.

'Not very much. Dad's all right, I suppose. But Mum –' He hesitated. Actually he didn't know what to say about his mum. After a moment he went on, 'Mum sort of tells you what to do all the time. She knows better than everyone else about everything.' Then he added sourly, 'But she's still managed to make a mess of her marriage. She chucked Dad out and made him think it was for the best.'

'So you really don't want to go back?'

'Not even slightly,' Henry said, then grinned to try to lighten the conversation.

Blue looked away from him. He couldn't be sure in the half light, but something made him think she might be blushing.

'Why don't you stay here?' Blue asked.

Henry stared at her in astonishment.

Glossary

Key:

FOL: Faerie of the Light
FON: Faerie of the Night
HMN: Human

Analogue World (a.k.a. the Earth Realm). Names used in the Faerie Realm to denote the mundane world of school and spots and parents who look like they might end up getting divorced.

Antiopa, Nymphalis (Nymph). Daughter of Queen Cleopatra, Princess of the Forest Faerie.

Apatura Iris. (FOL) Father of Prince Pyrgus and Queen Blue. Was Purple Emperor for more than twenty years.

Asmodeus. A smelly demon.

Atherton, Aisling. (HMN) Henry Atherton's younger sister and pain in the ass.

Atherton, Henry. (HMN) A young teenage boy living in England's Home Counties who first made contact with the Faerie Realm when he rescued the faerie prince, Pyrgus Malvae, from a cat.

Atherton, Martha. (HMN) Headmistress of a girl's school in the south of England. Wife of Tim Atherton, mother of Henry and Aisling.

Atherton, Tim. (HMN) Successful business executive. Husband of Martha Atherton, father of Henry and Aisling.

Beleth (a.k.a the Infernal Prince; the Prince of Darkness). Prince of Hael, an alternative dimension of reality inhabited by demons.

Black John. A demon.

Blue, Queen Holly. (FOL) Younger sister of Prince Pyrgus Malvae and daughter of the late Purple Emperor Apatura Iris.

Border Redcap. Sentient fungus that inhabits rocky areas of the Realm wilderness and sprays psychedelic spores when attacked.

Brimstone, Silas. (FON) Elderly demonologist and former glue factory owner.

Cardui, Madame Cynthia (a.k.a the Painted Lady). (FOL) An elderly eccentric whose extensive contacts have made her one of Queen Blue's most valued agents.

Chalkhill, Jasper. (FON) Business partner of Silas Brimstone and, secretly, former head of Lord Hairstreak's intelligence service.

Channel. A military medium used for communications.

Chevalier. Realm equivalent of a Knight.

Cleopatra. Queen of the Forest Faerie.

Comma, Prince. (FOL/FON) Half-brother of Prince Pyrgus and Queen Blue. (Same father, different mothers.)

Cossus Cossus. (FON) Lord Hairstreak's former Gatekeeper.

Countdown. A dangerous military precaution against kidnapping.

Creen. What Haleklind natives call Haleklind.

Demon. Form frequently taken by the shape-shifting alien species inhabiting the Hael Realm when in contact with faeries or humans.

Endolg. An intelligent animal that looks much like a woolly rug. Endolgs have a unique ability to sense truth, which makes them popular companions in the Faerie Realm.

Faerie of the Light (Lighter). One of the two main faerie types, culturally averse to the use of demons in any circumstances and usually members of the Church of Light.

Faerie of the Night (Nighter). One of the two main faerie types, physically distinguished from Faeries of the Light by light-sensitive cat-like eyes. Make use of demonic servants.

Faerie Realm. A parallel aspect of reality inhabited by various alien species, including Faeries of the Light and Faeries of the Night.

Feral Faerie. A wild, nomadic faerie people who live and hunt in the depths of the great primeval forest that covers much of the Faerie Realm. The Feral Faerie are not known to hold allegiance to either the Faeries of the Light or the Faeries of the Night.

Firstman. In Realm mythology, the first sentient creature created by the Light in the Garden of Haedon.

Fizz Parlour. Fashionable establishment specialising in giving patrons a mind-expanding experience.

Fluid Dark. What nomadic Trinians call demons.

Flyer, personal. A Realm aircraft roughly equivalent to a flying sports car.

Fogarty, Alan. (HMN) Paranoid ex-physicist and bank robber with an extraordinary talent for engineering gadgets. Fogarty was made Gatekeeper of House Iris in recognition of the help he gave to Prince Pyrgus, even though it was Fogarty's cat who nearly ate Prince Pyrgus in the first place.

Follower. Demonic spy.

Forest Faerie. The way you refer to a Feral Faerie if you don't want to give offence.

Gatekeeper. Ancient title used to describe the chief advisor of a Noble House.

Great House. Noble family.

Guardian. Spell-driven security hologram.

Hael. Faerie name for Hell.

Haelmind (a.k.a. Hellmind). The mental Internet of Hell.

Hairstreak, Lord Black. (FON) Noble head of House Hairstreak and leader of the Faeries of the Night.

Halek knife (or blade). A rock crystal weapon which releases magical energies to kill anything it pierces. Halek knives are prone to shattering occasionally, in which event the energies will kill the person using them.

Halek wizard. Non-human, non-faerie. Reputedly the most skilful of the magical practitioners in the Faerie Realm. Halek wizards typically specialise in weapons technology.

Haleklind. Homeland of the Halek wizards.

Halud. An exotic spice.

Haniel. Winged lion inhabiting forest areas of the Faerie Realm.

Hodge. Mr Fogarty's tomcat.

House Iris. The Royal House of the Faerie Empire.

The Illustrious Svengali. (HMN) A stage hypnotist.

Innatus. Nomadic Trinian shaman.

Kitterick. An Orange Trinian in the service of Madame Cardui.

Lanceline. Madame Cardui's translucent cat.

Laura Croft. (HMN) Henry's dad's new squeeze.

Levitator. Viewglobe fitted with an anti-gravity device.

Lien. A magical spell that compels the victim to act in a certain way.

Limbo. A dimension of reality temporarily inhabited by demons who are under a service contract.

Lucina, Hamearis, Duke of Burgundy. (FON) War hero and close ally to Lord Hairstreak.

Malvae, Prince Pyrgus. (FOL) Brother of Queen Holly Blue. Pyrgus likes animals a lot more than politics and at one time actually ran away from home to live as a commoner because of disagreements with his father.

McKenna, Paul. (HMN) A television hypnotist.

Memnon. (FOL) The Spicemaster (see below).

Nagel. A chieftain of the nomadic Trinians.

Niff (Hael wildlife). A heavily armoured, steel-fanged animal slightly smaller than a fox.

Nyman. A Leprechaun in Madame Cardui's service.

Ogyris, Gela. (FON) Daughter of Zosine Ogyris.

Ogyris, Genoveva. (FON) Wife of Zosine Ogyris and former lover of Kitterick.

Ogyris, Zosine Typha. (FON) Rich merchant from Haleklind, now living in Yammeth Cretch and closely allied to Lord Hairstreak.

Orion. The Communications Angel.

Ornitherium. An ancient bird-house.

Ouklo. Levitating, spell-driven carriage.

Pelidne. Lord Hairstreak's latest Gatekeeper.

Perin. Tiny amphibian renowned for spitting on its own forefeet when attacked.

Plack. Artificially created life-form.

Portal. Inter-dimensional energy gateway, either naturally occurring, modified or engineered.

Procles, Graphium. (FON) One of Hairstreak's Generals.

Quercusia. (FON) Comma's mother.

Refinia. A tropical disease of the Realm which causes severe swelling of the brain.

Ropo's. Popular coffee bar.

Severs, Charlotte (Charlie). (HMN) Henry Atherton's closest friend in the Earth Realm.

Silk Mistress. (FOL) Member of an (exclusively female) Guild trained in the control of spinners and the making of spinner silk into expensive and much-sought-after fashion items.

Simbala. An addictive form of music sold legally in licensed outlets and illegally elsewhere.

Slith. Dangerous grey reptile inhabiting forest areas of the Faerie Realm. Sliths secrete a highly toxic acid which they can spit across considerable distances.

Somme. A particularly bloody battle of World War One.

Spell cone. Pocket-sized cones, no more than an inch or so in height, imbued with magical energies directed towards a specific result. The old-style cone had to be lit. The more modern version is self-igniting and is 'cracked' with a fingernail. Both types discharge like fireworks.

Spicemaster. A Realm oracle who makes predictions with the aid of mind-altering spices.

Spy eye. A bugging device.

Stasis spell. A spell that freezes something into immobility, preserving it intact for as long as the spell lasts.

Stimlus. Personal energy weapon.

Tracker. Potentially lethal mechanised robot forming part of Hairstreak's new security system.

Transporter. Mr Fogarty's hand-held version of the thing they use in *Star Trek*.

Trinian. Non-human, non-faerie dwarven race living in the Faerie Realm. Orange Trinians are a breed that dedicates itself to service, Violet Trinians tend to be warriors, while Green Trinians specialise in biological nanotechnology and consequently can create living machines.

Tulpa. An intelligent thought-form.

Ward, Anaïs. (HMN) Henry's mother's lover.

Woodfordi. (FOL) A military Channel.

Yammeth Cretch. Heartland of the Faeries of the Night.

Yidam. One of the Old Gods who walked the Realm before the coming of the Light.